ISOLATION
THE HORROR ANTHOLOGY

ISOLATION

THE HORROR ANTHOLOGY

Edited by
DAN COXON

TITAN BOOKS

Isolation: The Horror Anthology
Print edition ISBN: 9781803360683
E-book edition ISBN: 9781803360690

Published by Titan Books
A division of Titan Publishing Group Ltd
144 Southwark Street, London SE1 0UP
www.titanbooks.com

First edition: September 2022
10 9 8 7 6 5 4 3 2 1

ISOLATION

THE HORROR ANTHOLOGY

CONTENTS

INTRODUCTION

As I write this, I'm on my eighth day of self-isolation, our entire household having contracted Covid-19. The experience is one you might be familiar with. Over the last two years, as the coronavirus pandemic has spread across the globe, it's ironic that one of the defining communal experiences has been isolation. Just as I am confined in my home, so are thousands of others across the country, and across the globe—all of us alone in our bubbles, together.

Of course, horror has always been aware of the dangers of isolation. From the Overlook Hotel to the *Nostromo*, there are perils awaiting us when we drift too far from society's faint circle of light. We have an inbuilt fear of straying outside our communities, of setting foot in the dark woods—a fear that, many thousands of years ago, might have saved our lives. There is danger in the unknown, and the farther you stray into the wilderness, the less you know. In space, no one can hear you scream.

More than the monsters that lurk on the shadowed fringes of society, though, the real danger comes from within. Humans are social animals, and away from the pack we start to lose our identity, question our reason; eventually, we lose our grip on reality. The Overlook may have ghosts in its halls, but it's Jack Torrance that they prey upon as he goes slowly mad. As Jonathan Maberry says in his Sam Imura story "Lone Gunman", reprinted in this anthology: "Alone, though, it's easier to be weaker, smaller, to be more intimate with the pain, and be owned by it." Isolation finds the cracks in our psyche, and works its way insidiously inside.

Isolation: The Horror Anthology encompasses all this and more. There are stories of madness and incarceration, and the loneliness that comes from rejection, or illness, or being caught in an abusive relationship. There are apocalypse stories, including new tales of the world's end from Tim Lebbon and Lisa Tuttle—because what could be more lonely than a planet gone silent? And as you'd expect, there are monsters too, from vampires and zombies to serial killers and mad gods, all of them sniffing weakness in the isolated and the lonely, circling, waiting for the kill.

Inevitably, Covid-19 rears its spiky head more than once. The pandemic has left scars on our collective psyche that will take years to heal, and some of these stories explore that loss, and the solitude we have all felt at times. One of the stories—Ken Liu's "Jaunt"—is barely a horror story at all, were it not for the shadow of fear and desperation that hangs over it as he imagines what the future might hold in the post-pandemic age.

Three days from now my quarantine period will end, and I'll be able to step out of my front door once more, into a world that sometimes feels like a pale imitation of the one we used to know. Hopefully I'll be able to see family and friends again, regulations permitting; I'll be able to walk the streets of the town I live in, browse the shops, eat in the cafes. As John Donne wrote four hundred years ago, "No man is an island, entire of itself"—we all need community and social interaction if we are to thrive. How else can we keep the darkness at bay?

DAN COXON
January 26, 2022

THE SNOW CHILD

Alison Littlewood

THERE'S a family building a snowman outside a little wooden house. A mother, dad, two kids: perfect. They pat down his sides, laughing at the woolly hat on his head, and then they are gone, left behind us. It's getting dark and I wonder that such young children are still playing outside, then remember it's only half past two in the afternoon.

This far north the sun is already fading, blue shadows draping the snow. I'm tired, and not just from the journey: a plane from Stockholm to Kiruna, the northernmost airport in Sweden, and then this bus, which is surprisingly full. But then, it doesn't go any further than Jukkasjärvi, busy with its ice hotel and reindeer centre and holiday lodges, its church and small supermarket, the clusters of wooden houses each painted a different colour. After this, I have to hope she remembers. I have to hope she is there. Beyond this is only the Arctic Circle and the dark and the cold; where my mother lives, there is nothing.

My unease creeps a little deeper into me. I should have come home sooner. I knew it every time we spoke on the phone, hearing the crisp brittle crust to her voice, the coldness beneath. But somehow one year turned into the next and then another, and anyway, it's nothing she didn't expect; it never did take long for her disappointment in me to become resignation. Our conversations consist of the same old expected phrases—*How are you? I'm fine. Good. Yes, soon, I hope. Take care of yourself. Goodbye*—all oddly formal, but we've been that way for so long I can barely remember anything else.

The last time we spoke, though, there *was* something else, a new edge to her voice, a jumpiness I hadn't expected. I'd pictured her huddled into a corner in the store, holding the payphone to her ear, fidgeting with the curly wire and glancing over her shoulder as if afraid someone else might hear.

Still, what did I expect? I'd left her out here all alone, with nothing but the snow and the night that closes in too soon. How could anyone live so remotely without it creeping into them—the cold, endless blue dark? I had wanted to wait for the spring, but that phone call had nagged at me, not the words but the way she said them, and so I'd told her I would come.

The bus slows and I wipe mist from the window, catching a glimpse of lights from the shop. It has grey walls, a yellow awning, a couple of snowmobiles parked outside: it's all just the same. I queue to get off the bus and catch snippets from the radio. Some kind of protest in Mälmo. The need for rent-controlled accommodation in Stockholm. A child missing from a village near Kiruna, presumed lost in the snow. I pull a face at that. She wouldn't be the first.

My sister, Alma, had been the youngest child, the *good* child. And she too was lost, wandering off one day into the trees, her coat as red as blood, her skin as white as snow, her hair almost as pale. To complete the fairy story her eyes ought to have been as black as ebony, but my sister's eyes were blue, like mine.

Snow had quickly covered her tracks. She never did come back, though my mother searched endlessly, leaving me alone in the cabin, young as I was. Sometimes I didn't eat. Sometimes I didn't shower for days, and when I asked about it she told me the oil on my skin would help to keep me warm. I never asked about my father; I had never known him. And even when Mother was there, she was not; as if the most important part of her had retreated, hibernating until this coldest of winters should pass.

Of course, it never did pass, despite Mother trying to act as if life was changeless. I know the cabin will be exactly the same. My room will be there, waiting for me. And Alma's, more deeply frozen still, everything just as it was when my sister was seven years old.

With a start, I realise that the bent-backed woman just emerging from the shop door is my mother. She goes to one of the snowmobiles, starts putting bags into its panniers. There's no trailer attached, as if she hasn't thought about my luggage, and I reflect that it's a good job I only brought my backpack. I'll have to wear it as we ride.

She turns and sees me, her reaction only a slight widening of her eyes, more lines carving her skin than I remember. *I'm here*, I mouth to her. I'm home: Tilda, the *other* sister. The one who never was quite what Mother wanted, who even now doesn't have a husband, let alone a child, the one thing that might have melted her.

My mother can't quite hide her disappointment in any of those things, but mainly, I don't think she has ever forgiven me for growing up.

It takes forty minutes: glimpses over my mother's shoulder of narrow white track, misshapen conifers lumpen with snow, shadows beneath them. Constant shaking and juddering from the uneven surface, the roar of the engine. Mother brought a spare balaclava and helmet, and my coat is windproof, though my feet are already freezing in my boots. It's minus twenty. There is a road out here, somewhere under the snow, but it won't be passable for weeks yet. I cling to her too-thin shape as Mother wrestles the snowmobile's handles, preventing it wandering from the path. All this way and all we've managed is *Hej* and a brief hug, her touch so light I'd almost felt I'd imagined it. Now it's impossible to talk, hard to see through the speckles of snow thickening on my visor. Mother never hesitates. She knows the way, letting the machine slow at just the right moment, though at first, despite the familiar windows, the snow-weighted roof, I don't recognise it.

The garden is somehow full of trees. No, not trees. I blink, scarcely taking it in, then it floods in on me all at once. I swing myself from the seat, wrestle the padded helmet off my head, pull the balaclava over my hair. Blink at what she has done.

The garden is full of snowmen, but they are more than that. These things are beautiful, obsessively shaped and wrought. They're not rough-rolled globes of snow but sculpted, refined, detailed. Not snowmen, but snow-children.

All of them are girls. All of them are shorter than me, about seven years old: just right. They are wearing Alma's clothes. I recognise a fleece covered in the printed teddy bears she used to love. A corduroy skirt she had begged for. I can't make out my mother's words as I step towards them; they reach me but distorted, as if I'm hearing underwater. Perhaps my ears are still ringing from the roar of the engine, though I don't think that's entirely it.

I stand in front of the nearest snow-child. Her face is not carved from compacted snow but from ice, set atop a snow body. I look at her smooth cheek, her nose, her chin. Her eyes look back at me, the clearest, palest blue.

"Do you see?" Mother's voice reaches me clearly now. "I knew you would like them, Tilda." When I turn, her smile is a little too wide.

There are objects, too, scattered around the garden. A ball. A wooden horse. A plastic doll with white-blond hair. Other things. A cuddly toy puppy, drenched and matted. Building blocks. All placed at the feet of children who will never play with them, never bend to pick them up. I stoop and retrieve an old book, a volume of fairy tales I used to love, the pages clumped and frozen, ruined.

"You see?" Mother crunch-steps to my side. This time, when she speaks, her voice is full of triumph. "They're real, Tilda. You do see, don't you?"

It is a long time before I can look at her. She stares back at me, unblinking, her expression one of purest joy.

I don't talk to Mother about the snow-children, not yet. I'm not sure what to say. I need to watch her first, decide what I should do. At first, she doesn't mention them either. She stows the snowmobile around the back of the shed then joins me inside. She speaks words of welcome, bustles about the kitchen, bends to the oven. I recognise the scent of her stew and realise I'm starving. She ladles it into bowls and we eat, her at one side of the wooden table, me at the other, stealing glances at one another. She asks me ordinary things. About my flat in Stockholm, out in the suburbs, far from the little streets of the Old Town so beloved of tourists. My job, nothing special, front of house in a fancy hotel. Whether I've met anyone interesting. *Not for a long time, Mother.*

I ask her little in return. It's difficult. So much here is the same, and I don't want to speak about what is different. It strikes me again that I should have come in the spring. At least then the snow-children would be gone, the land revealing itself, green emerging from the white. We fall silent and she takes to staring out of the window, just beyond my head. It's disconcerting, as if she's almost but not quite seeing me, and I can't help wondering if she's thinking of Alma.

Slowly, a tear runs down her cheek.

I sit up straighter. "Mother, what is it?"

She waves my words away. Wipes the tear away. I see it balanced on the crook of her finger, glistening.

"I'm just so afraid, Tilda," she says.

I can't answer. I don't know how.

She says, "I'm afraid they'll leave me. So afraid my daughters will melt away."

I picture a snow-child, her face made of ice. Droplets of water running down her cheek as the temperature rises. All of them becoming soft, misshapen, transforming into something else before they vanish.

I still can't speak so I go to her and wrap my arms around her shoulders. I feel the little rounded bones of her, hard and unbending. Pat the soft warmth of her hand. Then I clear the table, run hot water into a bowl. After the washing up, there's little to do—there's no television here, no DVDs or CD player—and we both say that we're tired. We agree to go to bed, though I have no idea what time it is at all.

The familiarity of my old room is expected, yet comes as a shock. I set down my pack, sit on the woven blanket covering the eiderdown, feel its slightly rough texture under my fingers. I look at the board games stacked in a corner, the ones I couldn't play after my sister left. The books, tilted this way and that, gaps on the shelf like pulled teeth. Has Mother offered my books, too, to those figures outside? I shudder to think of it; my books, old friends all, sodden and ruined at their feet.

I get ready for bed, donning an extra layer of thermals, two pairs of socks in case I should have to get up in the night. I didn't bring slippers but I spy my old moccasins, tucked under my desk. I feel nine years old again and I try to remember what it was like not to be alone but one of two. Alma slips away from me, though, as she always did; instead, the memory that comes is of my mother. The way my door would creak open and she would be standing there, like a ghost. The way she'd slip inside and snuggle the eiderdown under my chin, patting it down, moulding its shape to my body. That was how she used to tuck me in, before Alma left. With tenderness, with love, and without a word.

~

Sometime deep in the night—or the early morning—I wake from a dream, its shape rapidly dissolving into mist. I was walking between the trees, I remember that, but I don't know where I was going. All I could see was the forest and only the forest, nothing else.

Now I hear a sound, one that might have followed me out of my slumber. I remain motionless, scarcely breathing. Just as I decide that of course I won't hear it again, it wasn't even real, there it is: the soft, high sound of a child crying.

I tell myself that at any moment I will wake again, for real this time, but I don't because I'm awake already. The sound comes to me once more: a child's sob, followed by a stream of words I don't recognise. The voice is muffled, but I think it's a girl's. It sounds as if she's pleading to come inside.

It is morning, weak white light seeping over everything. It must be late; I've slept in. The sounds I heard last night seem distant as any dream and just as unreal as I swing my legs from the bed and into my old moccasins. They still fit perfectly.

I go to the window and open the curtains. I can't see the garden from here, though I half expect to see a little frozen face peering in, looking back at me. Of course I don't. There's only the side of a hill leading nowhere but into the boreal forest that clothes this latitude for miles and miles. I never did know why Mother decided to move here and I often wondered if it happened when my father left, or died, or when whatever happened to him happened, my mother turning her loneliness into something physical.

The clattering of pots and the hiss of a kettle call me towards the kitchen. I put my head around the door, afraid of what I'll find—*They're real, Tilda. You do see, don't you?*—but Mother is setting out bowls of steaming porridge, glasses of lingonberry juice and a pot of coffee. I can't help smiling at the old smells. I sit and she puts porridge and juice in front of me, no coffee, and I feel as if I'm nine years old once more.

"What would you like to do today?" She sing-songs the words, her voice a shade too bright. She glances at the window, as if she's already waiting for me to be gone.

I take a deep breath. "I thought maybe we could talk." I force myself to smile but she turns away, so I almost don't see her lip twist.

"I'm going to chop some firewood," she says. "You'll need it, I suppose."

I remember what she said about her snow-daughters melting: *I'm just so afraid, Tilda.* There's no sign of her worrying over that now. No sign of whatever madness came to meet her in the cold.

She shifts, as if she knows what I'm thinking. "Together, then," she says. "Let's go out, shall we?"

And so we do, both of us heaving sections of a fallen tree onto a block for Mother to cut into pieces before I remove the logs and stack them undercover to dry. She swings the axe easily, for all she looks so stringy and thin. But then, she's strong; she has to be, out here alone, with no one to help her.

I push aside the guilt that rises and look towards the front garden. I can see only one of the snow-children from here. Ripples of transparent hair flow behind her and one foot is almost lifting from the ground, as if she's about to skip away. Perhaps she is; perhaps she moved during the night. I wonder if she, too, has pale blue eyes—but I suppose she must have, like Alma's; like mine. Mother's children, all.

"Mother," I try to begin, "you don't really think they're real, do you?"

She swings the axe and there's a loud *smack* as she sets it quivering deep into the block. "Enough," she says. "We'll go inside now, Alma."

I stare at her. Has it been so very long? But surely she could never forget that it was Alma, the perfect daughter, who went missing; the other who was left behind.

She blinks. "*Tilda.* Come inside."

I don't move and she, too, glances at the thing she has made. "You must know the story," she spits. "Someone returns home. They find that the woman has a child, one she wished for really, really hard."

Someone, she said. In the story it was a husband who came home, I knew that, but that's not what she said.

"And she lives with the child, quite happily, a gift, a *joy*, until the sun comes and she melts." She strides over to me, grabs my arm, starts pulling me around the side of the cabin. There they are: snow-child after snow-child, gleaming in the light streaming from the pale white hole in the sky. "In spring," she adds, needlessly, and points. "This is Istapp. This is Snöflinga, and this—"

Icicle. Snowflake. This is what she has named them. "Mother, listen to yourself. Please. You made these things, you can't really think—"

She moves quickly. I feel the sting of her slap spreading across my cheek.

"You'll say nothing." She pushes her face up close to mine. "Nothing, you understand?"

She turns and stomps away from me, her steps squeaking and crunching in the snow. She doesn't look back, just opens the door, goes in and closes it after her, as if we'd had a normal conversation.

I put my hand to my face. It is already turning numb as the cold creeps into me.

Inside, Mother is doing ordinary things. Chopping carrots she must have bought at the store, half a world away. Scooping them into her stew-pot.

"Mother—"

"Nothing," she snaps, as if completing her earlier sentence. She doesn't look up at me.

"All right," I say softly. "I won't say anything, if you don't want me to." I'm already wondering what to do. I can stay with her a few days, but what about after that? I could give up my flat and my job, but the thought of being out here, caught up in her pretence…

I think again of the spring. Her delusions must end then, mustn't they? I'm not sure if I can last that long. I don't know if I can bear to watch her pain as all her work, her precious *children*, melt into the ground.

A sniff comes from somewhere behind me and I whirl about. A little girl is standing in the doorway. She is leaning against the jamb, staring up at me as slowly, slowly, a drip runs down her face. She appears to be about seven years old.

My mouth falls open. "What the—"

I feel, rather than see, Mother rush past. She steps in front of me as if to shield the child from the heat of my gaze and stoops to her. "There you are!" she says, half turning to me again. Her whole demeanour has changed. She looks happy. She looks *joyful*, her delight brimming over. "You see, Tilda. You see?"

I do see, but I don't understand and I can't move.

"I made her," Mother says simply. "She is my daughter. She's your sister, Tilda."

This child doesn't look anything like my sister. She isn't Alma. She's staring down at her feet and her features are half hidden but it's plain to see that her hair isn't blond. This girl's hair is black as ebony and she doesn't smile back at Mother or even look at her. From what I can make out, her expression is pinched, frozen. Her nose is running, another drip poised to run down her face.

I force myself to speak because someone has to say something, but I barely croak the word. "*Hej*," I try. "*Hej*."

The child jerks her head, but she gives no sign of recognition and I'm not surprised when she doesn't answer. Mother starts pulling at her shoulders, twisting her away from me, giving her a little push.

"She can't *talk*, Tilda," she says. "Not like us, not words we can understand. Don't you know anything?"

Yet the child wriggles her shoulders and pulls away from her. She sticks her arm straight out, pointing towards the window, and she does speak; she says a single word. "Mama."

I stare, but Mother doesn't. She starts guiding her along the hall, towards my sister's room. I can hear her voice, the bright tone of her response. "Yes!" she says. "So clever, my dear. That is your mother—you see her white cloak?"

I realise, as Mother closes the door behind them, that she is talking about the snow.

I am in my room, sitting on the bed, mobile phone on my lap. I've been trying to get it to work, though I don't know why I bothered. Mobiles don't work out here. Did I think they'd have built a signal tower in the wilderness since I came here last? Still, I turn it as if at any moment it will ring, connecting me to another world. I unlock it with my thumb, open the messaging service. The last one I had was from a friend at work. *Big night out when you're back!* We were planning a nice meal in the Old Town, never mind the expense.

That reminds me I'm hungry. Mother has emerged a couple of times from Alma's room, but mostly she's been in there. Muffled voices, rustling sounds, the rattling of dice then the sweeping of game pieces onto the floor. At least, that's what I thought I'd heard. It might be anything in there. A troll. A witch. Even Alma, her little face so serious, her eyes wide and blue and so very pretty.

I push myself up, walk along the hall, stopping to stare at the two-way radio tucked into its alcove. It's a last-mile service only, meant for emergencies, enough to reach the nearest neighbour at best. I hear a door open and quickly look away, continuing into the kitchen. There, I see what my mother has laid out on the counter: piles of meat, great joints of elk, all of it glistening and frozen.

Mother comes in, her feet shuffling, pace slow. She sits at the table, her back to me.

"Would you like some lunch, Mother?"

She doesn't answer so I look in the cupboards, rummage through tins, find some soup. I grab a pan from another cupboard, grimace at the dark crust around its rim.

"Mother?"

She doesn't even twitch. I run the tap, wash the pots before I use them. When did it get so bad? But it was like this before, I remember. I've been washing up since I was nine years old; since Alma went away.

I put the soup on to warm, watch as the surface starts puckering.

"We should eat," I say. "Mother, we'd better feed the child."

"My *daughter*," she snaps, correcting me.

"Yes." There's nothing else I can say.

She lets out a long sigh. "Don't make it too hot, Tilda. It might hurt her."

"Yes, Mother."

"Do you think they're melting, Tilda? I think they're already melting. Then it will all end. They'll come back next year, but they won't be the same, will they?" She twists in her seat and looks at me. "They're never the same."

Now I'm not sure it's just the snow-children she means.

"Oh, for goodness' sake," she snaps, "I'll do it." She strides towards me, pushes me aside. Starts clattering bowls onto the counter, one, two, three.

When they're full, I put out a hand and squeeze her wrist. "Let me do it," I say. "Let me feed my sister."

Her frown dissipates as she stares into my eyes. After a long moment, she nods.

When I open the door to Alma's room, the child is sitting on the bed. Her eyes are bloodshot and sore, her hair greasy, her fringe a little too long. She follows me with dark brown eyes, sniffing as I sit at her feet. I hold out the soup like a gift.

She shuffles closer, the bed shifting and sinking as she moves. I can smell her; clothes that have been too long in a musty cupboard, the oil of her hair. She is real, this girl. Flesh and blood. Did I really need reassuring of that?

I smile, dip the spoon into the soup and hold it out. She takes it, swallows. Takes it, swallows. She's hungry. She isn't made of ice and snow—but I knew that, didn't I?

She hasn't uttered a word, but one rises to the surface of my mind anyway and I whisper it to her. *Mama.*

The child lets out a gasp. She grabs my hand, slopping soup over the rim of the bowl as words burst from her. I can't make sense of them, but I see the hope that's suddenly in her eyes. She keeps looking at the window, as if at any moment someone might come, but out there it's already growing dark.

I wish I could ask her to explain where she came from. I wish she could tell me.

She can't talk, Tilda. Not like us; not words we can understand.

I recognise her voice, though. I've heard it before. I heard it during the night, not through a window, as I'd assumed, but through a door. Not pleading to come in, but crying to get out.

I stroke her back, shushing her as best I can, and try to remember what I'd heard on the radio on the way here. A child missing, from a village near Kiruna. Did they say where, exactly? Or where she was from? I can't remember, but plenty of tourists fly into that tiny airport in the far north of nowhere. Is this one of their children? And was she lost in the snow—or snatched from her family?

I picture my mother lifting the child's small form onto the snowmobile. Driving away, her arms around her. Loving her, this little daughter she'd found at last, after all these years. And the snow falling, falling, erasing all trace behind them, as if they'd vanished into a story. A happy ending for someone.

When I re-enter the hall, Mother is nowhere to be seen. I pause by the radio, flick the switch. It doesn't respond; no light appears. It has the feeling about it of something dead and I look under the little shelf, tracing the wire to its end. My mother has cut the cord in two.

I shoot out a hand and silence my alarm. I set it last night on a low volume, my mobile coming in useful at last. I knew I'd need to be up and out before the light came to wake me. I'm already dressed but I pull on my boots and an extra jumper and then my coat. I'll fasten it later, outside. I can't risk the sound of the zip waking her.

I sneak out into an early morning that isn't as dark as I expected. The sky at its zenith is black, the stars a bright glitter, but low on the horizon a green veil shifts and dances. The northern lights have come to help light my way.

There's no helping the sound of my boots on the snow but I stay close to the house, where it's at least been cleared in the recent past and isn't so deep. I go around to the back of the shed and tug the cover from the snowmobile, revealing its sleek shine, its gathered power. Then I push open the shed doors, ignoring the shadowed shapes of tools and machinery, everything needed to survive out here, and reach for the hook just inside. My fingers meet with nothing.

Of course the key isn't there. Had I really imagined she'd leave it for me?

I watch the lurid light stroking and slipping over the curves of the snowmobile, turning the snow the colour of sickness. I check the ignition but it's empty, a small black slot. So simple; so impossible. I stare into it, thinking of all the movies I've seen in Stockholm, the hotwired cars. Always so easy to drive away, but I have no idea how to make it start.

For the next couple of hours I keep to my room, wondering and wondering where she might have hidden a key. It might be anywhere.

She could have thrown it into the snow. Perhaps I'll find it come the spring, as the white retreats from the earth.

Then I hear sounds coming from outside: sharp cracks and spattering, something breaking like glass. I can't see anything from my window, so I pull on my coat.

In the front garden, the white figures are motionless. Nothing moves, nothing changes, not here, but I realise that something has. One of the snow-children is broken. Her jumper hangs from her, misshapen; one of her arms is missing. Her neck juts upwards, ending in glinting shards like a broken bottle.

Movement draws my gaze. A dark shape is shuffling, bent-backed, from the shed. It is my mother, the crone; the witch. She stoops and picks up something from the ground, clear and shining. It is the snow-child's head. It must be heavy, judging by her lurching gait as she moves back towards the shed once more.

I notice her axe, abandoned in the garden. Obscene among the toys lying at the children's feet.

Mother pauses. She cradles the child's head in her arms as if it were flesh and blood. "I have to save them," she says, before she goes back into the shed. A metallic sound is followed by the slight suck of a seal giving way.

The freezer. It had been just on the other side of that thin wooden wall, all the time I'd examined the snowmobile. My mother needs her stores after all, everything she might require to survive out here, spring and summer as well as winter.

I'm just so afraid, Tilda... I'm afraid they'll leave me. So afraid my daughters will melt away.

I remember the meat laid out on the kitchen counter. She's been emptying the freezer, I realise. Making room for them, her children; her daughters.

~

Mother doesn't seem tired from her labour. The snow-children are shattered, the stumps of legs and bodies lying on the ground. Mainly she seems to have taken arms, hands, heads. The things, I suppose, that are most *them*; the easiest to store.

Now she is making stew. Mounds of thawed meat litter the counter. It looks like an abattoir after the blood has drained away. She sears the flesh. The smell grows thick in the air.

I don't try to talk. Wherever Mother has gone, I know I can't reach her. She left a long time ago: she walked into the woods looking for Alma and she never came back again. She left me here alone.

I am not alone now, of course. Occasionally there is a rustle or some other sound from my sister's room, but the door doesn't open. It's as if Alma is in there, sulking at me, after I'd teased her perhaps, or pulled her hair, or dreamed up some game she didn't like.

I think of the snowmobile. I could try bending a paperclip and put it into the ignition. I could slip alcohol into Mother's coffee, get her drunk enough to tell me where the key is. But there's nothing to drink here. I remind myself she never cared for it, doesn't have that particular vice, and let out a dry splutter of a laugh.

Mother looks up. I freeze, but after a moment she resumes her work. Chop, chop, chop. One, two, three.

Along the hall, a door whispers open.

Mother's eyes flick to me, then she carries on. Chop, chop, chop; the sound is no different to before, but I know that it *is*. She's listening.

A footstep, so light, so quiet. Then another.

Mother slams down the knife and rushes to the door, pulling it open to reveal a little figure in a blood-red coat, her face blanched white as snow, her hair as black as ebony, the fairy tale at last, but she isn't going into the forest, oh no: because the witch is here, the witch is my mother, and the witch snatches her up and lifts her from the floor. The little girl squeals, *squeeeeeeals*, as Mother carries her back into Alma's room, *her* room now, and bangs the door closed. The sound isn't quite final, though. There are others: shouting, crying, muffled sounds, and I stare towards them, feeling that I've heard them all; I've felt them all, so many times, and I start to shake and feel water running down my face.

After what seems like an age, Mother emerges.

"Leaving," she snaps. "Always, they leave. Always. All my daughters."

She returns to the counter and picks up her knife. The sounds are brisk and sharp as she resumes her chopping.

It isn't until I'm quite certain she won't notice me, when I have turned invisible to her, that I step softly from the house.

The freezer is there. A monster of grey metal that can swallow an elk whole. I had half expected to see locks and chains, but there are none. Why should there be? No one ever comes here.

I reach out and lift the lid, adjusting my stance to take the weight. It makes the loud sucking sound of a hungry mouth and cold breath spills out. I look down and see lumpen shapes, just as I'd expected. She has been freezing them, her snow-children; saving them, keeping them safe from the coming spring.

There are finely formed fingers, almost transparent, frozen now for as long as she wishes. Locks of hair, curling and twining yet always keeping their shape. Faces look up at me: cheeks, noses, chins. Their eyes are all the same pale blue; sleeping beauties, all.

Yet I know there is more.

Always, they leave. Always.

I move the pieces aside, then start throwing them to the floor, these perfect things she has made. The things to which she has given her love, though it was never asked for, never expected; never earned. *All my daughters.* Ice shatters and scatters across the rough concrete and I don't care. I am glad to see them break.

All *my daughters*, she had said.

And there, beneath them, I find it. There are pieces of child everywhere, their bodies confused and jumbled together, but only one of them is wrapped in plastic.

The freezer is still half full of hands, arms, heads. They are packed around her, keeping her company. I ease them away from her, my fingertips numb, all feeling long since stolen away.

Pale hair, the shade of moonlight, is curled and crushed between plastic and the frozen dome of her skull. Glitter crusts her skin. Her eyes are white now, the colour of snow. I see all the perfect curves and planes of her, so well-remembered, so very pretty, just as she had always been.

Alma. My sister. My mother had found her after all.

I don't wait. Only the length of time it takes for my mother to go into the shed once more, and then I act: I thrust the long pole of a snow shovel through both door handles. She knows she's trapped at once. She doesn't shout or squeal; nothing so human. She just starts bang, bang, banging on the wood.

I run into the house. I'm wearing my coat. I touch my pocket, feel the shape of my phone; I can use its compass, keep trying for a signal as we go. I have a warm hat and gloves and two pairs of socks inside my boots. I'll grab her coat, too; she can dress on the way. I yank open her door and put my finger to my lips, the same in any language: *Shh.*

I point to the window. "Mama," I say.

Her eyes widen. She shuffles off the bed and holds out her hand towards me.

Then we're out. We're in the snow. I glance over my shoulder, as if someone might be watching us leave, but there is no one, only that relentless banging coming from the shed. I pause to pull the coat over the child's arms, slip gloves over her hands. Her fingertips are already pink with cold. She grasps for my hand and I hold hers tight as we walk towards the trees, wading into deeper snow. The hole where the sun should be is lowering in the sky, but I think there is time. There has to be time. I glance towards the cabin once more, and see our own deeply shadowed footprints trailing after us.

The sound of splintering wood carries clearly through the cold, clean air. Moments later, there is the roar of an engine.

The child looks up at me. Her eyes are wide and round and full of fear. I yank on her hand and we start to run, but it is slow, so slow. The tracks we leave are like those of an injured animal.

We duck under stunted conifers, dislodging snow from their branches, flakes whispering to the ground all around us. It is almost like fresh snowfall, almost like that day. No, not like that; we were playing then. *Let's play hide and seek, Alma. I'll come and find you. I promise.*

But we aren't playing now and I will not let her go. I won't send her away from me, all alone, so small, into the forest.

I pull on her hand, *faster*, as we crest the hill, reaching an open slope on the other side. Does the engine sound more distant now? A snatch of hope whips away from me on the breeze. No. She knows exactly where we are. She always knew I'd have to run south. It's just that she can't weave between the trees; she's going around them.

We start down the slope and I turn and see her, a black metal gleam growing larger, growling as it comes, like a fearsome beast. She's bearing down on us, close, closer, and I lift the child into my arms. For the briefest moment it feels like I'm holding a shield, then I throw her away from me, off to the side. I know she'll land safe. The snow is so soft, after all.

The next instant, I am struck. I am flying, flying through the air. I do not know when I land; there is little difference between the snow and the sky. For a moment there is nothing but white, it is all there is, and then the pain begins.

I do not need to see to know that I am broken into pieces.

My eyes, nose, mouth are full of snow. Cold sends a jolt stinging into my teeth and I splutter, feeling ice running down my skin, already melting. Distantly, my legs burn and throb and *insist*. I blink, trying to peer down at my body. The snow isn't pure; it isn't clean. The snow is tainted with me. All around, red crystals bloom, crimson flowers opening their petals.

Mother walks towards me. The crunch of her footsteps is loud, so loud. It hurts inside my head and I want her to stop and thankfully, she does. She looks down and I see myself reflected in her eyes: the disappointment that quickly turns to resignation as she kneels. Behind her, I glimpse another child, another daughter. Just as she was then, always seven years old. *Run*, I think, but she doesn't.

Mother leans over me. Her skin is flecked with ice, but she doesn't seem to feel it. She bends over as if inspecting me, but I feel something, *pat pat pat*, and realise that she isn't. She's pulling at the snow, mounding it around my body, moulding it to my shape. She means to keep me warm, and I feel the cold leaching from me, quickly fading away. *That's what a mother is*, I think, and allow myself to sink deep into the soft pillows. She is covering the blood. She's making me clean again. Making everything white and perfect; her lovely little snow-child. She starts heaping it onto me, over me, its weight like thick, heavy blankets. Mother is tucking me in. I tell myself she loves me best after all. And it is warm, so warm, the comfort settling into my flesh, wrapping itself about my bones. I can sense sleep waiting for me, not here yet but close, *kind*, and softly, I smile.

This is how she always did it, I think. With tenderness, with love, and without a word.

She has left a little hole for my eyes. Somehow I can see them peeping out, palest blue amid so much white. And I can see my mother. She is reaching for the child, holding her hand. She is taking my sister home. She's taking her to be with all her daughters; Mother is going to make sure that she is safe.

FRIENDS FOR LIFE

Mark Morris

I T was a week after Daniel's mother's funeral when the flyer landed on the doormat.

It came with a bunch of other junk—*Al's Pizzas! Leather Sofas at Half Price! Sell Your Gold for Cash!* Daniel was about to dump it all in the recycling when the flyer fluttered out of the pile in his hand and seesawed to the floor. Irritated, he dropped the rest of the junk into the brown plastic tub and bent down, grunting as his pot belly was compressed between his chest and groin. Picking up the flyer, he glanced at the bold blue lettering on its white background:

Feeling lonely? Isolated? No one to talk to?

Then why not come along to Hargrave Community Hall and make some FRIENDS FOR LIFE?

**Meetings held every Tuesday evening at 7 p.m.
Hope to see you there!**

Daniel's first reaction was a bilious surge of resentment. He didn't like the suggestion that years of crippling social anxiety could be eradicated simply by meeting up with other, similarly afflicted individuals.

And yet, just for a moment, before the realist in him—all bitterness and anger, brutalised by decades of being bullied, shunned and belittled—crumpled the flyer in his fist and thrust it deep into the recycling tub, a tiny, still-optimistic part of him thought: *But what if...*

Daniel was thirty-six. He was five feet five inches tall, and weighed a little over two hundred pounds. His shortness and squatness he had inherited from his parents, who had been so similar in stature that Daniel had often wondered whether it was this that had drawn them together. It was certainly this that had led to Adam Smedley dubbing his family "the Trolls", and afflicting Daniel with the nickname "Gimli". It hadn't helped Daniel's cause when he had pointed out that Gimli was a dwarf, not a troll. In fact, it had led to Smedley hooting, "Shut up, you *geek*!" and smacking Daniel so hard in the mouth that he had needed two stitches in his upper lip.

Even when Daniel's dad dropped dead of a heart attack two years later, while queueing at the deli counter in Sainsbury's, it hadn't stopped the bullying and name-calling. Daniel had endured Smedley's taunts and beatings until the bigger boy had eventually left school at sixteen and joined the police. Daniel himself had stayed on for his A-levels, and then got a job in the IT department of local firm Shaw's Finance.

Years of humiliation at the hands of Smedley and his cronies—which the rest of the class had found funny and entertaining rather than cruel and demeaning—had crushed his spirit and his confidence. Daniel had now been at Shaw's for eighteen years, exactly half his life, and in all that time he had never socialised with his workmates, never even attended the firm's Christmas party or summer BBQ. He had always used his mother as an excuse for why he had to get home—though now that she was dead, of course, he couldn't do that anymore.

Then again, with everything that had happened in the past two years, he no longer had to. Since the start of the pandemic, Daniel had been working from home, a situation that now looked set to continue indefinitely. At some point during the lockdown, it had occurred to Lionel Shaw that he simply didn't need to pay for quite so much office space to run his business. All that most of his employees required to do their jobs was a computer and a Zoom link.

And so Daniel, who had previously left the house he shared with his morbidly obese mother to go to work every weekday, suddenly found himself almost as housebound as she was. And at first, despite his mother's increasing demands, it had been a relief not to interact with other people. Other people made him feel ugly and awkward, not to mention stupid and inarticulate, even though he wasn't.

After a while, though, the novelty had begun to wear off, and it hadn't only been down to his mother's failing health. What was that old saying? *Be careful what you wish for.* Before the pandemic, Daniel had regarded his bedroom, with its games console and its floor-to-ceiling shelves crammed with books and DVD box sets, as his sanctuary. But when a sanctuary became somewhere you were *forced* to spend all your time, it started to become less like a sanctuary and more like a prison cell.

"*Dani-elll... Dani-elll...*" As time wore on, his mother's voice, which had grown increasingly reedy and more frightened as she neared her end, had become like a hot wire applied to his nerve endings, particularly as her demands had become not just frequent but continuous. Now that her voice had been silenced for ever, though, Daniel missed it desperately. Several times since her death he had woken in the night, certain he could hear her calling. And although his instinctive response as he had thrown back his duvet had been irritable resentment, the instant he remembered she was dead he had felt such a crushing weight of grief that he had collapsed back onto his bed, barely able to move.

Years ago, Daniel had read that grief and depression was like carrying a rucksack full of rocks on your back. Although he felt he'd been carrying such a rucksack for the past twenty-five years, so many more rocks had been added to his burden since his mother's death that now even simple things, like getting dressed or making a cup of tea, felt like an exhausting trudge up a steep hill. Today was Saturday, and it was in such a state, struggling through the fug of his grief, that he eventually set out that morning to pick up a few provisions. He was passing the chemist's on the High Street (no longer would he have to queue in there for his mother's many prescriptions) when a flash of blue letters on white caught his eye.

It was the same flyer he had received that morning. Certain words jumped out at him: *lonely... isolated... FRIENDS FOR LIFE!* He scowled and trudged on. But there was an identical flyer in the window of the butcher's shop, and another in the window of the barber's. And when he reached the little Sainsbury's over the bridge, there was one on the community noticeboard, its blue lettering jumping out amid the other notices about lost cats and music tuition.

When he got home, wheezing and sweating, he fished the crumpled flyer out of the recycling bin, smoothed it out and read it again.

Hargrave Community Hall... Tuesday evening at 7 p.m....

The Community Hall was only a couple of streets away, three minutes' walk at most. He had passed it on his way back from Sainsbury's.

Not that he'd go, of course. He couldn't face company right now. But maybe at some point in the future...

Though, more than likely, maybe not.

Perhaps it was fate, perhaps it was a subconscious impulse, but at 7 p.m. the following Tuesday, Daniel was trudging back from Sainsbury's with a few essentials he'd run out of since the weekend—bread, milk, cereal—when he noticed that the door to the Community Hall was ajar, and light was spilling out of it.

It was a bitterly cold night. September had given way to October, and as the days grew shorter, autumn was enshrouding the land in mist and fallen leaves. Daniel's breath fogged the air, and the fingers of his gloveless hands ached with cold. As he came parallel with the open door, he heard the comforting clink of crockery, and a brief ripple of laughter. He stopped, his breath rasping in his chest. Through the drifting fog of his own breath, he looked at the bar of welcoming light. He had been in the Community Hall several times with his mother, back in the days when she was still mobile. She'd been a great one for musicals, and had dragged Daniel along to local theatre productions of *Annie Get Your Gun* and *My Fair Lady*. Trawling those memories, he pictured what lay beyond that invitingly open door.

There was a short hallway, or vestibule area, with a door leading into a kitchen on the left, and male and female toilets side by side on the right. Straight ahead, at the end of the short hallway, another door led into the hall itself: a large, square, wooden-floored room with high ceilings and a stage at the far end, flanked by velvet curtains. When Daniel had last been here, the hall had been full of chairs, the majority of which were occupied, and he remembered how excited his mother had been, her eyes sparkling, her plump cheeks ruddy. The memory evoked a pang of grief, and was almost enough to make him turn from the welcoming band of light and resume his homeward trek. But before he could, a voice behind him, shy and hesitant, said, "Are you thinking of going in?"

The clench of sadness in Daniel's gut changed to alarm. He turned to see a woman, perhaps twenty years his senior. She was small, hollow-cheeked, frail as a bird. Dark hair flecked with grey peeked from beneath a woolly hat.

"Er…" Tongue-tied, Daniel stammered, "I'm not… I don't know."

"Why don't you try it? Everyone's very nice." The woman's voice was hesitant, diffident.

Daniel felt himself drawing in beneath his shell. "I don't think it's for me."

"You won't know unless you try it. My name's Angela. What's yours?"

"Er… Daniel."

"Do you live locally, Daniel?"

Vaguely he waved the hand that wasn't clutching his bag of groceries. "Couple of streets away."

"Why not pop in for a cuppa then? There's no obligation to stay for the duration. And at least it'd warm you up for the rest of your walk home."

Much to his own surprise, Daniel found himself nodding and following Angela through the doors of the Community Hall.

He hadn't known what to expect, but he was relieved to see there were only a handful of people here. He was relieved too that no one turned to assess him critically when he entered. Most people were sitting or standing around talking in pairs or groups of three. One man was standing at a trestle table below the hatch to the left of the main door, pouring himself a cup of tea from a big metal urn.

"Tea? Coffee?" Angela asked.

"Er… tea, please."

"Seeing it's your first time, I'll pour you one, but after that just help yourself. And help yourself to biscuits too. We've got a good selection this week. Custard creams and chocolate Hobnobs. Hello, Terry."

The man at the table, dressed in a brown sweater and black jeans, was tall, fiftyish, with a long, lugubrious face and thinning hair.

"Hello, Angela." He glanced at Daniel. "Hello. Are you a new recruit?"

"This is my friend, Daniel," Angela said. "We just met outside, so I dragged him in."

"Nice to meet you, Daniel," Terry said, extending a hand.

"Hi," Daniel said, and shook Terry's hand awkwardly after transferring his shopping bag from his right hand to his left. He was still getting over the surprise of Angela describing him as her friend.

She offered him his cup of tea, then realised he was still holding his bag. "Oh, sorry. Do you want to put your shopping down? You can leave it in that corner. It'll be quite safe."

"Oh… yeah. Thanks," said Daniel.

He turned to do as she had suggested, and when he turned back saw that Angela and Terry had been joined by a small, plump woman of about forty, with frizzy red hair and a beaming smile.

"Sorry to muscle in," she said. "I noticed a new face, so came over to say hi. I'm Liz."

"I'm Daniel," muttered Daniel.

"Liz started this group," said Angela.

"Oh," said Daniel.

If Liz noticed his awkwardness, she didn't show it. She said, "It's nice of you to drop in, Daniel. The more the merrier. How did you hear about us?"

"I had a… thing through the door." Flustered, his mind had blanked on the word *flyer*.

Liz seemed delighted. "Those were June's idea." She gestured towards a willowy woman in her seventies, who was chatting to a stooped man with a black beard. "Well, now you're here I expect you're wondering what we're all about?"

Daniel nodded dutifully.

"We're not a club as such," Liz continued. "There are no membership fees, no obligation to attend, nothing like that. We're just a group of people who meet every Tuesday evening for a chat and a cuppa and… well, that's about it."

"We have outings too," said Angela. "Sometimes, at weekends, we go on walks, or hire a minibus and go to the seaside, or sometimes to the cinema or the theatre. If there's ever anything anyone wants to do or see, and they fancy a bit of company, they just mention it here, and those who want to go along can do. Terry took a few of us metal-detecting the other Sunday. It was fun."

"But again, there's no obligation," Liz added, as if she sensed Daniel might be a bit overwhelmed at the prospect of so much socialising. "No one's going to judge you or put pressure on you if you don't want to join in. The whole point of these get-togethers is that they're casual, non-pressured, non-competitive, non-judgemental. I started the group about six months ago, after the restrictions eased, because I'd moved here from down south, and didn't know a soul, and like a lot of people was working from home. I decided to hire the hall on a weekly retainer, and then put an ad in the local paper. The first week there were three of us, and the next week a couple more came along, and now there are about fifteen of us. Some come every week, some just now and again. We've had people come and go, but we've got a nice little group going, haven't we?"

Angela and Terry were nodding. Angela said, "This group has been a lifeline for me. It stops me feeling lonely. Because that's what most of us are, or were before we started coming here, and there's no shame in that. Liz is lonely because she's far from home, and hasn't had the opportunity to make friends because of the pandemic. I'm lonely because I spend nearly all my time looking after my mum, who's got Alzheimer's. June's lonely because she's old and lives in sheltered accommodation…"

"My wife left me," Terry admitted, seemingly without embarrassment. "And it was only after she'd gone that I realised most of our mutual friends were *her* friends."

Angela laughed. "So you see, Daniel, we're all needy people. Not that I'm trying to put you off."

"Mum died," Daniel surprised himself by saying. There was a silence following his statement, but none of the three was looking at him as if he was something to be pitied or patronised. All he saw was genuine empathy and interest. It gave him the courage to go on.

"Just under four weeks ago. She'd been ill a long time, so it was a relief in a way. But still…"

Terry nodded in understanding. "A relief for her, but not much of one for you, eh? It doesn't matter how old or ill your mam or dad are, it still hits you like a train when they go."

"If you don't mind me asking," said Liz, "is your dad still around?"

Daniel shook his head.

"Any brothers or sisters? Aunties, uncles, cousins?"

"No… just me."

"So you've had to deal with all this on your own," said Angela. "That's tough."

"Looks like you found us at the right time," said Terry.

Angela smiled at him. "Give him a chance. He might decide he never wants to see any of us again after tonight."

Daniel surprised himself for the second time in as many minutes. "I won't," he said.

"Has anyone heard of the burning of the barrels?" Liz asked.

Everyone shook their head, Daniel included. It was three weeks since Angela had first enticed him into the hall, and much to his own surprise, not only had he been to every Tuesday meeting since, he had even been to both of the weekend outings the group had embarked upon that month—a trip to a local abbey owned by the National Trust, suggested by June, and a gentle tramp through some of the outlying villages, suggested by Barney, a retired science teacher and widower.

Daniel wasn't sure where his new-found hunger for company had come from. Perhaps his mother's death had pushed him beyond the bounds of solitude and isolation he was comfortable with; or perhaps it was simply that he had never been fortunate enough to find a more accepting and uncritical bunch of people before.

Certainly, he felt comfortable here. For the first time in his life, he felt as though he fitted in. As the weeks had progressed, he had found himself becoming less shy; had found his shell softening, crumbling. Angela, who had been the first to show him kindness, had become a particularly good chum. Daniel had found they shared the same quirky sense of humour; in fact, he had smiled and laughed more in the past few weeks than he had done in the past five or ten years.

"It sounds a bit sinister," June said now.

Liz laughed. "It's not really. Though it is dramatic. Perhaps even a bit alarming to outsiders."

"What is it?" Terry asked.

Liz was sitting on the edge of the stage, legs dangling, her frizzy red hair pushed back by a green Alice band. It was a foul night, and only seven of them had ventured out to the hall that evening. The wind and rain battering the building was causing the wooden rafters to creak overhead. But despite the conditions, the chunky iron radiators were pumping out plenty of heat, and Daniel, hands wrapped around his mug of tea, felt warm and cosy.

"It's a Bonfire Night tradition where I come from," Liz continued. "There are twelve pubs in the village, and each year, on November fifth, a dozen villagers are chosen, and each one carries a barrel of burning tar from one pub to the next. The first villager will carry the first barrel from pub one to pub two. Then the second villager will carry the second barrel from pub two to pub three, and so on."

"Like a tag team," said Terry.

Liz smiled. "Exactly. Tradition dictates that the first four barrel-bearers are children, the next four are women, and the last four are men. At the twelfth pub, the chosen villager carries the final barrel to the village square and uses it to light the huge bonfire that's been built there. Once the fire's been lit, we all eat and drink and make merry.

The whole village comes out to watch and celebrate. The streets are packed. It's great fun."

"Sounds rather pagan," said June.

"Not to mention a health and safety nightmare," said Angela.

Liz laughed again. "The tradition has certainly got pagan roots. The story goes that the fire was carried through the streets as some sort of cleansing rite, to burn away evil spirits."

"Or disease perhaps," suggested Barney.

Liz nodded. "Could be."

"So doesn't anyone ever get injured?" Angela asked. "I mean, burning barrels and crowds of people sounds to me like an accident waiting to happen."

"No one ever has as far as I know," Liz said, shrugging. "Or if they have, it's never been reported."

"Why are you telling us this?" asked Colin, who was the bearded man June had been talking to the first time Daniel had entered the hall. Like Terry, he had once been married, but after he and his wife had separated, she had moved to Spain with her new husband and taken their twin sons with her. Colin was quiet, reserved, and all Daniel knew about him was that he worked for a food packaging company, and that he loved cricket.

"Well, Bonfire Night's coming up in a couple of weeks, and I'm thinking of going back there for the weekend—if I don't, it'll be the first time I'll have missed it, and it's a big part of the village's social calendar. And... well, I just thought, if any of you were interested, I could hire the minibus and we could make a weekend of it. My uncle owns a hotel in the village, so I'm sure he'd give us a good rate. I know it's a bit further afield than where we'd usually go, but..." She shrugged. "Anyway, it's just a thought."

"Where is this village?" asked June.

"Wiltshire," said Liz. She grimaced. "It's probably a silly idea. I know it's a hell of a trek."

"A bit too much of a trek for me, I'm afraid," said June.

"Me too," said Barney. "I don't mind travelling if I'm going on holiday, but it's a long way just for a weekend."

"I'd be up for it," said Terry. "You know me—history buff extraordinaire. It sounds fascinating."

"Me too, if I can get a care nurse for Mum," said Angela.

"What about you, Colin?" said Liz.

He hesitated, then shook his head. "Probably not. Sorry."

"Daniel?"

Daniel glanced at Angela. She raised her eyebrows in a way that clearly meant: *Go on, it'll be fun!* He knew she had no romantic designs on him, which suited him just fine. He had no experience of women in that regard, and would have run a mile if Angela, or any other woman, had shown any interest in him beyond the platonic.

He looked from her to Liz, and then he did what had recently become natural to him: he smiled. "Why not?" he said.

"Hello."

"Daniel?"

"Yes," Daniel said warily, not immediately recognising the voice.

"Sorry to call you at home. It's Liz. I'm afraid we have a bit of a situation."

"Oh. Right," Daniel said. He had never been good on the phone. He was not a natural conversationalist, and the silences made him nervous.

Luckily, though, Liz was already talking again, rapidly and breathlessly. "There's been a slight cock-up on the minibus front. I'm afraid it's been double-booked, which means we can't hire it for our trip to Wiltshire this weekend. As there are only four of us, I'd offer to take us in my little car, but it would be too much of a squeeze, especially with our luggage, so I hope you don't mind, but I've booked train tickets for the 3.10 train on Friday for you, Angela and Terry. They're all paid for, so you don't have to worry about that. All you have to do is turn up at the station, go to the ticket machine, and put in your credit or debit card—it won't be charged. Then you just type in your collection reference, which I'll text to you now. Is that okay?"

"Er…" Daniel tried to take in everything she'd said to him. "Yes, okay."

"I'm going to drive down to Wiltshire beforehand, so I'll meet you all at the station. Sorry for the inconvenience. It's a pain, I know."

"It's… it's okay," Daniel said.

"Lovely. Thanks for being so understanding. I'll see you on Friday. Bye."

"Bye," Daniel mumbled, but she had already rung off. Next moment his phone buzzed in his pocket. He pulled it out and saw it was a text from Liz, who he must have given his phone number to at some point, with the collection reference she'd promised—a string of numbers and letters.

The abrupt change of plans unsettled Daniel, but he supposed it would be all right. In fact, it would probably be more enjoyable travelling by train, as long car journeys often made him feel sick. With his phone in his hand, he sent a text to Angela, who was only the second person he'd ever texted, besides his mother. The text was short: *Have you heard from Liz? She's just told me about the change of plans for Friday.*

He waited a while, but heard nothing back, which was unusual for Angela, as she usually replied fairly quickly. Then he remembered her looking for her phone at the weekly meeting last night.

"Are you all right?" he'd asked her, as she'd rooted through her shoulder bag, a worried expression on her face.

"I can't find my phone," she'd said. "I'm sure it was in here."

"Maybe you left it at home," Daniel said.

She chewed her lip. "Maybe. But I don't usually forget it when I go out. I like to have it with me in case the nurse needs to ring me about Mum."

She'd taken everything out of her bag and checked the pockets of her coat, but her phone hadn't been there. Daniel knew she travelled to the Community Hall by bus, and wondered whether it had fallen out of her pocket. He didn't say anything, though, for fear of worrying her. In the end she'd shrugged and said, "Oh well, it's not here, so it *must* be at home."

"I'm sure everything will be all right," Daniel had said.

"Yes," she'd replied, "I'm sure it will be."

But she'd looked distracted and anxious for the rest of the evening.

When Daniel stepped off the train it was already dark. He looked up and down the platform, feeling out of sorts. The sight of Liz hurrying towards him, waving madly, at least helped to assuage the gnawing sense of disorientation he'd been feeling ever since the train had pulled out of York station. Liz's welcoming grin changed to a look of puzzlement as she reached him.

"Where are the others?" she asked, tilting her head as though they might be crouched behind Daniel, playing a trick on her.

"I don't know," Daniel said. "They weren't on the train."

"Did you call them?"

"Angela's not answering her phone. I think she might have lost it. And I don't know Terry's number."

"Let me try," Liz said. She produced her mobile, jabbed at the screen, then held the phone up to her ear. After a moment she said, "It's ringing," and then she frowned and said, "Voicemail." She paused, presumably waiting for the message to finish—Daniel couldn't hear anything above the grumbling of the departing train—and then she said, "Terry, hi, this is Liz. The train's here and so is Daniel, but he tells me neither you nor Angela were on it. Presumably there's been some sort of mix-up. Call me when you get this message."

Moving the phone away from her ear, she jabbed at it again. "Calling Angela now," she said, and listened for a while. Thirty seconds later she lowered the phone with a frown, then switched it off with her thumb and dropped it back into her pocket. "No answer. I wonder what's happened. Do you think they both decided not to come?"

"Angela wouldn't have without telling me," said Daniel.

Liz frowned. "Yes, it's very strange. Oh well, perhaps they'll turn up. In the meantime, I ought to take you to your hotel so you can leave your bag and do whatever you need to do. The lighting of the first barrel is less than an hour away."

"All ready?" said Liz, who was waiting for Daniel in the foyer.

Daniel nodded, forcing a smile, though in truth he felt unsettled, and somewhat uncomfortable in Liz's company. She was a perfectly nice person, but Daniel had never spent any one-on-one time with her in the few weeks since he'd started attending the Tuesday night meetings.

He supposed it would be okay, though. It wasn't as if they had to sit and chat over a drink or a meal. They'd be walking about, surrounded by crowds, following the route of the burning barrels through the narrow streets of the village. There probably wouldn't be much time for conversation—at least not until the end of the evening, when the bonfire was lit and the party was under way in the village square.

Perhaps at that point he could feign tiredness and head back to the hotel. He'd probably be doing Liz a favour. This was her home, after all. There were more than likely people she wanted to catch up with—family and friends.

"Let's head over to The Plough then," she said, clapping her gloved hands together and beaming at him from beneath her pink bobble-hat. "That's our first port of call."

She led the way down the steps of the family-run hotel and out onto the street. There was already a steady flow of people heading towards the centre of the village, all of them wrapped up against the bitter cold, their collective breath coiling like vapour from a steam train. The mood was one of celebration. People were smiling, chatting, laughing; the children were running around, waving sparklers and shrieking joyously. There was a charred smell in the air, but it wasn't unpleasant. It was like wood smoke blended with something aromatic.

"It's so wonderful to share this experience with a new friend," Liz said, her face glowing with happiness and rosy health.

Daniel wished Angela and Terry were here—the presence of either of them would make him feel less awkward, less as though this was some kind of weird date. He wondered if Liz felt the same; if she was simply making the best of things in an effort to put him at ease. The notion that she might be drew a smile out of him. "It's great to be here," he made himself say.

She reached out, and for an alarming moment he thought she was going to take his hand. But instead she simply touched him briefly on his coat sleeve, and with childish glee she said, "Come on."

The streets grew more congested the closer they got to The Plough. The people seemed to know to leave the centre of the street clear, instead packing onto the pavements, and milling around what appeared to be a ramshackle market stall where it looked as though drinks were being served. Just outside the door to the pub, glimpsed through the bobbing heads of the crowd, Daniel saw a small wooden barrel, standing on a piece of coarse brown sacking. The barrel was open at the top, the interior coated thickly with tar.

"Wait here," Liz said. "Don't move."

Before Daniel could respond, she turned and disappeared into the crowd.

For a few seconds he saw her bobble-hat jinking among the crush of people, like a bright pink boat on a dark sea, and then it sank out of sight. He stood where he was, seemingly the only solitary person within a chattering tide of humanity. Where had Liz gone? Had she seen someone she knew? He was just wondering whether he should follow the crowd if she wasn't back by the time the first barrel-bearer set off on their journey, when two people in front of him moved aside and she popped out between them. Her gloved hands were held tight to her chest, and at first Daniel thought she was clutching a pair of tiny binoculars. Then she extended her left hand towards him, and he saw she was holding a small plastic glass, like a shot glass, brimming with amber liquid.

"Every pub here brews its own beer," she said. "It's traditional to have a little taster at each one along the route. Keep your glass with you, so you can use it again."

Looking around, Daniel now noticed other people knocking back mouthfuls of ale, or clutching their own tiny glasses, having already done so.

He took the proffered glass, mumbling, "I don't really…" But before he could say "drink" his voice tailed off, not least because Liz was already knocking back her own mouthful and wasn't listening to him. He suddenly decided it was good she hadn't heard. He didn't want her to think him a party-pooper. Although he wasn't keen on beer, he tilted his head back and swallowed it quickly, like medicine. He braced himself for the bitter taste, and was pleasantly surprised by how sweet it was; in fact, it was delicious.

Liz grinned at the expression on his face. "Good, eh?"

"It's… great," Daniel said.

"There's more where that came from. Oh, here she comes."

Liz was looking towards the pub entrance, and Daniel looked that way too. A girl no older than nine or ten, her head wrapped in a headscarf, was emerging from the pub doorway, smiling shyly and waving at the crowd, who were cheering and applauding. The girl was wearing a pair of thick black gloves that reached almost to her elbows, and made her hands look cartoonishly large, but aside from that, there were no particular concessions to the dangerous task she was about to undertake. A bearded man stepped out behind her and arranged what appeared to be a canvas shawl on her shoulders. Then he hoisted the barrel up and heaved it onto her back. The girl, stooping a little to accommodate its weight, reached up and gripped it tightly.

Next, the bearded man produced what to Daniel looked like a giant matchstick—a length of wood, its end wound tightly with a bulb of dark cloth—and held it up, to more cheers. Another man stepped out of the crowd and lit the bulb, and immediately it burst into flames. The bearded man applied the burning brand to the tar-smeared barrel on the girl's shoulders, and that too erupted into flame. Daniel gasped as the flames leaped three or four metres into the air, but the rest of the crowd, Liz included, were cheering and whooping, their faces wreathed in grins. At once, the girl began to run along the street, the fire from the barrel streaming behind her, casting a wash of orange light across the faces of the delighted onlookers. Although the mood was celebratory, almost rapturous, Daniel couldn't help thinking the briefly illuminated faces looked demonic, ghoulish, like a row of Halloween pumpkins.

As one, the crowd began to move, following the girl. Liz plucked at his sleeve encouragingly, and then Daniel too found himself being carried along by the eager crowd, his feet moving so fast he felt in danger of stumbling and falling.

He didn't, though, and two minutes later the crowd was slowing, stopping. Daniel saw they were now at the second pub, The White Hart, the sign of which, depicting a snow-white, antlered stag, its head twisted to regard the arrow piercing its hindquarters, was creaking as it flapped in the wind.

Upon reaching the pub, two men hurried forward, both wearing flame-retardant gloves, and took the burning barrel from the girl's shoulders. Lowering it to the ground with a clunk, another man came forward and doused the flames with a fire extinguisher. Straightening up, the girl raised her hands in response to the crowd's cheers, a wide grin splitting her sooty face. She was swept up and carried around on someone's shoulders, while members of the jubilant crowd reached up to shake her gloved hand as if she were a celebrity.

Other members of the crowd, meanwhile, were gravitating towards another of the ramshackle market stalls set up to the left of the pub doorway. Before the crowd engulfed them, Daniel caught a glimpse of four women bearing glass jugs filled with frothing amber liquid. With great speed and efficiency, the women were filling up the dozens of glasses held out towards them.

"Have you still got your glass?" Liz asked, holding out a hand.

"Yes," said Daniel, and passed it to her.

"Back in a sec," she said, and plunged into the crowd.

She reappeared just as a second child, a boy this time, gangly and freckled, emerged from the pub. Daniel took his glass from Liz, and after a moment's hesitation he again tilted back his head and tipped the contents into his mouth.

If anything, this second mouthful of ale was even more delicious than the first. It was heady and spicy, and the word that immediately entered his mind was: *nectar.* He felt it suffusing his body with warmth as it trickled into his stomach. When Liz asked him if it was good, he giggled as if she'd said something funny.

"Nectar," he said, releasing the word in his head.

Liz laughed, then let out an excited whoop as the barrel that had been hoisted onto the boy's shoulders leaped with flame. Immediately the crowd was off again, carrying Daniel along with them. He felt as if he were floating, flying, as they set off after the second barrel-bearer. Liz, in her bright pink hat, was giggling so much that Daniel couldn't help laughing too. Although their view of the barrel-bearer was blocked by the sheer number of people in front of them, there was no fear they'd lose track of him. The flame from his barrel leaped into the night sky. Writhing in the wind, shedding sparks and gouting black smoke, it was like some elemental force, some sprite leading its followers in an arcane dance.

By the time they reached the fifth pub, The Harvest Moon, Daniel felt as though the crowd had become a single entity, and that he was an integral part of it. The four mouthfuls of ale he'd consumed had smoothed his jagged edges, erased his inhibitions. No longer did he feel like an outsider here. No longer did he feel awkward or uncomfortable in Liz's presence. He threw back his fifth mini-glass of ale with no hesitation, and gasped as it fizzed in his head like synaptic fireworks. He felt happy. So happy.

"I'm having *such* a great time," he said.

"I'm glad," said Liz. "It was so great that you joined us when you did. It was meant to be."

"I think so too," said Daniel. "If I hadn't found you—found you all—I don't know what I'd have done."

The fifth barrel-bearer was a woman, and the barrel larger this time. The fire, when it was lit, leaped high into the night—five, six metres. Daniel roared his approval along with everyone else.

By the time they reached a pub called The Boxing Hare, Daniel's vision was blurring and he was beginning to lose count.

"Is this the eighth pub or the ninth?" he asked, his tongue feeling too big for his mouth.

Liz laughed and handed him another mini-glass of ale. "Does it matter?"

"Not really," Daniel said, laughing, and knocked back his drink.

The next pub was The Lost Crown, and Daniel noticed that the barrel-bearer this time was a broad-shouldered man with a tattooed neck and shaven head. Was this the first adult male barrel-bearer, or the second? Or maybe it was the third? All Daniel could recall was the barrels themselves, their flames clawing at the night sky, and sometimes even swirling into the pressing crowd, although no one appeared to have been hurt.

Deciding to ask Liz, he turned, but she wasn't there. She must've gone to get the drinks. The prospect of knocking back another mouthful of nectar filled him with delicious anticipation—but when the barrel had been lit and the crowd had begun to move off in pursuit of the departing barrel-bearer, she still hadn't returned. Dismayed at the prospect of missing out, he made his way through the tail end of the crowd towards the familiar trestle table with its overhead canopy, where the women had been distributing the drinks.

Seeing they were packing away, Daniel asked, "Is there no nectar left?"

"Nectar?" said a large, florid-faced woman with an amused expression.

"Beer. Has it all gone?"

"You got a glass, lovey?" another woman asked. This one was younger, her blond hair tied in an elaborate plait.

"My friend's got it."

"Who's your friend?"

"Liz, er…" For the life of him, Daniel couldn't remember her surname. Instead he gestured vaguely at his own head. "Pink hat."

"Oh, I know Liz," said a third woman, sharp-faced and dark-haired. She pointed down an alley between The Lost Crown and the building next door. "I saw her going down there."

"Why?"

"No idea, lovey. Perhaps she wasn't feeling well."

"Or maybe she had a secret assignation," said the large woman, and cackled.

Daniel looked at the narrow gap the woman had indicated. In the darkness it was nothing but a black strip, barely wide enough for two people walking shoulder to shoulder.

"I suppose I'd better see if she's all right," he mumbled, aware that the crowd following the latest barrel-bearer was growing ever more distant.

The large woman winked at him. "I suppose you'd better."

"Before you go, though…" said the fourth and youngest woman, and held out one of the small glasses, brim-full of golden liquid. "Wouldn't want you missing out."

"Thank you," Daniel said. He took the glass and swallowed its contents, to approving laughter. The drink went straight to his head, making everything spin. He staggered past the trestle table and the four women, and entered the mouth of the alley. Behind him, booming and discordant, their laughter seemed to follow him.

Eventually, though, it faded, and Daniel suddenly realised how alone he was. For the last hour or so, he had felt an integral part of a swarm, a flock, a shoal, but now he felt... not exactly cast out, but a little bereft at the knowledge that his absence would not detract one iota from the crowd's enjoyment.

Staggering along the alley, his thoughts muzzy, his body not quite feeling as though it belonged to him, he wondered again where Angela and Terry were, why they hadn't turned up. Had they not received Liz's message about the tickets? When he found Liz, he'd ask her whether she'd actually spoken to them. Perhaps, having been unable to reach them, she'd simply left them messages, or sent them texts? If so, it might explain why Angela wasn't here, having lost her phone a few days ago.

The alley was dark and silent, and contained no sign of life. "Liz," Daniel called, his voice echoing off the dank walls either side of him. "Are you in here?"

No reply. Where could she have gone? Could the ale have affected her so much that she had lost her bearings and was now wandering around, confused?

He reached a T-junction—another alleyway, as narrow as this one, stretching to his left and right. He looked in both directions, but this alley too was unlit, and after ten metres or so the faint glint of light on the damp walls faded to blackness.

"Liz!" he shouted again, but there was no response. Perhaps he ought to turn back? But when he looked over his shoulder, he realised he was no longer alone. The alley behind him was now occupied by a dark, bulky figure carrying a burning barrel on its back. Flames were leaping from the barrel, six, seven metres into the air, the walls on either side writhing with reflected light.

Despite the soporific effect of the alcohol, Daniel's stomach clenched with fear. The figure was maybe twenty metres away, but marching remorselessly towards him. Daniel knew there was no way he could wait and let the figure go past—there simply wasn't room. And besides, he had a horrible feeling that the figure was here not despite him, but *because* of him.

All he could do, then, was go forward. But which way? Left or right? As if about to cross a road, he glanced quickly both ways, and suddenly realised the decision had been made for him. To his left, emerging from the darkness, was a flicker of flame, which Daniel quickly realised was a second barrel-bearer. The alcohol seemed to coalesce into a queasy, pounding terror in his head and gut. Feeling slow and uncoordinated, he went the only way he could—to his right.

At first he walked quickly, trying to maintain his dignity, trying to convince himself this was all some silly mistake. But another glance back at the silhouetted figure, above which flames were leaping, caused his nerve to fail and he broke into a stumbling run. Within seconds his breath was rasping in his chest, his lungs labouring, his right side burning with a stitch as painful as a knife wound. Never had Daniel been so aware of his own lack of fitness. Never had he been gripped by such acute and primal terror, not even when Adam Smedley and his sneering friends had cornered him at school.

The alley, still narrow, still enclosed by high stone walls, curved to the left. Following the curve, Daniel saw another T-junction ahead of him.

His heart leaped. Here was potential salvation. If he could only choose the right direction in which to turn, he would be out of the path of the two barrel-bearers, and his ordeal would be over.

But upon reaching the junction, he again realised that the choice had been taken from him. Thirty metres to his left was a third dark figure, flames coiling upwards from the barrel on its shoulders. Seen from a distance, and with no light to provide definition, this barrel-bearer, like the others, appeared demonic—faceless, featureless, the flames that flowed from its hunched form seeming to emanate directly from within it.

So terrified was Daniel now that he began to blubber like a child. Turning right again, he stumbled and staggered, unsure whether it was the alcohol that was making him slow and clumsy, or simply the debilitating effects of his own terror. There was a part of him that wanted to curl into a ball, shut his eyes, deny this was happening. He even briefly wondered whether this was a nightmare, whether he'd suddenly wake with a jolt and find himself in his own bed, or back on the train.

He came to another junction, and again, to his left, was a fourth barrel-bearer. There was no question about it now—he was being herded, manipulated like a rat in a maze. But to what purpose? Again, with no other option, he turned right, and a minute later, panting, sweating and sobbing, he came to yet another junction. Reaching it, he prepared to again look left, expecting to see another dark figure, another leap of flame.

But this junction, as he approached it, seemed different. The others had been characterised by only a slight variation of darkness between the walls on either side and the one that faced him; in effect, the facing wall at the end of each alley had resembled a dark grey door set into a black wall. The gap between the enclosing walls here, though, was lighter and composed of different textures. There was a suggestion of depth and space, which gave him a surge of hope. Could this be the end of the maze? Was he about to emerge into somewhere that would provide him with more opportunities to escape his pursuers? The prospect energised him, and he put on a spurt of speed. He burst from the alley, and suddenly sensed movement all around him. Disorientated, he faltered, looking around wildly—and then relaxed. He was back among the crowd. He saw heads turning towards him, smiles appearing on faces, nods of approval.

But almost immediately his relief turned to disquiet. No, he wasn't *among* the crowd. Instead he had emerged into a narrow channel *between* them. He was in what he guessed must be the village square that Liz had mentioned; certainly, it was a large open area surrounded by buildings. Daniel, though, was still as confined as he had been in the alleyway, except this time the walls were composed not of stone but of people. They were packed tight, shoulder to shoulder, having formed a kind of honour guard on either side of him.

Thinking the best way to hide from his pursuers was to merge with the crowd, Daniel moved towards the wall of people on his left, expecting them to shuffle apart, allow him to squeeze between them.

But to his dismay and alarm, they stood firm, refusing to let him in. They were not aggressive towards him, they even continued to smile. Yet when he approached them and said, "Excuse me," all those within reach simply stretched out their hands and gently pushed him away.

"I just want to…" Daniel said, but a woman interrupted him. Shaking her head and pointing to her left, she said, "That way, dear."

Daniel looked in the direction she was indicating. Perhaps fifty metres away, at the end of the human corridor, was something that, due to his disorientation, he hadn't even registered when he had first emerged from the alleyway. It was a vast hill, twenty or more metres high, wide at the bottom, tapering to a mound at the top.

No, Daniel suddenly realised, *not a hill. A bonfire.* He remembered again what Liz had said at the meeting a couple of weeks ago—how, once the bonfire had been lit, the villagers would eat and drink and make merry.

Wiping tears, snot and sweat from his face, he stumbled towards the bonfire, looking left and right. All around him villagers were smiling, nodding, urging him on. Whenever he got close to them, though, be it on his left or his right, they reached out, gently pushed him not only away, but towards the vast mound of wood and debris dominating the centre of the square. If even one of them had been hostile or aggressive towards him, Daniel, frightened and confused, might have responded in kind. But they weren't. They were gentle, encouraging. Scared as he was, even now he wondered whether he had misinterpreted the sense of threat that this situation implied, whether he was simply worrying unduly about a harmless quirk of village tradition.

At last he reached the bonfire. He looked up at it, and then he stepped forward and placed his hands on the tangle of planks and twisted branches and broken items of furniture, half thinking that perhaps he could make his escape by tearing a route right through the middle. But it was as impenetrable as barbed wire. In despair he turned to face the crowd, who were all looking at him, all smiling and nodding eagerly.

"I don't like this," he said, his voice as plaintive as a child's. "I don't want to be a part of this. I've had enough."

Just then, there was a flicker of light at the far end of the corridor of villagers, and the first of the barrel-bearers, who had pursued him through the maze of alleyways, stepped out of the dark gap from which Daniel himself had emerged minutes earlier.

Daniel's heart clenched, and, gripped by panic, he turned again to the huge bonfire in front of him. Instinctively he hurled himself at it, his only thought being that if he could make it up and over the huge mound, he could yet escape.

And amazingly, fuelled by the adrenaline of sheer desperation, he found himself making progress. The vast mound was so solidly constructed, the individual items that formed it so tightly wedged, that as he hauled himself up, he found handholds and footholds a-plenty. He gasped, and sweated, and shook, and cried, and his heart whacked painfully in his chest, but he kept going. He climbed five metres above the ground, then ten, then fifteen.

When he was twenty metres above the ground, a wave of dizziness engulfed him. As black spots danced in his eyes, he clung for dear life to the jags of wood he had been using as handholds. Long seconds passed, and then, at last, the dizziness faded. Now, for the first time, Daniel became aware that the crowd below him were cheering loudly. Still clinging to the mound of wood, he twisted to see what was happening.

Below him, he saw that all four barrel-bearers had now emerged from the alleyway, and had placed their barrels in a semi-circle at the foot of the bonfire. Each of the four was now standing back from their barrel, looking up at him. For an awful second, illuminated by the yellow firelight, each of them seemed to wear the grinning, mocking features of Adam Smedley. But then the illusion passed, and the faces of the four men swam and changed and became those of people he didn't recognise.

Then the line of men stepped apart, two to one side, two to the other, and someone Daniel *did* recognise stepped between them. Still wearing her bright pink bobble hat, Liz raised her head, beaming up at him. In her hand she held one of the brands that had been used to ignite the barrels earlier.

"Thank you, Daniel," she shouted. "You do our village the greatest honour, and we love you and will always remember you for it."

As the crowd burst into a fresh wave of cheering and applause, Liz thrust the brand into the wall of fire created by the combination of the four burning barrels, the bulbous end instantly erupting into flame. Then, without hesitation, she tossed the brand through the wall of fire and onto the bonfire.

Some of the smaller bits of debris at the bottom of the bonfire caught light, and instantly started to spread. Black smoke curled up towards Daniel, making him cough.

Turning back to face the mound of timber in front of him, Daniel again frantically began to climb. Behind him, far below, the cheering of the crowd became wilder, more jubilant. But louder still was the hungry crackling of flame, which, though he wouldn't stop trying, Daniel knew he could never outpace.

SOLIVAGANT

A. G. Slatter

It's Monday morning when Magda Doubinsky discovers all her chickens are dead.

Slaughtered.

Every egg crushed too.

A poultry genocide.

Even from here I can see the bright red flecks on the snow. Not just near the ramshackle coop, but scattered the length and breadth of the front yard. Feathers too, although only the dark-coloured ones really show.

There's nothing wrong with Magda; she's a nice old lady. The neighbours can't imagine who'd do this sort of thing as they gather outside her house, clucking, offering sympathy to the distraught woman. Magda's been in the garden all morning now; she's shifted from seeking help and howling to simply telling whoever walks by what's happened. Gathered quite a crowd, she has. The attention's paying her back a thousandfold, so I guess that's something. Making a connection with one's fellow humans.

Who would do such a thing?

Who indeed?

I'll have to go out soon, go across the road, stop peeking through the dusty blinds that I really need to clean. Go and make my presence known so no one looks in our direction. There's some leeway, everyone knows I work late (because everyone knows just about fucking everything in this teeny-tiny town), stocking shelves at the Mart on Carrow Street, and I sleep late as a result. But there's only so much grace that buys you—folk are naturally suspicious of those who don't conform to the norm. My own mother used to regard anyone who wasn't an early riser as some sort of deviant. Possibly still does.

"You shouldn't have done it," I say in a low voice.

He can't hear me, of course, slumbering dead as he does. We've been here, what? Six months? It's been nice. Settled. Quiet. Then he fucking does this. He always does something like this.

A batch of cookies can be whipped up in under twenty minutes, and hand-delivered to Magda's door. I'll make myself presentable while they're in the oven, remove last night's makeup that's a little like a melted clown face because I was too lazy to take it off when I got home. A new layer applied will cover a myriad of sins. I head to the kitchen.

"Tea, dear Kitty?"

Magda's delighted with the offering; no one else had thought to bring anything to sweeten their sympathy. When I turned up, she shooed the stragglers of her audience and ushered me inside. It's dark; smells nice in here, clean, and sort of like spices and potpourri. Like stepping into the specialist bath and bedlinen shop on Main. It shouldn't do so well in such a small place, but apparently it's hit the town's weak spot for long, luxurious soaking and high thread count sheets.

"Thanks, Magda, yes." Through the dim hallway lined with old photographs—like really old, daguerreotypes and tintypes, plus a few faded ones from maybe the 1970s or '80s but nothing later than that.

I wonder if all these people are dead, and there were no children to keep the line going, no one to take new photos. I don't look too close, don't ask questions about lost families. The kitchen, when we step into it, is surprisingly bright. A lot of windows, a lot of clear glass rather than the ones at the front that're frosted and coloured in spots, with heavy curtains to keep out the sun. Feels like two different buildings.

"Sit, sit."

I obey—it's a bad habit—and slide onto a bench seat against a wall; outside's a backyard, overgrown, almost tropical-looking but for the snow on every branch and leaf. There's a long heavy table in front of me, an ancient refrigerator in a nook, a woodfire stove that looks like it came with the ark but is keeping the room toasty warm. Warmer than our whole house on its best days. That's the problem with renting, and renting cheap: lucky if there's a lick of insulation. If there is, it's probably asbestos.

She's little, is Magda, quite tiny. Surprisingly so—after a few seconds of staring as she bustles around the space, I start to think she might actually be shrinking before my eyes. I blink, shake my head. I'm tired, a little dizzy, a little anaemic. I look again: she's stabilised. Short, but normal short.

"Milk?"

"No, thanks. Black's good, whatever you've got."

"I mix my own blends! My mother used to do it, and her mother before her."

Ah, crap. What have I let myself in for? But when she puts the pretty floral teapot in front of me, with the paired pretty floral cups (their glaze a little crazed with age—but aren't we all?) the steam coming from it smells intoxicating.

"Rose petals, blackberries, lavender, a little lemon peel—every batch is different because I don't measure anything. I like surprises." She smiles until she doesn't because, I imagine, she's remembering what she found this morning. Poor Magda. Poor chickens.

"Are you okay, Magda?" I ask as she pours the tea, then hurries back to the counter to collect the cookies I brought—transferred from my dingy plastic plate to an ancient porcelain thing, much better than anything I own. "I'm so sorry about… you know."

"Not very pleasant to wake up to," says she, eyes darkening and narrowing behind big black-framed glasses. But the hand that passes me the teacup on a matching saucer doesn't shake. This little old lady's not for the frightening it seems. Still, I wonder how she'd go if she knew what had done for her chickens? She finishes kindly, "But you didn't do it."

I never do anything.

"Maybe a fox?" I suggest. "A big one. A mean one."

"Maybe," she says, grabbing a cookie like it's done her wrong. "Or something."

I reach over, take one; still soft, the warmth is fleeing, though the dot of jam is just under molten. Not bad. I could have eaten them at home, but then I'd miss out on the company. Why today, though? Of all days? Why come over today? It's no sort of anniversary, nothing that might make me nostalgic. And I've seen so much grief over the years, my own, other people's—why this little old lady?

Funny how death can bring people together.

Yeah, real funny.

"And how are you, Miss Kitty? Seen that boyfriend of yours lately?"

"Some," I say. "He travels a lot. I'm alone a lot. It suits us."

"Well, I guess folk like their space." She nods, chews. "Delicious. No one bothers you in that house on your own?"

"Nope. How about you?" *Chickens notwithstanding.*

"No one's tried to break in here since 1985." She sits back with a smile, as if the memory is very pleasant, and a shiver runs up my spine, does a tumble-turn at the base of the neck, and runs back down.

"What happened in 1985?" I ask.

"Just some silly boys got taught a lesson." A wider smile, surprisingly white teeth, and I think she's kind of boasting, bigging herself up. As if she could have done anything; maybe there was a husband here then, who took care of matters. I imagine a big bear of a man with hands like hams. Suddenly I regret coming over; but equally I want to tell her everything. That I'm sorry, really sorry, and I know who did it. And I'm really, really sorry.

Instead I swallow down the last mouthful of cookie, drink too fast the tea that's still hot. The burn on my tongue, in my throat as the liquid passes by, is a sort of a comfort—I'll regret it later—but for now it's an intensity that breaks through the daily numbness. I stand.

"Well, I'd better go, Magda. I've got a few chores to do before work tonight. Thanks for…" I gesture around. "Let me know if I can do anything to help."

"You've done enough, Kitty. Thank you for your kindness. The Kane boys are going to clean up the bodies soon, and Abel Tasker's bringing more chickens tomorrow."

"Do you need any help paying for them?" I reach for the wallet in my back pocket, remember I left it at home because why would I need it to visit a neighbour? But it doesn't matter because she's shaking her head. I'll go to the feed'n'seed and put a hundred bucks of credit on her account, just to smooth things along. My conscience mostly.

"I'm not impoverished, Missy, thank you very much." But she doesn't sound offended. I'm reminded of my Great-Aunty Ede who could tell you off without making you feel bad. Should have been a diplomat, should Ede. My hostess walks me out.

"Bye, Magda."

"Bye, Kitty Lang."

I can feel her eyes on me as I cross the road, but when I turn at my door to wave, she's gone.

~

I hate the cans.

They're unreasonably heavy. Peas are the worst. Or second worst. Any of your canned meats are hefty but you kind of expect that. Peas, though? Seriously. Should definitely be lighter than they are.

The advantage of cans is that they fit together nicely, a good and simple system of interlocking. Boxes not so much. Boxes are kind of ass when it comes to stacking; too light, especially cereal, easy to knock over. Then you've got to start again, and *then* Beanie Donaghy, Night Manager at the Mart, wants to have a word with you, thank you very much. I try to avoid those chats. I really do my best to do so.

However, sometimes it is apparently unavoidable.

Like an hour ago when I had to restack a bunch of Reese's Puffs, which meant I was behind a schedule of some sort but of which I was not aware, because Lord forbid I should finish anything early. Beanie had subsequently walked along all the aisles and stuck bright yellow Post-its on anything she felt was not my best work. I couldn't help but feel she'd made extra slog for herself just because she didn't like me—my makeup in particular and my attitude in general. And the attitude, I guess, because I go out of my way to be an asshole at times; but the makeup's a masterpiece and should be acknowledged as such. I don't know why but there's just something about Beanie that makes me slather on that extra layer of black eyeliner, one more slick of red lipstick, and ensure my hair's dead straight, with the bangs cut precisely just below my brows so it always looks like I'm peering from behind a curtain. I do this because I once heard her boyfriend tell her I was hot and maybe she should try that look sometime. Which, coincidentally, was around the time Beanie decided she didn't like my attitude. I mean, seriously. I don't want her dumbass boyfriend, but I do like irritating a woman stupid enough to think I do.

It's been a long six months.

"Hey, baby."

His voice in my ear, and I didn't even hear him come up to me. I should be used to it. It shouldn't make me startle after all these years. But it does. Has a different effect nowadays. Once it would send me into a fever of want, how quiet he was, how he'd just appear. It's been a while since I felt that way; now I'm just afraid. And it makes me feel even more alone than I usually do when I'm sitting in whatever house in whatever town we've washed up in, and he's sleeping in a cellar or beneath the floorboards, up in the attic or in a crawlspace, anywhere the sunlight can't find him.

And I don't make friends anymore because if—*when*—he finds out, they get treated like Magda's chickens and we have to move all over again. It's always him. Except once in the early days. That was all me.

I did something terrible, and I'm sorry for it, but there's no going back and fixing it, is there? It wasn't that girl's fault, and he'd never intended anything except making a meal of her; I tell myself I can't remember her name. I didn't know any better then, and he was all I had. He'd taken everything else, hadn't he? But because I was so new to him and his life, I was terrified he'd replace me quick-smart if I wasn't good. Didn't realise how far he liked to push and tease my insecurities because it made me obedient, didn't it? Fearful and obedient. I didn't realise *then* that you don't throw away someone like me so easily, even if you tell them every day how worthless they are. Compliance is a price above rubies, after all.

The red hair's always a surprise, no matter how many times I see him, kept long and in a ponytail. The scattering of freckles across his nose and cheeks, a little faded but still evident, green eyes, thin lips, big ears. Black T-shirt stretched across a chest that's wide but not muscular, greyhound belly I used to love to slide my hand down, heavy boots, long legs in black stovepipe jeans, black leather jacket over the top the only concession to winter. It's been a long while since that's made me burn. It's two a.m., almost my quitting time. There's a glow in his cheeks, a false warmth. Stolen. Hopefully not from around here; hopefully he did what he's meant to: go elsewhere, another town, running as fast as he does, riding the night, leaving no trace.

"Why?" I say.

"Why what?" Feigned ignorance.

"Why Magda's chickens?" I want to beat him around the head with this can of beets.

"Magda? First name basis? Have you made a friend, my kitten?" And his tone's dangerous so fast.

"Don't be an idiot. Everyone calls her that." I shrug like I don't care. "She's an old lady, she's done you no harm. And what did the chickens ever do to you? It was stupid."

"Maybe I was just feeling… foxy." He laughs. It's a loud bark that manages, somehow, to echo around the Mart. Sure to attract Beanie, who's probably watching me on the security cameras to make sure I'm not pocketing canned ham or other high-value items.

"Stupid," I say again. "Shitty. You'll draw attention and I'll have to get us out of here."

"But you're so good at it—"

"Lang? What did I tell you about goofing off with friends?" Beanie rounds the corner of the aisle faster than you can imagine, her heeled boots click-clacking. Man, she must have been booking it from the little office out back. *Nothing, Beanie, you told me nothing because I don't have any friends and no one's ever visited me before.* Not even him. The fact he's here tells me he's getting ready to start some shit.

But I don't say any of that. I bow my head, look out from under my bangs (because a little passive-aggressive fucking never hurt anyone, and it feeds whatever whirlpool of ache lives within me) and speak very softly. "I'm sorry, Beanie."

"I should fire you." Her lips, smothered in a peachy pink gloss, pucker like an asshole as if she's considering it. She's a reasonably attractive girl, it's just her personality that leaves a lot to be desired. And it's cute she thinks I think she can fire me, however, speaking of passive-aggressive fucking; her dad owns the place and he hired me and he's got tastes his little girl doesn't want to know about.

Oh, nothing creepy, but Big Bill Donaghy—terror of the loading dock, darling of little old ladies with handfuls of coupons, and scourge of the town council's rezoning ambitions—has a penchant for being told what to do and ridden around as if he's a pony with a bit in his mouth. Once a week we meet at a Motel 6 a couple of towns over. He doesn't seem to care if anyone thinks it's an affair—eligible widowman as he is—but certainly wouldn't want anyone knowing what it *really* is. And Billy-boy's aware he's unlikely to find anyone else in Hope's Bluff who's going to keep his secrets for a low-paying job of restocking shelves plus an extra envelope of tax-free cash every week. There's a notice in the window I want to see: *"Man seeks rider. Will provide own saddle. No funny stuff."*

Maybe it is a little creepy. It's just so hard to tell anymore.

"Beanie, is it?" The only sign of mockery is that Cinna's voice rises a couple of notches. There's that shiver, doing its thing up and down my spine again, but Beanie's too dumb to know what's good for her. I swear that girl would hear a rattlesnake shaking its booty and go right on over to have a word with it about the noise it was making and would it mind keeping things down. I don't like her, but not enough to see her at the end of his fingers, dangling with her cute clicky-clacky boots a foot off the ground. Although maybe it'd be funny? No. No, it would not.

"Cinna," I say gently. "Do what you will. I can't be bothered with her at the best of times."

Beanie's expression is priceless. The least I could do is hate her. Isn't indifference just the worst?

Cinna narrows his eyes, long nose almost twitching as if he might sniff the lie on the air. But I haven't spent all these years around him without learning a thing or two. If I don't care, why would he? He loses interest faster than you can imagine, it's as if a light goes out.

"Cinna?" Beanie says, only she pronounces it "sinner" and I think maybe I can't save her; maybe she's determined to be dead. But then he laughs. Should have known that would tickle him.

"I'll see you at home, Cinna. Beanie, I am sorry, it won't happen again." I look at the man who's the only lover I've ever known and say quite clearly, "I'll be there soon."

He wanders off, deprived of his fun. He might wait outside, hang around and spy on me to make sure I don't detour, don't drop in on any *friends*. I learned that after a while, that it wasn't worth it, making connections.

Beanie stares at me for a moment, then decides there's nothing more to add, nothing that wouldn't sound stupid. Or stupider. She turns around, click-clacks back towards the office.

Me? I grab another can, lift it into place, notice my hand's shaking enough to blend the beets. Resting my head against the price strip on the edge of the shelves, realise how it might be sharp if I pushed at just the right angle, just hard enough. How it would be to have warm red drip down my face. To feel *anything* acute instead of this dull, constant lonely ache. But I don't. That'd ruin my makeup.

Sluggish when I wake, the curtains keep the room dark.

The marks in the soft underflesh of my upper arm will be pink and they throb; he didn't need what he took, but he *wanted* to take it. Because I'd yelled at him when I got home, stupidly fearless, hating him for drawing attention. So he chewed. Teaching me a lesson. *What have you learned? Are you going to be a good girl, Kitty?* Gone, now, from the bed with its saggy mattress, back in the basement where the one window's been painted over black. In a tea-chest he had before I met him. Hardly a traditionalist. When he was made, someone stuffed him in and he can't seem to be parted from it; it's where he had his first rising.

What woke me? The phone flashes that it's almost eleven a.m., but there's no alarm, no ringing. *Thud*. I shake my head, instantly regret it. *Thud thud*. Someone kicking a wall? Or the sides of a tea-chest? No. He never rouses in the light time. *Thud thud thud!*

"Miss Kitty Lang? Are you alright in there?"

Magda, knocking on the front door.

Damnit.

No one knocks but the Mormons and the JWs and the occasional guy from the gas company looking to read the meter.

I should never have gone over there. Should never have shown my face. Baked cookies, had tea, what the fuck was I thinking? No one would have had any reason to look to our doorstep, to think Cinna might have been around, might have been given to chicken slaughter when he couldn't get what he really wanted. When he was bored. When he decided the rules didn't apply.

Don't kill someone, just bleed 'em a little.

If you've *got* to kill 'em, then make it fast. Don't toy with 'em.

Never a child.

Always old people who've had a life already.

Roam out of town—*don't* shit on your own doorstep.

A list of rules repeated like a mantra. Like a decaying orbit, chipped away by circumstance, excuses and whim.

Don't come to the house, Magda, he can smell you when he wakes. He'll know you've been here. Think that because I expressed concern I care. That you're important to me. That you're a friend. A pet.

He always kills the pets first.

Roll up, out of bed, stumble across the bedroom because during the day I'm careful of light, trip on the dining room rug, stub my toe on the corner of the coffee table, make it to the door. Fling it open. Squint into the bright winter, all that snow reflecting back at me. From Magda's expression I can tell I look like shit. Though there's something about what he does to me that makes the ageing slow down, without the thick makeup I look… older. Sicker.

He, however, just doesn't age. Eternally a teenager, with all the entitlement and cruelty and arrogance that entails. Never got the chance to grow out of it. Or that's what I tell myself even though I know it's a choice. He got away with being an asshole when he was warm because he was pretty and fun; he continued to be that way because why wouldn't he? I'm shivering, just in a singlet and pair of boxers, and I realise too late she can see all the marks he's made on the canvas of me over the years.

"Are you okay, Kitty?"

"Just a little under the weather, Magda." My voice is ragged, throat sore from dehydration. I clear it, but that doesn't fix anything. "Can I help you with something?"

She holds up a casserole dish. "I thought you might like a homemade meal that you didn't have to cook yourself. Just heat it up. It's mac'n'cheese, not that boxed crap."

My favourite. I'm reaching for it before I think, then I stop. She looks at me, curious as an owl. "You can't be here, Magda. I can't take that."

I clench my fists, pull them back to my sides. Her expression falls, but the casserole dish stays up high, an offering.

"Kitty Lang, I can tell something's wrong in your life. And I'm willing to bet it's that no-good boyfriend of yours. I had one of those myself and I know how to—"

"Sshh! Magda, you've got to go because I can't protect you!" And slamming the door in her face, I turn, put my back to the wood and slide down it into a boneless puddle of person. I hold in the sobs until I hear her leave, out the squeaky garden gate, snow boots shuffling across the freshly salted road.

I really could have done with some of that mac'n'cheese. With something someone else had made just for me. Not just trouble.

I take a break, stand outside in the darkness of the Mart parking lot. Bummed a cigarette from Effie on the registers even though I don't smoke but I just want the comfort of that tiny speck of heat and light. The orange flare in the dimness, while I jitter on the spot, my heels tap-tap-tapping on the asphalt. The advantage of the smoke is that it almost covers—or at least obscures—the stink from the dumpster where things are rotting. I think about Magda and I imagine what's happening at her little house.

Cinna's crossing the street, silent and sleek, graceful as any dancer or killing machine. Leaps over the fence like he's got wings, then slinks through the yard. Scoping the locks. He doesn't need an invitation. Prefers not to have one. Besides, what fun is permission? He'll wait for the lights to go out, the blue flicker of the television to die against the windows. Magda's old. He won't take his time. Won't get much out of her. But he'll do it because he wants to.

Who'll discover her? Can't be me. Won't be me. She lives on her own. Maybe the Kane boys checking the branches on those trees; maybe Abel Tasker will drop by, see how the new chickens are going. Find Magda Doubinsky doesn't answer the door and worry because she's aged and alone. They'll break in or maybe someone's got a key. Find her wherever Cinna left her. Maybe he'll make it seem like an accident, a heart attack. Or maybe he won't bother, he'll let it look like what it is. Folk often won't believe because they just don't want to. But there'll be some who know better.

I'll need to start making plans in the morning, leave a passing-decent interval before we go. The lease is almost up, not that it matters. I'll tell Beanie Cinna's got a new gig, a permanent one, in another place, a big city. Chicago. Yeah, Chicago's good. Meanwhile, we'll go in the opposite direction, find another little pitstop on the way to the world. I'll shed Kitty Lang like a coat, pick a new name from the false identities at the bottom of my bag, all those old licences, stolen, recycled over the years. Take Billy-boy's rolls of cash from the cave I hollowed in the mattress.

Fill the newish Ford F-250 with gas; pack the few bits of clothes we carry. When Cinna wakes one night soon, we'll load his tea-chest, strap it down; roll on into the night. Or maybe I'll need to meet him in the agreed-on place, the spot we always choose when we arrive: somewhere out of town, an old barn, abandoned farmhouse. In case of emergency.

"Kitty Lang!"

Beanie's voice scares me shitless. I was so far away, so deep in figuring what I need to do to get us outta here. Don't know how long I've been on break. Enough of a stretch for Beanie to lose her shit, apparently. I stub the life from the cigarette and hurry towards the automatic doors of the Mart, towards the artificial brightness and Beanie Donaghy with her halo of light and her clicky-clacky boots.

She's shaking her head as I walk by; she says, "Kitty Lang, I ought to—"

And I snap. Flow at her like an oil slick until I'm right in her grille, lips drawn in a snarl and growling, "What, Beanie? What the fuck you oughta do?"

Maybe she sees all the years in my face that I normally hide. Maybe she sees how many of them I've been alone despite a constant companion I should have ditched an eon ago; how deep that isolation has eaten into me. Maybe it's just the sawing tone of my voice, but she steps off, hands going to her crotch as if she maybe just peed herself a little with fright.

A few moments, me hanging there in the doorway like a threat to see if she's got a snappy comeback, but nope. Just Beanie and her mouth dangling open. I straighten, jam my hands into the pockets of my jacket, go back to stacking cans. I can do that even with tears blurring my vision.

But late in the afternoon, when I finally wake, when I go to check the mailbox for bills, I see Magda in her garden. She's feeding the new chickens, throwing corn kernels, bright yellow bits of sunshine on the snow. The old lady notices me—no wonder, I'm like a fucking garden gnome by the dead rosebushes—and raises a hand. A tentative wave. I'm so happy and relieved, I wave back. I'm so happy and relieved, I leave my own yard and go across to her in my dressing gown and slippers, shivering my ass off like a belly dancer. I'm so happy and relieved that I throw my arms around her tiny, scrawny form and cry on her like I'm trying to drown her in the deluge.

There's more tea. This one tastes like liquorice, which I wouldn't normally like. But it's soothing.

"Now," she says as she sits, puts a bowl of mac'n'cheese in front of me, and I realise I haven't had anything for about a day. My stomach's curling back against my spine. Next there's a plate of chocolate cake; I use my fingers like a bad child, eating too fast and get the hiccups and heartburn. Doesn't slow me, though.

"Now," she says again when I'm washing it all down with more tea, "tell me."

And I do.

What he is, what he's done.

What I've done.

How, when I got home this time, I didn't say anything to Cinna. To do so would have been to feed his urge to destroy, whatever made him want to take away anyone or anything I might care about. He'd just repeat what he'd been doing all these years. Any friends early on as we moved around the country, before I learned not to connect. Of the family I'd had, only my mother remained because there'd never been any love lost between us. My father and sisters, four aunts, two grandparents: all gone. All the same way. All in one night. It's one of those historic true crime cases, like Villisca, those axe murders or the start of them anyway, before they crisscrossed states like a bloody tapestry. Unsolved.

Although I read something a few years later where my mother said it was me; that I'd killed them, then fled. But it wasn't. Not really, he just followed me home. And no one's ever managed to find us. I think Momma's in one of those old people places now; she sold her story, made some money I should think. I used to keep track of her from sheer curiosity. It's sixty years she's been dining out on those lies. Feathered her nest telling folk how her oldest daughter did some terrible thing because she could believe it of me just because we didn't get along. Or maybe she's dust too, the last link to my once-upon-a-time.

I tell Magda how he's been the only person I've had in the world for so long. How maybe I was less afraid of death than of coming back from it, which was what he threatened at least once a month. It would hurt, he'd say, it would hurt a lot—and I'm a coward that way.

Darkness has fallen again while I've been here, talking and eating and crying with Magda hovering over me like a concerned grandmother, a proper one, like I used to have. It's the first time in forever that I haven't felt it happen, haven't sensed how it drops like a curtain across the world. It's only when I turn my head—look outside, see my reflection against the black mirror night makes of the window—that I hear him moving.

Through Magda's winter jungle of a yard, around the house—I've known him so long, I can *feel* it. But oh my God, there was that moment: that moment when *I did not* and what a glorious moment of hope that was. Freedom tastes almost metallic-new on my tongue, right up until I spot him out there, and he comes close, starts to tap on the glass. Then I see his expression, and his fingertips as he pulls away are blistered.

"What have you done? Magda?" I ask breathlessly. No wonder she was safe last night; he couldn't have gotten in even if he'd wanted to.

"I told you, I had one like that myself," she says and tweaks up the sleeves of her shirt to show the raised scars in the crooks of her elbows, faint yet distinct, "but I also had a grandmother who knew a thing or two about handling his type."

And she looks right through the pane, right at Cinna, with all those faded marks on display, and she gives him the finger. Twice, both hands rising like knives to the ceiling, and she calls him something so coarse it shocks even me, but I also want to write it down to use later myself. If I have a later.

"Magda," I sort of breathe her name as a warning. "Don't antagonise him."

I want to ask more questions, find out how she does this, but then she steps to the window, chin jutting, and stares him down until he melts back into the blackness, and that just takes my breath away. "He can't get in here. We'll deal with him tomorrow."

"He might run." Cinna's got his own keys to the Ford, but he doesn't tend to drive, not on his jaunts—easier to trace licence plates, less so a man who can slip between shadows. He likes me to do it, besides, loves a chauffeur.

"He won't go anywhere until he gets you, girl."

The way she says "girl" sounds a little like "bait" and I am not comforted by that.

"He won't go anywhere until you're with him or dead. They don't like rebellion. They break your spirit. Make it so you've got no one left in the world. Kill anyone you care about."

"Kills the pets first," I say quietly.

She steps away from the window, rests a hand on my shoulder. "Is there anyone else he might go after, Kitty? Anyone at all?"

And even as I'm shaking my head, even as I'm thinking *He can't get in here*, I'm picking at another thought. It starts small, but it's insistent. Like a fluffy white dog that wants your attention. And you don't wanna kick it because, hey, it's just a little dog. So soon enough it's hanging off the hem of your jeans, gnawing.

He can't get in here, no.

But he knows where to find Beanie.

~

So I'm running down the street, towards the Mart and its lights bright as a fucking spaceship. All I can think is that I don't want to die, I don't want to die how he's going to kill me, and I don't want to come back. And I really don't want to die for someone called "Beanie". I mean, fuck it. What sort of name is Beanie anyway?

But I don't need any more deaths on my conscience.

Not even Beanie's.

Fuck it.

I left the house with Magda yelling on the doorstep. Stopped in at home to put on some actual clothes, because if I'm going to die I don't want it to be in my slippers and robe. And I'm on foot because I found he'd taken the truck. Lucky nothing's far from anywhere in Hope's Bluff. But the blacktop's icy and I keep sliding, haven't fallen over yet, so I'm sort of surfing along the rime-kissed roads. To my credit I stay upright until I get to the parking lot, then I misjudge the step up to the kerb, and finish by rolling onto my feet, the right knee bruised, but the jeans untorn.

Effie's on the register, looking so bored she just might die. Got to love teens. "Where's Beanie?"

The girl looks at me, barely moves a muscle yet manages to convey that the "boss" is out back. I limp along the aisles, doing a headcount to make sure the evening staff are all present and accounted for; that he hasn't decided to extend his massacring skills from chickens to people. Slap my hand against the office door. Panic for a few seconds, thinking it's locked, then remember I need to turn the handle.

It opens, almost swatting Beanie as she sits, boots up, at the desk that's too big for the little room. There's a romance novel in one hand and a powdered donut in the other.

"Beanie! Thank God." Not something either of us ever thought to hear from my mouth. "Have you got your car here?"

Sometimes the boyfriend drops her off. "What—Lang?"

"Do you have your fucking car?" I yell. She drops her donut, *poof*, snowstorm on her black sweater.

"Yes!" she yells back, trying to clean up.

I reach in and grab her wrist, pull her upright. "Keys?"

"Pocket."

"Good, c'mon." And I'm dragging her along behind, this girl I don't even like but don't want to see die, trying to figure out my plan—because do I have a plan? The fuck I do.

And I am out here with nothing on me, not a weapon of any sort because I am dumb.

I am the stupid girl who accepted a Coke from a cute boy in a drugstore. I'm the stupid girl who let him walk her home, after she'd told him all her secrets. I'm the stupid girl who woke one night not too many days later to find most of her family dead in their beds. And I'm the very stupid girl who got in the 1961 Ford Pickup with Cinna when he told me to, even though he was covered in blood and grinning from ear to ear. Because there was nowhere else to go, and only my mother left.

Clicky-clack, clicky-clack, clicky-clack. Her boots sound like train wheels on tracks. If I drag her any faster she'll start puffing steam. She gets out: "Where are we going?"

And it's interesting to note that Beanie is simply *obeying* me—maybe she's just like her old man, likes to be ordered around a bit—and I'm thinking, *Yes, Kitty Lang, where are we going? Just where the fuck are we going?* And I think how maybe she's a lot like me, how I've been trained to be, because there's a certain relief in obedience, in abdicating responsibility.

"Beanie, we are going for a drive. We are going to drive until we come to the sun again." And I sound like Peter Pan with his "second star to the right and straight on until morning" bullshit. And I'm dragging this girl behind me because I know I've been mean. Because when I saw her expression the first time her father favoured me over her and she mistook its nature, I didn't correct her. I let her heart break a little and I just played on it like an asshole. I'm dragging her behind me because of that other girl whose name I won't remember, but whose face I'll always see painted red by my hand, because I was afraid of being alone—except it just made me more alone, didn't it? Did not see that coming.

We're heading past the registers, Effie raises a brow and it probably counts as a heavy calisthenics programme for her. Out the automatic doors, where we pause for a second for Beanie to point to her new red Ram 1500, then we're stepping (carefully) down from the kerb and moving towards it as she *bloops* the key, and the taillights flash. She hands me the keyring when I open my palm.

"Well, when are we coming home?"

"Yes, Kitty, *when* are you coming home?"

Cinna's voice is cold as an ice storm and he's standing in the middle of the parking lot where he wasn't a moment ago. No sign of the truck, but then there wouldn't be, would there? Around the corner or in an alley where I couldn't see it. All he had to do was wait. Because I'm a stupid predictable girl he trained too well.

"Just go away, Cinna. Just leave me be. Leave me here."

"But that's not how the game's played. I don't like being alone on my own." He grins.

"I'm tired. I'm old. Let me go."

"Oh, baby, you look so good for your age! Very well preserved." But he puts a finger to one cheek, as if considering. "Although you're a little slower nowadays, and getting ornery. So, maybe it is time for some new blood."

He hasn't moved but he doesn't need to. He can stand in the one spot all night and never seem any less dangerous. He looks at Beanie.

"Lang, what's he—"

"Hush, Beanie."

"Now is that any way to speak to your successor?" drawls Cinna. She wouldn't last a week. He'd snap her neck after the third question in a row.

"Lang, why's he—"

"Beanie, quiet."

"Does she have your organisational skills, though?" He takes two steps—one forward, one backward, like the start of a dance.

"Lang, how's he—"

"I swear to God, Beanie, if you don't shut the fuck up I'm gonna marry your dad and you're gonna have to call me 'Mom'." Which, as threats go, is quite surprisingly effective.

"C'mon, Kitty Lang, one last chance. What do you say? Let's go now and I'll forget you did this." He holds up his hand, palm forward, and I can still see the blisters from whatever sacrament's on Magda's windows. "You and me, alone together. Forever."

It takes everything I've got to drag an answer up from the bottom of what's left of my soul. To not do what's easiest, what's habit. To not abdicate. To not obey. I say, "No."

And then push Beanie out of the way because I know what's coming. Push her out of the way just as he reaches me, nails longer and sharper than they've any right to be, and he wraps one hand around my throat, hooks the meat of my upper arm with the other and rips. It feels like someone's cutting my strings; and it'll start hurting in a moment. Behind him I can see something small moving surprisingly fast, what looks like a baton clasped in one hand. I shouldn't watch, shouldn't stare, should just listen to the patter of my own blood on the ground. But I can't help myself, I do stare, and Cinna moves, doesn't he? And though she's surprisingly fast, she's still too slow. Because Cinna fucking moves.

Not very far but just enough so whatever Magda is trying to stick in his back goes into the right not the left side of his ribcage. His expression spasms, and smoke rises from whatever's embedded, but he drops me and swings around, one arm describing a wide arc until the back of his hand catches Magda in the face, lifting her off her feet and sending her flying across the lot. She hits the dumpster with a resounding clang. She hits so hard I half expect her to shatter.

I struggle-sit and watch Cinna fight to get hold of the stake she's stuck in him. White wood, maybe ash, maybe rowan. Not enough to kill him, not in the right place, but enough to hurt. His fingers grasp it, pull, let it go as soon as it's out—fresh burns on his palm livid in the lights from the Mart. Cinna staggers a bit, straightens, stares at me as if my betrayal was the last thing he could have predicted. He points a blistered finger at me.

"I'll see you—you know where to go." His tone makes it clear I'm to conform. That he anticipates obedience. As always. Then he's gone— not as fast as usual, however. Normally I blink and he's vanished, but this time I see him limping away.

Beanie rolls up from wherever I threw her, then helps me and we limp over to Magda. I'll never get the details about what happened in 1985, never get that mac'n'cheese recipe, never have those random tea brews again. The old lady's broken, head at the wrong angle, eyes staring, her black-framed glasses fractured on the ground beside her. But her expression's serene—that's what strikes me. She wasn't afraid, there's no horror there. She wasn't terrified of Cinna. She'd faced her own worst once and I guess nothing was ever scary after that. She looks so tiny, so light, but I know she's going to be a considerable weight in my chest.

It's five hours before the sheriff lets me go.

And that's with Beanie vouching for me, saying I'd tried to help, pointing at the wound on my shoulder that the doctor at the little hospital shook his head over as he sewed me up. There's a bottle of painkillers in my pocket for when the injection wears off. The sheriff, who's got the worst breath, tries to get me to say it was a bear or mountain lion—and I do not know how that's going to make Magda any less dead. Beanie just insists it was a knife; I don't bother to correct her. Eventually the deputy gently escorts an interrupting Beanie outside; I call after him that he should get her coffee and a donut because, well, it seems only fair.

I tell the lawman it was Cinna. I give him the licence plate of the F-250; I don't believe they'll find it, though. There are too few cops around here, no resources—why do you think we've always chosen places like this? Nope, the truck'll already be hidden inside that old barn ten miles outside of Hope's Bluff; he'll expect me to be there too, come nightfall, like the obedient girl I am. Sheriff's picked over the remains of the stake, half eaten away by Cinna's blood, still can't get his head around the idea that sweet little old Magda stabbed someone with it.

Dawn's breaking by the time he tells me not to leave town.

Beanie's waiting in the lot, sitting in the driver's seat of that bright red Ram 1500, door open, her clicky-clacky boots dangling. She's sipping a coffee and got one hand buried in a Krispy Kreme bag. So, that's something, I guess.

"Need a lift?" she asks, and her voice is kind of small, like she's worried I'll just tell her to fuck off.

I consider it a second, for old times' sake, then say, "You got a prybar in that thing?"

She nods, looking vaguely offended that I'd ever doubt it. I nod back, climb into the truck.

We don't go home. There'll be what can generously be termed a *police presence* going through everything I own. They won't find anything, but I don't want to be around while they're making a mess. Picking through the few artefacts of my life that actually meant something to me.

We don't go home, though, because I'm expected elsewhere.

Beanie's obedient, following my directions. She even lets me finish the last of the glazed donuts. It takes a while to get where we're going because the roads are windy and the place is well hidden behind thick stands of trees and rises, perfect for an illegal still or meth lab or general lair. We drive right up to the barn and Beanie's suddenly less obedient when I tell her to stay in the truck.

In fact, she's downright obstinate and insists on following, saying: "I *know* what I saw." She gets out and goes to the toolbox in the back, rummages, hands me a compact prybar, sturdy; takes an impressive claw hammer for herself and slides a pink boxcutter into a pocket.

"You won't need that," I say, and hope I'm right.

He hasn't even bothered to padlock the doors and we push them way, way open. The barn's still dark as barns are wont to be, but there are spears of light coming through all the holes in the walls, so many it's as if some Bonnie and Clyde shootout happened here.

There's the F-250, midnight blue like it's part of the shadows. Closed, but not locked, streaks of blood bubbling away some of the paint on the driver's side. It takes a little time to find the tea-chest, however; he's made a bit of an effort, made a cubbyhouse with some old bales of hay. Between us, we demolish the fort and drag the crate out into the day.

I lever the lid off, then kick the front panel in, a creaking of nails, a splintering of wood. In the seconds before the cold winter sun does its job, I see him there in the bottom of that box, curled around himself like a sleeping fox or a snake, oblivious. He looks so small, smaller than Magda, and I can't believe I've been afraid of him all these years.

Then that pale wiry body begins to smoke, shrinks further, bursts into flames, even the red hair kind of burning in on itself until there's nothing left. Just like that, he's gone. The person I've known for the longest time. The person who's made me the loneliest. The worst. Yet, somehow, I can't help but feel like my chest's got a hollow ring to it.

I look down at myself, at my hands; I touch my face.

Got to admit, I sort of thought I might go too. That whatever linked us would pull me after him. But there's no change. No sudden ageing, no wrinkling, no inferno. There's just Beanie looking at me, waiting for an explanation, and me not knowing where to begin.

LONE GUNMAN

Jonathan Maberry

1

THE soldier lay dead.
  Mostly.
But not entirely.
And how like the world that was.
Mostly dead. But not entirely.

2

He was buried.

Not under six feet of dirt. There might have been some comfort in that. Some closure. Maybe even a measure of justice.

He wasn't buried like that. Not in a graveyard, either. Certainly not in Arlington, where his dad would have wanted to see him laid to rest. And not in that small cemetery back home in California, where his grandparents lay under the marble and the green cool grass.

The soldier was in some shithole of a who-cares town on the ass-end of Fayette County in Pennsylvania. Not under the ground. Not in a coffin.

He was buried under the dead.

Dozens of them.

Hundreds. A mountain of bodies. Heaped over and around him. Crushing him down, smothering him, killing him.

Not with teeth, though. Not tearing at him with broken fingernails. That was something, at least. Not much. Not a fucking lot. And maybe there was some kind of cosmic joke in all of this. He was certain of that much. A killer of men like him killed by having corpses piled on top of him. A quiet, passive death that had a kind of bullshit poetry attached to it.

However, Sam Imura was not a particularly poetic man. He understood it, appreciated it, but did not want to be written into it. No thanks.

He lay there, thinking about it. Dying. Not caring that this was it, that this was the actual end.

Knowing that thought to be a lie. Rationalization at best. His stoicism trying to give his fears a last handjob. *No, it's okay, it's a good death.*

Except that was total bullshit. There were no good deaths. Not one. He had been a soldier all his life, first in the regular army, then in Special Forces, and then in covert ops with a group called the Department of Military Sciences, and then freelance as top dog of a team of heavily armed problem-solvers who ran under the nickname "the Boy Scouts". Always a soldier. Pulling triggers since he was a kid. Taking lives so many times and in so many places that Sam had stopped counting. Idiots keep a count. Ego-inflated assholes keep count. A lot of his fellow snipers kept count. He didn't. He was never that crazy.

Now he wished he had. He wondered if the number of people he had killed with firearms, edged weapons, explosives, and his bare hands equaled the number of corpses under which he was buried.

There would be a strange kind of justice in that, too. And poetry. As if all of the people he'd killed were bound to him, and they were all fellow passengers on a black ship sailing to Valhalla. He knew that was a faulty metaphor, but fuck it. He was dying under a mountain of dead ghouls who had been trying to eat him a couple of hours ago. So… yeah, fuck poetry and fuck metaphors and fuck everything.

Sam wondered if he was going crazy.

He could build a case for it.

"No…"

He heard himself say that. A word. A statement. But even though it had come from him, Sam didn't exactly know what he meant by it. No, he wasn't crazy? No, he wasn't part of some celestial object lesson? No, he wasn't dying?

"No."

He said it again, taking ownership of the word. Owning what it meant.

No.

I'm not dead.

No, I'm not dying.

He thought about those concepts, and rejected them.

"*No,*" he growled. And now he understood what he was trying to tell himself and this broken, fucked-up world.

No. I'm not *going* to die.

Not here. Not now. Not like this. No motherfucking way. Fuck that, fuck these goddamn flesh-eating pricks, fuck the universe, fuck poetry two times, fuck God, fuck everything.

Fuck dying.

"No," he said once more, and now he heard *himself* in that word. The soldier, the survivor, the killer.

The dead hadn't killed him, and they had goddamn well tried. The world hadn't killed him, not after all these years. And the day hadn't killed him. He was sure it was night-time by now, and he wasn't going to let that kill him either.

And so he tried to move.

Easier said than done. The bodies of the dead had been torn by automatic gunfire as the survivors of the Boy Scouts had fought to help a lady cop, Dez Fox, and some other adults rescue several busloads of kids. They'd all stopped at the Sapphire Foods distribution warehouse to stock up before heading south to a rescue station. The dead had come hunting for their own food and they'd come in waves. Thousands of them. Fox and the Boy Scouts had fought their way out.

Kind of.

Sam had gone down under a wave of them and Gipsy, one of the shooters on his team, had tried to save him, hosing the ghouls with magazine after magazine. The dead fell and Sam had gone down beneath them. No one had come to find him, to dig him out.

He heard the bus engines roar. He heard Gipsy scream, though he didn't know if it was because the hungry bastards got her, or because she failed to save him. Impossible to say. Impossible to know unless he crawled out and looked for her body. Clear enough, though, to reason that she'd seen him fall and thought that he was dead. He should have been, but that wasn't an absolute certainty. He was dressed in Kevlar, with reinforced arm and leg pads, spider-silk gloves, a ballistic combat helmet with unbreakable plastic visor. There was almost no spot for teeth to get him. And, besides, Gipsy's gunfire and Sam's own had layered him with *actual* dead. Or whatever the new adjective was going to be for that. Dead was no longer dead. There was walking and biting dead and there was dead dead.

Sam realized that he was letting his mind drift into trivia. A defense mechanism. A fear mechanism.

"No," he said again. That word was his lifeline and it was his lash, his whip.

No.

He tried to move. Found that his right hand could move almost ten inches. His feet were good, too, but there were bodies across his knees and chest and head. No telling how high the mound was, but they were stacked like Jenga pieces. The weight was oppressive but it hadn't actually crushed the life out of him. Not yet. He'd have to be careful moving so as not to crash the whole stinking mass of them down and really smash the life out of him.

It was a puzzle of physics and engineering, of patience and strategy. Sam had always prided himself on being a thinker rather than a feeler. Snipers were like that. Cold, exacting, precise. Patient.

Except…

When he began to move, he felt the mass of bodies move, too. At first he thought it was simple cause and effect, a reaction of limp weight to gravity and shifting support. He paused, and listened. There was no real light, no way to see. He knew that he had been unconscious for a while and so this had to be twilight, or later. Night. In the blackness of the mound he had nothing but his senses of touch and hearing to guide every movement of hand or arm or hip. He could tell when some movement he made caused a body, or a part of a body, to shift.

But then there was a movement up to his right. He had not moved his right arm or shoulder. He hadn't done anything in that quadrant of his position. All of his movements so far had been directed toward creating a space for his legs and hips to move, because they were the strongest parts of him and could do more useful work longer than his arms or shoulders. The weight directly over his chest and what rested on his helmet had not moved at all.

Until they did.

There was a shift. No, a twitch. A small movement that was inside the mound. As if something moved. Not because of him.

Because *it* moved.

Oh, Jesus, he thought, and for a moment he froze solid, not moving a finger, hardly daring to breathe, as he listened and felt for another twitch.

He waited five minutes. Ten? Time was meaningless.

There.

Again.

Another movement. Up above him. Not close, but not far away, either. How big was the mound? What was the distance? Six feet from his right shoulder? Six and a half feet from his head? Something definitely moved.

A sloppy, heavy movement. Artless, clumsy. But definite. He could hear the rasp of clothing against clothing, the slither-sound of skin brushing against skin. Close. So close. Six feet was nothing. Even with all the dead limbs and bodies in the way.

Jesus, Jesus, Jesus.

Sam did not believe in Jesus. Or God. Or anything. That didn't matter now. No atheists in foxholes. No atheists buried under mounds of living dead ghouls. There had to be someone up there, in Heaven or Hell or whatever the fuck was there. Some drunk, malicious, amused, vindictive cocksucker who was deliberately screwing with him.

The twitch came again. Stronger, more definite, and…

Closer.

Shit. It was coming for him, drawn to him. By breath? By smell? Because of the movements he'd already made? Five feet now? Slithering like a snake through the pile of the dead. Worming its way toward him with maggot slowness and maggot persistence. One of them. Dead, but not dead enough.

Shit. Shit. Shit. Jesus. Shit.

Sam felt his heartbeat like a hammer, like a drum. Too fast, too loud. Could the thing hear it? It was like machine-gun fire. Sweat stung his blind eyes, and he could smell the stink of his own fear and it was worse than the reek of rotting flesh, shit, piss, and blood that surrounded him.

Get out. Get out.

He twisted his hip, trying to use his pelvis as a strut to bear the load of the oppressive bodies. The mass moved and pressed down, sinking into the space created as he turned sideways. Sam pulled his bottom thigh up, using the top one as a shield to allow movement. Physics and engineering, slow and steady wins the race. The sounds he was making were louder than the twitching, rasping noises. No time to stop and listen. He braced his lower knee against something firm. A back. And pushing. The body moved two inches. He pushed again and it moved six more, and suddenly the weight on his hip was tilting toward the space behind the body he'd moved. *Jenga*, he thought. *I'm playing Jenga with a bunch of fucking corpses. The world is fucking insane.*

The weight on his helmet and shoulders shifted, too, and Sam pushed backward, fighting for every inch of new space, letting the weight that was on top of him slide forward and into where he'd been.

There was a kind of ripple through the mass of bodies and Sam did pause, afraid he was creating an avalanche. But that wasn't it.

Something was crawling on him. On his shoulder. He could feel the legs of some huge insect walking through the crevices of jumped body parts and then onto his shoulder, moving with the slow patience of a tarantula. Nothing else could be that big. But, this was Pennsylvania. Did they have tarantulas out here? He wasn't sure. There were wolf spiders out here, some orb weavers and black widows, but they were small in comparison to the thing that was crawling toward his face. Out in California there were plenty of those big hairy monsters. Not here. Not here.

One slow, questing leg of the spider touched the side of his jaw, in the gap between the plastic visor and the chinstrap. It was soft, probing him, rubbing his skin. Sam gagged and tried to turn away, but there was no room. Then a second fat leg touched him. A third. Walking across his chin toward his panting mouth.

And that's when Sam smelled the thing.

Tarantulas did not have much of a smell. Not unless they were rotting in the desert sun.

This creature stank. It smelled like roadkill. It smelled like...

Sam screamed.

He knew, he understood what it was that crawled across his face. Not the fat legs of some great spider but the clawing, grasping fingers of a human hand. That was the slithering sound, the twitching. One of *them* was buried with him. Not dead. Not alive. Rotting and filled with a dreadful vitality, reaching past the bodies, reaching through the darkness toward the smell of meat. Of food.

Clawing at him. He could feel the sharp edges of fingernails now as the fingers pawed at his lips and nose.

Sam screamed and screamed. He kicked out as hard as he could, shoving, pressing, jamming with knees and feet. Hurting, feeling the improbably heavy corpses press him down, as if they, even in their final death, conspired to hold him prisoner until the thing whose hand had found him could bring teeth and tongue and appetite to what it had discovered.

Sam wrestled with inhuman strength, feeling muscles bulge and bruise and strain. Feeling explosions of pain in his joints and lower back as he tried to move all that weight of death. The fingers found the corner of his mouth, curled, hooked, tried to take hold of him and rip.

He dared not bite. The dead were filled with infection, with the damnable diseases that had caused all of this. Maybe he was already infected, he didn't know, but if he bit one of those grublike fingers it was as sure as a bullet in the brain. Only much slower.

"Fuck you!" he roared and spat the fingers out, turning his head, spitting into the darkness to get rid of any trace of blood or loose flesh.

He wanted to vomit but there was no time, no room, no luxury even for that.

And so he went a little crazy.

A lot crazy.

All the way.

3

When the mountain of dead collapsed, it fell away from him, dozens of corpses collapsing down and then rolling the way he'd come, propelled by his last kicks, by gravity, by luck. Maybe helped along by the same drunk god who wanted more of the Sam Imura show. He found himself tumbling, too, bumping and thumping down the side of the mound, the jolts amplified by the lumpy body armor he wore. Kevlar stopped penetration of bullets but it did not stop the foot-pounds of impact.

He tried to get a hand out before he hit the pavement, managed it, but at the wrong part of his fall. He hit shoulder-first and slapped the asphalt a microsecond later. Pain detonated all through him. Everything seemed to hurt. The goddamn armor itself seemed to hurt.

Sam lay there, gasping, fighting to breathe, staring through the fireworks display in his eyes, trying to see the sky. His feet were above him, one heel hooked over the throat of a teenage girl; the other in a gaping hole that used to be the stomach of a naked fat man. He looked at the dead. Fifty, sixty people at least in the mound. Another hundred scattered around, their bodies torn to pieces by the battle that had happened here. Some clearly crushed by the wheels of those buses. Dead. All of them dead, though not all of them still. A few of the crushed ones tried to pull themselves along even though hips and legs and spines were flattened or torn completely away. A six-year-old kid sat with her back to a chain-link fence. No legs, one hand, no lower jaw. Near her was an Asian woman who looked like she might have been pretty. Nice figure, but her face had been stitched from lower jaw to hairline with eight overlapping bullet holes.

Like that.

Every single one of the bodies around him was a person. Each person had a story, a life, details, specifics. Things that made them people instead of nameless corpses. As he lay there, Sam felt the weight of who they had been crushing him down as surely as the mound had done minutes ago. He didn't know any of them, but he was kin to all of them.

He closed his eyes for a moment and tried not to see anything. But they were there, hiding behind his lids as surely as if they were burned onto his retinas.

Then he heard a moan.

A sound from around the curve of the mound. Not a word, not a call for help. A moan. A sound of hunger, a sound of a need so bottomless that no amount of food could ever hope to satisfy it. An impossible and irrational need, too, because why would the dead need to feed? What good would it do them?

He knew what his employers had said about parasites driving the bodies of the victims, about an old Cold War weapon that slipped its leash, about genetically modified larvae in the bloodstream and clustered around the cerebral cortex and motor cortex and blah blah blah. Fuck that. Fuck science. This wasn't science, anyway. Not as he saw it right then, having just crawled out of his own grave. This was so much darker and more twisted than that. Sam didn't know what to call it. Even when he believed in God there was nothing in the Bible or Sunday school that covered this shit. Not even Lazarus or Jesus coming back from the dead. J.C. didn't start chowing down on the Apostles when he rose. So, what was this?

The moan was louder. Coming closer.

Get up, asshole, scolded his inner voice.

"Why can't I just lay here and say, 'fuck it'?"

Because you're in shock, dickhead, and you're going to die.

Sam thought about that. Shock? Yeah. Maybe. Concussion? Almost certainly. Military helmets stopped shrapnel but the stats on traumatic brain injury were staggering. Sam knew a lot of front-line shooters who'd been benched with TBI. Messed up the head, scrambled thoughts, and…

A figure lumbered into sight. Not crawling. Walking. One of them. Wearing mechanic's coveralls. Bites on his face and nothing in his eyes but hunger and hate. Walking. Not shuffling or limping. Not even staggering, like some of them did. Walking, sniffing the air, black and bloody drool running over its lips and chin.

Sam's hand immediately slapped his holster, but there was no sidearm. He fumbled for his knife, but that was gone, too.

Shit. Shit. Shit.

He swung his feet off the mound of dead and immediately felt something like an incendiary device explode in the muscles of his lower back. The pain was instantly intense and he screamed.

The dead mechanic's head snapped toward him, the dead eyes focusing. It snarled, showing bloody, broken teeth. And then it came at him. Fast. Faster than he'd seen with any of them. Or maybe it was that he was slowed down, broken. Usually in the heat of combat the world slowed down and Sam seemed to walk through it, taking his time to do everything right, to see everything, to own the moment. Not now.

With a growl of unbearable hunger, the ghoul flung itself on Sam.

He got a hand up in time to save his skin, chopping at the thing's throat, feeling tissue and cartilage crunch as he struck, feeling it do no good at all except to change the moan into a gurgle. The mechanic's weight crashed down on him, stretching the damaged muscles in Sam's back, ripping a new cry from him, once more smothering him with weight and mass.

Sam kept his hand in place in the ruined throat and looped his other hand over, punching the thing on the side of the head, once, twice, again and again. Breaking bones, shattering the nose, doing no appreciable good. The pain in his lower back was incredible, sickening him even more than the smell of the thing that clawed at him. The creature snapped its teeth together with a hard porcelain *clack*, but Sam kept those teeth away from him. Not far enough away, though.

He braced one foot flat on the floor and used that leg to force his hips and shoulders to turn. It was like grinding broken glass into whatever was wrong with his spine, but he moved, and Sam timed another punch to knock the ghoul over him, letting his hips be the axle of a sloppy wheel. The mechanic went over and down, and then Sam was on top of him. He climbed up and dropped a knee onto the creature's chest, pinning it against the place where the asphalt met the slope of corpses. Then Sam grabbed the snapping jaw in one hand and a fistful of hair at the back of the thing's head with the other.

In the movies snapping a neck is nothing. Everyone seemed to be able to do it.

That's the movies.

In the real world, there is muscle and tendon and bone and none of them want to turn that far or that fast. The body isn't designed to die. Not that easily. And Sam was exhausted, hurt, sick, weak.

There was no snap.

What there was… was a slow turn of the head. Inch by inch, fighting against the ghoul's efforts to turn back and bite him. Sam pulled and pushed, having to lean forward to get from gravity what his damaged body did not want to provide. The torsion was awful. The monster clawed at him, tearing at his clothes, digging at the Kevlar limb pads.

Even dead, it tried to live.

Then the degree of rotation passed a point. Not a sudden snap, no abrupt release of pressure. More of a slow, sickening, wet grinding noise as vertebrae turned past their stress point, and the point where the brainstem joined the spinal cord became pinched inside those gears. Pinched, compressed, and then ruptured.

The clawing hands flopped away. The body beneath him stopped thrashing. The jaws snapped one last time and then sagged open.

After that Sam had to finish it, to make sure it was a permanent rupture and not a temporary compression. The sounds told him that. And the final release of all internal resistance.

Sam fell back and rolled off and lay side-by-side with the mechanic, their bodies touching at shoulder, hip, thigh, foot, Sam's fingers still entwined in the hair as if they lay spent after some obscene coupling. One breathed, the other did not. Overhead the moon peered above the treetops like a Peeping Tom.

4

The moon was completely above the treetops by the time Sam got up.

His back was a mess. Pulled, strained, torn or worse, it was impossible to tell. He had a high pain threshold, but this was at his upper limit. And besides, it was easier to man up and walk it off when there were other soldiers around. He'd seen his old boss, Captain Ledger, brave it out and even crack jokes with a bullet in him.

Alone, though, it's easier to be weaker, smaller, to be more intimate with the pain, and be owned by it.

It took him half an hour to stand. The world tried to do some fancy cartwheels and the vertigo made Sam throw up over and over again until there was nothing left in his belly.

It took another hour to find a gun, a SIG Sauer, and fifteen more minutes to find one magazine for it. Nine rounds. Then he saw a shape lying partly under three of the dead. Male, big, dressed in the same unmarked black combat gear as Sam wore. He tottered over and knelt very slowly and carefully beside the body. He rolled one of the dead over and off so he could see who it was. He knew it had to be one of his Boy Scouts, but it still hurt him to see the face. DeNeille Shoopman, who ran under the combat callsign of Shortstop. Good kid. Hell of a soldier.

Dead, with his throat torn away.

But goddamn it, Shortstop's eyes were open, and they clicked over to look at him. The man he knew—his friend and fellow soldier—did not look at him through those eyes. Nothing did. Not even the soul of a monster. That was one of the horrors of this thing. The eyes are supposed to be the windows of the soul, but when he looked into Shortstop's brown eyes it was like looking through the windows of an empty house.

Shortstop's arms were pinned, and there was a lot of meat and muscle missing from his chest and shoulders. He probably couldn't raise his arms even if he was free. Some of the dead were like that. A lot of them were. They were victims of the thing that had killed them, and although they all reanimated, only a fraction of them were whole enough to rise and hunt.

Sam placed one hand over Shortstop's heart. It wasn't beating, of course, but Sam remembered how brave a heart it had been. Noble, too, if that wasn't a corny thing to think about a guy he'd gotten drunk with and traded dirty jokes with. Shortstop had walked with him through the Valley of the Shadow of Death so many times. It wasn't right to let him lie here, ruined and helpless and hungry until he rotted into nothing.

"No," said Sam.

He had nine bullets and needed every single one of them if he was going to survive. But he needed one now really bad.

The shot blasted a hole in the night.

Sam sat beside Shortstop for a long time, his hand still there over the quiet heart. He wept for his friend, and he wept for the whole goddamn world.

5

Sam spent the night inside the food distribution warehouse.

There were eleven of the ghouls in there. Sam found the section where they stored the lawn care tools. He found two heavy-bladed machetes and went to work.

When he was done he was in so much pain that he couldn't stand it, so he found where they stacked the painkillers. Extra-strength something-or-other. Six of those, and six cans of some shitty local beer. The door was locked and he had the place to himself.

He slept all through the night.

6

When he woke up he took more painkillers, but this time washed it down with some trendy electrolyte water. Then he ate two cans of beef stew he cooked over a camping stove.

More painkillers, more food, more sleep.

The day passed and he didn't die.

The pain diminished by slow degrees.

In the morning he found a set of keys to the office. There was a radio in there, a TV, a phone, and a lockbox with a Glock 26 and four empty magazines, plus three boxes of 9mm hollow points. He nearly wept.

The phone was dead.

Sam turned on the news and listened as he loaded bullets into the magazines for the Glock and the single mag he had for the SIG Sauer.

He heard a familiar voice. The guy who had been here with the lady cop. Skinny blond-haired guy who was a reporter for a ninth-rate cable news service.

"*This is Billy Trout reporting live from the apocalypse...*"

Trout had a lot of news and none of it was good. His convoy of school buses was in Virginia now and creeping along roads clogged by refugees. There were as many fights among the fleeing survivors as there were between the living and the dead.

Typical, he thought. *We've always been our worst enemies.*

At noon Sam felt well enough to travel, though he considered holing up in this place. There was enough food and water here to keep him alive for five years, maybe ten. But that was a sucker's choice. He'd eat his gun before a week was out. Anyone would. Solitude and a lack of reliable intel would push him into a black hole from which he could never crawl out. No, the smart move was to find people.

Step one was finding a vehicle.

This place had trucks.

Lots of trucks.

So he spent four hours using a forklift to load pallets of supplies into a semi. He collected anything that could be used as a weapon and took them, too. If he found people, they would need to be armed. He thought about that, then went and loaded sleeping bags, toilet paper, diapers, and whatever else he thought a group of survivors might need. Sam was a very practical man, and each time he made a smart and thoughtful decision, he could feel himself stepping back from the edge of despair. He was planning for a mission, and that gave him a measure of stability. He had people to find and protect, and that gave him a purpose.

He gassed up at the fuel pump on the far side of the parking lot. A few new ghouls were beginning to wander in through the open fence, but Sam kept clear of them. When he left, he made sure not to crash into any of them. Even a semi could take damage and he had to make this last.

Practical.

Once he reached the crossroads, though, he paused, idling, trying to decide where to go. Following the buses was likely pointless. If they were already heading south, and if Billy Trout was able to broadcast, then they were alive. The last of the Boy Scouts were probably with them.

So he turned right, heading toward the National Armory in Harrisville, north of Pittsburgh. If it was still intact, that would be a great place to build a rescue camp. If it was overrun, then he'd take it back and secure it.

It was a plan.

He drove.

There was nothing on the radio but bad information and hysteria, but there were CDs in the glove compartment. A lot of country and western stuff. He fucking hated country and western, but it was better than listening to his own thoughts. He slipped in a Brad Paisley CD and listened to the man sing about coal miners in Harlan County. Depressing as shit, but it was okay to listen to.

It was late when he reached Evans City, a small town on the ass-end of nowhere. All through the day and into the evening he saw the leavings of the world. Burned towns, burned cars, burned farmhouses, burned bodies. The wheels of the semi crunched over spots where thousands of shell casings littered the road. He saw a lot of the dead. At first they were stragglers, wandering in no particular direction until they heard the truck. Then they walked toward him as he drove, and even though Sam didn't want to hit any of them, there were times where he had no choice. Then he found that by slowing down he could push them out of the way without impact damage to the truck. Some of them fell and he had to set his teeth as the wheels rolled over them, crushing and crunching things that had been people twenty-four hours ago.

He found that by driving along country roads he could avoid a lot of that, so he turned the truck out into the farmlands. He refueled twice, and each time he wasted bullets defending his truck. Sam was an excellent shot, but hoping to get a head shot each time was absurd, and his back was still too sore to do it all with machetes or an axe. The first fuel stop cost him nineteen rounds. The second took thirteen. More than half a box of shells. Not good. Those boxes would not last very long at that rate.

As he drove past an old cemetery on the edge of Evans City, he spotted smoke rising from up ahead. He passed a car that was smashed into a tree, and then a pickup truck that had been burned to a shell beside an exploded gas pump. That wasn't the source of the smoke, though, because the truck fire had burned itself out.

No, there was a farmhouse nearby and out in front of it was a mound of burning corpses.

Sam pulled the truck to a stop and sat for a while, studying the landscape. The moon was bright enough and he had his headlights on. Nothing moved except a tall, gently twisting column of gray smoke that rose from the pyre.

"Shit," said Sam. He got out of the truck but left the motor running. He stood for a moment to make sure his back wouldn't flare up and that his knees were steady. The SIG was tucked into his shoulder holster, and he had the Glock in a two-hand grip as he approached the mound.

It was every bit as high as the one under which he'd been buried. Dozens upon dozens of corpses, burned now to stick figures, their limbs contracted by heat into fetal curls. The withered bones shifted like logs in a dying hearth, sending sparks up to the night where they vanished against the stars.

Sam turned away and walked over to the house.

He could read a combat scene as well as any experienced soldier, and what he was seeing was a place where a real battle had taken place. There were blood splashes on the ground and on the porch where the dead had been dropped. The blood was blacker even than it should have been in this light, and he could see threadlike worms writhing in it. Sam unclipped a Maglite he'd looted from the warehouse and held it backward in his left hand while resting the pistol across the wrist, the barrel in sync with the beam as he entered the house.

Someone had tried to hold this place, that was clear enough. They'd nailed boards over the windows and moved furniture to act as braces. Many of those boards lay cracked and splintered on the floor amid more shell casings and more blood spatter. He went all the way through to the kitchen and saw more of the same. An attempt to fortify that had failed.

The upstairs was splashed with gore but empty, and the smears on the stairs showed where bodies had been dragged down.

He stepped to the cellar door, which opened off of the living room. He listened for any kind of sound, however small, but there was nothing. Sam went down, saw sawhorses and a door that had been made into a bed. Saw blood. A bloody trowel. Pieces of meat and bone.

Nothing else.

No one else.

He trudged heavily up the stairs and went out onto the porch and stood in the moonlight while he thought this through. Whoever had been in the house had made a stand, but it was evident they'd lost their battle.

So who built the mound? Who dragged the bodies out? Whose shell casings littered the yard?

He peered at the spent brass. Not military rounds. .30-30s, .22, some 9mm, some shotgun shells. Hunters?

Maybe.

Probably, with a few local police mixed in.

Why come here? Was there a rescue mission here that arrived too late? Or was it a sweep? The armed citizens of this rural town fighting back?

Sam didn't know.

There were dog footprints in the dirt, too. And a lot of boot and shoe prints. A big party. Well-armed, working together. Getting the job done.

Fighting back.

For the first time since coming to Pennsylvania with the Boy Scouts, Sam felt his heart lift. The buses of kids and the lady cop had gotten out. And now someone had organized a resistance. Probably a redneck army, but fuck it. That would do.

He walked around the house to try and read the footprints. The group who had come here had walked off east, across the fields. Going where? Another farm? A town? Anywhere the fight took them or need called them.

"Hooah," he said, using the old Army Ranger word for everything from "fuck you" to "fuck yeah." For now it meant "fuck yeah."

East, he thought, was as good a direction as any. Maybe those hunters were protecting their own. Sam glanced at his truck. Maybe they could use some food and a little professional guidance.

Maybe.

He smiled into the darkness. Probably not a very nice smile. A hunter's smile. A soldier's smile. A killer's smile. Maybe all of those. But it was something only the living could do.

He was still smiling when he climbed back into the cab of his truck, turned around in front of the old house, found the road again, and headed east.

SECOND WIND

M. R. Carey

HERE's my problem with dead people: they fall apart.

Okay, I grant you, the transition to being a stiff is a shock to the system. You wake up one morning, and you feel like shit: death warmed up, as they say, or rather death cooling rapidly towards background ambient. You feel for a pulse: not verifiably present. But is that because it's not there, or because you're a klutz and you don't know how to take a pulse?

Okay, you can't feel a heartbeat, either. That's ominous, because you're so scared by this time that your heart should be racing, not parked at the kerb with the handbrake on.

You draw a ragged, stressy breath... and it just stays there. Nowhere to go. Your body isn't metabolising oxygen anymore, and your formerly autonomic functions are all unplugged from the board. The pressure doesn't build. You could keep that breath pent up behind your teeth for a minute, an hour, a day and a half, and you're never going to feel the slightest need to let it out again.

The sign on the door just flipped, from OPEN to CLOSED. This is it. Grammatically, you can never start a sentence with "I am" again. It's *was* all the way.

But that's no reason to let up, is what I'm saying. Too many people use death as an excuse, and I'm sick of hearing it. The world's still out there, people. It's not going away. The rules of the game didn't change because you croaked, and if you don't get back in the saddle you're gonna end up trampled and covered in horseshit. Your choice.

I used to be a stockbroker, which is probably what killed me. Or rather, being a *great* broker is what killed me—having the kind of obsessive edge that took me to the top of the NASDAQ while most of my respected peers were still flossing their teeth and picking out a tie that matched their hand-stitched braces.

It's a tough gig, don't mistake me. Tough as hell if you're doing it at the level I was used to. I guess it's a bit like riding a log flume must be. Only instead of logs there are hundreds of millions of euros rolling under you, behind you, and you know damn well that if you lose the flow and try to stop it before it's ready, you'll go down and never see daylight.

So yeah, there's a certain level of stress that you live with. I won't say "thrive on", because that's macho bullshit: the adrenalin surge is pleasant for about a half an hour, tops; after that your body starts shaking itself to pieces and you're swallowing heartburn. A day in the dealing room is a day in the slaughterhouse: you come out of it with other people's blood and sweetmeats spattered on your shirt, and that's if you've done okay. If you messed up, it's your own tripes you're wearing.

I had my first heart attack when I was twenty-six. I usually tell the story so it happened on my actual birthday, but in fact it was the day after. I'd been out all night, flying high on wings of coke and frozen Stolichnaya, then I showered, popped a few dexies and went back to work. The two guys I was with, they did the same thing, more or less, but they flaked out in the course of the morning—sneaked off to the room with the folding beds that the management lays on for quitters, to keep the crash at bay with a snatched half hour of sleep. I kept right on going, because I was on one of those flux-market tumbles where nobody knows what's happening and you can squeeze the shit from one exchange to another. Too good to miss.

But like in a bad movie, I start to get a reverb on my hearing. Well, what the hell, right? I don't need to hear properly to see the numbers scrolling up the screen. I'm doing fine. Better than fine. I'm making the pissant competition breathe my farts and think they're good fresh air.

And then I'm on the ground, with a couple of invisible sumo wrestlers sitting on my chest. That's aggravating, I think as I black out.

Three days at the Portland Clinic on caviar and Tenecteplase. Back in the saddle, clip clop, clip clop. Because the guys who stop never start again, and that's the gospel truth. I've seen it enough times to know that it's a natural law.

The second attack caught me by surprise, because this time I wasn't even working: I was with a woman—using "with" to denote the act of coitus. Normally I'm pretty good at sex: I can reach a plateau and stay there for as long as I like until my partner of choice is ready to join me for the final pull towards the summit. On this particular occasion, however, the lady had to struggle out from underneath my inert body and call the emergency services. I'd been wearing her panties as a party hat, and I still was when I woke up—not at the Portland but at the Royal Free. Paramedics must have ripped off my diamond cufflinks, too, but how the hell do you prove it? When you're unconscious, people can take all the liberties they like.

So that was two, and the doctors said I should expect strike three to come over the plate pretty damn soon if I didn't change up and get myself some Zen-like calm. I didn't waste any time on that prescription: I am what I am, and I play to my strengths. What you've got to do here, I said to myself, is to choose the least appalling out of a clutch of really shitty options.

So, what were the options? Well let's take a little tour, why don't we, and see where we end up.

The dead started coming back a few years ago now, around the turn of the new millennium. Actually it probably started a whole lot earlier than that, but that was when the trickle turned into a flood. Some of them come back in the spirit, some in the body. An acquaintance of mine, a guy named Castor who makes what he humorously calls a living as an exorcist, says it's all the same thing with different wrappers. Zombies are people whose ghosts cling to their own dead flesh out of fear or stubbornness or sheer habit, and learn by trial and error how to get things moving again. You hear crazier stories, too—human ghosts ram-raiding animal bodies and doing a little forcible redecorating. Formative causation, they call it, or some other bullshit periphrasis: you look like what you think you should look like, at least most of the time. But the animal soul is still in there with you, and when you're at your weakest it will try and slip out from under. That, the so-called experts tell us, is what werewolves are.

Ghost, zombie, or loup-garou: those were the options I was looking at, assuming I didn't just go gentle into that good night like some passive-aggressive moron. So I planned accordingly, in between strike two and strike three. I had a shed-load of money put by already—salted away against a retirement I clearly wasn't going to live to enjoy. Now I put some of that cash to work, although first of all I set up a Celtic knot of offshore-registered shelf companies to handle my assets: dead men can't legally own jack shit, but corporations are immortal. I bought a lot of real estate, because the property bubble was going through a wobble and there were some really sweet deals to be had. Partly I was just diversifying my holdings, but I was also looking for a place where I could set up *post-mortem*. What I needed was a pied-à-terre that was both huge and invisible—standing on its own grounds, because nosey neighbours would be the last thing I needed.

I settled on a disused cinema in Walthamstow, the Gaumont. It was going for a song, despite having a Cecil Masey façade and most of the interior fixtures and fittings still intact. Nineteen-thirties vintage, and it had never been either burned out or turned into a bingo hall. It had been a porno theatre, briefly, but I wasn't too worried about sticky carpets. In fact, I wasn't worried about the auditorium at all. I stripped out the projection booth and fitted it with a bespoke arrangement of air-conditioning and freezer units. Temperature and humidity control were going to be key.

Somewhere around then was where my personal extinction event happened. RIP, Nicholas Heath: no flowers or known grasses, by request. But I'd been expecting it. It was a bump in the road, nothing more. I'd already decided which kind of dead man I was going to be, and I'd made sure that the funeral parlour would hold off on the burial for at least a week, to give the other shoe a chance to drop.

To be honest with you, I don't like to talk about that part of it. Some people say they see tunnels, blinding white lights, heavenly messengers or moving stairways. I didn't see a damn thing. But I did have the sense of not being completely in control, and that really scared me. I mean, for all I knew it could be a lottery. Maybe you didn't get to choose which way the ball would bounce. I might find myself looking like Casper the friendly white sheet, or Lassie, or in some other stupid, inconsequential, unworkable shape. Or nothing at all. Not all the dead come back, even now.

But I did: and I came back as me. I sat up on the morgue slab, signed myself out, collected my effects and hit the road. Forget about statutory notice, or packing up any of the stuff from my apartment. Dead men aren't covered by contract: my job was gone, my *casa* was someone else's *casa*, and the landlord had probably already changed the locks. I headed straight for the Gaumont, bolted the doors and got on with the job.

It was good timing, in a way: I'd finally got the air-conditioning units working properly at two degrees Celsius, and I had the place all set up to move into. Which was just as well, because it was the last moving I did for a while: the fucking rigor mortis hits you right after you sit up and look around, and for the next twenty-four hours it's all you can do to roll your eyes to the heavens.

So I'm lying there, in the dark, because I didn't get a chance to turn the lights on before my muscles seized up, and I'm running through the list in my mind.

Rancidification.

Black putrefaction.

Butyric fermentation.

Dry decay.

These, collectively, were the joys now in store for me. And every second I wasted meant more hassle later, so as soon as the rigor passed, I spat on my hands—figuratively speaking—and started taking the appropriate measures.

Rancidification, the first stage, is far and away the most dangerous. That's when all the fluids in your body rot and go sour. The smell is fucking indescribable, but that's not what you've got to worry about. The souring releases huge quantities of gas, which builds up in your body cavity wherever there's a void for it to collect in. If you don't do something about it, the pressure of the gas can do huge damage to your soft tissues—rip you open from the inside out. But if you make incisions to let out the gas, every hole is a problem that has to be managed at the putrefaction stage.

I got a long way with some ordinary plastic tubing, which I shoved into a great many places I'm not keen to talk about. In the end I had to make some actual incisions, but I kept them to a minimum: I was also helped by an amazing substance called Lanobase 18, which is what undertakers use to soak up the fluid leaking from your internal organs and turn it into an inert, almost plasticised slurry.

As far as the putrefaction stage went, I was already ahead of the game just by having a cold, controlled space of my own. No insects to lay their eggs in my mouldering flesh; no air- or ground-borne contaminants. I used that time to start the embalming process; I needed it because by now my stink had matured into something really scary. I kept having to pour cologne onto my tongue to blitz what was left of my airway and nasal passages, because even though I wasn't inhaling anymore the smell was still getting through to me somehow.

By the time I hit phase three, I was more than half pickled—and now it started to get easier. What was left of my flesh changed its consistency, over the space of a couple of weeks, into something hard and waxy. Adipocere, they call it. It's kind of unsettling at first, because it doesn't feel like anything even slightly organic, but it has the huge upside that it doesn't smell of anything much. I could live with myself now.

Dry decay mainly affects your bones, through a leaching of organic compounds called diagenesis, so I just let it happen and turned my attention to other things.

Unfortunately, I'd missed a trick or two while all this was going on. I had the projection booth itself and the adjacent generator room armoured up like the fucking Fuhrer-bunker, but I hadn't bothered with all the ground-floor doors and windows. I didn't think I'd need to: the Gaumont had stood empty and undisturbed for so many years, who was going to pay it any attention now?

But the keyword there is *undisturbed*. I'd had a whole lot of kit delivered when I was setting up my freezer and air-conditioning arrays, and I'd had some guys in to reinforce the upstairs walls and doors. I might as well have put out a welcome mat: I was telling all the neighbourhood deadbeats that the cinema was now inhabited, and that it might contain something worth stealing.

In point of fact, it didn't: everything that was valuable was locked away behind steel bulkhead doors up on the first floor. But that didn't stop a variegated collection of scumbags from breaking in downstairs, smashing the windows and ransacking what was left of the old furniture, looking for something they could purloin, pawn or piss into. Some of them had even moved in, and were now squatting in the auditorium or the storerooms behind it.

First things first. I made some calls, using one of the false names and email addresses I'd set up for my offshore holding company, and hired some guys from a private security firm to come in and clear out the squatters' little rat nest. They threw everything and everyone out into the street: then they maintained a presence while I got the builders to come back in and make the place secure.

Steel shutters on the ground-floor windows; steel bulkhead doors over the old wooden doors, attached to I-beams sunk two feet into highway-mix concrete. I had the work team coat the windowsills and door frames with green anti-vandal paint, too: the losers could still sleep in the doorway if they wanted to, but I wasn't going to make it comfortable for them and that was as far as they were going to get. As a dead man walking, I was too vulnerable: I wanted to have the freedom of the building, without worrying about who I might run into. In any case, this was my retirement home now: why the hell should anyone else get the benefit of it? That's not how life works—take it from a dead man.

Relaxing isn't something I do all that well, but now I felt like I could finally slow down and take stock. I'd ridden out the roller coaster of physical decomposition, at least to the point where I could maintain a steady state; I had my place secured and my lines of communication laid down so that I could get what I needed from the outside world without dealing with it directly.

I took a day off. Watched some movies on cable. Opened a bottle of Pauillac and sniffed the wine-breath, since drinking it without any digestive enzymes was an idiot's game.

It was half a day, actually. Half a day off. By the afternoon I was restless, worried about what I might be missing. I fired up the computers—three of them, each registered with a different ISP and apparently logged on in a different time zone—and put some of my money back into play on the New York exchange.

That was a good afternoon, and an even better evening. Stress couldn't touch me now—look ma, no glands—I couldn't get tired, and I didn't need to take bathroom breaks, so I kept going steadily through a fourteen-hour session, not logging off until the exchange closed.

Then I switched to the Nikkei-Dow and did the same, for another five hours.

Man! I thought. This is… you know… liberating! Death means never having to wipe your ass again; never getting pulled out of the zone by your body's needs, or by someone else blabbing in your ear like they've got something to say. It means you can keep going forever, if you want to.

Of course, forever is a long time. A long, long, *long* fucking time.

On day three, the deadbeats broke in again. They'd actually sneaked back while the concrete was still setting, and pushed one of the steel plates up out of line, so they could work it loose later with a crowbar. I could hear them doing the same thing with the door of the projection room, my holy of holies.

Yeah, dream on, you verminous little bastards. That door, and the wall it was set in, was about as porous as a bank vault: not needing to breathe meant not having to cut corners where personal security was concerned. All the same, I couldn't stop thinking about what would have happened if the door had been open—if I'd been down on the ground floor picking up my mail or something. I couldn't take that risk again.

This time I thought it through properly: defense in depth was what I needed, not one big-ass door with one big-ass bolt on it. I had the builders—none of whom ever met me in person, of course—completely redesign the ground floor, replacing all the existing walls with steel bulkheads and at the same time putting in a whole lot of new ones. I took my inspiration from the crusader forts of the late Middle Ages, turning the Gaumont into three separate keeps, one inside the other. There was just a single vault door connecting the outer keep with the middle one, and then a second linking the middle keep with the inner one. Other doors were devoid of bolts, locks or handles: they were all independently lockable via a computer-controlled system, and the first thing I did was to slave the whole damn thing to the main server up in the projection booth. I put in some CCTV cameras, too—dozens of them, set up so there were no dead angles. I could check out any given stretch of corridor, any given room, and make sure it was clear before I opened the doors and took a stroll.

What? This sounds like overkill? Well it wasn't. I was thinking things through, that's all. Every fortress can turn into a trap, so every fortress needs a back door. And this particular fortress needed a mail slot, too, because for some of the things I was doing online I still needed physical documents, physical certification, actual rather than digital signatures. It's stupid, but it's true: some parts of the world haven't started surfing the electron tide yet, and they only believe in what they can hold in their hands. Hah. Maybe not so stupid, when you think about it.

So now I could swing back into top gear, stop watching my back. And believe me, I did.

To tell you the truth, I got lost in it. I must have spent a week or more at a time just bouncing from one exchange to another in an endless, breakneck rhythm. You know those velodromes, where the racers ride their bikes almost horizontally on the canted walls? Well, that's what I was like. The only thing that kept me touching the ground at all was my unthinkable velocity. Which is fine, so long as you never slow down.

But gravity's going to have its way with you sooner or later.

It was subtle at first—subtle enough that I didn't even realise it was happening. I missed a spike here, wrapped up slow on a closure there: not big things, and not connected. I was still coming out ahead, and still in control. It took me a couple of days to realise that I was too much in control: that I was going through the motions without feeling them, and making conscious decisions instead of letting instinct play through me.

I tied down, cashed in and logged off. Sat there in silence for a while, staring at the screens. A wave of grief swept through me, and I don't care if that sounds stupid: a sense of bereavement. Nicky Heath was dead. I hadn't really got that fact in my head until then.

If you stop, you never start again: my own golden rule. But I didn't feel like I could touch the keyboard right then. I was afraid of screwing up; afraid of hitting some rock I would have seen a mile off back when I had a functioning endocrine system. *Look ma, no glands.*

I think I must have been hearing the noises in the walls for a while before that: bangs and scrapes and scuffles, muffled not by distance but by the thickness of the brickwork and the layers of steel plating. But now I let myself listen to them: jumbled, discontinuous, slightly different each time. It wasn't the freezer unit, or the big electrical generator downstairs. The only things that made noises like that were living things. People. Animals. Members of the big but still exclusive club of entities-with-a-pulse.

I turned on the CCTV monitors and did the rounds of the cameras. She wasn't hard to find, once I started looking: she was in the outer keep, way down on the ground floor, in a blind stretch of corridor between two of my self-locking doors—nowhere near the big steel portal that led through into the middle zone.

It was still a nasty shock, though. Sort of like scratching your balls and coming up with a louse.

Going by what I could see, she was one of the homeless people I'd cleared out when I first moved in: probably in her early twenties, but looking a damn sight older, huddled in way too many layers of clothes in a corner made by the angle of a wall and a door. She had dirty blond hair and a sullen, hangdog face. Hard to tell anything else, because she was folded down into herself, knees hugged to her chest and head down. It was probably cold down there, in spite of all the layers.

Where the hell had she come from? She couldn't have been in there since the last invasion, because I wouldn't have missed her, and in any case she'd be dead by now. There wasn't anything to eat or drink down there, and she clearly hadn't brought anything in with her that she couldn't carry in her pockets.

I backtracked with the cameras until I found the smoking pistol: a vent pipe for one of the freezer units that had been run through the outer wall of the building. She'd just hit it with something—a hammer or a stone—again and again until the flimsy metal bent back on itself far enough for her to squeeze through. That had let her into a part of the building that was on the route I used when I went down to collect the mail. She must have scooted through a door or two that was unlocked when I came through, and then got caught in the dead-end stretch of corridor when I made the return journey and locked up again.

She'd tried to get out: those were the sounds I'd heard. She'd hammered and clawed at the door and probably screamed for help, but only faint echoes had come up to the projection room, and I'd been too absorbed in what I was doing to decipher them.

Now she looked to be in a bad way. The monitor only resolved in black and white, but there were dark patches on her hands which I assumed were probably blood—most likely from trying to pull on the edge of the door-jamb—and when she briefly came out of her huddle to grab a gulp of air I saw that her lips were swollen in a way that suggested dehydration.

I got up and paced around the room, trying to think it through. I wasn't capable of panic, but I felt a dull, blunt volume of unhappiness expand inside me, like those goddamned intestinal gases back in the first stage of decay.

I could just let her die, was the first thought that came to mind.

I could open up the doors to let her back out the way she'd come, but she might be too weak to move. She might die anyway.

If I opened the doors, someone else could get in. Safer just to leave her.

But someone could have seen her climbing inside, and not coming out again. Someone might be looking for her right now, or calling the police, or crawling through that hole with torches and crowbars and...

No, nobody else had found the hole. The CCTV cameras didn't show any movement or activity either in the room where the vent let out or anywhere else in the outer keep. I should have put more sophisticated alarms in, I thought irrelevantly: movement sensors, infrared scanners, or something. I shouldn't have let this happen. Now here I was, already guilty of false imprisonment or some such bullshit, with the police probably searching the whole damn neighbourhood and Christ only knew what kind of trouble to look forward to if she was found here, alive or dead or anywhere in between.

I stopped pacing because I'd come up hard against a wall. I wanted to punch it, but that would have been a really stupid thing to do: no blood flow, so no scabbing, no skin repair. Any wound I opened in my own flesh would stay open unless I sewed it shut.

I stared at the wall for maybe five minutes, galloping through the same rat-runs inside my head. When I'd done it enough times to be sure they always ended up in the same place, I got moving again.

I had no choice. I had to bring my uninvited guest up to good-as-new spec before I cut her loose, much as I ached to do that. I had to make sure there was no harm and no foul.

I found a bucket the builders had left behind, and a washbasin in what had once been a cleaner's cupboard behind the projection booth. I cleaned the bucket out as far as I could, then filled it with cold water. I flicked some switches on the main board, releasing the locks on all but one of the doors between me and the woman—leaving just the door that she was leaning against.

Then I went downstairs, let myself out through the inner and middle keeps, and made my way around to her stretch of corridor. She must have heard me coming, because when I turned the last bend I caught the sound of her fists banging on the other side of the door, and her voice, muffled through the thick wood, telling me she was stuck.

I left the bucket of water right in front of the door and went back up to the projection booth. I watched the woman on the CCTV hook-up: she was still hammering and shouting, pushing at the door, thinking or at least hoping that someone could hear her.

I re-locked all the other doors before opening just that one. Since she was leaning her weight against it, she just tumbled through when it opened. She saw the bucket, stared at it with big incredulous eyes, and finally cupped her hands and drank from it. She coughed up a storm, and vomited a little, too, but she was alive, at least. That was a good start.

Food was more of a problem, because unless there were a few hardy rats down in the basement somewhere, there was nothing edible in the entire building. I got around that by going to the Ocado website, whose online order form allows you to specify exactly where you want the food to be dropped off. I specified the mailbox, which was actually a double-doored receptacle like the ones post offices use—big enough to take thick bundles of legal paper, and as it turned out, big enough for a bag of groceries, too.

I ordered stuff the woman could eat cold, to keep things simple: turkey breast, bread rolls, a bag of ready-cut carrot slices, a few apples. I added some fun-sized cartons of orange juice, and then on an impulse a bar of Cadbury's Dairy Milk.

This time I had to approach her from the opposite direction, since she'd gone through the door to get to the water bucket, and was now on the other side of it. It didn't matter: from the master board up in the projection booth, I could open up any route I liked, and make absolutely sure of where she was before I moved in, did the drop-off, and retreated again to the booth and the CCTV monitors.

At the sound of the lock clicking, she went scooting back through like one of Pavlov's dogs.

She wolfed the food down like she hadn't seen bread since the Thatcher years. It was a pretty unedifying sight, so I turned off the CCTV and left her to it for a while.

The next time I checked she was done. The floor was strewn with wrappers, apple cores, a crumpled juice carton. The woman had spotted the camera, and was staring at it as though she expected it to start talking to her. Actually, it could do that if I wanted it to—the cameras came with a mic and speaker rig as standard. But I didn't have anything I wanted to say to her: I just wanted her to eat, drink, wash, fix herself up and get the hell out of there.

Wash. Oh yeah. I ordered some more groceries, and added soap and shampoo to the list—not to mention another bucket. The next time I fed her, I left both drinking water and wash water, but she didn't take the hint—maybe because the water was cold. Too bad. I didn't have any way of heating it up, and I wasn't running a guest house.

I spent about three days feeding her up. On the second day I left her some plasters and antiseptic for her fingers, which she ignored just like the wash water. On the third day I made a similarly useless gesture with some clean clothes, ordered from the Asda superstore at Brentwood with the same drop-off instructions.

Okay, so my reluctant house guest wasn't interested in personal hygiene even on a theoretical level. I don't know, maybe the dirt acts like insulation out on the street: and maybe after the first month or so your panties get welded to your privates past the point where you can take them off. Maybe not, though, since she had to be managing to piss somehow. Following that thought through, I realised it was probably a good thing that the cameras had such crappy resolution. I could see the corner she was using as a latrine, now that I looked for it, and I sure as hell didn't want to see it any clearer.

Well, the bottom line was that she had to go out looking no worse than when she came in: I wasn't under any obligation to make her look better.

On day four I drew her a map, showing her how to get back to the vent pipe, and left it with the food. Then I threw the lock on the door behind her, and all the other locks leading back to the outer wall and her exit point.

She examined the map as she ate her breakfast, which was croissant and apricot jam. She'd shown a real taste for pastries by this time, and none at all for fresh fruit or cereal.

But after she'd finished, she didn't make a move to step over the threshold. She just wiped her mouth on the napkin provided, dropped it into the water bucket—which always drove me crazy because I had to fish the fucking thing out again—and settled back down against the wall.

What was she playing at? She had to realise I was allowing her to leave.

"Come on!" I shouted at the monitor. "Get out of there. You're free as a bird. Go!"

She settled into her characteristic, head-bowed huddle. She couldn't hear me, of course.

Impulsively, I flicked the microphone switch on the CCTV board. I'd never used it before, so I had no idea if it even worked, but a light flashed on the board and the woman jerked her head up as though she'd just heard something: a click, maybe, or else a little feedback flutter from the speaker.

"Hey," I said. "What do you think you're doing? Time to go, lady."

She blinked twice, her face full of comical wonder. She took her time about answering, though, and when she did it was kind of a *non sequitur*.

"Who are you?" she demanded.

"The owner," I said, and then, not to be put off, I repeated, "Time for you to get out of here."

She shook her head.

I blinked. "What do you mean, no?" I asked, too incredulous even to be pissed off. "This is my place, sweetheart. Not yours. You're not wanted here."

The woman just shrugged. "But I like it here."

The way she said it made me want to go down there and upend the water bucket on her head. She sounded like a little kid asking if she could stay a bit longer at the beach.

"How can you like it?" I demanded, really annoyed now. "It's a… it's a fricking corridor. What, you like sleeping on concrete?"

"That's what I was doing outside," she said, calmly enough. "And at least here I don't have homeless guys wanting to charge me a blow job for a place by the fire."

"Because there is no fire."

"But there is food."

"Food's off," I said bluntly. "That was the last of it."

The woman put her head between her folded arms again, as a way of telling me the conversation was over.

"I mean it," I said. "Food's off. You stay here, you starve to death."

She didn't answer. Fine, so she wanted to be alone. I turned off the sound and left her to it.

"Dumb bitch," I said to the monitor, even though she couldn't hear me now.

That was going to be the first item in a varied agenda of invective, but I realised suddenly what had just happened: what was *still* happening. I was angry. I'd managed to get angry, somehow, even though on the face of it I didn't have the necessary equipment any more.

If I could do anger, then presumably I could do other flashy emotional manoeuvres, too. Quickly I fired up my computers and logged on to my US trading board. I didn't surface for five hours, and by that time I was three hundred thousand up on the day.

Saint Nicholas was back, with gifts of ass-kickings for all.

After I closed out on the day, I checked in with the woman. She seemed to be asleep, but she stirred when I clicked the mic back on.

"What's your name, darling?" I asked her.

"Janine," she muttered, looking muzzily to camera.

"I'm Nick."

"Hi, Nick."

"You can stay here tonight," I said. "Tomorrow we'll talk."

But we didn't. Not much, anyway. I made a food drop at 6.00 a.m., before she was even awake, then came back upstairs and logged on. I had another good day on the markets, and the day went by in a blur.

I did order a folding bed, though, and some blankets and pillows to go on it. I picked a local store that could deliver immediately, had them leave it round by the back door and lugged it in myself after they'd gone. It made my skin prickle just a little to be in the outside air again, even though it wasn't a warm day or anything. Just psychosomatic, I guess.

Over the next few days I furnished Janine's corridor pretty lavishly. *She* furnished, it, I should say: all I did was buy the stuff and bring it to the door, then let her choose for herself where to put it. I'd started to leave the mic on by this time so she could tell me what she wanted: a chair and a table, a kettle for making tea, a chemical toilet, even a little portable DVD player and a few movies for her to watch while I was busy on the trading boards.

The weirdest thing of all, though, was that I actually started talking to her while I was dealing. It seemed to help me concentrate, in some way I couldn't quite define. Most of the things she liked to talk about were stupid and irritating: her favourite celebrities, previous seasons of *Big Brother*, her hatred for supermodels. I just made "I'm still listening" noises whenever they seemed to be called for, and channelled the aggravation into some world-class short-selling.

It got so that if Janine actually shut up for a while, I'd throw in a question or two to get her talking again. Questions about herself she didn't like to answer, except to say that she was living on the street because of something that had happened between her and her stepfather back when she turned eighteen. I got the impression that it had been a violent and dramatic kind of something, and that the stepfather had got the worst of the deal.

"He came on to you?" I asked, genuinely—if slightly—curious.

"I suppose. He came into the bathroom when I was showering one morning, and tried to get in with me."

"That's pretty unequivocal," I allowed.

"Pretty what?"

"Clear-cut. Hard to misinterpret."

"Yeah, right. So I smacked him in the mouth with the showerhead, really hard, and then I ran out."

"Naked?"

"No, Nick. Not naked."

"Then you were showering in your street clothes?"

A pause. "I didn't run out straight away. He fell down and hit his head. I had time to grab some stuff."

This was in Birmingham, Janine told me, as if I could possibly have mistaken her accent. She'd taken a bus down to London the same day, hoping to stay with a friend who was studying Hairdressing and Beauty at Barnet College. But the friend had acquired a boyfriend, and wasn't keen on that arrangement. She passed Janine off to another girl, whose floor she occupied for a while. Not a very long while, though: there was an argument about the rules for the use of the bathroom, and she was out on her ear again before the end of the week.

I was starting to see why Janine wasn't big on washing.

"So what about you, Nick?" she asked me, when we'd been doing this for maybe a week or so. "What do you do for a living?"

"Well," I said, "when you put it like that, Janine, the answer has to be nothing."

"I can hear you typing away up there," she said. "Are you writing a book?"

"Yeah," I lied. "I'm writing a book. But it's not to earn a living."

"How come? You're already rich?"

"I'm already dead," I said.

That remark led to a very long silence. The next time I checked on her, she was asleep.

In the morning, she asked me if she could see me.

"The cameras only work one-way," I pointed out.

"I don't mean on the cameras. I mean, you know, face to face."

"I'll think about it," I lied.

But she wouldn't leave the idea alone: she kept bringing it up last thing at night, when I was logging off and cashing in. I kept being evasive, and she kept going quiet on me, which was really annoying. I'd say goodnight, get nothing back: she went to sleep each night surrounded by a miasma of hurt silence.

In the end it happened by accident. Almost by accident, I should say. When I unlocked the doors one morning so I could drop off a food delivery, I flicked one switch too many. She was waiting for me as I turned the corner, leaning against the open door with her arms folded in a stubborn, take-no-prisoners kind of pose. The crazy thing is, I sort of knew on some level that I'd done it—that I'd opened the final door and removed that last degree of prophylaxis between us. I just didn't let myself think about it until we were face to face and it was too late to back out.

She stared at me for a long time in silence. Then her face wrinkled up in a sort of slo-mo wince. "You look horrible," she said.

"Thanks," I answered inadequately. "You say the sweetest things."

That made her laugh just a little, the sound pulled out of her almost against her will. She took a few steps towards me, then stopped again and sniffed the air cautiously.

"What's that smell?" she wanted to know.

"Which one? I have a complex bouquet."

"It's like… antiseptic, or something."

"Formaldehyde, probably. I'm pickled inside and out, Janine. It's why I don't smell of rotten meat."

"You smell of that, too."

I bridled at that—like some living guy accused of having bad body odour. "I don't," I said. "I went to a lot of bloody effort to—"

She made a gesture that shut me up—kind of a pantomime of throwing up her hands in surrender, except that she only threw them up about an inch or so. "I'm sorry," she said. "You're right. You don't smell rotten. You just *look* like you should smell rotten. Your skin is all waxy and sweaty, and I can see stitches in your neck."

My carotid artery was one of the places where I'd inserted a trocar to draw off some of my bodily fluids way back when I was fighting the war on rot. "Don't get me started," I advised her.

So she didn't.

"Show me where you live," she suggested instead.

She stayed upstairs with me for an hour or so, wrapped in three coats against the cold. Then she retired back to her little home sweet home and spent the rest of the day watching movies. Musicals, mostly: I think she was plugging herself back into the world of the living to make sure it was still there.

The next day I bought her a couple of hot water bottles, and she was able to stay up in the projection room for a little longer. I didn't mind the bottles, so long as she kept them under the coats so the heat stayed right against her skin. The thermostats were still set at the same level, so the room didn't warm up at all, and she didn't come close enough to me for the heat to be a problem.

I think that was the first day I forgot to lock her in, and after I'd forgotten once, it kind of felt like going back to that state of affairs would be a slap in the face to her—a way of saying that I'd thought I might be willing to trust her but then decided I didn't after all.

That thought raised all kinds of other thoughts, because it suggested that I *did* trust her. There was no reason why I should. Back when I was alive, I'd never felt more for people like her than a kind of queasy contempt, mixed with the unpleasant sensation that usually translates— by some spectacular whitewashing process—as "there but for the grace of God".

But God doesn't have any grace, and I don't have the time or the temperament for helping lame ducks over stiles. If I meet a lame duck, generally speaking, I make duck a l'orange.

So what the fuck was going on here, anyway?

At first, I justified it to myself by counting up my market winnings. Janine could make me feel things again, as though my endocrine system was pumping away like it did in the old days—and that gave me a lot of my wonted edge back. But plausible as that explanation was, it was ultimately bullshit. After a week or so, I was spending more time talking to her than I was in managing my portfolios. A week after that, I wasn't even bothering to log on.

At this point I was even making a loss on the deal, because I kept buying her stuff. It wasn't even stuff she needed to live anymore: it was chocolates and beer and donuts and even—I swear to God—a fucking hat.

You're probably thinking that there was some kind of a sexual dynamic going on. Janine certainly thought so. When I presented her with the final little *chatchke*—the straw that broke the camel's neck, so to speak—she stared at it for a long time without reaching out to take it. She looked unhappy.

"What?" I demanded. "What's the matter? It's just a necklace. See, it's got a J on it, for Janine. Those are diamonds, you realise. Little ones, but still…"

She looked me squarely in the eye—no coyness, no pissing around. "Do I have to blow you to sit at the fire?" she asked.

I thought about that. I wasn't insulted: it was a fair question, I assumed, given the way she lived outside on the streets. I also wondered for a split-second if she might be offended if she realised how far I was from being attracted to her. She was dirty, she was as skinny as a stick and she had bad skin. Back when I had a pulse, I would sooner have had relations with a greased oven glove.

"There is no fire," I reminded her.

She nodded slowly. "Okay then," she said, and took the necklace.

But the writing was on the wall, because once I figured out what it wasn't, I couldn't hide anymore from what it was.

That shitty old poem: it's not lame ducks you help over stiles. It's lame dogs.

I watched Janine sleep that night, and I knew. I let myself see it, instead of hiding from it. I knew what I had to do, and I knew I had to do it soon. But shit, it was nice, you know: watching ghost expressions chase themselves across her face. Hearing her breathe.

The next morning I gave her a roll of notes—maybe fifty grand, maybe a little more—and told her to get lost.

She cried, and she asked me what she'd done to hurt me. I told her she'd figure it out if she thought about it long enough. When she asked about the money, I said it was a one-off payment: she should use it to get the hell away from here, and not talk about me to anyone she knew on the street, or else I'd have all the homeless schmucks in Walthamstow climbing up my drainpipes.

She cried some more, and I knew she didn't buy it. It didn't matter, though: that was the closest thing to an explanation I could give her. I walked her down the stairs, through the maze, all the way to the door. I unlocked it for her. She stepped across the threshold, then turned to stare at me.

Neither of us said anything, for the space of three heartbeats. Maybe four: my memory isn't reliable in that respect.

"Imagine if the necklace had been a collar," I said.

She nodded. "I get it," she said.

"And if I fitted a little leash to it. Took you out for walkies."

"I said I get it, Nicky. I don't think it was like that."

But I knew she was wrong. Old ladies have their cushion dogs, their ugly little pugs and pekes and chihuahuas: some dead guys, however appalling and unconscionable and sick and wrong it sounds, have homeless women.

"Thanks," Janine said. "For the money. It's more than I've ever had in my life."

"You're welcome," I said. "Rent a flat. With a bath, or a shower or something. Both, maybe. Go for the win."

She refused to be insulted. She just gave me a slow, sad smile.

"It's not good for you here," she said.

"It's great for me here. Two above freezing. Low humidity. A perfectly controlled environment."

"Stay in the world, Nicky," she murmured, her eyes still brimming in a really unsettling, organic way.

"Is that the same as the street?" I countered. "I'll pass, thanks."

She made like she was going to hug me, but I raised a hand to ward her off and she got the point: no body heat or radiated thermic energy, by request.

"Bye, then," she said, with a slight tremor in her voice.

"Bye, Janine," I said.

"Is it okay if I write to you?"

"Why not? So long as you make sure there's adequate postage."

She turned and ran, pretty much, across the car park and out of sight around the corner of the building. That was the last I saw of her.

I waited to see if she was going to come back: it seemed quite likely that she might do that—think of one last thing to say, or ask if she could stay one more night or something. I gave her ten minutes, in the end, despite getting that prickly feeling again from having real, unfiltered air flow across my flesh. Finally I shut the front door, did a quick round of the outer circle to make sure I hadn't taken on any more unwanted passengers, then went back upstairs and locked myself in again.

It was really quiet. Quiet as the tomb, as they say, except for the freezer units humming away behind the far wall. I thought about going down and blagging one of Janine's DVDs, but they were all feel-good shit that would make me want to hurl.

I didn't really feel like going online: the vibe was wrong, which meant the best I could hope for was adequate. But finally, around about midnight, I fired up my digital engines of destruction and got back in the hot seat for a few hours of Far Eastern mayhem. Because it's still true, you know? Still gospel, in my book.

The guys who stop never start again.

UNDER CARE

Brian Evenson

I

IN the morning a nurse would come, though whether this was the same nurse every time he couldn't be sure. All their faces looked alike to him, as if they were one face. Sometimes he tried to make conversation. Whenever he did, the nurse responded with inarticulate and vague murmurings until his own words dried up. They would both remain silent for the remainder of the time it took for her to pinch the tube that came from his side firmly closed with her thumb and forefinger and then draw the other tightened thumb and forefinger with agonizing slowness down the tube, forcing the pale, yellowish pink fluid out of it.

If he tilted his head just right, he could see where the tube jutted from his side. He had groped along his ribs with one hand and felt the strips of tape affixing the tube in place. *Where does it lead?* he wondered. *Lungs?* How deep did the tube run? Into a lobe of the lungs themselves or just the cavity that contained them?

He didn't know. Perhaps the thoracic cavity, but there was, curiously, no pain when he breathed in and out, no tenderness when he palpated the spot on his side where the tube ran in. It was as if the tube had been there a very long time, long enough to become part of his body.

His thoughts often ran in such directions, growing slightly unhinged. He needed someone to talk to. If he had someone to talk to, his mind would stop churning. The nurses, unless it was just one nurse, were (or was) no help. He couldn't talk *to* a nurse, only *at* her.

"How long have I been here?" he asked the nurse, one of the nurses, the next time she knocked softly and then, without awaiting an invitation, entered the room. She made a mumbling noise in reply. Not words precisely: there was nothing meaningful, not even in the intonation, for him to interpret. Perhaps she was speaking, saying words, and something was wrong with his mind so that he couldn't apprehend them as such. And perhaps he too was mumbling, not fully articulating the words that, to the ear of his mind, felt so distinct and clear.

For that matter, was the first time he remembered seeing the nurse actually the first time? Even on that putative first occasion, his first memory of the nurse milking the tube, he had felt absolutely no pain when he breathed.

At least none he could remember.

But pain was something you remembered, wasn't it?

The way the nurse moved, her slow, deliberate, perfectly calibrated motions as she milked the pale, yellowish pink fluid down the tube, made him struggle to think of her as human.

He stared at her hand, the veins standing out on the back of it, as she held his tube pinched closed. If he stared long enough and she held still enough, he could make out, just barely, the gentle pulsing of the blood within the veins. Was that possible? Whether it was or not, he still saw it. He stared at that faint movement just beneath her skin, and as he stared, he listened to the sound the pinkish yellow fluid made as it left the tube to drizzle into a container somewhere below. What sort of container? Metal, perhaps, judging by the tone the patter of the fluid made, but beyond that he didn't know. The container was under the bed, out of sight, and though at the end of each session she carried something away, she always, perhaps deliberately, positioned her body so that he never saw what it was.

What was she doing with the fluid? If she was merely emptying it, there was a sink in the little bathroom connected to his room. But she never went into that bathroom to empty the container. Instead, proffering an inarticulate noise, she carried it out the door.

Once she was gone, he found himself staring at his own hand, the back of it, at the three prominent veins running through his wrist and toward his knuckles. No matter how long he stared, he could not see blood pulsing through them. This didn't mean anything, he tried to tell himself—though he wished he had someone else to tell him this, to reassure him. It would sound more credible coming from someone else. But he only had himself.

He could, in his head, work out a logic for his failure to see. For instance: his brain, so coordinated with the beating of his own heart, compensated for the pulsing in advance. He wasn't seeing the blood pulse because his brain saw it not as information but noise. Or the IV on his arm had filled his veins with enough saline to make the pulsing invisible. Or perhaps what he thought he was seeing on the back of the nurse's hand was just his brain playing tricks on him.

Or perhaps, he thought later, in darkness, waiting for the nurse to come again, he and the nurse were not the same sort of being at all. He continued to think this idly, from time to time. Mostly he didn't believe it. But that he believed it at all, even if only for brief stretches, troubled him.

He did not leave the bed. He never had, at least so far as he could remember. He understood, logically, that there must have been a time before this room. He sensed vaguely that he had a past, but he was having a hard time bringing that past into focus. Any house he imagined struck him as plausible, as something he might have seen in a movie or might have visited. A red-brick house with a white picket fence, for instance. Could he have lived in that? Certainly. Had he? He didn't know. Plausible was a long way from certain. No matter what he imagined, nothing quite rang true.

Why do I not leave the bed? he wondered. Could he, if he so wanted? His IV could no doubt be easily disconnected, either by pulling it out of his arm or by disconnecting the Luer lock. The catheter was more complicated, but if it had been inserted it could be withdrawn. Other than that, there was only the tube in his side keeping him there. It seemed to be connected or anchored to something, but there was enough slack to it that he probably could, if he wanted, sit up and edge out of the bed and then, as he had seen the nurse do, disconnect the tube from whatever held it in place.

I should do that, he told himself.

But he didn't.

Soon, he told himself, *soon*.

One of his questions to the nurse early on, perhaps the third or fourth visit of hers that he remembered, had been: *What hospital am I in?* This was the only time he found her seamlessly fluid motion interrupted. For just the briefest moment, a second or two, her whole body had stuttered, stopped. And then she had begun to move normally again, as if nothing had happened. She was making a sound which at first he thought must be the same non-committal murmurings she always made, but no, there was something different about it. What? He couldn't quite decide. But it was, he was sure, different.

Only once she had finished and was halfway out the door did he realize what the sound he had been hearing must be: she had, in her own way, been laughing. But why? Because this wasn't a hospital after all? Because he didn't know where he was? Because he had asked the question before, perhaps many times, and couldn't remember having done so? Something else entirely?

Or perhaps it hadn't been laughter at all. Perhaps he had been wrong to hear it as such.

But if not laughter, what could it possibly be?

Am I in a hospital? he wondered. The bed seemed a hospital bed, could be raised or lowered by applying pressure to a series of buttons inset in one of the plastic siderails. Were there other places such beds were commonly found? He didn't know.

He looked around. An ordinary room, plain walls, a series of cabinets. A window with a partially drawn blind, darkness behind it. There was always darkness behind it. A partly open door that revealed a section of tiled wall and the porcelain edge of a sink. Another door, the main one, always shut except for the few seconds it took the nurse to pass in or out. When she opened it, he made an effort to look into the hall. He had never seen anyone in it, only a brief flash of empty hallway, the only noise the squeak of her rubberized shoesoles as she walked in or walked away.

Is anything to be gained by doubting this is a hospital? He pondered this a long while. *No*, he finally decided. Or rather, if there was something to be gained, he could not see what that something might be.

I am in a hospital, he told himself firmly, and almost believed it.

II

There followed a long period when everything seemed the same from one day to the next, the motions of the nurse precise and unvaried, his own time in the bed monotonous, no significant change. How long that went on, he couldn't say. It felt so much the same that soon it started to feel like no time was going by at all, as if he were simply repeating the same day over and over.

He tried to break free of this by affecting a casual banter with the nurse, or nurses, seemingly without success. No matter what he said she gave the same response. She was there for only a few minutes a day in any case, leaving him mostly to his own devices, to sleep or to stare at the dark window. *Do I have a call button in case I need her?* he wondered, but there was nothing that looked like a call button among the buttons inset in the siderail, just two buttons with a triangle pointing up and two buttons with a triangle pointing down.

"Marry me," he said to the nurse as he stared at the veins on the back of her hand, just to see what she'd say. She responded the same way as always. "What would I have to do to convince you to lift me from my bed and carry me out to see another patient, any patient?" Same response. He was just formulating something else to ask, involving how much he would have to pay her to hurl him through the window, when suddenly she froze. One hand had pinched the tube closed and the other was milking the fluid down it when she simply stopped mid-gesture and became utterly, completely still. She was bent over him, awkwardly. She wasn't even breathing, or was breathing so shallowly he couldn't detect it.

"Hello?" he asked.

Silence.

"Are you all right?"

Silence.

This went on for fifteen, perhaps twenty seconds, as if she were a piece of machinery that had been inadvertently switched off. He reached up and touched her face. It felt cool to the touch but still felt like skin, more or less.

And then, as suddenly as she had stopped, she began moving again. But instead of simply continuing with the task she released her hold on the tube, stepped back from the bed, and crouched down until she was out of sight.

Surprised, he tried to lean over the side of the bed to see what she was doing. But by the time he had edged over far enough all he could see was the crisp white cap covering the crown of her head.

He was opening his mouth to speak when he heard from below a sucking sound, then a lapping, as if he were listening to a dog drink. *No*, he thought, *it can't be. She wouldn't...* But no, another part of him was saying, *How can you know what she would or wouldn't do? You have no idea what she is capable of.*

She glanced up and he hurriedly looked away. Had she seen him looking? He wasn't sure. It wasn't possible to be sure, but he hoped she hadn't. He closed his eyes and kept them tightly shut.

A moment later he heard the rustle of her skirts as she stood. He felt her hands brush him as they grasped the tube again and continued to force the pinkish yellow fluid from it. He counted slowly to three and then opened his eyes. She was looking at him, her gaze seemingly the same as always, incurious, her face free of any expression of menace or anger or joy, and so perfectly clean that it was almost possible for him to believe he hadn't seen it, almost possible to convince himself that when she had looked up from where she crouched on the floor there hadn't been pinkish yellow fluid trickling from one corner of her mouth.

He pretended nothing was wrong. His heart was beating in his throat, but he made a concerted effort not to look away too quickly. He reminded himself he shouldn't stare unduly either. It was a question of showing neither fear nor interest, of meeting her eyes exactly as long as usual, no matter how fast his heart was beating. Did he succeed? Well enough, he supposed, since after a few moments she finished her task and, as usual, left the room.

He waited until the squeak of her shoesoles had faded down the hall. He let out all his breath at once, and then, abruptly, panic began.

Not yet, he told himself, *not yet*, and forced himself to count slowly to one hundred. All the while he imagined the nurse turning around and coming back, coming for him.

He forced himself to stay calm. When he reached ninety-two he abandoned the count and tried with trembling fingers to disconnect the Luer lock, but couldn't unplug it somehow. He kept at it until his trembling and panic were so bad that he resorted to biting the lock until it broke and finally separated. Saline began to leak from the ruptured line, slowly soaking the bed.

He held his breath, listened. No squeaking of shoesoles, no sound of any kind.

No matter how hard he tugged, the catheter wouldn't come free. Even though he couldn't feel any pain, he could tell from the blood beginning to ooze down the tube that if he tugged any harder he would permanently damage himself. In the end he managed to lean far enough out to unplug the catheter tube from the bag that it drained into. He left it loose and dangling.

It was an effort to leave the bed. He moved slowly, rocking his hips from side to side until he reached the edge, and then he slid out and over, slowly descending until his toes found the floor. Only gradually did he shift his weight fully onto his feet and legs. When he was sure he could stand, he did, balancing against the bed with the heels of his hands. He couldn't straighten because of the tube, the tension in it. He bent a little and groped his way down the tube and found, finally, hooked onto the frame below the bed, a metal clip that held the tube in place and kept it closed. Bending and stretching now, face pressed to the mattress and arm extended as far down as it could go, he managed to loosen the clip enough to work the tube free.

He straightened. The open tube was drizzling, spattering his bare feet. Pushing off the bed, he made for the door.

From the doorway, the hall seemed like any hall: floor covered in linoleum or something roughly equivalent, plain white walls marred and scuffed where a gurney or something gurney-like had struck in passing, lightly buzzing fluorescents regularly inset in the ceiling. He moved forward and stepped into it.

The journey was not easy. His legs were unsure of themselves, still learning how to walk again. He moved very slowly, all the while the pinkish yellow, unless it was yellowish pink, fluid dripping over his shins and feet and onto the floor, leaving a sticky, irregular trail.

He braced his palm against the wall to steady himself and crept along. He came to a door, out of breath. Before he could think whether it was a good idea to do so, he had opened it and peered in. It was a room just like his own, but empty. And not exactly like his own, he realized: the walls were not white but pale pink.

Though as he edged his head around the frame and looked at the wall just beside his face, he realized with a start that it was not painted pink after all but instead misted with blood, speckled so finely and so regularly that the white and the red looked a single color unless viewed, as he was indeed viewing it, from very close.

~

Appalled, he closed the door and continued on. There was still no one in the hall, no sign that anyone else existed. He could still hear his tube and his catheter dripping. Probably he should fold over the ends of both tubes and hold them tightly in his fist so as not to leave a trail. But he didn't have the strength.

Another door. He almost passed it without opening it, but then thought, *What if it is a way out?*

When he turned the handle the door made a hissing sound, like an airlock. Inside was a room like his own, nearly identical, empty. The bedclothes were disarranged, as if someone had just left. *Where is everybody?* he wondered.

But the room felt wrong. It appeared slightly out of focus, as if either just coming into existence or just going out of it. It would be a mistake, he felt, to enter. This time, he didn't even dare allow the plane of his face to cross the threshold.

Is it too late to go back? he wondered. *Return to my bed, pretend nothing has happened?* He looked behind him at the slick, discolored trail he had left. Was it really possible all that fluid had come from his own body? *Yes*, he realized, *it is too late.*

Another door, shivering slightly in its frame from whatever difference in pressure existed between the hall and the space behind the door. He hesitated, his hand resting lightly on its handle, and then passed on. He was not sure he wanted to know what was inside.

~

There, at the hall's end: a door. It was different from the others he had passed, doubled and large. As he came closer, he saw it could be opened by pressing a red square on the wall before it.

He worked his way forward, toward the square, and when he reached it pressed it. With a gentle hum, the doors swung apart.

Inside was a small room, smaller than he had been led to expect from the nature of the doors that led into it. Around a circular table sat three nurses. They were motionless, all in the same posture, heads bowed, hands resting gently on the table. They were not moving. They did not seem to be breathing.

Where their faces should have been there was nothing at all, as if their skin had been stripped away to expose the damp underflesh beneath.

They sat unmoving, an enameled metal basin lying on the table between them. On the far side of them was another door, a wire mesh glass panel in it showing only darkness. It could be a way out. But he would have to pass them to reach it.

As silently as he could, he began to follow the wall around. He would have to pass close behind the back of one of their chairs, but after that it would be easy. With a little luck, he'd be able to sidle silently through the door before the nurses sprang back into motion. With even more luck, the door would be unlocked and would lead him out of this place and into the company of other humans.

He was nearly to the chair when he made the mistake of glancing at the bowl on the table. At this angle, its interior was visible now. It was, he saw, full of yellowish pink fluid. Something floated in it, half-submerged. He was quietly nudging his way around the chair when with a slurp it bobbed to the surface. He made the mistake of looking. It was, he saw, a face. The nurse's face.

He was still staring when the face opened its eyes and looked at him. Startled, he stumbled, bumped the back of the chair.

Immediately the faceless heads snapped upright, and their hands began groping, grabbing one another and breaking away, struggling with one another. They were—he realized as one of the hands climbed the edge of the basin and closed on the face, only to be struck away by another hand attempting to do the same—fighting over who would have the face.

Abandoning caution, he hurried toward the door. It was locked. Through the wire mesh glass nothing was visible but a vast darkness.

He stumbled away, fleeing back the way he had come. One of the nurses had managed to gain control and was lifting the face to affix it. *How long*, he wondered, *before she comes after me?*

There was a red square on this side too. He pressed it. With a gentle hum the doors slid open.

There was no point in fleeing, but he fled nonetheless, hoping something would occur to him before the face caught up with him.

But nothing did.

HOW WE ARE

Chikọdịlị Emelụmadụ

MY mother was extraordinary, so they say. *They* being my grandmother, who is raising me.

They say my mother had the power to make anything grow, and the will to keep it so. She carried me within her for nearly two years. We talked often then, her voice in mine in hers, flowing streams of endless conversation. She told me about herself, about those bits that she hid from everyone. Some of these things I forgot. Others I learnt by myself. One cannot hide from one's own mind. One day she simply said "Enough," and I slid out of her, wet and shivering. She pulled me to her bosom, but I had been born with all my teeth, and hunger. Instead of suckling I'd bitten her and drawn a mouthful of her blood. They say she sprang, pulled me off, slapped me. Not with spite, you understand, more surprise, hurt. I understood. We had been one entity not long ago, she nourished me, nurtured me, protected me within herself long after she should have, and in turn what had I done but supped on her bones, crumbling her teeth to shards? What had I done but turn what she had grown from her own body into a weapon against her? No wonder she hit me.

They say the birthmark draping half of my face is because of this immediate post-natal violence, a dark grey-blue bruise, like ube.

They say my power came from her blood, but the hurt I caused soured it. Now instead of growing things I infect them, hurt them.

I can kill them too.

Grandmother needs my pain for her medicine. On Afọ days, we go to the market where we peddle tinctures and potions and creams. Grandmother shares a stall with another woman—rents from her, really—even though I have never seen this woman, Eunice, sell any of her wares. If it is a good market, Grandmother will gladly part with Eunice's share of her profits. If it is bad, she will try to hide her monies in my pants. Eunice may be half blind, but she has hearing like a dog, she always knows how much we make. Nobody else will share a stall with Grandmother, not for how much she wants to pay. Grandmother is stingy and her mouth is bad. I wonder how Eunice stands her.

Besides, it is not really her they come to see, but me. Maybe it is the side effect of this power which plagues me. I can infect; therefore, I see infection in the body, weakness, aches, rot. I can tell when it is hopeless, though I never do, not while Grandmother can sell them a bottle of salve. I don't even need to touch a person to see where the break is, where harm has entered the electric path around the body. No, the touching is for something else, when the crowd gathers to witness me, and Grandmother on its fringes gives me her special sign. Grandmother is discerning and cautious, and we never get caught. A peculiar tinge of gold jewellery, rich cloth, the right cut of jib, and the sign comes. These ones I must touch. These I must give something only she can cure. Not for long. Grandmother's cure helps but its effects never last. We have patrons and pay home visits. Not many, not even a few, smaller than that—but those we have, Grandmother will ensure we milk them dry, both of money and life. That is my specialty. Incurable stuff. Soaps and solutions help, but not forever.

Business is booming.

Grandmother likes to force me to listen to her stories, ever since I was little and my mother ran away. I am my mother's penance, and so I sit and absorb Grandmother's verbal venom. She loves to talk about her beloved father, the notorious poisoner, so skilled that his poisons were undetectable, incurable. To be poisoned by my late great-grandfather was to die painfully and horribly. People feared him and many curried his favour. He is the only person of whom Grandmother speaks almost lovingly, as his life brought them riches. For a man who grew no crops, nor hunted, he had meat and fish aplenty for his family at every meal, especially as no other families would join them. So what if—he was known to boast—his daughters remained unmarried? He was rich enough to cater for them until they grew old and decrepit. Rich enough, powerful enough until some young talented upstart poisoner tested his mettle. Great-grandfather's death lasted eight agonising months, and afterwards his family absconded, hiding from their father's enemies, changing their names—here Grandmother spits into one of her tonics. Only Grandmother had the courage to try and follow in her father's trade. She had none of his skill for suffering, no creative ways to seduce and prolong a bout of death. The closest she could come involved a numbing sleep which, while it quietened the sufferer, did nothing to properly alleviate their pain.

For my mother, Grandmother has nothing but scorn. The woman who birthed me not only turned Grandmother's blood-gifts from bitter to sweet, but when the fullness of her powers came about, powers which equalled her ancestor's, she refused to make money off them, wandering the villages and giving herself away to all who needed her.

Good-for-nothing waste of talent! Grandmother spits. Do you know what she stole from me? Before her, my cures lasted. And what did she do with my power? Nothing! Spreading her laps for an ordinary "How are you?" from common men and women.

Grandmother's hands tremble whenever she talks about Mother. Such is her rage that the knife she is using to whittle a chewing stick from a branch of bitterwood slips and buries its blade in the side of her index finger. Grandmother hisses. She does not suck the blood, but instead opens another bottle and squeezes her finger into it. She glares at her finger as if it has personally betrayed her.

Still stealing from me, she says. All I do is mention her and my essence comes pouring out of me. You see this, Gifty? You see how wicked your mother is? Tueh! she spits again.

I mind my business and turn the plantains frying in the pan. Grandmother mumbles but does not demand a response from me.

When I was little, Grandmother could not abide my silences. She would jump up and whatever was in her hand would lash my skin, bruise it, break it. One day, I clung to her ankle as she hit me with a wooden spoon for not finishing my food—

Bastard! Wasting my money! Your fool of a mother should have taken you!

Afterwards, a few hours later, the ankle blistered and burst and blistered over again. Grandmother, following the first fact-finding wince that punctuated her exploring fingers, had looked at me properly, not out of the corner of her eye as she was wont. Her face, lost in thought, seemed almost kind.

Come here, this child, she said. I came. Can you do this again? She pointed at her ankle. I knelt down and touched the unblemished one. Only her knowledge of herbs stopped the skin from bursting open like overripe fruit. The battering ceased that same day. I was six.

The plantains are hot and golden, slightly crisp around the edges like Grandmother likes them. She slides five, six scalding slices into her mouth before I get a chance to serve them with the beans, stew, and fried beef. Grandmother sighs with pleasure when she bites into the meat.

Tomorrow now, some foolish man will come and turn your head and you will take all your gifts to his household, she says. Even your mother could not cook like this.

If only.

Grandmother does not like to mix her stew with the beans, prefers to let the red sit on top of the black-eyed beans like molten magma on a mountaintop, scooping both layers together. Prefers to let her tongue do the mixing. She eats her fill, drinks her cup of water and burps, before giving me her nod, assent. I am allowed to eat now. Grandmother picks her teeth, watches me like a guard dog. It is all an act, this permission to eat, left over from the days when she could and did deny me food often. I am bigger than she is, stronger and wider too. The thing which keeps me bound is more than strength or size. Grandmother is the only family I have ever known. Despite the crowd I attract at the marketplace and in the village squares, I have no friends, no other family—cannot so much as touch anyone without imparting some malaise or other. It is a lonely life, a life filled with the echoes of other people's living. I have no doubt that Grandmother would get by with her talents, but me, what use would I be to anyone? What point is it telling people where they ail if I cannot then provide the relief that is so desperately needed? I am not my mother. There is nowhere for me to go, so I stay.

I can perform wonders in a cooking pot, they say. I take Grandmother's word for it. Despite the pleasure I take in its making, food has no taste in my mouth, never has. For years I complained to Grandmother, and she beat me, thinking me ill-mannered, ungrateful. Hurt, harm to the body, aches, fugue states, those things I can smell, perceive, taste.

I shovel my food down for sustenance, wash the dishes and clean the kitchen.

We retire without locking our doors. Nobody would dare attack us.

Tuesday is Eke, and before the cock has crowed thrice in the compound across the street, I have readied our wares for sale. Grandmother likes Eke Awka the best out of all the markets we visit. Big, bustling, and situated in the state capital, Eke Awka is the second largest in the state, the biggest being Main Market at Onitsha, but we never go there. Not when it attracts thousands daily. Grandmother is cautious, afraid even, that somebody will figure out what I do and steal me away to use for their own misdeeds or kill me. There are many skilled poisoners, dibias, medicine men from as far as Kogi, towards the north. She is afraid that some ambitious poisoner or herbalist from Calabar or Benin will challenge her, and she will fail. She is afraid about what this means. Grandmother does not go anywhere or try anything if she is not already sure of its outcome. I have learnt from her and keep to myself.

We leave without breakfast. On Eke days, as is our custom, Grandmother stops at the akara sellers at Gbalingba Square. Huge, wide pans full of bleached palm oil simmer, and the brown akara balls bob up and down, turned over by perforated spoons the size of shovels. Soon they are done, scooped up and dumped in woven baskets lined with newspaper. It is brisk, hungry business. Already there are a few barrow and truck boys waiting for the heavy breakfast which will see them through to the afternoon. Eke days are busy and there is much money to be made. Not one of these boys will risk losing trade by stopping for lunch until the swell dies down.

Gifty, Gifty! How bodi? Mama Chioma is the most buxom of the akara artisans. She is also my favourite. She greets Grandmother and her smile gleams in her slick face. Fat, Christian Mother arms jiggle rhythmically as she stirs the spiced bean paste in preparation for dropping into the oil. Chioma, her daughter, slices whole loaves of bread, stuffs them with the akara, and prepares akamụ, baptising the corn pap with sparkling cubes of sugar and splashes of evaporated milk, before handing off to the next customer. The boys eat standing, squatting, perching on the overfull wooden benches.

How much own? Mama Chioma asks. The usual? I nod. Her arms move, dropping the paste with her fingers into the oil. Grandmother casts a lazy, practised eye over the assembled patrons, but her gaze does not hold genuine interest. These are not her desired clientele.

The akara is ready. Mama Chioma shakes off the excess oil in the spoon and wraps the balls, still shrieking from contact with the heat, into newspapers. She places the package in a black polythene bag and stretches out her hand. I open my bag and allow her to drop the bundle within, making sure not to touch her skin with the sliver of mine appearing between my long sleeves and the gloves I wear. Grandmother hands her the money.

Bye-bye nụ! Mama Chioma waves. She smells like a heap of cashew fruits that have fallen under the tree, heavy and heady and sweet.

We settle down for breakfast in Agnes's stall. Agnes is the woman from whom Grandmother rents space on Eke days, a woman with a wide mouth and dull, bulging eyes who looks but does not see. Grandmother's hands are swift, and she cuts and drugs the akara before serving Agnes's portion. Grandmother has kept Agnes her mind-slave for a long time, each dose wearing off just as Eke day comes around. We will keep most of what we make at this stall and still Agnes will thank us, as though we are the ones doing her a favour. Whatever other money she makes, Agnes gives away to the priest in the white-garment church she attends. Grandmother says Agnes has been asleep since long before they met. Some people are better off that way.

The akara has not yet gone down my gullet when the first customers arrive. Agnes sells occult artefacts, badly printed books in esoteric languages, framed symbols, carvings, perfume oils, holy water, sacred money pencils and pens. Sometimes Agnes is slow to give change, so I try to help. Grandmother makes a sound in her throat, but I don't mind her. It is the least I can do after what we have taken from Agnes.

I have sweat running down the sides of my face by the time the sun sits in the middle of the sky. Sickness reeks in the heat. I call out to a man whose blood flows tight and fast in his veins. He smells of dirty laundry. The man waves a dismissive hand as he hurries away.

You have high BP! I call after him. Do you want to die? Grandmother cuts eyes at me, smiling with her teeth as she wraps up a package for another customer. We do not mention death, even if it is round the corner. We take the hopeless, those who have a slow, steady decline. Knowledge of immediate and certain death makes people stupid and reckless. And the suddenly dead always seem to have angry relatives wanting their money back.

I smell Buchi in the crowd before I see her, the smell of petrichor, heady and delicious. My armpits begin to sweat, but I keep my head, touching the woman with the gold bracelets almost up to her elbow as Grandmother has indicated. Buchi's presence is a breeze, blowing away all the odours in my head, and it is with shame that I touch the woman's hands. She is in the peak of health, her blood metallic, full, and rich. Her laughter is incredulous when I feel her wrist, sure of itself, of her body. I regretfully send a message to her ankle.

You have a swelling that is about to appear, somewhere on your legs, I say. It is not dangerous.

Is that all? Grandmother smiles crocodile wide. Search well, she says. She is desperate, wanting me to give the woman something malignant. Even the moisture collecting in the woman's cleavage smells wealthy.

She said she sees nothing, what did you want her to find again?

the woman asks Grandmother. A wariness has entered her eyes at Grandmother's careless words.

Buchi draws nearer as I touch the woman's wrist again. I consider giving her an accompanying cyst on her wrist, or an ulcer in her stomach, but these also show up quickly and it would be unfortunate for her to suspect me of anything. There are three rings on her ring finger. Rich husbands bring problems too.

No, nothing, I say, withdrawing my hand. The woman leaves a few notes in front of me which Grandmother tucks into the waist of her wrapper before they have even touched the table. Some of the gathered disperse, disappointed not to get a free show of a rich woman breaking down. The poor love nothing more than to see the wealthy reduced to nothing. Disgusted, Grandmother turns away and walks through Agnes's shop, past the sleeping woman, into the small inner room to compose herself. I slip my glove back on.

Can you really tell when people are sick? Buchi's smell makes me dizzy. I want to sit, but Grandmother does not believe young people should sit without reason, so there is no chair for me. Buchi repeats the question.

Yes, I reply.

Even when we were in school? Is that why you didn't play with anybody? It must have been pepper for you, all the sickness you knew about. Did you know Mrs Anigbo had cancer? That she was going to die?

I am wondering why after all this time Buchi is talking to me in the market, after all this time of me rebuffing her friendship in school, and turning a blind eye to her everywhere else. Buchi can say one million words in a minute, the same as when we were in primary school, when she tried to be my friend, asking me all sorts of questions while I sat under her heady perfume and tried not to formulate an answer. Eventually even her persistence could not hold out against my taciturn nature, and she drifted away with her many friends and admirers. Our schoolmates added one more reason to why I must be unpleasant and avoided at all costs. Nobody rejected Buchi's friendship.

Touch me, she says. And my heart vomits heat all over my insides. I stare at her, overwhelmed, flabbergasted, scared. Tell me if I have any sickness, now. Buchi is insistent.

I can already smell that she does not. An excess of oils under the skin on her face, minute blockages, painful yes, but not deadly. I shake my head, no.

You haven't even touched me yet, she laughs.

I don't want to, I reply.

Why not? Buchi's eyes are black, the bones in her face sharp as knives.

I am delivered from the peril of lying by Grandmother, who clears her throat behind me. Buchi greets her, teeth flashing, eyes disappearing almost into her face. Grandmother's response is a grunt.

I hope you are not just here, gisting with your friends when there is work to be done? she asks.

She is not my friend, I say.

Buchi stares at me. She says goodbye and winds her way through the throng in the market, taking her scent with her. For the rest of the day, I put the rod back in my spine and cast Buchi out of my mind. Grandmother must never know how I feel.

The man with high BP comes back, and as a mercy I touch him and wear down the wall in one of his arteries. Grandmother will not chop his money more than once.

Some nights when Grandmother falls asleep, I slip out and take a walk to clear my head, to feel something other than other people's illnesses, their tastes, my own flesh, or the inside of my gloves. Grandmother owns a modest bungalow, encircled by a low wall and not much else. Leaving is easy, no squeaky gates to open. The night, between patches of generator-made light, is impenetrable, but I know my way around. Nobody bothers me here, in this village. All those nights of wandering around with my gloves off, laying hands on trees while the night cooled itself. My hands know the feel of leaf, of bark thick and corky, or thin like the husk from groundnuts. I have felt fruit, inedible, spiky, or furry. Trees do not get sick like people do, at least not from me. Their embrace is all I have enjoyed for years.

Tonight, the thoughts in my head cause me to cower in the dark, to skip quickly through pools of light. Buchi's parents are three miles away, in one of two duplexes shared by four families. I tell myself I don't mean to go so far, hence the wrapper around my waist, concealing my nightgown, my stretched-out, frayed sweater against the chill. These are home clothes, to be hidden from all eyes except mine and Grandmother's. I tell myself this, hiding my destination from myself.

The compound gate is still open. I observe a set of boys' quarters behind a low hedge that I cannot remember being there before, past the almond tree in the middle of the compound—somebody is doing well, expanding. I dart behind the duplex, eyes searching in the dark. No sane person would visit at this time of night, alone, on foot. I cannot afford to cast a shadow over the white-blue illuminations coming from the two ground-floor flats. There is the smell of stale Egusi soup coming from the one flat closest to me, but the next one smells of—I breathe deeply—yam porridge and first rains.

The back door to the flat clatters open. At the same time, the night swells with the laughter of young men from the boys' quarters behind me. Both things cause me to freeze. Buchi sees me before I can step back fully into the shadows.

Gifty? she calls. Gifty?

I step forward.

What are you doing here? Buchi drops a bag of rubbish into the outdoor bin and comes towards where I am standing. Instantly I grow dizzy again and the air hots up.

Did you come to see me? she asks. I think you said I wasn't your friend? Am I sick? Did you come to touch me?

Her questions, so many of them. My head swims and I put my hands up to stop my head from rolling off my shoulders.

What is it? She is whispering and her breath tickles the hairs on my top lip. Do you want to come inside?

No, I manage. I turn to leave, and Buchi blocks me.

Come inside, she says. It is late and your house is far.

She knows where I live. Everybody in school did, the better to avoid it. Buchi reaches for my hand and stops herself. She turns towards the back door again and slips inside without waiting to see if I am following. After a moment, her head slips out again. She beckons. I go to her.

The corridor is even darker than outside had been, and the only light comes from the TV in the parlour. The concrete floor is cool against my bare feet, but the walls still carry some warmth. There is the intense smell of gmelinas about the house which no other scents can mask. Somebody is dying.

Buchi's room is less than half the size of mine, it appears to be a converted store near the kitchen and away from the rest of the family. Her bed has been pushed to the wall, but boxes, bags, and cartons line the other three walls. There is a hint of louvre panes by one partially blocked window, a massive cross hanging near the ceiling with Jesus still on it. A glow-in-the-dark rosary is curled up on her pillow. Her room is small, secluded, perfect. My guard is up.

I feel her smile in the dark.

Who is dying? I ask.

The smile vanishes.

My mother, she says, and I taste the tears collecting in her throat.

We lie side by side, facing each other in her narrow bed. It is agony, my muscles stiffening to hold me in place. Buchi tells me everything, things I know none of her admirers could have known—tragedy repels company—things which I hope she has told nobody else.

You can really see sickness? she asks again.

See, smell, sometimes taste, I tell her.

What does it smell like?

All sorts of things. Your mother smells of gmelina fruits.

I hate that smell, she says.

I concur; me also.

The generators supplying electricity to various houses in the neighbourhood begin to power down one by one. Buchi swallows. Her saliva is sticky, thick, gluing her tongue to the palate. Her hand finds one of my gloved ones. My heart throws up its contents again.

And when you touch them? Is it bad-bad? What do you see?

I try to explain about the electricity. It sounds stupid.

So, it doesn't pain you? Why don't you touch people, then?

I withdraw into myself. In my mind, I am already on the road home, slipping back through the unlocked door and into my bedroom before Grandmother awakens. Tonight, has been a mistake. What had I been hoping would happen? What was this need to apologise for not calling her my friend? The desire to unburden myself shrinks back from telling her what my touch really does, the hundreds Grandmother and I have infected, have killed over the years. What would Buchi think of me then, a plague, lying in her bed?

Buchi is silent, her breathing even. I assume she has fallen asleep and prepare to climb out of the bed.

Why are you running? she asks. Her lips on my eyelids are startlingly hot. She kisses my sweaty nose. Turbulence from my stomach, fresh dust notes in my nostrils. I jerk back even as my face rises to meet hers.

Wait! I say.

You don't have to touch me, she says. I will touch you.

I am despicable. I am weak. I have killed her.

Her tongue at the entrance to my mouth brings the rains down upon me, upon us both, a monsoon, thrashing and curling around us, and we are swept away.

I have been watching Buchi for signs of illness, or infection from my hands, and, finding none, our friendship thaws, thrives. I am not sure how this has happened, but I am unwilling to try touching someone else in case it is a fluke of some sort. Nothing goes out of me when we touch.

I slip out frequently to see Buchi. Never the same days or times, but she is always waiting regardless. We are careful of the university boys in the boys' quarters, we know how they behave, what they will do if they suspect how we are.

My days off are the days Grandmother makes special potions with secret ingredients. Those days are filled with reading and helping Buchi take care of her stepsisters, of her dying mother and despondent father, a civil servant who slumps in front of the TV upon his return, whether there is electricity to power it or not. I help her to divert attention from her stepmother, rushed and harried with teaching and side hustles, indifferent to both Buchi and her own children, and upset by them at the same time. I wash Buchi's hair.

It is a strange setup, and yet I prefer it to what Grandmother and I have, the oceans of distance between us, physically, in her bungalow, and otherwise.

Buchi tends to her mother, a small woman, made smaller by disease, a pile of bones covered in thin, brown skin. Buchi turns her with more ease than she does her sisters and wipes her bedsores.

My parents divorced when we were in school, she says, but my mum couldn't go home to the Philippines. Her parents disowned her for marrying my dad, so she stayed here, but my father met someone else that he wanted to marry. Then she became ill…

Buchi's confidences come without prompting. She talks to me as though she is talking to herself. I stare at the woman on the bed, the woman whose eyes are half open, breath coming in painful gasps, stopping for seconds at a time.

I wish she had gone, Buchi says.

She drops the face towel into the bucket of Dettol and tepid water. I wish Mummy would die, she has suffered enough. When she dies, I will go to my uncle in Lagos and find my luck there.

I can come with you.

The declaration tears out of me forcefully. The notion of being without Buchi is like endless night. I had borne it before when I knew no better, but not now, not after I have been kissed by the warmth of the sun. I cannot think to stand the yawning, grasping aloneness that will result from her departure. In that moment, I understand my mother, why she left. It was not because I bit her, tainting her powers within myself. It was not the possibility of her gifts fading like Grandmother's, or her certain cruelty. It was that people need other people, their souls, their spirits, to bloom and grow. Was that not, after all, why I stayed with Grandmother? For a shallow semblance of the same? My mother gave away her gifts for free, to Grandmother's chagrin, but in so doing, she opened up and gave of herself as well. That is living, that is being, and I am ashamed of how long it has taken this knowledge to emerge from deep in my subconscious. Is this something I learnt, or something my mother revealed to me?

Buchi's hand slips beneath my waistband with ease. Can you help me? she asks. I taste the tears again. Can you help my mother to stop breathing?

I pull the searching hand away. Who said I can do that? I ask.

Can't you? she counters.

Clouds gather all day without rain to back up the threat. Nevertheless, it has the same effect as if it were raining. People dart about the shops and exit the market quickly, hoping to avoid the downpour, the inevitable flooding which brings traffic to a standstill.

I mull over Buchi's request in my mind, one eye on the sky, the other on passers-by. I smell a stroke coming in one person, the bitterness of burning tyres creeping up the electric pathway, but before I can say anything, the man in question scurries away. The odour of spoilt chicken livers as the woman before me stops to finger Eunice's wares—the baby in her womb is dead already. I think of saying something.

If you are not buying, please don't block my front, says Grandmother, making use of her famous bad mouth. The woman places a protective hand on the swell of her stomach as she walks away.

Grandmother smiles at me. You have not been cutting your hair, she says. It is now long, and nobody will plait it for you. Nobody can touch you, remember? Or do you know something I don't? Grandmother's smile is rare and never in my direction. It frightens me, its appearance. Coupled with the weather, it is as though I have soldier ants stinging me all over.

Another customer materialises, and Grandmother gives the sign. I stare the man down. Him? He wears a safari suit, grey and ordinary, and a pair of leather sandals. His hair and moustache have been combed. He is plump, but nothing about him screams wealth. His hands hover over the bottles and jars but his eyes search elsewhere. Him? I stare at Grandmother, who looks back unblinking.

Is this all you have? asks the man.

What are you looking for? I reply.

The man looks uneasy. I open my eyes and nose wide, and I know he will not tell us women, not even with blind Eunice pretending not to listen. His is a man's problem.

Perhaps my granddaughter can touch you. She will know what ails you. Grandmother kicks me, making certain to connect with the bottom of her sandaled foot.

No! The man jerks away before I can reach him. He hurries off.

He did not have much, I say to Grandmother.

We need money, God knows. It is not as if you are doing your job, disappearing all the time. Where do you even go, sef?

Nowhere. I realise immediately that I have given the wrong answer. Grandmother smiles, nonetheless.

Secretive, just like your mother.

I am distracted by the smell of fresh dust and whirl around without my usual caution. The crowds are sparse, and Buchi's smile is wide, noticeable as she bounds towards our stall. I try to signal her with my eyes to dim her happiness, but Buchi is oblivious. Behind me, Grandmother croaks like a frog.

Buchi does not touch me when Grandmother is around, but she does not need to. I wear the imprint of her hands on my skin. Buchi is also taken in by Grandmother's crocodile smiles. She bumps me, tries to make me smile, jokes, she and Grandmother between them, passing anecdotes over my head. My body is taut with worry, taunted by anxiety. Buchi is used to being adored. She does not see that Grandmother is not like other grandmothers are meant to be. I want Buchi to leave. Grandmother's eyes flit from her to me even though I have not moved from my place since she appeared. The clouds are stained with charcoal.

Maybe we should pack up now, Grandmother says.

We never pack up early, not until the market closes for the day—and even then, we linger at the buses, doing last-minute deals on potions— but I am relieved. Pressure has built up in my ears and this way, I can walk Buchi to her bus stop and relieve some of it.

I pull Buchi out of the shop under the pretence of the rain and escort her to her stop.

What is doing you? she asks.

You can't come to our house.

Why? She fiddles with her scapular, placing the one brown square over her chest so that it lines up with the one on her back.

The magnitude of it, how to explain that silence is the most frequent visitor in our house? That Grandmother cannot be trusted? She will look and she will see and there is no telling what she can do with what she sees. Grandmother can destroy anything with her mouth. What if Grandmother says something of the work that we do, our real work? Tells her what I have done to countless others? Will Buchi still like me then? I must keep them apart.

Grandmother is wicked, I say.

Hia! Buchi hisses. If she is wicked to you, be wicked back. You have a mouth too.

Buchi thinks everything is easy. My mind is full of things to say but my tongue has tied itself the way it normally does when things are too much. Buchi normally talks for both of us.

Have you thought about the thing I said? she asks. About my mother?

I sigh. Yes, I say.

Are you going to do it for me?

How are you expecting me to do this thing? I am searching again for what Buchi knows or suspects of what I do.

Buchi looks away. I would do it myself if she was not my mother, she says. I would do it for you.

I turn it over in my mind. I have never killed anybody before, not in the way she is asking me, not as a mercy. I have been passive, letting Grandmother direct and place my hands just where she wishes. Selfish as well, for a roof over my head and the lie of family. Passive and selfish. That is all I know how to be. Buchi is asking something else entirely.

I don't want her to suffer.

Buchi shrugs. Will it be more than she is suffering already?

My head hurts.

Do it next week. Should we say Wednesday? Let me give the little ones time to get ready, you hear? Just do it fast. If I could do it myself...

A drop of rain slaps me on the head, another on the cheek. Buchi squeals and runs for the bus without saying goodbye, but I do not mind. I need more time to think.

There are things you don't dare think about when nobody wants you, things that you cannot afford to ponder because they open you up to the risk of painful discovery. I never asked Grandmother questions about my mother, not where she went or where she was living or why she did not come to see me. It did not matter, because I still felt the residue of my mother's essence from sharing her mind, and even though I missed her fiercely, I know she loved me, loved me enough to wreck her body to keep me protected. I know that whatever caused her to leave must have been unbearable, and as I grew, I knew Grandmother to be that cause. It is hard to compete with the memory of a dead ancestor. Grandmother used up all her love on her own father. The rest of us she merely uses.

But I have also settled, in ways that my own mother chose not to, and in so doing I have wasted the sacrifices she made for me. I think I now understand love and I understand sacrifice, and Buchi by one simple act is asking for both. It is time to be neither passive nor selfish. I am resolved.

That night, when she opens the back door to me, it is with the solemnity that the occasion deserves. Buchi touches her lips to mine softly and leads me by the hand. Snoring comes from the parlour, little snuffles from all over the house. I have come late on okada, after most of the rain has subsided, to avoid the inevitable misstep and drowning in overfull roadside gutters.

Her mother's breathing sounds much worse. The gmelina smell suffocates me. I deliberately avoid looking inside her with my eyes, as there does not appear to be any use for my gifts.

She sounds really bad, I whisper. Maybe we should just let her go on her own.

No, Buchi whispers back. Sometimes she is like this, and we think she will die, but it has been eight years.

She takes my hands, pulling my gloves off one by one. Buchi places them down on her mother's chest. The thin skin clings to the ribcage, fragile. I could shatter them if I pushed down, but that sounds like extra misery for the woman struggling for every breath. I could wrap my hands around her throat, I am strong enough. I could put the flat pillow on her face and cut off all air.

How will you do it? Buchi asks. She puts her index finger in her mouth.

Turn around, I tell her, and she obeys. I try what comes naturally, sending her every infection and disease I have ever conjured up. At once the electric pathway within her goes haywire, explosions going off, things burning. My heart echoes the panicked beating beneath my hands, the breathing shallow and fast. I have never felt such power, nor held such intent in my mind. I push until the brain inside the eggshell skull collapses. I raise my hands, pick my gloves off the bed, and slip them back on. For once, the smell of my handiwork nauseates me.

I've finished, I say.

Buchi turns back around. Her jaw hangs open. She is not supposed to look like this, she says. There is blood coming out of the corpse's bulbous eyes, the ears and nose.

What did you do to her? she asks. Her own eyes are wide. It is as if she too is seeing me for the first time.

The rains continue almost nonstop all weekend long and into the next week. The trips to the markets are miserable, sodden affairs. There is little profit, but Grandmother insists on earning what there is, first at Agnes's and then at Eunice's. The market seems emptier, and not just because most people take shelter in different shops. Buchi has not been to see me, and I, recalling the horror on her face at my handiwork, cannot bring myself to visit. Grandmother watches me but leaves me to my thoughts for most of the morning, chatting with Agnes when she is not serving customers. Agnes makes the noise in her throat that means agreement though I am unsure to what extent she understands.

Forget that one, says Grandmother, and it takes me a while to figure out she is talking to me.

She talked too much. They always promise the world, then, before you know it, they are running from the magnitude of your power, and you are pregnant and alone.

My mind scrambles to comprehend what has come out of Grandmother's mouth. I stare at her, and she stares at me. I wonder how much she knows, what she knows.

Although, in your case, it is a blessing you cannot get pregnant like that. That one has not known suffering, real suffering. How can you be your true self with such a one?

I stare at her some more.

Close your mouth, before flies enter. You think because I am old, I do not see things? The man that sired you was the same, attracted to your mother but overawed by what she could do. Where is he now? She is still looking for him, your useless mother. But you, there is a lot more to you. You and my father are similar. Let the chatterbox girl go, you will find another.

Inside me it is warm, in a way I have never felt. Grandmother does not say any more on the matter, but what is said cannot be unsaid. I am buoyed by her words, seen, accepted, all ill-will forgotten. It lasts a while before doubt descends.

She can touch me, I say. I can touch her, and she does not get ill.

Nothing new under the sun, Grandmother says. Of course she has figured it out too. That is the reason she has spoken. That is why she can say, Leave the chatterbox girl. A bit of residual doubt remains—is Grandmother being amenable so that I do not leave like my mother did? I put the thought away.

When it is clear we will make no more money today, I ask Grandmother if I can go for a while, counting on her to say yes, which she does. Something has opened up between us. It makes me brave. I am determined to face Buchi, on my own terms, in the daylight, instead of crawling to her at night. I did as she asked, and this silence is the thanks I receive? Throwing a shawl over my head, I race for the next bus in line. It is half full, and I must wait for it to fill with passengers before we can leave; however, I am not fazed. Time stretches before me, crammed with possibility. Perhaps it is not just Buchi I can touch without harming, maybe there are more, hundreds, thousands more. Nothing new under the sun.

The sun breaks through dark clouds and it is raining and sunny at the same time. Some of the passengers clap, delighted. A child in its mother's lap begins to sing the rainy-sunny-day song popular among schoolchildren. I smile, recalling doing the same at his age.

Buchi's compound is different in the daytime, gate wide open, silent, except for the droplets of water slapping the thick, broad leaves of the almond tree. Standing by the front door feels strange to me, as does knocking, but I do it anyway. There is no response. I dash around to the back door and find it ajar.

To another, the smell would be unbearable, but to me it is merely unpleasant and familiar. I smell my handiwork all over the house.

The first room holds the bodies of the two stepsisters in bed, arms around each other, dark blood congealed on the bedding. Their mother is curled up on the floor in her own rufescent excrement. I open the rest of the rooms in a rush.

Buchi! Buchi! I shout. Other bodies: her father slumped in work clothes, briefcase clutched in a dead fist, his body blocking the front door. Her mother's body lies where I last saw it. It reeks the most.

I find Buchi with her head and shoulders in the toilet. Her nightgown is stained and bloody. The world swims, thunder smashes down around us.

Buchi! I try to lift her out but some of her hair comes off in my hand. The scalp beneath is bloodless. I throw the hair down, try again, standing over her, lifting up and out. Her eyes are glued shut, her face watery.

No, *my* face is watery. I am crying and my tears splash all over Buchi's unmoving features. Ugly sounds, loud in my throat, deadening my ears.

The ants are back, swarming all over me, pinching and biting, and I rush out the door and towards the centre of the compound. I put my hands on the almond tree and I push every bad feeling, every scrap, every ounce of whatever is in my blood into the tree, into the ground, into the sky.

Take it! I shout. I don't want this anymore.

Lightning slices through the air, the smell of plastic burning. I am covered suddenly by leaves, falling violently to the ground. From the ends of my toes, the grass begins to wither, spreading out across the compound towards the boys' quarters, and beyond.

THE LONG DEAD DAY

Joe R. Lansdale

S HE said a dog bit her, but we didn't find the dog anywhere. It was a bad bite, though, and we dressed it with some good stuff and wrapped it with some bandages, and then poured alcohol over that, letting it seep in, and she, being ten, screamed and cried. She hugged up with her mama, though, and in a while she was all right, or as all right as she could be.

Later that evening, while I sat on the wall and looked down at the great crowd outside the compound, my wife, Carol, called me down from the wall and the big gun. She said Ellen had developed a fever, that she could hardly keep her eyes open, and the bite hurt.

Carol took her temperature, said it was high, and that to touch her forehead was to almost burn your hand. I went in then, and did just that, touched her forehead. Her mother was right. I opened up the dressing on the wound, and was amazed to see that it had turned black, and it didn't really look like a dog bite at all. It never had, but I wanted it to, and let myself be convinced that was just what it was, even if there had been no dog we could find in the compound. By this time, they had all been eaten. Fact was, I probably shot the last one around;

a beautiful Shepherd, that when it saw me wagged its tail. I think when I lifted the gun he knew and didn't care. He just sat there with his mouth open in what looked like a dog's version of a smile, his tail beating. I killed him first shot, to the head. I dressed him out without thinking about him much. I couldn't let myself do that. I loved dogs. But my family needed to eat. We did have the rabbits we raised, some pigeons, a vegetable garden, but it was all very precarious.

Anyway, I didn't believe about the dog bite, and now the wound looked really bad. I knew the real cause of it, or at least the general cause, and it made me sick to think of it. I doctored the wound again, gave her some antibiotics that we had, wrapped it and went out. I didn't tell Carol what she was already thinking.

I got my shotgun and went about the compound, looking. It was a big compound, thirty-five acres with a high wall around it, but somehow, someone must have breached the wall. I went to the back garden, the one with trees and flowers where our little girl liked to play. I went there and looked around, and found him sitting on one of the benches. He was just sitting. I guess he hadn't been the way he was for very long. Just long enough to bite my daughter. He was about her age, and I knew then, being so lonely, she had let him in. Let him in through the bolted back door. I glanced over there and saw she had bolted it back. I realized then that she had most likely been up on the walk around the wall and had seen him down there, not long of turning, looking up wistfully. He could probably still talk then, just like anyone else, maybe even knew what he was doing, or maybe not. Perhaps he thought he was still who he once was, and thought he should get away from the others, that he would be safe inside.

It was amazing none of the others had forced their way in. Then again, the longer they were what they were, the slower they became, until finally they quit moving altogether. Problem with that was, it took years.

I looked back at him, sitting there, the one my daughter had let in to be her playmate. He had come inside, and then he had done what he had done, and now my daughter was sick with the disease, and the boy was just sitting there on the bench, looking at me in the dying sunlight, his eyes black as if he had been beat, his face gray, his lips purple.

He reminded me of my son. He wasn't my son, but he reminded me of him. I had seen my son go down among them, some, what was it, five years before. Go down in a flash of kicking legs and thrashing arms and squirting liquids. That was when we lived in town, before we found the compound and made it better. There were others then, but they were gone now. Expeditions to find others they said. Whatever, they left, we never saw them again.

Sometimes at night I couldn't sleep for the memory of my son, Gerald, and sometimes in my wife's arms, I thought of him, for had it not been such a moment that had created him?

The boy rose from the bench, stumble-stepped toward me, and I shot him. I shot him in the chest, knocking him down. Then I rushed to him and shot him in the head, taking half of it away.

I knew my wife would have heard the shot, so I didn't bother to bury him. I went back across the compound and to the upper apartments where we lived. She saw me with the gun, opened her mouth as if to speak, but nothing came out.

"A dog," I said. "The one who bit her. I'll get some things, dress him out, and we'll eat him later."

"There was a dog," my wife said.

"Yes, a dog. He wasn't rabid. And he's pretty healthy. We can eat him."

I could see her go weak with relief, and I felt both satisfied and guilty at the same time. I said, "How is she?"

"Not much better. There was a dog, you say."

"That's what I said, dear."

"Oh, good. Good. A dog."

I looked at my watch. My daughter had been bitten earlier that day, and it was almost night. I said, "Why don't you go get a knife, some things for me to do the skinning, and I'll dress out the dog. Maybe she'll feel better, she gets some meat in her."

"Sure," Carol said. "Just the thing. She needs the protein. The iron."

"You bet," I said.

She went away then, down the stairs, across the yard to the cooking shed. I went upstairs, still carrying the gun.

Inside my daughter's room, I saw from the doorway that she was gray as cigarette ash. She turned her head toward me.

"Daddy," she said.

"Yes, dear," I said, and put the shotgun against the wall by the door and went over to her.

"I feel bad."

"I know."

"I feel different."

"I know."

"Can anything be done? Do you have some medicine?"

"I do."

I sat down in the chair by the bed. "Do you want me to read to you?"

"No," she said, and then she went silent. She lay there not moving, her eyes closed.

"Baby," I said. She didn't answer.

I got up then and went to the open door and looked out. Carol, my beautiful wife, was coming across the yard, carrying the things I'd asked for. I picked up the shotgun and made sure it was loaded with my daughter's medicine. I thought for a moment about how to do it. I put the shotgun back against the wall. I listened as my wife came up the stairs.

When she was in the room, I said, "Give me the knife and things."

"She okay?"

"Yes, she's gone to sleep. Or she's almost asleep. Take a look at her."

She gave me the knife and things and I laid them in a chair as she went across the room and to the bed.

I picked up the shotgun, and as quietly as I could, stepped forward and pointed it to the back of my wife's head and pulled the trigger. It was over instantly. She fell across the bed on our dead child, her blood coating the sheets and the wall.

She wouldn't have survived the death of a second child, and she sure wouldn't have survived what was about to happen to our daughter.

I went over and looked at Ellen. I could wait, until she opened her eyes, till she came out of the bed, trying for me, but I couldn't stomach that. I didn't want to see that. I took the shotgun and put it to her forehead and pulled the trigger. The room boomed with the sound of shotgun fire again, and the bed and the room turned an even brighter red.

I went outside with the shotgun and walked along the landing, walked all the way around, came to where the big gun was mounted. I sat behind it, on the swivel stool, leaned the shotgun against the protecting wall. I sat there and looked out at the hundreds of them, just standing there, looking up, waiting for something.

I began to rotate and fire the gun. Many of them went down. I fired until there was no more ammunition. Reloaded, I fired again, my eyes wet with tears. I did this for some time, until the next rounds of ammunition were played out. It was like swatting at a hive of bees. There always seemed to be more.

I sat there and tried not to think about anything. I watched them. Their shapes stretched for miles around, went off into the distance in shadowy bulks, like a horde of rats waiting to board a cargo ship.

They were eating the ones I had dropped with the big gun.

After a while the darkness was total and there were just the shapes out there. I watched them for a long time. I looked at the shotgun propped against the retaining wall. I looked at it and picked it up and put it under my chin, and then I put it back again.

I knew, in time, I would have the courage.

ALONE IS A LONG TIME

Michael Marshall Smith

AFTER Mr. Jones died, and the funeral with family, his son stayed on in London for a week to clear the house.

The heart of the task, the first pass at it, anyway, was selecting keepsakes to pack and ship; objects to remind him of these people now gone, especially the versions of them before their decline. A slow one, in his father's case, more rapid with his mother, leaving the old man adrift for twenty years except for regular carer visits in recent years, and less frequent but longer ones from his son and his family. The last of these, stopping by alone while on a business trip, had been three months before. This was a source of guilt, though they'd continued to speak every day on the phone until the end, which—as so often— came suddenly, with no time to get back to say a final goodbye. He was gradually making his peace with this. When you've loved someone that deeply for that long, there's a limit to what "goodbye" means. His father had seldom been one for overt sentiment, and what's left unsaid is often fuller than words could have encompassed, for better or worse.

You can't hang on to everything, and in most cases it was easy to make the call. He kept nothing from his old bedroom. If he'd wanted those few souvenirs of teenage life he would have retrieved them at some point in the last thirty years. With his parents' possessions he decided he needed a protocol, to avoid being excessively swayed by sentiment.

So he elected to assume he *wouldn't* take something—California is a long way from England, and there was a limit to how much old stuff he could expect his wife to welcome—*unless* it met one or more of three criteria: it was a strong reminder of childhood; it was something he knew one or both parents had prized (rather than merely inheriting, it's easy to end up keeping some object that even your great-great-grandmother never much cared about); he found it objectively attractive, or believed his wife might. He knew, for example, that she'd always admired the 1960s sideboard, though God knows where they'd put it. As it happened the sideboard also met both the other criteria, and he could remember his wife and mother happily chatting about it years ago, so he put a Post-it note on it.

He moved through the rooms, one by one, accounting the lives of people now disappeared. You can't allow yourself to feel every feeling that presents itself during this process: sometimes you have to watch the emotions float past, acknowledging them, but not allowing yourself to drown. He noticed how some objects he might have thought possessed resonance no longer did: without someone at the center of the web to confer connection, things return to being random things. In the back of the closet in his father and mother's bedroom, for example, he found a blue handbag. A quick glimpse inside showed it to be still full of bits and pieces, but there was no point sorting through them: after this long, they would make no sense to him. If it had been the large, black leather one he remembered from his childhood—back when your mother's handbag was one of the main storing-places in the world, a key accessory of one of the two pillars of your reality—he might have wavered. He didn't recognize this one, so... no.

He noticed also how, while in the house, he lost almost all sense of his own identity. Death returns us to archetypes. He was not, for now, the person with a career and family and history of his own. He was a role. He was The Son.

He left the living room until last. It had formed the center of his father's last years, and remained by far the most psychically charged. Also, there was simply *so much stuff*.

Not hoarder-style: his father had been methodical all his life. Everything was neatly arranged, meaningful. Some of it too meaningful, albeit in trivial ways. Piles of books he'd bought for his father as birthday or Christmas gifts, organized by subject. With some he remembered the moment of purchase, turning the volume over in his hands, deciding whether his dad would be likely to enjoy it, if this book might even rekindle engagement in a once-enthusiastic academic mind. Some now looked read. Others, especially given in the last couple of years, did not.

Those were all easy. Charity shop. But the rest of the stuff... he realized he'd better make more coffee before starting. This was going to take a while.

On his way out of the room he noticed something on a shelf. A small, lidded pot, about an inch high and two inches across, made of some silvery metal, burnished to a reflective shine. After a moment, he recognized it.

And frowned, surprised to see it there.

Karen's phone rang as she was walking into the driveway. She'd been lost in thought, or lack-of-thought, and the noise made her jump. The ringer was off, as it always was when she was at work, but the vibrate was strong enough to make her bag buzz loudly. It sounded like a bullying little drill. Whenever she got home for the evening she turned vibrate off and put the ringer on low instead. It didn't ring often. She quickly reached for the phone before it could go to voicemail. Peter took it personally if his calls weren't picked up—even when he must have known she was with a client. He ran the schedule, after all. No personal calls allowed during working hours. Just Peter. He was the boss.

"Hello, dear," he said. That sing-song lilt, in full effect within two words. As if he was a professional but friendly member of cabin crew on a long-haul flight, who'd tell you off if your hand luggage wasn't stowed before take-off, yet might also discreetly find you an extra glass of wine, should you need one in the dark lees of an intercontinental night. Karen knew, however, that while Peter was certainly professional, in his own way, he was not friendly. Not really. He might as easily decide to withhold that glass of wine. Just because he could. "Wanted a word."

"It'll need to be quick," she said. "I've just got to Mr. Jones's. I'm due in… three minutes."

"I know. Mr. Jones is why I'm calling."

"Oh?"

"I had a visit earlier. Might be a bit of a thing."

"With?"

"The son."

"Why? I told you. He visited yesterday. While I was there."

"You did tell me that. And I'm sure you were charming to him."

"He seemed nice enough. Here on business, he said. I left him with his dad."

"It appears he stayed a little while after you'd gone, catching up. What with him living in America, and all."

"Okay, but… so?"

"Seems he's quite observant."

Karen's heart did a heavy little thump. "Oh."

"Indeed. He was waiting outside the office when I arrived this morning. He was… I'd characterize him as 'concerned.'"

"What about?" In her spare time, the evenings and weekends when she had little to do, Karen was an avid reader of mystery novels.

From the library, or picked up cheaply in charity shops. In one, she'd encountered the assertion that when being interrogated it's best not to volunteer inessential information. Don't answer questions you're not being explicitly asked. This conversation with Peter, though on the surface about him telling *her* things, felt like unsafe ground. Talking with him often did.

"A number of things. Cleanliness, for a start."

"I've told you," Karen said, defensively. "Two one-hour sessions a week isn't nearly enough. It's a big, old house. And Mr. Jones does nothing to tidy, never mind clean. It's not his fault, to be fair. His mobility's got worse and worse. Just rounding up and washing the cups and plates he's left around the place uses up a good ten minutes while I'm there."

"I explained this. Told the son how his father could be difficult about some things, too, when you're only trying to help."

Washing clothes, for example. Mr. Jones only tackled it once a month, and so both he and the house were permeated with that fusty-sweet old person smell. He was, however, fiercely protective of his washer/dryer: a concern that it might for some unknown reason stop working was far stronger than the desire that his clothes be clean. Despite reassurances that she was perfectly capable of working the machine (it was a similar model to the one she had in her flat), Karen had been brusquely banned from tangling with it. Several times. A few minutes after the last occasion, Mr. Jones apologized, quietly saying he didn't mean to cause offense, it was just the way he was, he hoped she understood.

Karen did. He was old. You stop being a person and become a fretting bundle of abstract nouns instead. Tiredness. Discomfort. Anxiety. Irritation. Oldness, in sum. Just a piece of oldness, huddled in an armchair bought many years before, once of good quality but now sagging and bearing the claw scars of long-dead cats, a tattered throne in a room that's too dark in the afternoon—because, for some old person reason, you won't put the lights on.

"The son wants to double the hours. Starting next week."

"Oh," she said, surprised. The rate for their services was far from cheap (a large chunk of it went to Peter, of course, leaving Karen on the edge of solvency most of the time). It was interesting how many relatives found that the bare minimum required to keep their elder's life ticking over was all they could afford. That, and not five minutes more. "Well, that's good. Mr. Jones has always been funny about the idea of more help."

"Evidently the son is persuasive. Mr. Jones asked for you to handle the additional sessions. He likes you, apparently. Or is used to you, anyhow."

Karen knew her boss wasn't being pointlessly undermining. When you're old, actively *liking* someone is seldom the point anymore. You want what you're accustomed to. Something that won't unnerve or confuse. No disturbances in the force. She'd been present on more than one occasion when Mr. Jones had become visibly alarmed at the sound of a letter dropping through the letter box, upset at a harbinger of potential chaos, something that might derail his carefully minimized existence. They were only ever junk mail and circulars, yet still he worried. "And you'll—"

"Already on it, dear. I'll post up a new schedule imminently. You'll have your car back soon, will you?"

"Yes, Friday, it's just in for a service. Look, it's almost time—I'd better go."

"One more tiny thing."

She waited, not speaking. She sensed this was not a time to utter a single unnecessary word.

"Observant, as I said. The son. And subtle. On his way out the door after our *chat*, he asked if all my girls had undergone police background checks. I said of course they had."

"And I have. You know that."

"I organized it myself. But that only answers his apparent question. Not the one behind it. The son's leaving the country this afternoon, he said, but stick to *light* duties for today, just in case. Okay?"

"Will do. Look, I really gotta go now. Mr. Jones gets super-anxious if I'm late."

ALONE IS A LONG TIME · 175

"Old people, eh? Go on then."

Though it was now 11:01 and she knew Mr. Jones could be waiting behind the front door, leaning heavily on his crutch, phone in his tremulous hand, on the verge of calling her or else going straight to the office to chase her down—she was mildly surprised there weren't already search helicopters circling overhead—Karen paused a moment, in order to be able to smile at him when he opened the door. The honest, open smile with which she liked to greet all her clients, one of whom (Mrs. Smith, now dead, but a cheerful old bird until the end) had told Karen made her look "years younger."

The honesty of the smile was important. To get there, Karen allowed a feeling of guilt to pass through her, as many times before. There was no point to it. What's done was done, and there are some rivers you can't swim back up.

She set off down the path to the front door, exuding capable cheerfulness. Mr. Jones wouldn't be pleased to see her. Not really. Merely glad that the anxiety of her brief failure-to-be-here had been relieved. His mind would immediately move on to something else, worrying at some other non-problem, reducing her to a tidying shadow glimpsed out of the corner of his eye, as he sat there in his chair, a king in exile from life, mind turned inward. Meanwhile a stranger moved around his house. Not family. Hired help.

What does it do to your sense of worth, knowing that the people who visit do so only because they're paid to come? And what does that arrangement meanwhile do to those visitors, whose care and attention is bought by the hour?

Karen supposed she already knew.

After exchanging the usual brief pleasantries, she got right to it. Working tactically, too. Karen remembered once, long ago, her grandmother telling her that if time or opportunity was short, you could make yourself feel fresh by just brushing your teeth, splashing water on your face, and quickly washing your feet. Karen had made recourse to this wisdom in the refuge, and found it achieved (in terms of how you felt, anyway) a good eighty percent of what a nice long bath would have done.

So, prioritize.

Kitchen; lower bathroom; Mr. Jones's bedroom; the area around his chair in the living room. Her next appointment wasn't until one p.m., and only fifteen minutes' walk away. Throw in a free half hour (but don't let Peter know—he wouldn't approve, despite it being her time and her choice). Lean into the products and bleach. If the son happened to drop in for a goodbye on his way to the airport, he'd be able to *smell* how clean the house was, the moment he walked in the door.

She tackled the kitchen and bathroom first. It actually felt good to do it more thoroughly than usual. She didn't enjoy skimping. There's no pleasure in a job badly done.

On the way to the stairs she glanced into the living room to see Mr. Jones dozing in his chair, newspaper collapsed across his lap like a mountain range, the state in which he appeared to spend much of his day. She'd probably have to disturb him when she did that room, but let him sleep for now. In fact…

No. Not today. Not for the boss, and not for herself.

She started onward, then stopped. Something looked a little different about the room. Something small. She took a step back, peered, couldn't tell what. Not important. Work to do.

Up in the bedroom she put discarded clothes in the washing basket. Used the dust-buster to suck crumbs off the floor and out of the bedding (Mr. Jones seemed to spend most of the night at least half-awake, evidently passing the time nibbling dry biscuits). Remade the bed itself, though the sheets really needed a wash now—the old-person odor was notably stronger here than downstairs. He wouldn't let her, however, and they wouldn't be dry by the time she left. She tidied the objects strewn across the dresser: comb, keys, small change.

After listening in case of movement from downstairs—once, just once, Mr. Jones had suddenly appeared outside the bedroom while she was cleaning, though that was six months ago, before his mobility got worse—she silently pulled open the top-right drawer of the unit. There, as had been his custom since Karen started working for him, lay his wallet, alongside a tattered envelope of cash. She knew the wallet held a bank debit card, along with a VISA credit card, and a small, tattered photograph of his late wife. Twenty years gone, but still smiling down from various other faded photos around the house. Karen also knew that once a month he got a cab down to the bank to withdraw enough to pay for things like his gardener, the place that delivered his newspaper, and little bits of shopping when he still used to go out.

She'd never taken anything from the drawer. However vague an old man might be about laundry or personal hygiene or the use-by dates of food in the fridge, they tend to remain surprisingly sharp about how many bank notes they have.

She closed the drawer carefully, and as she straightened, caught sight of herself in the mirror on the dresser. What did that reflection show? A woman of thirty-eight. Living by herself in a flat not far from the tube station. A face and figure that wasn't bad, surely, yet didn't seem to do the trick on dating apps. Not for kind men, anyway. Just the other type.

She pushed away the thought (or rather, like the guilt earlier, let it pass through and out the other side), and gave the mirror a quick wipe.

By the time the bedroom was done, the time was 12:07. She went back downstairs—glad to confirm that yes, a wave of bleach and pine scent hit you as you reached the ground floor—and stood outside the living room. Mr. Jones was still dozing, half the newspaper now on the floor. She wondered how she'd feel if this was her own father. He'd never made it to anywhere near this age, passing away in the night from a cardiac event. Presumably, more than she felt now.

Actually, the room wasn't bad. She quietly arranged and plumped the cushions on the couch, tidied a few small pieces of furniture, fetched the dustpan and hand brush and collected up dust and crumbs. Next, she flattened the two small rugs: these seemed to present an obvious deathtrap for someone who could only get around with a crutch or, increasingly, a Zimmer frame, but she'd asked if he wanted them rolled up and stowed somewhere, and the offer had been firmly declined. They'd most likely been acquired by his wife, thirty or more years ago. Their presence and position was part of the lonely amber in which he was trapped.

Finally she gathered up the pieces of the newspaper and interleaved them back together, folding the whole back to neatness, and leaving it where it'd be easy for him to reach when he woke again. Assuming, of course, he was truly asleep. The borderland between that state and being awake seemed to expand in the old. Perhaps, in fact, that's what death was, and where its dominion lay: the point in life where this middle ground swelled and swelled until it filled all the time in the world.

It was 12:22. She should leave soon. She found herself, however, remaining in the center of the room, wondering what in here had caught her eye before she went upstairs.

Hard to tell, in a room this cluttered. Well, not cluttered—it wasn't untidy. It was simply… *very full of things*. Old paperbacks on many shelves. Piles of non-fiction hardcovers. Other, much older books— Mr. Jones had once been an academic, apparently, a widely traveled anthropologist. A professor, in fact, hard though that was to imagine now. Photographs of family members, including his son standing with a nice-looking blond woman and two children, somewhere far away. A shelf entirely populated by primitive-looking pottery birds from Mexico. A cabinet full of dusty soapstone ornaments from China, along with three long lines of much smaller things made of ivory. These little Japanese figures were called *netsuke* (she'd had to look it up, it was pronounced more like "nidge-key," or at least that's how Mr. Jones said it—a year ago he'd been more talkative, and had told her stories about a few of the things in the room). Many, *many* other things, from a row of pots from South America to pieces of sinuous glassware from Sweden and a few gray ornaments made by Inuits and some small painted boxes from Russia.

A museum of a life. A shared life, presumably, as it seemed hard to believe the same sensibility could have valued all of these things. Karen suspected the birds and pots had been the choice of the late Mrs. Jones; the rest most likely her husband's.

When she'd taken things, it had been from the latter group. She reasoned that objects you acquire for yourself, after a certain number, don't stick in your mind as clearly as something you've inherited from someone now gone. She couldn't tell you how many mystery paperbacks she now owned, for example, and had in fact been known to buy the same one twice. The objects she'd inherited from her mother, however, or the small collection of things her ex-husband had given her when they were first going out, back when he was sweet and before everything had gone wrong... she remembered each of those.

So, a piece here, a piece there. The first a small glass bowl, found hidden and forgotten behind other things. This had been a careful choice: if he noticed, all she had to do was say she'd given it a clean, and replace it. He didn't notice.

Then a piece of soapstone, again chosen from the back of the shelf. One of the Russian lacquer boxes, then another. Over time, four of the many netsukes—two of which had turned out to be surprisingly valuable. By that point they were being sold via an associate of Peter's. He'd asked her flat out, one day when they were alone in the office, how often she took things from their clients. Her shock at his matter-of-factness, and the guilt it wrote across her face, made denial pointless. So after that, they had an arrangement. One she couldn't back out of.

Because Peter wasn't friendly. Not really. Not at all.

In two years, only a dozen things. Okay, two dozen. At least. None had been missed. Mr. Jones didn't care about them anymore. Didn't notice.

But by the sound of it… his son had.

Probably not specifically, or his conversation with Peter that morning would have taken a much harder turn. More likely he'd just noticed that one shelf or other looked a little less… full. More of an impression than actual knowledge. Strong enough to raise with Peter, subtly. Not certain enough to raise hell.

But if he cared that much, why was he living so far away? It was Karen who was tending Mr. Jones's world, not him.

Then she spotted it.

The thing that had caught her eye. She walked over to a shelf in the corner, a couple of yards behind Mr. Jones's chair. A pot. Small. Made of some silvery metal.

After a quick glance to check Mr. Jones was still asleep, Karen reached out to it, tapped it with a fingernail. *Tink*. Hollow. The metal sounded thin, too.

It was extremely shiny. Like a mirror.

Odd that it was so highly polished, in this room full of tarnish and dust. She hadn't cleaned it, or even seen it before. He must have retrieved it from a drawer since her last visit, decided to display it. Otherwise she'd definitely have noticed it. It was very attractive.

Easily portable, too.

Though not today, and not soon. If he'd put it there since her last visit, he'd be more likely to notice if it disappeared.

She bent down, bringing her face close. The reflection, curved though it was, pleased her. Something about the surface caused it to work like one of those filters you get in social media apps, the ones that make you look smoother, younger. Better. More like the kind of woman that men might want to actually sit and talk to in a pub, instead of just seeing how quickly they can get you drunk enough to leave; the beer's expensive in here, love, let's get a bottle of wine and go back to your place, you said you live nearby.

Karen moved her head closer to the pot. The reflection of her face got a little bigger. The rest of it reflected…

She blinked.

The rest of it showed a wall, cream-colored. To one side, partially obscured, a painting. Or a print, at least. But…

She half straightened, glanced behind her. Saw what she knew she'd see. One of Mr. Jones's bookcases, filled with old, yellow-spined paperbacks. That was strange.

She turned back. The reflection in the pot was the same as it had been. A wall, no bookcase. And the painting on it. She moved her head to the side to see it better… and caught her breath.

Mr. Jones stirred in his chair, but it was only a dozing realignment. Karen barely noticed.

She was staring at the painting in the reflection. She recognized it. Knew it well. A pale woman, eyes open but not alive, floating on her back in a pond. Well, not floating. Drowned. Ophelia. An inexpensive reproduction of a famous painting, the one thing of her grandmother's that Karen had liked and kept.

That… was *really* strange.

She reached out for the pot. Maybe if she picked it up, the reflection would change to what it should be. If Mr. Jones woke and saw her holding it, she could say she was cleaning it.

She couldn't seem to pick it up, however. It shouldn't be, it was small, but it was very heavy. There was something odd about the feeling of the metal, too. It was so shiny it felt wet.

And now she couldn't seem to detach her hand from it.

She bent over, concerned now, trying to pull away. Couldn't. The reflection seemed stronger, too—so clear that it almost looked as if her hand was *inside* the pot. Then her wrist and forearm, too. And further, and further, until the reflection seemed to sinuously expand, filling her entire visual field.

Starting to feel genuinely afraid, Karen turned, trying to root herself back in where she was. She didn't see Mr. Jones's living room, however. She saw her own flat.

"*What?*"

She spoke without thinking. Glanced across to see if she'd woken the old man, but he wasn't there. The only things around her were her own. The couch she sat on to watch television some nights, without noticing much about what was on. The chair where she read her mystery novels, almost all of which had the same plot, in which angry men hurt women and then were caught, a comforting if inaccurate fantasy. Several pot plants, pointlessly alive.

But something was wrong about the room.

Over there, on the right, should be the door to her kitchen, with its too-clean surfaces and fridge half full of ready meals and inexpensive wine and, once in a great while, a treat for dessert, affordable only because she worked for Mr. Jones.

It wasn't. The wall of her own living room surrounded her in a complete circle, like the outsides of the silver pot, or a cell. She ran over, and banged her fists against the wall. They made a soft, sharp, *tink*ing sound, like fingernails against thin metal.

"Let me out," she said. And then shouted it. Then screamed.

It echoed back, a tinny little sound.

A while later, Mr. Jones roused himself and made his way—very slowly, very carefully—to the kitchen. He'd found himself wanting a cup of tea, spent a period measuring the strength of this desire against the projected labor involved, and finally decided it was worth it. Just about.

He put the kettle on. Selected a vessel. The mug was chipped. They all were. He had stopped caring about this sometime before he stopped even noticing. A mug was a mug. If it held tea, its essential function remained unimpaired.

As he waited for the water to boil he looked out through the window to the driveway. He did this quickly, as usual. He felt he ought to know how it looked out there. But knew looking would confirm that it was getting overgrown, a fact he would feel he should do something about. In fact, it was more that he felt that he *should* feel that. In reality... he'd stopped caring much about that, too.

Then he was struck by a thought.

He looked at the clock on the shelf above the sink. Half past two. She must have left by now, but he didn't remember it happening. He turned to the door that led out into the hall.

"Karen?"

No answer. He poured hot water into the cup, sighed, and made his way halfway to the door, an expenditure of energy he hadn't allowed for. "Karen? Are you still here?"

Nothing came back. Maybe she'd said goodbye. He didn't recall such an exchange, but knew he wasn't retaining things as well as he used to. If you're a man once able to walk into a room of a hundred students and give an hour's lecture, without notes, on a culture's entire magical beliefs, you know the parameters of your mind pretty well. Are able to notice, therefore, when shadows start to gather in the corners of that space, when it becomes as dusty as your house, and you can't walk across it with a confidence you once took for granted. That there were days when you were unable to successfully traverse that internal room at all, instead remaining stranded in the middle, incapable of constructing the sentence that would get you to the door.

He tried her name one more time.

Then he noticed, out in the hallway left neatly by the wall, a blue handbag. And belatedly recalled something he'd done in the middle of the night, in response to a careful question from his son about whether

he was sure all his possessions and mementoes in the living room...
were still there. Remembered making his careful way down the stairs,
to the study in which he used to write, and digging something out of
the lowest drawer of one of the filing cabinets. Something he'd bought
long ago, for rather too much money, but never displayed. Until now.

Interesting.

Mr. Jones decided that events would doubtless unfold.

He went back to the counter, fished the teabag out of the cup, put it
in a saucer left nearby. This regime had been instigated by his wife, as
she liked to put the bags in the compost at the bottom of the garden.
The idea of making it down there seemed laughable now. It must have
been a year, at least. Probably two. Every few days he emptied the
contents of the saucer into the bin. But he put the bags on the saucer
first, nonetheless. We honor our ghosts.

Hampered by having to carry the mug of liquid, the journey back
to his chair in the living room took three times as long as the outward
leg. When he eventually sat down, exhausted, he thought he heard
something, faintly, from the shelf behind.

A quiet *tink*ing sound. Then something that sounded like a desperate
cry, coming from a very long distance.

As he sat slowly drinking his tea, he noticed the newspaper had
been put neatly where he could reach it. Must have been Karen. That was
thoughtful of her.

But it didn't change anything. What was done, was done.

Three months later, his son stood near that chair, now empty, looking
down curiously at the pot on the shelf behind.

He remembered it. Something about his father having bought it at
a bazaar or souk or somewhere in Africa, many years before. He didn't
recall it ever being on display, however. His mother had never liked
it. Odd that it should be out. He was pretty sure it hadn't been when

he visited that final time, when he'd left the country thinking at least he'd talked his dad into accepting a little more help. A few days later, on the phone, his father had observed the carer had been replaced with another, after failing to turn up the next day. He hadn't seemed to care much.

The son picked up the pot, turned it over. Ultimately it was merely another of the objects for which he felt nothing in particular. So the little silver-colored object (it wasn't actually made of silver, instead an obscure alloy whose properties had been known in some cultures for a long time, though seldom discussed, and usually dismissed as metaphor) wound up in a store that was home to many cluttered stalls of such unwanted objects—old crockery and forgotten books and racks of tired pieces of clothing that had quite some time to wait (possibly forever) before they might be considered appealingly retro.

It was put amongst a crowd of other things on a battered old white bookcase, and initially priced at twelve pounds. A few years later, that was reduced to eight. It's likely to stay at that price forever, as the person who owns the stall long ago forgot it's even there.

Though the curious or bored pick it up once in a while, they always put it back, and no one ever holds it long enough to hear anything from inside.

CHALK. SEA. SAND. SKY. STONE.

Lynda E. Rucker

1

CHALK. White and burnt orange, graffiti-scarred. Brown sand. Grey sea, reflection of a grey sky, but infinite tones of grey. Grey as though it's the only colour in the world and the only colour the world needs. Stones among the shells, round and smooth after countless seasons tumbling in the ocean.

Claire had found her hag stone among those stones and shells, slipped a bit of thread through the riven hole and wore it around her neck. She figured she needed all the protection she could get.

She has come to know this stretch of shoreline intimately. She has walked it twice a day, sometimes more, for five months in one direction or another. It has been a kind of pilgrimage, but towards what she is uncertain, and she feels no wiser for it; she still feels brittle. She still feels damaged. She still feels herself.

Overhead, gulls soar, climbing and plummeting on gusts of wind, their wings spread wide.

2

Margate sits facing the North Sea, nearly but not quite on the easternmost tip of what had been an island until the late Middle Ages. Roman legions had once walked these shores, maybe even Julius Caesar himself. This area has been inhabited by humans for thousands of years, and the chalk upon which it is built and which rises in whitened cliffs above the sea is something more than ancient; it is the stuff of deep time. It's warm in the sun when she presses her palms against it, warm as it would have been a hundred million years ago when the whole world was warm, when there were forests instead of ice at the North Pole, when the separate continents were still breaking and drifting apart, when ankylosauruses and iguanodons and ornithopods roamed this stretch of shoreline or its Mesozoic equivalent. Today their winged descendants pluck meat from dead crab in rock pools and tear apart soggy bags of abandoned chips.

In a thousand years or more, maybe archaeologists will unearth the remains of the clanging arcades along the seafront. By then it will all be lost: the retro neon announcing the entrance to the Dreamland amusement park, the brutalist architecture of the building that looks like a tower block but is home to luxury flats, the white stark geometry of the Turner Contemporary Gallery. There will be no echoes at all of squabbling families on the beach, runners on the promenade, Down-From-London hipsters quaffing local ales and imaginative cocktails and poking round second-hand shops in the Old Town alongside triumphant, resentful Brexiteers.

This, she thinks, is what people become right before they turn into ghosts: flat characters you can sketch with a word or two. She knows because she has become one herself: *the grieving widow.* It is an easy and comfortable way of being. You can wear the words as a shield. Except that widows are supposed to be old. She is only forty. She ought to have been twice that age before this came to pass.

For five months, she has lived in those final moments of Vikram's life on the motorway. They told her he didn't suffer, but how would they know? Surely they said that to everyone. She cannot stop thinking about it even though she knows what these are called: intrusive thoughts. She knows because like everyone in the English-speaking Western world of a certain class, she is schooled in therapy-speak. Everything can be fixed with the right doctor or the right pill.

Magic spells, she thinks. Handfuls of beans.

If a beanstalk grew before her now, she would climb it, up and away.

She had visited the spot where it happened even though everyone told her she shouldn't. She had stood on the verge with the cars and the lorries rumbling past. There was no sign that this had been a crash site, let alone the spot where her world had come undone. She understood then why people lay flowers and other mementoes at such sites, to mark them as a place where a portal had opened and devoured the life they thought they had. But she felt nothing. This was unsurprising, as the single certainty she possessed was that nothing could ever happen to her again. She wasn't sad; she was empty. Not the grieving widow but the hollow widow.

Your friends, she found, however dear they are to you, give up on you after a while if you can only wait them out. It was such a relief when they stop ringing and texting. As for her family, they are worse than useless. She believes they are secretly relieved. Several years earlier, they had shocked her with their opposition to the marriage. It had been nothing that they said but all the things they didn't, and the looks that passed between them.

His own family might have been a comfort but they are not here: they are all in India. She'd had to phone his sister there to give her the news, and she felt like a monster doing it, as though it were somehow all her fault. It *was* all her fault. Everything changes when a butterfly flaps its wings on the other side of the world. Alter one action or inaction and everything changes again. She could have made things different, had she only known.

She has yet to tell a single soul that the last thing she and Vikram did together was conceive a child.

Because of this, Claire doesn't mind so much being hollow. This means there is more room for their child to become who she is. (Claire is sure she is a girl.) She is not like those other pregnant women with their hopes and fears and ambivalences. She feels like a pure vessel, with no plans for herself and no expectations for her daughter. This must have been how God felt in those early days, when the earth was without form and void: *Let there be light.*

3

Two days after she lost Vikram, she left the flat they'd shared in Camden Town and took the train to Margate, where her recently deceased grandmother's house sat vacant while Claire's mother and uncles argued over what to do with it. Claire found the key where it had always been, under the blue flower box in the window to the left of the door. It smelled musty inside. Claire's mother and uncles had moved her grandmother to a home a few months earlier, and she had declined rapidly there.

Claire had not been there for more than a year, but the worn carpet in the foyer with the rose pattern was the same as ever. The place was tidy but neglected, drifting dust motes on the air and mouse droppings in corners. Claire took stale bedding out of a wardrobe and hung it outside. It was a cold afternoon, and she sat on the deck overlooking the back garden as the dusk gathered, wrapped in a blanket and sipping a cup of tea. She rang her parents and told them about Vikram. She thought she was doing it well, explaining it factually and succinctly, but it seemed that it did not come across this way. Apparently this was not how a grieving widow was supposed to sound, and they were alarmed that she had waited two whole days to tell them. What did two days matter when decades stretched ahead of her? Was Vikram any more or less dead? Her mother said something about her being in shock and, well, Claire guessed so; you would be wouldn't you?

She did not ease their worry and confusion when, in response to her mother's insistence on driving down to London the next day, she told them where she was and that she didn't want to see anyone. No, there would not be a service. She couldn't answer their questions. She couldn't tell them what she needed to tell them, what she needed to do, which was just to stop. To disappear. The absolute relentlessness of time, moving along as it did, was abominable. She had come to some kind of temporary truce with them by the time she put her phone down, an agreement that, for the moment at least, they would let her be.

There was a fox at the bottom of the garden. It looked like it had found something down there to eat, although the garden was a long and narrow one and it was too far away for her to say for sure. The fox eventually padded its way closer to the house, and then it saw her. Claire sat very still, and it decided she was not a threat and came closer. She wanted to run away with it. She wanted to become something wild, to scavenge in the marshes and the estuaries and the mudflats and lose herself amid the rotting barges and layers of silt. Her eyes met those of the fox. She knew in that instant that she was a mother although the life inside her was but days old, and that the fox was not an *it* but a *she*, a mother as well. She silently told the fox that when her cubs were born she could bring them here, that it was a sanctuary. The fox lowered her head and slipped into the night.

4

She had to go back up to London, to sign certain papers, to pick up his ashes. She spent a single, agonizing night in their flat and vowed never to do so again. The next day she borrowed her friend Ana's car to drive up to the crash site, where she learned nothing. The act of driving itself was horrible, and she wished she'd taken Ana up on her offer to accompany her. Back in London, she grabbed the few things she cared about, stuffed them in a suitcase, and caught the last train to Margate. Walking through the empty streets after midnight, accompanied by the comforting rattle of her wheeled suitcase, she felt almost peaceful.

Then there was still more paperwork to do regarding Vikram; how was it possible that departing this earthly plane spawned so much bureaucracy on it? Some of her friends packed up her flat for her. She told them to keep the furniture or sell it or throw it out, she didn't care. But what about her job, they said. What about it? She was signed off work for now; as for later, did any of it really matter? Ana and her partner Stefan drove out with her belongings, *sans* the furniture. Claire had to put on the mask of a regular human being for several hours. She knew she should offer to let them stay the night, but she couldn't bring herself to do so.

When they finally left, she went to bed for three days. She barely ate; she didn't really sleep much either. Three was the magic number, wasn't it? The number of fairy tales. After three days she rose from the dead. After three days she started to walk, and on the third day after that, she found the hag stone. She actually found three of them, and she took the third one that she found.

And then the world halted. A sickness had been rolling across countries and continents like a great darkness, and it had reached England at last; as though a light were switched off, the country stopped, overnight.

It was extraordinarily satisfying, an actual apocalypse to match her personal one.

And it meant that even less was expected of her. She might never have to return to the office, and so she found herself able to work again, in fits and starts. The inanity of the spreadsheets and video conferencing and looming performance review were no more bearable.

But the tedium of it all does not seem to weigh on her as heavily. Now at least she doesn't have to see anyone, and after a few ghastly "happy hour" Zoom sessions she declines virtual meetups as well. Now her family, who had been making some protesting noises about her taking up semi-permanent residence in her grandmother's house, go quiet. Everything is so quiet. The streets are empty. It's bliss.

It also gives her an excuse for not seeing a doctor, which she hadn't wanted to do anyway; a doctor who would note her down as a "geriatric mother" and who would want to run tests and talk to her about the risks inherent in her ageing eggs, her ageing uterus, her ageing birth canal, as though women over thirty-five haven't been doing this for millennia. She does not want the baby to be exposed to their clinical rooms, their sterile observations.

She is surprised at how much she, a dedicated Londoner, takes to the landscape. They had visited Margate often when she was a child, staying with her grandmother and spending endless summer days on the beach, but they had never ventured past the main sands then, and after she grew up she thought she would never live anywhere but London, even as housing prices spiralled and more and more of their friends left and the city felt more and more unliveable. Now she can't imagine ever going back. She had always thought cities were the only places where anything happened but she has discovered that this is untrue, that the chalk and the sand and the sea and the sky and the stones are in a state of constant, exquisite change. She has begun to think of herself and her daughter as bound to these ancient shores by a kind of umbilical cord, and the notion is not an unwelcome one.

Less welcome: she has also begun to sense a presence in her grandmother's house. It isn't a presence like that of the fox. In fact, it could almost be said to be the fox's opposite: where the fox was fur and flesh and heartbeats and blood and shit and afterbirth, this is— it is gossamer. It is barely there, but it creates a chasm in its barely-thereness. It is a lacuna.

At first, she attributes her sense of it to many things: an overactive imagination, for one. She has read about a kind of sleep disorder that can make you think there is someone in the room with you. Apparently this may be the origin of fantasies about alien abduction, and older delusions: that a neighbour was bewitching you, that a demon was watching you. And yet, over time, as the sensation persists—even when she is not asleep—she begins to wonder: why not? Why not a witch, a demon, a ghost? Why is it more plausible that it should be our own mind and not one of those beings?

She notices it not just when she wakes in the night but also in the liminal hours between sunset and evening—that time her grandmother used to call *in the gloaming*—and just before daybreak. She has taken to rising with or before the sun, and it is often there in the shadows left by the departing night.

She hasn't decided whether to be afraid of it. It does not seem to be either Vikram or her grandmother, although she has the idea that ghosts are depleted of their essence, no longer the beings they once were, so she might not recognize either of them.

She has no idea what it wants, or why it is there.

In the night, she wakes, clutching the hag stone with both hands like she's praying.

5

During that spring, the fox comes to visit a few times with her cubs. They are wary and stay near the bottom of the garden. Claire never has that sense of communion with her again, so she hopes the fox knows that she and her cubs are indeed safe there. She does not want to think of them when they are not in the garden, about the world and the many dangers that await them there. She wishes they could simply live in the garden with her, but she supposes that would make them captives, and they would be unhappy. They would rather be free than safe; this, she reminds herself, is what separates wild animals from domesticated ones.

Outside, in the garden, that's one thing. She is less sure about the inside of her grandmother's house and the yawning empty thing that shares it with her. It occurs to her that she must have brought it with her from their flat in Camden. It must have been what drove her from there, although she hadn't realized it at the time. She had imagined that the weight of memory was too much for her, but it was this absence, and its tempting promise of oblivion. It seems to dissipate without walls to contain it, though, so she redoubles her explorations, spending more and more time outside of the house. One day she packs a lunch and walks miles and miles, goes as far as Reculver, the crumbling remains of a Saxon monastery built atop the even older remains of a Roman fort built atop who-knew-what: those fantastic colonizers, the Romans, and then the invaders who followed them, had obliterated the language and the history, and all that was left hid inside stories and rituals whose origins and true meaning were long forgotten.

On the path to Reculver she is startled to encounter the Wantsum Channel, or what is left of it. It's merely a depression in the earth now, where once it had been a strait that separated Thanet from the mainland. You would never notice it but for the informational sign. She imagines ships churning through the landscape.

When she finally gets to Reculver, she feels let down. It's a striking sight yet, unlike the wholly unremarkable Wantsum Channel, it's as though the life has been leached from the place. Too many visitors, she thinks, although of course there's no one there right now, and the visitor's centre and cafe are closed.

Claire eats her lunch on the headland with the ruins behind her, looking down at the sea and across the water.

6

The truth is that she can scarcely bear to be in the house any longer. The emptiness has been expanding. At night, when she can sleep, she dreams that the presence is smothering her, stealing her breath. Sometimes she hears it in the next room, or on the stairs, or anywhere that she is not. It's maddening, the way it is always just out of reach until she's at her most helpless. When she closes her eyes, it's next to her; a moment later, when she opens them, it's drawn back into the shadows. She always senses it just behind her, or just outside her peripheral vision, or just out of sight of the doorway she's looking through.

7

We have forgotten what things are called. We don't know the names of things any longer.

She read this somewhere and she's been haunted by it ever since because it's true. It seemed less urgent back in London, but here, her ignorance is inescapable. She can't name the birds—"gulls" and "not gulls", that's all she's got—or the stark and ragged wild flowers at the top of chalk cliffs. She takes photos of the flora and uploads them to an app that makes identifications. Large bindweed the app tells her. Alpine speedwell. Red valerian.

Instead of looking at things through the phone on her camera, she ought to look at them through her hag stone. Her grandmother had been the one who told her about them. You're supposed to be able to gain a kind of second sight by looking through one, glimpse another world. She holds on to it like a promise, for when she needs it most. As long as she doesn't look she can believe in its power, that there might be a way to go somewhere else. When she touches the stone, it feels warm, almost alive.

She keeps clicking and uploading and thinking that her grandmother would have known what all the birds and plants were as she knew the names of her children and her grandchildren. Would have known them like she knew her prayers, those murmured words under her breath that were a near constant in her final years. Claire had thought that knowledge was boring when she was young and now there was no one to teach her.

It feels like losing the words for things is a kind of dotage for all of humanity. We're all losing our grip on what's real, she thinks. Maybe that's okay; bindweed and speedwell and valerian and all the rest can go back to just being. When humans die out, it won't be the way we imagine it now; it won't be an asteroid strike, or choking on smoke from forest fires, or drowning in encroaching seas, or a disease we can't defeat. Instead, humans will become like ghosts, increasingly insubstantial, not understanding that their time is over and that the world has moved on without them. Walking through walls and floating on parapets but still trying to carry on, trying to go to meetings and send emails and not understanding why they can't sync their Google calendars with anything any more.

She remembers something she'd asked her grandmother once: *Does it hurt to be a ghost?*

She can't remember her grandmother's answer.

8

No one has paid her grandmother's TV licence that year, and notices about this delinquency are slipped through the mail flap regularly as if anyone cares any more with an apocalypse on. Only the apocalypse, it seems, has been averted. On the BBC, to which her grandmother had remained devoted to the very end, they talk about "reopening" and "back to normal"; they feel like words from foreign places.

That summer, there are parties all up and down the beach; "raves", the press calls them, quietly appalled. Up early, Claire sometimes encounters the detritus of these bacchanalian rituals: rubbish everywhere, human waste, partygoers sleeping it off in the sand or half-collapsed tents. It's shocking and inevitable, a surge of vitality and a defiance in the face of death.

She is more acutely aware of the changes of the season than she has ever been before, but the passage of time on the calendar has never seemed more meaningless. She's getting texts from friends again. She ignores them. Her mother rings her. Now that things are "going back to normal", has she thought about what she's going to do next? Claire says non-committal things and then turns off her phone.

At some stage, she turns her phone back on and there's a series of texts from her line manager at work that increase in formality and urgency, from a breezy, "Heya, haven't seen you on the company Slack this week" to "RING ME". Claire turns the phone back off.

Her belly is growing firm and round, her face is puffy. She is supposed to be glowing, but she doesn't feel glowy. She's starting to feel the child moving about inside her, and she begins to take it swimming. The air is warm but the icy water is almost unbearable; still, she likes nothing better than to sink below the surface, stay there for as long as she can hold her breath.

Other times she just stands on the shore and listens to the crashing of the waves like a lullaby.

9

There is nothing for it but to try to speak to the emptiness. It has consumed the entire house. She can barely get in and out now. Sleep, or anything else, is out of the question. It is loud, as well; she had not noticed this initially but now it is a roaring desolation. She wonders how long it will be before the neighbours notice.

She used to be funny, so she leads with that: "We have a saying about beware staring into the abyss because it will stare back at us. I feel like I may have taken this to an extreme."

Nothing. Her mind trips through the cliched dialogue of horror cinema: *Who are you? What do you want? Why are you doing this?*

It would be like asking those questions to a wind howling down from the Arctic or the remnants of a tropical storm surging across the Atlantic and Ireland and Wales to this farthest eastern stretch of land, to batter the waves against the sea wall before it perished somewhere in Europe.

In the end, it seems easiest to relinquish the house. It was never hers anyway.

It's a grey, moody day down in the harbour, and that seems to be keeping people away. She turns and walks east. A couple of miles in that direction, before she rounds the peninsula and finds herself almost touching-distance with Europe, is the old smugglers' cove, Botany Bay. Its chalk cliffs and sea stacks meet brown sand against grey sea and grey sky and slippery, treacherous stone underfoot. It's full of secret caverns and ghosts and, almost certainly, lost treasure.

She picks her way carefully.

She has come here so many times; there is something otherworldly and untamed about it, even when it's crowded with swimmers and sunbathers and jet skiers. But today there's no one around.

There are so many things she could do. She could turn around and go to the train station and buy a ticket to her mother's house, or back to London, go to Ana and Stefan's. She could "recover" to talk in circumscribed ways about her breakdown. She could get her job back. She could lead a sensible life of restraint and muted colours and small emotions. The lacuna might never find her and her daughter.

It's time. Claire reaches for the hag stone round her neck. She holds it tight in her fist for a few moments.

She lifts it to one eye, and she peers through it to the other side, the other world.

Gulls wheel and scream at one another above an empty shore.

READY OR NOT

Marian Womack

1

THERE is a birch tree at the edge of the back garden, that bends over the next-door neighbour's on the other side. It looks as if it is trying to get as far away as possible. Miraculously, in a north-facing suburban garden, it happens to be a fairly majestic tree. She knows the birch tree protects children; she just doesn't know why she has this knowledge, where it comes from. A novel, probably.

The vet had presented her with three options. To burn the cat and give her back the ashes. To burn the cat and disappear the ashes, so she wouldn't have to see anything, or deal with anything. Or, the third option, to give back the cat to take home with her, so she could bury him in her garden. This option had sounded wrong to her, unclean. But then she saw the prices on the piece of paper she had to sign to allow them to euthanise him, and meekly said that she would take him with her. And here she was, under the birch tree, digging again at the same little spot. *I could put it where I put the other him three months ago*, she thought, for the last thing she wanted to do was to tell Julian about him, and flushing him down the toilet seemed barbaric to her. So she said nothing, took some paracetamol for the pain, excused the whole thing as strong PMS and then a heavy month, and brought him back there, to the garden. The thought that her beloved Baptiste would now keep him company was comforting.

The only thought now was, would the rats dig him up? Would the rats dig them up? There was nothing else to do, better not to think about it.

There she was again. Alison was sure: her neighbour was on the other side of the garden fence. The fence was high, and she could not see her. But she knew, she could sense the old woman walking around the garden, nipping here, nipping there, removing a sneaky bud, crouching down to kill a weed. Now and again a twig snapped under her feet, grass waved at her passing, a coal tit would fly out to make way for her. The old woman had that quality, of being there, of disappearing. Alison had not heard her leave the house. As she moved the energy changed, until she knew that the woman was standing against the fence again, staring into the vine-rotten wood, right in front of Alison and her tree.

Ready or not, here I come.

Where was Julian? Why had he left her alone?

The old woman had never talked much to them, or at all to Alison. She had spoken to Julian on a few occasions about issues connected to their respective gardens, the need for him to trim it a bit here and there. As far as Alison remembered, the old woman had never exchanged a word with her, like those ladies who hardly acknowledged her, did not include her in the conversations.

It was Julian who used to say that she was going to get them. This was his particular joke. He would draw a picture for Alison's benefit, their elderly neighbour in front of a cauldron, a ladle moving of its own accord. Some familiar lurking nearby, making itself useful. A toad, perhaps. Or a bird. They knew she had no cats, that she despised cats.

Alison could not tell half the time if he was being serious or joking. He sometimes used jokes to discuss painful, traumatic issues, or to attack her, and other times jokes were simply jokes. This was how they interacted, second-guessing each other. Then the thing with the cats happened.

Some neighbours from the street got kittens. It happened like this: they had two small children, and wanted to find something to keep them entertained during the long periods of confinement. These neighbours lived in one of the prettiest Victorian cottages, an immaculate academic dwelling. They had never been invited inside, but at some point the neighbours had put their house on the market, and Julian looked at the pictures online and had admired, jealously, their collection of books. As if they themselves did not have enough books, occupying every single available wall, the whole of the spare bedroom filled with boxes, more boxes in the garage, modular bookshelves everywhere. The neighbour was a Shakespeare scholar, and he gave the cats pretty Shakespearean names. They were beautiful cats, black with white paws and bellies, the kind that everyone remembers from children's stories. Their neighbours let them out of the house, that was their mistake. And they hunted. People started finding dead birds, unwanted offerings at their front doors.

Why did they do nothing to protect them? Julian claimed not to be at all surprised when one of the cats appeared in the apple tree that stood in the little patch of green right in front of the old woman's house, dead with his guts spilling out. The other one was never seen again.

"She got them at last!" was all he said, an odd, manic smile dancing on his face. Alison thought that it was the first time she has seen him look scared of being right. Being right was important for Julian.

It was the violence that got Alison. If it really had been the old lady, why do it like that? She could have poisoned them, for instance, but instead she chose to do something unspeakable. It broke the street, whatever community had been built up in its makeshift way. Until then, neighbours had congregated in their doorsteps with mugs of tea and coffee on Sunday mornings, just to keep check of who was still alive behind their doors. Now, all this stopped abruptly. There was a silent acknowledgement that something else was going on, something that had been easier to ignore in the days when everyone went about their business, had meetings to attend, jobs to perform, shopping to do. Now, there was nowhere to go, and the little street was all their world. And that world was smaller somehow.

The academic neighbours with the immaculate book-lined house moved out soon after.

2

One thing she missed was *that* noise, the *clack clack clack* of Baptiste's little paws on the wooden floor. But that was all. An advantage of Julian's unexpected desertion was that the house without him was silent. She had no idea where he was, or what he might be doing. It was comforting. For too long she had been secretary, organiser, maid, and everything else in between. Without Julian prancing around, she could go out into the garden, kept secluded by the overgrown sumac, walk to the birch tree, and have a sneaky cigarette—he would certainly not approve. Later on, she could sit in front of the computer and check the early twentieth-century Japanese edition of *Alice* that was going, incredibly cheap, to the highest bidder. It was a little life of sorts, only her, the acrid cigarette, the pacing up and down to the tree.

The birch tree. She knew she would have to do something about it, plant some bulbs, perhaps in the spring. The turned earth looked terrible, brought horrid thoughts. The smell was much more powerful than she had expected. She put out the cigarette and walked the stone path back to the conservatory door, all the time wondering if her neighbour was following her progress on the other side of the fence. So quiet, so still… But a stillness that had some dense purpose within it. What purpose, exactly? The unanswered question. Alison opened the door, went back inside, closed the door; only then she noticed it, her heart quietly racing inside her ribcage.

The thing is, the neighbour's dead cat had hit them hard, for back then Baptiste was still alive. Baptiste, their fat slow house cat, who had thankfully never been let out. Whenever Alison looked from her bedroom window, Baptiste would come and sit on the windowsill and purr, looking to the outer world. Alison knew what he wanted, for her to open the window so he could smell the outside. She was wary of doing this, as once, in the old neighbourhood, he had fallen asleep on the windowsill, and dropped three storeys from their rented apartment. She had another reason not to want to open the window. She was scared of letting something else in. The cat followed, with his old, watery eyes, the progress of some birds strutting around the messy garden.

And there she was. Very straight, unmoving. From her vantage point, Alison glimpsed a faded pink fleece through the green and the branches. What was she doing? That was the first time she had seen her like this, staring at the fence without moving, like a child who had been punished. There was some oddness in her position. The old lady was shorter than her, with a stocky upper body and short legs, strong and lean arms for her age. She had hardly any neck, and her head was too big for her body. She reminded Alison of a puppet, the way she stood. Her head was covered by a mane of white hair that she cut over her shoulder and in a lopsided fringe, and never put up. It was difficult to explain why that big round head with no neck made her so scary. Dusk fell, the twin suburban gardens folding themselves into evening hibernation. Why was she there? What was she doing? It looked as if she was about to turn, and go and search for someone hiding.

Ready or not.

Slowly, slowly, the old woman started turning in her direction, until she was staring at them, Alison and Baptiste. Alison had waved at the woman through her fear; those were the earlier days, the days when she still thought her neighbours and co-workers would include her despite looking so decidedly *not-from-these-parts*. The old woman did not react. She just continued looking in her direction, white hair quite unruly, black eyes dark beyond understanding. It was probably the distance, but they looked completely black, not eyes, but two dead pebbles. The next few days, Alison would have nightmares about them.

Alison's stomach had contracted, and she walked backwards in fear, painfully hitting her calves on the bed. She could still see her from the bedroom window. Suddenly, with a jerking movement, the woman turned around and started furiously working, pruning and cutting and dragging things in a wheelbarrow, the very image of industry, that little old lady, with white hair, no neck, and a round and thick head, too big for her diminutive body, that old lady strong beyond her years. The image was suburban, normal. Except it was not.

There is no one else doing this. The street is deserted. Everyone else is inside their homes, watching television, preparing themselves for another long weekend with nowhere to go. There is no one else because all the other gardens are showing the desolation of winter; that is, except *her* garden. A garden suspended in time, a somehow not-quite-winter garden. An impossible, unnatural oddity, pruning, digging, planting, when everybody else's strip of grass is brown and muddy and dead, and will remain so for months to come. How to explain the impossible? she wonders, for a fragment of a second. Then, it all goes up like smoke, and she forgets. How easy it is not to see, how easy to close a door when something is slightly off-kilter, stamping our own image on the disturbance, the image of the reality we know to be true.

But nonetheless there is something decidedly unnatural about the whole thing, her disproportionate doll-head, her evergreen garden, her stubborn immobility. Did she look out again? Was she brave enough? What did she see? Alison couldn't distinguish the woman's features, but somehow she could tell she was smiling. Between the shadows and the greenery she could glimpse the yellow shade of her small teeth.

Alison knew, at that moment precisely, that her neighbour would get her one day, exactly as Julian had predicted, and that she knew she would get her one day. They both knew it; they had just been playing cat and mouse.

3

Bad luck came with the house. A square building, four walls and a flat roof, part of a row of ugly nineteen-sixties terraced houses. The terrace sat at the end of a quaint street, opposite a much prettier row of Victorian two-bedroom cottages. The terraces were ugly houses, cheaply built, not enough insulation to cope with the heatwaves or the cold winter. It belonged to Julian's parents, but she had lived in the place for nearly two years, looked after it, spent a considerable amount of her own money on its upkeep.

The faults of the house were plenty. The north-facing back garden was a dark, shady patch of green, perpetually wet. There was a conservatory facing it. It wasn't badly put together, but it had certainly seen better days. When Alison and Julian first moved in, they discovered that one of the roof glass panels leaked. It cost them a small fortune to repair it, roughly Alison's monthly salary. The reality of the arrangement with Julian's parents had taken shape in front of her eyes at that moment. They owned the house, but they weren't landlords, did not want to behave as landlords, did not want to be bothered with problems. It was a rude awakening. Alison had not expected to have to come up with that kind of money for an urgent repair not covered by the already expensive house insurance. The whole thing left her stressed and worn out.

It had been the cost of the repair that had surprised her, and she would spend weeks agonising over one thing: the roof had six glass panels in total. What on earth would she do if they all started leaking? Would she have to spend half a year's salary fixing them? She lost sleep over this, took to obsessively checking the panels, heart leaping in her chest whenever it rained.

So that was it: they would live rent-free, but they would do everything that needed to be done, including paying whatever tax was due on the property, as well as being responsible for the home insurance Julian's parents had chosen, even if it did not cover the house's main problems. They were the problems of swift decrepitude, of the obsolescence of cheaply built houses, of worn-out things; the typical problems of a house in need of endless rounds of maintenance, where all fixes were temporary, and something always needed to be done. Julian did not have a job yet, and Alison found herself paying for all the monthly bills and all repairs.

Alison would eventually grow to hate the house. It wasn't that she wasn't thankful to Julian's parents. The housing situation had reached almost catastrophe event levels: everyone she knew who owned property or rented within the town's perimeter was helped by some wealthier older relative. Some adjuncts had made headlines by living out of their cars. Garden sheds and garages and even old-fashioned bolthole-style disused bunkers in back gardens were rented out to young hourly paid academics, the workforce who kept the town's illustrious institution going in exchange for no future retirement payouts, nor the job security necessary to put down roots and start a family. Meanwhile, academics from earlier generations, who were wealthier for the simple reason of having been born decades before, in the long-gone times of free education, a healthy job market, a free national health service at the point of need, and sensible house prices, were placidly sitting on half-empty properties all over town. The situation was untenable.

Alison did not feel comfortable for one simple reason: she had no way to prove that she lived in the house. A German national, the issue of proving residency to stay in the country turned out to be tricky. When Julian had mentioned the house, she had supposed there would be some kind of rental agreement in place; however, for some reason that Alison could not fathom, Julian's parents refused point-blank to draw up a contract. They did not want to be landlords, they repeated; they did not want any kind of responsibility over the property. With rent-free living quarters, it made sense that Alison paid for everything. But there is nothing free in the world, of course, and Alison's payment was in the form of losing control over her own life arrangements, at a delicate geopolitical moment. Fear and acute anxiety ensued, as she worried she was not getting anywhere in terms of proving residency. She consulted an immigration expert, gave him a copy of the letter Julian's parents had written to "prove" she lived in their house. Her worst fears were realised when he explained such a document would not have any validity for her legal residency purposes. She agonised over the whole thing, found herself in her own personal limbo. The only role that was permitted to her was that of a passive enabler: she had to yield to others' decisions, and provide the money to put them into action. She might agree with something or not, or might wish that a particular item was changed or repaired, but she was not allowed to cast a vote. Every time she tried to suggest that something needed to be done, Julian would cut the problem off at the root by having a huge row with her. He was not very good at looking beyond his needs, and not happily drawn into conversations about things that did not interest him. Alison could only look on as things deteriorated around her: the black mould that infected most of the north-facing walls, the old stove that only worked when it wanted, with an extractor on top that did not work at all, the bad lighting in the kitchen which meant that they cooked in the dark and, most contentious of them all, the lack of wardrobes and storage places.

Like a surprising number of English houses, the terrace was conspicuous for the absolute lack of closet space. As Alison understood it, before she and Julian were due to move in, his parents had suggested that a wardrobe of some sort needed to be built somewhere. Julian's mother had even gone as far as sending them to have a look at the recently installed wardrobe of one of her friends, so they could have an idea of what was possible. However, for some reason this had never progressed from the planning stage, and the proposed closet never materialised. As a result, Alison kept her good clothes, the skirts and blouses and long dresses and cardigans she wore for work, in an array of dusty cardboard boxes that were spread around the little spare room and the landing. Then a strange dynamic brewed, one of those so typical of Julian and his family—impossible to anticipate, unavoidable, sticky once she was covered in it—where it became suddenly so easy to dismiss her opinions as irrationality: every time Alison asked when the wardrobes were going to be installed, she got a kind of exasperated look coming from Julian, who, most of his books up on shelves, had already forgotten everything about the need for some storage. This saddened Alison. It reinforced her idea of how little Julian understood her life, the casual throwing around of words, "alien", "migrant", the endless questions and statements prefaced by "you are not from these parts". It was painful to have confirmation of how little Julian understood, how little he knew, or cared to know. He was accusing her now of worrying too much about her clothing of all things, of being some sort of princess. This was ridiculous. Alison did not have many good clothes, or even expensive clothes, only the ones she used for work. Why was this so important? he repeated.

It was true, Alison tried to explain, that Julian turned up to meetings with editors—he was trying to become a full-time translator—or with senior college tutors—he was trying to get some hourly paid teaching going—in old T-shirts with holes in them, third-hand trousers straight out of charity shops, and shabby sports jackets inherited from his dad. But it was he who could do those things: this off-hand, shabby-chic manner of existing wasn't possible for everyone. Alison found it very difficult to explain to him in a way that he could understand, that he could relate to: with his blond hair, and his blue eyes, and his boyish smile, it did not matter what Julian was wearing, for he always belonged. Alison, a mixed-race foreigner, with "not quite the right look" about her, as someone had once put it, was required to always appear immaculate. Very patiently, as if explaining something to a child, Alison had tried to clarify all this to Julian, how she had to prove she belonged three times more than him. How she was held to higher standards, how she needed to keep as neat and prim as possible merely to be taken seriously, to be considered professional, not its opposite, and other not-so-pleasant monikers that quickly attached to her if she let her guard down. She did not say other things, perhaps harder for him to understand, like how tiring it was to live like this, how exhausting it was to be constantly judged and prejudged. Alison was not sure at all that her husband of four years got any of it.

She had to do something. There was absolutely no help coming, not from the in-laws, not from Julian. Eventually, Alison gave up and, trying to be practical, she spent some money on flat-pack wardrobes instead, in truth not much better than cardboard boxes, but at least it meant she could finally hang some of her things. She bought one for her clothes, one for Julian's, and another one to hang the coats and other heavy garments. When they arrived, she despaired. They were so badly designed that there were things that still did not fit in them, as now she realised there was also the linen to contend with, all the sheets and towels, that still had absolutely no place to go, and remained in the boxes. So Alison bought some plastic boxes as opposed to cardboard ones. They were piled up on the little landing, or occupied the dusty space underneath the bed. She reflected sadly on the situation: she was living in worse conditions than when she was a student. Julian at least was happy.

Sometimes events take on a life of their own. By then Alison was feeling overwhelmed. She could not have articulated the reason, but soon she found herself in tears every time she looked at her fat plastic boxes. Filled to the brim, they were so heavy that she could not handle them. Julian had to be asked to take them down from the pile, put them on the floor, put them back again in their pile, every time Alison needed to take something in and out of them. This, of course, exasperated him, put him on edge. He even accused her at some point of asking him to move boxes too often on purpose. If she did not ask him for help, he would also get offended, accusing her of hoping to drop one of the boxes on her foot, so she could have more reasons to complain. Hence, a further dynamic was established: whatever Alison did, or said, or didn't do, or didn't say, she would be sure of annoying him. And so it went on.

Alison started imagining what she would do if Julian died; if he, for example, had a sudden heart attack. She would not be able to face telling her in-laws, who were sure to blame her and the whole sorry mess for it. Would she be better off putting him under the birch tree, with their unborn child? Or perhaps fit him in the bigger, sixty-four-litre plastic box?

Needless to say, a childish squabble over boxes wasn't everything. Sadly, things were still going to get much worse. Alison's health was rapidly deteriorating. She found herself in physical pain quite often, her immigration-related anxiety reaching astronomic proportions. Then Alison's unhappiness was the thing that started being questioned. The narrative put forward went like this: Alison was, to all effects, a guest in the house, and should be nothing but grateful. Again, she felt that she could not explain properly, or that she would not be understood. Perhaps she was unhappy because Julian never allowed her to forget that she was a recipient of his charity. Without any unpleasantness, Julian knew how to place her under a sort of constant obligation to be grateful, and not to complain. There was no explicit uttering of this. All Julian had to do was to repeatedly mark his ownership of the place, subtly; but Alison understood. It was behind every assumption that he should not help with the upkeep, or even the cleaning, or that he was to be exempt from putting his shoes on the shoe rack under the stairs that she had bought, or even on a protective rug in the entry hall, but stubbornly out of it, leaving marks of mud on the carpeted floor that Alison was expected to clean. She was, in essence, assuming the awkward position of some kind of house-help in exchange for free rent. To try and avoid the unsavoury dynamic, Alison started insisting once more that she wanted to pay some rent, no matter how little. She didn't feel she could stand living like this, she insisted; unpleasant conversations ensued.

She started hating herself. How difficult would it be to live in a car, like those plucky adjuncts did? She had no money to go anywhere on her own, to fulfil her dream of renting a place, sign a piece of paper that stated she had an address, and to upload said piece of paper to the immigration portal. When, eventually, Julian's parents decided to put the house in his name, again he insisted that Alison should see it as some sort of lucky break that she had got thanks to him: now she would never be homeless in the ancient and overpriced town. But Alison could not reconcile her idea of herself with the narrative of leeching off her partner. That was not the way she wanted to think about herself. She had always had jobs and grants and scholarships, holding several part-time positions simultaneously at times. She had always felt proud of this part of her identity. Why did Julian insist on erasing it? Who was she, in fact, if he erased that? Someone she herself did not recognise, or want to know. Was Julian even aware that he was erasing that part of who she was, or had he never known her at all? He was not only forcing her to be exactly that person she despised, but also, cruelly, he was insisting that she should be grateful for being forced to become it.

She had shouted all of the above, but still there was no recognition from him. She felt utterly alone. Eventually, Julian called her an ungrateful bitch.

Still, she tried to explain once more that she was not being ungrateful, but simply that she had been forced into the rather uncomfortable position of losing control over her own living space. In this, she felt, both Julian and his parents were equally to blame. As the argument worsened, Julian told Alison that he hoped she died in a ditch, and someone came and raped her dead body. Alison was so shocked by those words that she wrote them down in her notebook that evening, her whole body shaking. She did not want to forget that he had said them to her. "Your smelly cadaver," he had said, "your rotting smelly cadaver." This was the person she had almost had a baby with.

4

She had, somehow, willed him to go. She could admit that much to herself. There was no coming back from the past few months.

Baptiste had noticed her loneliness, and he came up to her lap more often than ever. It was almost as if he was trying to comfort her. But he also spent the nights going up and down the stairs, his little paws going *clack clack clack* over the wooden floor, no doubt looking for Julian. But he was legally her cat, she thought, even if he had chosen Julian as his true owner. His companionship would not last long. Soon, he started getting thinner, and thinner, and thinner, until he weighed practically nothing. It was shocking to take him in her arms, a whole creature, no weight. Even a doll had more substance. Unable to go out into the world, Alison searched the web for extra special and expensive cat food to tempt him. He was gobbling it all up and yet still losing weight. The progress was fast, the vet shocked at his cadaveric expression when she saw him, alerting her that nothing was to be done as soon as she looked at him.

Still, she would see him after the end, many times she saw him. She had first thought that another cat had got into the house, when she first heard the *clack clack clack*. And then the animal jumped on her bed by the same corner Baptiste liked, and she felt the same non-weight on her body.

She was paralysed with something close to fear. Then, she fell asleep, and thought about it no longer. Some days she would still hear him upstairs, hear the *clack clack clack* of his paws, see him leaving a room out of the corner of her eye. She put it all down to stress, loneliness.

She checked under the birch tree often, to make sure the earth looked the same. She decided she would plant the bulbs soon. This was a good, proactive idea. Then she went to have dinner, and, beans on toast on her lap, she tried to find something to watch. She was very proud of these little activities, which reinforced her capacity of acting "normal". She discovered that the streaming service did not work. The message on the screen was clear: the account had been discontinued. She remembered: this was one of the few things Julian had sorted, paid monthly from his own private account. It seemed that Julian had terminated their subscription. She would have to get it fixed. The whole idea was too much. She could read a book; but her reading pile had not gone down at all during the whole confinement. If anything, it looked bigger, more menacing, although she did not remember buying many books at all. It filled her with dread, feeling more guilty as the months passed, unable to read due to that guilt, the whole cycle perpetuating itself *ad nauseam*. Where did the books come from? She looked at them: they mostly had a library stamp. Had she taken them out, or Julian?

Alison went to bed earlier than she used to, and lay there, thinking. Waiting for the *clack clack clack* of her dead cat. Thinking about the birch tree at the edge of the back garden. And then she realised something: she hadn't had her period since Julian left. She truly hoped she wasn't pregnant, it would be too soon to do it all again: she had not yet managed to clean all the earth from under her nails. Perhaps her period had stopped due to stress. Perhaps her periods were ending. About time, she thought.

The problem of having a baby, Alison rationalised, was that, during the first few months of the baby's life, looking after a baby meant in fact succeeding in keeping the baby alive. And, Alison feared, she might not be up to protecting a newborn, or an infant, or a toddler, from peril. Or even worse, that Julian would wash his hands of it all, and she would not be able to cope on her own. There were other (irrational) fears, of losing the baby, somehow, to something that lurked in the shadows, among the crevices, in those liminal spaces we don't consider: landings, corners, spaces we use to go from room to room, or from her house to the vet, her only condoned outing in five months. A fear that there is a blank spot in all corners where the pavement becomes invisible for a second, and you cannot see the child anymore, only the brambles the council forgot to trim.

She lay there, thinking these thoughts. A friend had once explained how she saw a ghost one night while breastfeeding, but she was so tired it didn't matter. She could see the end of the stairs from her side of the king-size, where she sat at night to breastfeed, and they usually left the door of the bedroom ajar because they had a little kitty that wandered in and out of the room during the night, *clack clack clack*. One night she was sitting up breastfeeding, too sleepy to hold her head up, too tired to check her mobile phone. Then she saw her. A woman halfway up the flight of stairs, looking directly into the room, looking directly at her, a woman unknown to her, a dead woman. She says that was how her brain computed the information, almost mechanically. A woman who should not be there, conjured up in a little child's and mother's most sacred moment. There was something disturbingly meaningful about it. As soon as she was baby-free again she went back to sleep, not a second to lose.

Alison looked to her slightly opened door, and found to her surprise that she could also see the end of the stairs into the little landing. She was waiting and waiting, until she heard the *clack clack clack*, the cadaveric expression, the dead cat jumping onto her lap, unable to leave entirely. And she knew, as her friend knew, mechanically, that he was protecting her, somehow.

She thought she saw her then, short, old and wrinkled, fiery white hair, dead eyes, pointy teeth. Alison was so scared at that moment that she levitated a few centimetres above the bed, pure energy finding a release through her pores. And then she fell asleep, and the next morning it was all long gone into the realm of nightmares and half-patched scraps of thoughts, ideas, securely interpreted as dreams. Still, she was beginning to understand something, to remember something. She just wasn't sure what, yet. Think Alison, think. It was very important to remember, to try to place this vague feeling. *Why did Julian leave me here?* No, that is not the question. *Why did Julian leave?*

5

"Hello?" The telephone rang, would it be Julian? Alison had almost not answered. She could not remember the last time someone had rung the landline, as everyone communicated via apps that seemed to her progressively more and more difficult to understand.

"It's me, dear." Alison's heart froze inside her chest. It was *her*. Why was she calling? "I was wondering if Julian could do something for me."

"Julian is not in, not right now." She was very careful not to give away the truth, that she was completely, indefinitely, alone. "Can I help?"

It was nothing, nothing at all. And she was so sorry to bother Alison. But the thing was, there was a continuous scurrying sound in the space between the two houses, a narrow gap between her wooden garden fence and the brick wall that had been added to Julian's house to build the conservatory. A trapped rat, or a hedgehog.

Alison's stomach contracted. She had been so worried about rats, almost obsessively. Since the confinements started, and due to the inactivity in the streets, the closed restaurants and shops, rats had become bolder. Without their usual supply of rubbish they had got closer to houses than ever, sometimes even getting into them in their search for food. Alison was forced to open the windows regularly in her ongoing fight with the black mould, but she was terrified when she did so. What if a rat, or rats, were going to get in? She usually sat at the end of the sofa to read or to knit or to watch television, as close to the wall as possible, the warmest spot in the room. And yes, now that she thought about it, she had heard the noise many times in the previous few days. Could there really be rats trapped there? Until now, she had imagined them climbing the outer wall. But then, this could only be her imagination; for she could also imagine *her* climbing the outside wall, feasting on the rats, listening inside Alison's house.

Her neighbour explained once again, in case Alison's English was not up to scratch. That she thought the noise came from a small animal, trapped between the brick wall of their conservatory and her garden fence. But she was too old and could not navigate the narrow space, did Alison understand?

"Do you understand, dear? I need you to go and look, and do whatever needs to be done. Or you can always send Julian when he is back home."

She had obviously done it on purpose. The whole conversation sounded like a way to get Alison to acknowledge that she could not do it because she was on her own. Or maybe she had brought the rats somehow to torment Alison.

She said that she would go. She was too scared to come clean about being on her own. Although something told her that her neighbour knew.

If Julian were here, he would laugh at her so hard, at her strange fears of the little, harmless lady. But then again, he had also put the idea in her head, that the old lady would come to get her. So she put her rubber boots on, took a torch from the kitchen drawer, and set out. And out she went, to look around the conservatory. Thick bushes, undergrowth. The fear of small baby rats, of rats' nests, biting at her feet. Impossible to advance without damaging her cardigan, without catching it on the branches. A narrow stretch, impossible to see the dark ending, manoeuvring inside without thinking.

She became trapped, momentarily. And the world stopped for a moment. Unable to move, her brain started racing, how to suss her body out, little by little. She could do it, if she wasn't so anxious. She only needed to calm down, which in turn increased her anxiety.

What is the scurrying, right there? Like the sound of a knife scratching a china plate.

She sees it then, the diamond of light, kaleidoscopic shapes that dance among themselves, opening the point in space to her, and she sees it, all that there is to see, and she understands.

Julian's hand had stopped in a sort of rictus, a scratching position. What is he doing, hiding here? From the witch, or from Alison? Not Alison, she will make it out, won't she? The last thought is for her baby. What exactly? She cannot remember. What about her and the baby?

LETTERS TO A YOUNG PSYCHOPATH

Nina Allan

Denn im Grunde, und gerade in den tiefsten und wichtigsten Dingen, sind wir namenlos allein, und damit einer dem andern raten oder gar helfen kann, muß viel geschehen, viel muß gelingen, eine ganze Konstellation von Dingen muß eintreffen, damit es einmal glückt.

Because we're alone, basically, in the deepest and most fundamental things especially we are alone. For one human being to have even the slightest chance of helping or advising another, so much has to happen, so many things have to fall into place. A whole constellation of stars has to align, really, or there won't be a hope in hell of it coming off.

(From 'Letters to a Young Poet',
Rainer Maria Rilke)

1

You do realise that if this is the path you go down, you'll be alone forever? You're a child of the pandemic, I hear you bragging; you know more about being alone than my generation ever will. Let me tell you, kid, you don't know jack. You believe you have learned about isolation but what you have learned in truth is mostly the opposite: the art of living in warrens, in cosy burrows, tightly packed as leverets and as dependent, waiting anxiously for the next directive and with the capacity for independent thought all but lobotomised. To thrive in your endeavour, you will have to relearn solitude, internally most of all.

Through the nights we spent under curfew I felt within myself the urgency of solitude, of sneaking abroad alone, and above the law. I did not choose to act, not then, but it was necessary for my sanity that I felt the possibility of acting, if I so desired.

You think you're alone now, that the power and thrust of your ambition has set you apart, but I am here to remind you that what you are experiencing is only a foretaste of what you will be facing. Laws against murder exist for a reason. Not that those in positions of power give a fuck about the rest of us—so long as we're killing our own they'd leave us to slit each other's throats from now until the next millennium before they could be bothered to shift their arses and put a stop to it. But imagine the chaos, the risk of contagion, the spillover effect. That's what laws are for, mainly—to stop the crap we have to put up with leaking into their groundwater, their hot tubs and infinity pools, their rooftop fountains in Monte Carlo or wherever.

But that's not the kind of law I'm referring to—if you were scared of the cops, we wouldn't be having this conversation. Cops are just cops at the end of the day, no braver and no less stupid than anyone else, and I should know, seeing as I've served on the force for twenty years. I'm talking about the existential laws of the universe, the proverbial line in the sand, and what I'm saying is if you cross it, there's no way back. You kill someone and it's like any other traumatic experience: you'll be in a place you won't fully understand until you've been there. A dangerous place—high mountains and steep descents and blood-red sunsets. Unforgiving. The resting place of angels, or devils. Once you've been to that place you'll know how little difference there is between the two.

You're eager to know how it was for me, the first time, but you're getting ahead of yourself. The nature-nurture debate has run on for centuries with no clear winner. There are those who believe in bad blood, that killers are born, not made. How else would you get two lads from the same estate—with the same bad dad, even—brought up side by side in the same house, same school, same shithole community centre, only one of them ends up running his own auto-repair shop and the other goes down for murder with no hope of parole?

It tends to be the god-botherers who are keenest on the *evil will out* doctrine. They slurp it down like manna from heaven, and they each have a dozen feel-good parables to illustrate how it's not your background that's important but what you make of it. But I find the do-gooders just as annoying, the ones who rabbit on and on about how if everyone had an equal start in life there'd be a lot less violence, a lot less jealousy, a lot less madness. Drowning in their liberal guilt. They're patronising, most of them, and terrified. So terrified of the people they're purporting to help they can barely look them in the eye. Bleeding hearts like that will never understand darkness, not in a million years.

For sure you can go on the rob because you want a new pair of trainers, but it's not that. Lusting after gaudy baubles has nothing to do with it. The reasons for violence are as many and various as the number of murderers. What you need to look for is how they get started, the inciting incident. Mostly the inciting incident is painfully banal: Barry has one too many, gets into some flak with a low life he saw eyeing his girlfriend then beats him to a pulp in the pub car park. A constellation of chance events, in other words; any other day of the week and it wouldn't have happened. Then there are the fuckers who get in too deep with a problem—gambling, embezzlement, till-skimming, pick one—and don't see any other way out except removing the trouble at what they perceive to be its source. What those dimwits never understand is that ninety-nine times in a hundred the source is them. Sex and drugs and rock 'n' roll. Especially sex. Most times men kill other men, but it's when they kill women they make the headlines and there's a reason for that, too.

It makes a story, doesn't it? The kind the do-gooders like to wallow in like pigs in shit.

There were two inciting incidents for me, or one that led directly to another. Call it chance, if you want. I prefer to think of it as an epiphany. However you choose to look at it, the result is the same: before, there was nothing—a schoolboy's life, uninformed, uninspired, undirected, the background hum of the present tense. After, it was as if I'd found my vocation, my reason for being.

The whole of existence took on colour and form. Suddenly, I was the hero of my own story, the king of all I surveyed. That's better than any drug, take it from me. The teachers and the ministers, the cops and the prison guards and the bloody psychiatrists won't ever admit that, but it's true. You must know that already, though. Why else would you have written to me in the first place?

2

I had a friend, Carly, and we went way back. If I was egging the pudding I'd say we grew up together, but it wasn't like that, not quite. Carly and I fell in together at secondary school. We weren't what you'd call a natural pairing. Carly was smart, like, nerd-smart. He was fifteen when we first started hanging out together but he was already working his way through a set of calculus problems even our maths master struggled with—I know that because he said so himself. Mr. Mahmood, I mean, our maths teacher. He was grooming Carly for Oxford. I was good at maths but only in comparison with the other kids in our year—sit me next to Carly and I looked like a moron. Not everyone would get this, but that's what I liked about him, what first made me notice him. That he was good at something, and enjoyed it, and even though he was ragged like a bastard over it he did not give a shit.

What did he see in me? Fuck knows. That I was a loner maybe, that I never joined in the ragging—not because I imagined I was Jesus but because I thought the eejits who got off on giving someone a hard time for being wired into their life rather than hanging around the precinct smashing beer bottles and catcalling old ladies were dumb fucks. I didn't want anything to do with them, or their determination to flush their lives down the toilet.

I didn't know what I did want—only not that. I envied Carly, I suppose. Because he cared about things, he was interested in things. We'd go off for hikes sometimes, down the canal basin, or even take the train out to Epping Forest. Carly kept on at me to sign up for the foundation course in computer science they'd started running at our local HE college. I'd do well with computers, he insisted. The combination of mathematics, logic and practical outcomes would suit my aptitude for putting two and two together without veering off into the black hole territory of higher mathematics. That's what Carly said, or something like it. I began to think I might have found something—something I was actually good at—that my life might turn out less of a fuck-up than I'd feared. One in the eye for my dad, at least.

But then Carly was murdered.

It was a stupid thing, a hideous, rash action of the kind you read about in the tabloids: A-grade student killed by louts. They pleaded not guilty. Claimed it was an accident, a joke that got out of hand.

We was just messing about, said one of them.

He slipped, said another.

How were we supposed to know that he couldn't swim?

They were all kids I knew. You might say we grew up together and you would be right. Two of them certified toe-rags, the third a shambolic waste of space who wanted to impress them. In the days after Carly's death, the air seemed to keen with his absence, a high, clear vibration, the kind you get when you rub your finger around the rim of a wine glass. The thing about loss is there's no way to describe it that doesn't sound like a cliché, that doesn't ring false, like you're protesting too much, trying to drag the attention back to yourself.

I couldn't get it into my head that Carly was gone. That certain things had happened that day, a whole sequence of small occurrences—Carly happening to be down by the river after dark for some fucked-up reason, those three gits getting chucked out of a mate's house by said mate's mother—that might not have mattered one bit if they'd happened on a different day, or at different times, or if even one of that series of events had run a different course. As things stood, it was like watching a game play out, those spidery lines of force, the submarine and the battleship drawing closer and closer together, blue dots on a radar screen. Like that scene in *Alien*.

I never knew about the girl, Georgia Dicker. The girl Carly was supposed to have been in love with. The reason he was down by the river in the first place, mooning about in the dark.

He never said a word. I felt a hollowness at my heart each time I thought of it. I kept telling myself: he would have told me, there just wasn't time.

I kept thinking: what else didn't he tell me?

I started to wonder: what if our friendship was a lie, and he thought I was scum? Just another lout off the estate, a part of his past he was getting ready to move on from?

Carly was gone, and he was even more gone, if that makes sense. Like it wasn't just his life that had been snuffed out, it was everything that mattered in the world. Everything that mattered in my world, anyway.

You've heard of existential angst, the howling void? I tipped right into it. I could feel myself sinking, the water closing over my head, rank with duckweed and old crisp packets and all the other assorted crap losers chuck into rivers under cover of night.

3

The second inciting incident was reading Marlon Hayward's memoir of his time in Afghanistan. You might not remember Marlon Hayward, he's before your time, but his book about the reality of being a soldier became a bestseller. Because of the graphic violence, I suspect. There were plenty who said it should never have been published, a row that blew up all over the media a second time when *Nowhere Man* was shortlisted for a major prize.

Two years after his book came out, Hayward headed back to Afghanistan, this time as a journalist. He claimed he wanted to find out what happened to some of the Afghan soldiers he came into contact with the first time round, but no one's seen or heard from him since. His memoir is still in print, though, if you're interested, which you should be. Hayward writes about his experience of war, which is thrilling and sickening enough to test anyone's staying power. But what sets his book apart, at least for me, is the way he writes about killing in general, in the abstract, philosophical sense.

A well-known critic who didn't like the book called it a naked re-tread of *Crime and Punishment*. Could be the bloke skipped over the chapter where Hayward takes a hatchet to Dostoevsky's work, calling it supine and gutless. *As if Raskolnikov needed to justify his actions*, Hayward writes. *As if anyone needs a reason to kill. Killing is an art, like everything else. I do it so it feels like hell. I do it so it feels real…*

You could call Hayward an arrogant bastard, showing off his literary street cred like that. I prefer to think of it as him flipping the critics and the Oxbridge tossers the double 'v' he knew they deserved. Anyone can learn to quote the classics and paraphrase dead poets. But none of it matters, not when the chips are down. None of it ever did.

What Hayward is saying is that the only way to remove the fear of death from your life—the only way to live—is to confront it head-on. To snatch power from God or the devil or the void, whichever you fear most, to take back what is yours, what belongs to you by right. To discover that you can kill and feel no guilt, just the heady rush of knowing you have escaped the tawdry human fate of toeing the line.

No one asks to be born. Life is a level playing field, and those who try and force you to believe otherwise are not acting in the service of morality but in their own self-interest.

4

I joined the police straight from school. I know my mum was disappointed—she'd hoped I'd go to college, do that degree in computer science I was forever banging on about before Carly was killed, but she knew better than to press the point. I was not in the mood to argue, shall we say. She came round pretty sharpish in any case. Being a cop was a proper job, not like dealing skunk round the back of McDonald's or nicking cars off the street and flogging them on to one of the cut-n-shuts that ring-fence Dagenham.

My dad thought I was doing it to spite him. Trying to be funny, was how he put it. We've not spoken in years, yet every time I look in the mirror, there the fucker is, staring back at me like he's my own doppelganger. Dostoevsky was obsessed with doppelgangers. Could be he had the same experience. Like being followed home by a lunatic. Like seeing the devil creeping in beneath your own skin.

I started out like any other rookie PC: hours stuck inside a patrol car with some other loser, cruising the perimeter roads of the less dangerous estates through the grim November evenings, breaking up the odd pub fight, trying to keep the lid on things, cautioning pilled-up fourteen-year-olds who gave their names as Dee Vader or Tommy Gunn or Maggie Thatcher. The kid who did that didn't have a clue who Thatcher even was, just a name she'd picked up from the gutter and tried on for size.

I noticed she came up before the junior magistrate two years after that. Her real name was Bryony Clayden. She had coke scabs round her nostrils and a jagged scar down her arm from wrist to elbow.

What she was doing in the dock, God only knows. Should have been in a women's refuge, by the look of her. Either that or put down.

The stuff you see. The whole gamut from fucking boring to Dante's *Inferno*, the dividing line growing fainter and more contested from year to year.

On one level, I guess I did become a cop to piss off my dad. I had fantasies of drawing up beside him in the squad car just as he was being kicked out of the Grapes of Wrath, lying in wait for him outside the betting shop where he's upstairs doing deals with his dodgy mates. Not that anything we had on him seemed to make much difference. There's a dozen cops and more who've nicked him for real, yet one way or another he's back out on the street again, six months max.

Quick as a cockroach, my pa; sneaky as a silverfish. A waste of time thinking about him, even if those thoughts and dreams do involve shoving him up against a cell wall and setting tasers to stun. My real reason for becoming a cop had nothing to do with him, or not directly. Deep down, I had the idea that joining the force might help me with my problem.

Because I did see it as a problem. Back then I did, anyway. I guess I thought standing close to the dung heap might help hide my own stink.

That learning about violence—how it operated, how it proliferated, how it gummed up the works of the very machine designed to control it—

might provide some relief, a channel for my fascination, a legitimate use of the substance I was becoming addicted to.

A methadone for murder, if you can believe it.

I hated most of my colleagues, though. Thugs chasing thugs, what's the difference?

It was like I could hear Carly, telling me what an idiot I'd been.

He didn't sound angry, though, he sounded sad, which was typical of Carly, which was how I came to thinking about the effort he'd put in, back before he was murdered, persuading me to get on that computer course, convincing me I had a talent and I should use it.

Fuck you, Carly, I thought. I knew he had something, though. My growing impatience with the status quo, my rising contempt for the insects I was forced to call equals—I knew my anger would land me in trouble, sooner or later. I had been disciplined twice already—trivial matters, verbal warnings only, but the discontent inside me was swelling into rage. I needed more from my days, not just a reason to get up in the mornings but a guiding obsession. Carly thought I was good with computers, fine, I would be good with computers. I started looking into how I might get a transfer to digital forensics.

5

Turns out Carly was right, goddamn him. I should have known myself well enough to realise that breaking up pub fights, keeping the sewers clear of street rats, was never going to offer me the mental sustenance I was looking for. The cops I'd worked the beat with all had pipe dreams of making detective, swaggering around in leather jackets, putting the frighteners on the local guvnors like in *Line of Duty*. Most of their dreams were doomed from the outset. Becoming a detective involves the exercise of the imagination, and for most of those gits—what my half-brother Tobey always used to call the uniformed wing of the criminal fraternity—imagination was an optional extra for enjoying porn. None of them ever said as much, at least not in my hearing, but I know they looked upon digital forensics as a jumped-up desk job.

Like I say, they were gits, too numb in the skull to understand that digital forensics is a whole other world. It offers a portal to another world, anyway: a cesspool of intrigue and treachery and perversion hovering barely beneath the surface of known reality. The police service is obliged to offer trauma counselling for some of the shit we have to wade through. The guys dealing meth and adult videos out of basements in Tottenham? They're just the foot soldiers. The criminals—the real criminals—mostly never set foot outside their own postcode. Their own front doors, come to that. Why would they, when they can rule their kingdoms of filth from the calfskin settee in the front room, during the ad breaks in Formula One or *WrestleMania*?

Paedos, pornographers, psychopaths, and sometimes all three. Fraudsters, gangsters, common-or-garden drug dealers, embezzlers on the citywide scale, pimps and human traffickers, gangmasters, navigators of the dark web who operate a find-and-deliver service for, like, anything; seriously spaced-out individuals who I can only compare with the stalkers in that novel about the alien trash dump by those dead Russian brothers. Stalkers too, obviously, the ordinary kind, the kind who rifle through their victim's private business like a Dylanologist through garbage.

You get acquainted with them all in this job, all so painfully vulnerable to being spied on if you know how to look. They make it easy because they are careless. That's the scariest thing of all—the ludicrous carelessness of almost everyone, like wandering off down the street leaving the front door wide open, your illegal activities, your diseased proclivities laid out like museum exhibits for anyone to sneak inside and take a piss on.

I spy with my digital eye, something beginning with 'S'. Slimeball, sicko, sonofabitch, usually all three.

I developed a feel for a lead, a talent for hacking into encrypted files like a sniffer dog latching on to a scent. Signature codes are like that for me, they have a subtext, a texture, a smell like a physical trace, like actual atoms, bleeding into the atmosphere and stinking up my airspace. The higher-ups in the boot room took to calling me the digital bloodhound. I'd grin and bear it, laugh along with them, best to be friendly at least on the surface and it's not so difficult to be friendly when you're having fun.

There was one mark I became obsessed with, an international art dealer called John Cross who traded child pornography under the radar. Cross was forty years old and a millionaire. He had a higher degree in art history from the Courtauld Institute and a sackful of influential friends. You remember that news story from a few years back about a paedophile ring involving government ministers? This was the real deal, and John Cross was sitting right at the heart of it. He'd been investigated before, a number of times, but the bastard always came out clean.

I was handed the file not long after I graduated to having my own office. A fresh set of rumours had surfaced and so the case was being reopened. Everyone knew there was something fishy but that was the problem—Cross was slippery as a fish and clever with it. No hook to hang him on. It was my job to find one, and in the end I did. Took me more than a year to get there but I'd learned not to worry about time. The difficulty of the assignment was part of its beauty, the sense that I'd finally come up against an opponent who was worthy of me.

A bad man, but a clever man. The two don't always go together but this time they did, and the excitement of the chase annulled the feelings of rage I had, at least for the duration.

Once I knew I had him, something shifted. But we'll come to that.

6

Cross's weak link was a Dutchman named Claes van Oosten, a high-class art dealer like Cross, but with a previous, proven link to the porn industry. Van Oosten had a six-month suspended sentence for possession of indecent images, a charge that dated from way back, before social media. I would guess that few if any of his current associates even knew about it. Van Oosten was still in his twenties at the time, and impressionable. He hadn't realised what he was getting into, or at least that was the angle his lawyer took and clearly it worked.

Van Oosten twenty years later looked clean as a whistle. His daddy was something in shipping, and the family were major benefactors of the Rijksmuseum. I only became interested in van Oosten because he kept cropping up in Cross's schedule—the two of them would meet up for lunch or dinner every time Cross was in Europe, which was once a month at least. I had a long list of Cross's contacts, and I was vaguely watching all of them, but van Oosten was so present it was almost irritating, like he was getting up in my face deliberately. I even went across to Amsterdam once, to get a look at him on his home turf. Easy enough, seeing as I already knew where he was going to be for most of the weekend. Sleek as a Siamese cat, van Oosten, credible and presentable with it. Johnny Cross might have matched him in terms of intellect, but in terms of personal style he was a local yokel.

Once I'd verified the link between them, things speeded up nicely. I had Cross every which way, up to and including a series of security shots at a motorway services near Chelmsford, meeting up with the courier and personal driver for a disreputable individual who had once been part of the Epstein set. I took a pride in that dossier, which in terms of conclusive, damning evidence was a thing of beauty. I made sure every last detail was in order, mailed it up to the boot room via our encrypted server. Then I went after Cross.

The time-stamp on the file was 20:04—a reasonable time to be logging off for the day, none of your all-night obsessive Zodiac stuff. The boss would usually be opening his inbox around 7:30—bit of a stickler, Monash, bit of an eager beaver—and all other things being equal, Cross would be safely in custody by nine o'clock. But the hours between were mine, a temporal vacuum. A space of emptiness in which the devil could do his business.

Or I could do it for him.

Now you might be asking me what the point was, why take the risk? I'd spent the better part of two years plus overtime gathering the goods to get that scum put away, so why soil my hands with him? I'm here to tell you that proving the case was never the goal for me. Nailing the evidence was something I did for form's sake, like ticking items off a checklist. Making sure in my own mind that I had the right guy. Even with a judge with half his marbles missing, Cross would be looking at fifteen years tops. With good behaviour and a prevailing wind he'd be out in ten, possibly eight.

The thing with guys like Cross is, they're born assuming the law is on their side, that it's a means for enforcing their inherent superiority— and guess what, they're right. The truth is, I hated John Cross, hated him personally. All those overseas junkets and two-grand suits and Michelin-star dinners and the best he could come up with as a life goal was dealing kiddy porn?

I kept thinking about Marlon Hayward, the way he'd called Dostoevsky gutless for having Raskolnikov destroy himself through guilt. Hayward says Raskolnikov doesn't just have the right to kill the old pawnbroker, he has a duty—she's a usurer, a drain on society, and a child-abuser into the bargain. The girl he kills by mistake is collateral damage and as a soldier, Hayward says, collateral damage is something you accept as part of the job.

I read *Crime and Punishment* something like five times after reading Hayward, and the book seemed laughable to me. Not laughable as in no good, but as in what the fuck? Dostoevsky had faced a firing squad, yet he'd put his boy through all that agony for the sake of a human dishrag you wouldn't wipe the floor with. His brain must have gone soft while he was in the gulag, I reckon. But still, I couldn't stop reading him. He has a way of telling a story, a way of sliding in amongst the low life. Like Dickens has, only closer to the knuckle, closer to the dirt.

There's a passage in *The Brothers Karamazov* where the oldest brother, Ivan, the bad-tempered angsty one, is telling his Jesus-loving brother Alyosha about the time the devil appears to him in his bedroom, dressed in a cheap jacket and slacks and promising him the key to paradise. All you have to do, says Old Nick, is accept that all the glory, all the joy, all the peace you're about to experience is founded on torture, on the degradation and abuse of an innocent child. You'll never have to see that child or answer for your choice but you'll know about it. Everyone in paradise knows, but they don't discuss it.

When Ivan asks why, the devil tells him it's none of his business, let's just say it's the price of his entrance ticket, and Ivan—and here we have to assume it's Dostoevsky himself speaking, because if there's one thing I learned from reading *Crime and Punishment* it's that Dostoevsky hasn't a clue about letting sleeping dogs lie—says no. No way, he says, you can fuck your ticket. And the thing is, in my head John Cross had become the opposite of that. In my head, John Cross was the fat, selfish prick who accepts the devil's bargain, who makes his fortune off images and ideas you wouldn't want to come across in your worst nightmares, especially not if you have kids, and after signing the shipping manifest he gets into an air-conditioned cab and glides off to an embassy reception, blathering on about Mondrian or Chagall or whoever.

I could not let that lie. I intended to deal our Johnny the hand he was owed.

7

This was all cock, you realise. The fact is, I wanted to kill him. I had decided I was going to commit a murder, and this was my excuse— that the man I was going to kill deserved what was coming. I knew if I was careful—being a cop had taught me that at least—I could get away with it. No previous history of violence—nothing beyond the odd after-hours *contretemps*, anyway, nothing that counted—and you more or less said it yourself: if I'd already nailed the bastard, why would I kill him?

I have no taste for Grand Guignol. I would argue that Grand Guignol—basement torture rooms, elaborate kidnap plans, extravagant devices—is an excess of egotism, the kind that sooner or later will get you caught. I had no desire to get caught, no hankering to show off my criminal ingenuity to my erstwhile colleagues. What I wanted was to change history, just a little bit. To swerve it sideways a notch, to hear the barely audible click as one version of events diverts to a different track and time alters forever.

There was no way for me to know what would change, or what would not change, as the result of John Cross's exit from the world, and you should know enough of me by now to understand that I didn't care.

The point was that his death would happen, and I would be responsible.

The fact that no one would know? I found the idea of my anonymity heady as wine.

I chose a weapon entirely suitable for the matter in hand, a particular brand of knife that happened to be popular at the time amongst the city's hoodlums. Not one of the fashion brands—expensive, difficult to conceal and unreliable, mostly playthings for amateurs—but a simple, bog-standard hunting knife with a titanium-steel blade. I overtook him in a deserted underpass—he'd been to a concert and gala reception at the Festival Hall—and then, once I was certain we were alone, I pretended to have lost my way and doubled back. I tutted and sighed then glanced at my watch—the fluorescent display flashed brightly in the semi-darkness as I angled my wrist. A second later I was shoving him up against the wall of the underpass. I remember the muffled thud as his head hit the concrete, the contrasting softness of his flesh, like putty, as I slipped him the knife.

He went down with barely a sound. I twisted the blade and then withdrew it, stepping carefully to one side as I did so to avoid the blood spatter, a movement that felt so natural and so fluid it might have been choreographed. I pocketed the handkerchief I had wrapped around the handle, later depositing it with the remains of a carton of chicken wings in a waste bin outside Dalston overground. I enjoyed those chicken wings. They anchored me in the moment. On some level, they seemed like the only proof I had of what I had done.

After ditching the chicken carton, I carried on up the road to my flat like on any other night. I put a load in the washing machine, poured myself a scotch, then turned on the TV. I don't recall what was on. I was concentrating on my breathing, listening for the sound of police sirens. In the end I nodded off, the background murmur of the television mutating into the sound of a station announcement in the dream I was having. I was at Euston in the early morning, waiting for Carly. We were going on a camping trip to Loch Lomond. Carly was late, and I was feeling pissed off because he was never late. I looked at my watch, then woke up with a start, heart thumping. I turned off the TV and went to bed, still thinking about the dream.

It seemed like an omen, somehow. Carly and I had been planning to go on that exact same trip, the week after we finished our A levels. We had even bought the train tickets. I still have mine, stashed away in the suitcase where I keep that kind of stuff. They're faded now but still legible, pieces of a past that never happened.

8

The few worries I had about the murder could be summed up in one word: coincidence. Would people find it suspicious, that John Cross happened to get himself killed on the same night his cover was blown?

This was a chance I had to take, and my instinct proved correct. The idea that the digital bloodhound might be Cross's murderer never seemed to cross anyone's mind. The fact that I had helpfully provided a whole case file of credible suspects and their possible motives made me something of a golden boy back in the boot room, at least for a day or two.

The forensics on Cross were limited, not to say rudimentary, and in the end the case was shelved, with everyone tacitly agreeing that the killer must have been an underworld contact that went bad, and given the feast of filth we now had on him the bastard had it coming.

I held my breath, on hyper-alert for whispers and rumours, but none surfaced. I waited for the fuss to die down then took the week's leave I had owing and booked myself a ticket on the overnight train to Glasgow. I felt I owed it to Carly, to finally follow through on that trip of ours. Glasgow's a massive sprawl, but unlike London you can hop on one of the local buses and be hiking through open countryside in under an hour. I'd purchased a small tent, and there were plenty of pubs and petrol stations where I could get a cooked breakfast or dinner and have a wash and brush-up.

Mostly I was alone. The rain pissed down from time to time but more often than not the weather was fine, fine for walking, anyway, and so I kept on going, inhaling the heady scents of trees and rain-soaked granite, the tea-coloured streams frothing and rushing in their narrow gullies and down the mountainside.

I gave no thought to the man I had murdered. So far as I was concerned, John Cross was already a non-person, a torn-out page of history. From time to time I wondered how things were going back in the boot room, if any unfortunate details might have come to light, but such questions were minor and fleeting and did not bother me. In my solitude I felt free—freer than I had ever done. There were times I thought about not going back, about picking up some bum job— one of the petrol stations where I stopped for a sandwich had been advertising for a shop manager—and simply living, drawing my pay packet every week and spending the weekends as I was doing now, walking in the hills and spotting eagles, leaving the whole sordid human enterprise behind.

It's not really you, though, is it mate? I could hear Carly saying, and although I was loath to admit it, I knew he was right. There was something calling me back to London—not just the stink of the boot room, but the feeling that always enveloped me when I was in the city: the sense of timelines converging, the weight of history if you like, the stench of other people's stories, each of them a grimy mystery that needed solving.

In London I could disappear. More surely than I ever could in the mountains, I could slide around any corner and be lost in the crowd. A communal entranceway or a supermarket car park, a floodlit loading bay or a tube station forecourt or a greasy spoon. Diesel fumes and dog dirt. The icy glint of diamonds in a Bond Street window.

And murder, of course, all those irksome personal tasks I was bound to perform. The cut-and-thrust, the roar of static, the black dust of oblivion. An end that I had caused, that points-change in the small hours, the *thunk* and click that only I—and for a second, my quarry—would ever hear.

That's the thing with an addiction: you keep going back.

9

I tracked down Georgia Dicker because I had to. I needed a project, something to keep my mind occupied, or rather to help me forget what almost happened with Rudi Ginelli. Rudi was a close call, you might say a warning. Stalking Georgia was an amusement. Getting involved with her was never on the menu. Which only goes to show how much we kid ourselves.

Rudi Ginelli was a new boy, a blue-eyed wonder, a trainee with the

Armed Response Unit and the kind of smart-alec loudmouth you either love or hate. Needless to say, I hated him. He'd done nothing to earn my hatred. Our paths rarely even crossed, only every time they did I kept getting the feeling he was familiar, that I knew him from somewhere, and so of course I went digging.

Turns out Rudi Ginelli is a cousin of Petey Blakemore, one of the tykes who did for Carly. Ten years younger than Pete, so they could hardly have been close, especially given that Petey was still banged up, but once I knew who Rudi was, there was no unknowing it.

I went for him in a crowded bar. Accused him of spilling my drink, though it was I who spilled his, right down his poncey Italian shirtfront, then cuffed him so hard his nose started gushing like a fucking waterfall. Dislocated his jaw, though I didn't realise that at the time. Took five other lads to pull me off him, and then I blacked out. Some kind of seizure, the docs said. Apnoea. When I came round I was lying on the floor with a circle of faces staring down at me like I'd fallen down a manhole, which was sort of how I felt. Lights before my eyes—visual disturbances, they called them—and a sound like heavy breathing right through my body.

I was suspended, pending medical examination. They stuck so many wires on me I felt like Frankenstein's monster. In the end they wrote it down to stress, handed me a month's compulsory leave and a written warning. I knew what it was, though—liquefied rage. Rage over Carly, and a thirst for killing so intense and all-consuming it was like my body was being attacked by a new kind of virus.

My addiction was back, full force. What scared me was not the compulsion but how out of control it was. I had to put measures in place, for my own protection. I stopped hanging out with the boys from the boot room, stopped drinking—or very nearly—and started on my Georgia project. Slow, careful, restful work, just what the doctor ordered.

More fool me.

I wanted to know if she remembered him—Carly, I mean. If he still meant anything to her, or if he was just some guy she knew from way back and would rather not think about.

I was curious, or that's what I told myself. Her people had kept her out of the papers—well they would, wouldn't they? Mummy and daddy in the civil service, private school. Fuck knows how she and Carly managed to meet. I'd only found out about Georgia in the first place from one of the guys from Carly's maths class, the boffins who were being groomed for higher things. Kid with cerebral palsy called Tim Westenra. Looked like he had some wasting disease but he was flattened by Carly's death, I could tell.

Does Georgia know? I remember him saying to me in that lisping voice of his. Has anyone spoken to Georgia?

I stared at him like he was a creature from another planet. I don't think he'd ever spoken to me before that. We were both still in shock. Carl's girlfriend, he insisted. I turned and walked away without saying a word, although later I wished I hadn't. I wished I'd shaken him like a piggy bank until he'd given up every last shred of information in his twisted head.

On the day of Carly's funeral I saw a girl standing on the street outside the crematorium. She was wearing a grey coat, her long red hair streaming over the collar like molten copper. We stared at each other, did that dance you do where you're trying to step past someone without bumping into them. Then she was gone, and I was left there feeling like an idiot without knowing why.

I've had girlfriends over the years, but none you'd call serious. If any of them started looking that way I'd bail.

What is it with you and this Greta Garbo shit? Reena said to me once. *You want to be alone.* I don't get it. You're not getting any younger, you know.

Reena is a prostitute. I pay her for sex but not for her friendship. The friendship's real.

Once bitten and all that, I said to her. A bluff, a blind—I don't like to talk about personal stuff and Reena knows it—but maybe there was some truth there, anyway, a part of me that had been, I don't know, *vanquished*.

By Carly or by Georgia, or by the knowledge that I could never get inside their world.

You see what this shit can do to you? Talking, I mean. When I first typed Georgia's name into Google I wasn't expecting to find much—just the usual fake LinkedIn listings for people who weren't who you were looking for or who didn't exist, and that's pretty much what I got. It didn't help that I had precisely nothing to begin with, just a name that could have been anyone's, and the fact she was living in Walthamstow the year Carly was murdered.

She could be living on the fucking moon now for all I knew.

She wasn't, though, she was living three tube stops away. She was working as a studio technician at a local art college and she'd just split up with some tosser named Theo.

Theo, I ask you. You couldn't make it up.

10

Georgia Dicker won a place to study art at Central Saint Martins but dropped out after a year owing to what are now euphemistically referred to as 'mental health concerns'.

In actual human speech, Georgie had anorexia and almost died. She was chuffed to get the studio technician job because the college were sponsoring her to study part-time, so she could finish her degree.

The break-up with Theo had thrown her back a bit but she was getting over it. She felt like her life was finally back in gear. She showed me some of her work: tiny porcelain cups and bowls that looked like doll's house furniture but were actually part of a multimedia installation she was working on to do with art behind closed doors.

Some people say they don't care if they're being spied on because they have nothing to hide, she said, but what that proves is how little they know about the value of privacy. We all have something to hide—we just don't always know who from.

I recognised her the second I saw her, in a pub she went to sometimes, right around the corner from the college. All that copper-red hair. I told her later it was love at first sight. The strange thing is I wasn't lying.

You make me feel safe, she said. You being a policeman, I mean. She laughed. I know it's a horrible cliché but I haven't felt safe like this, not since I was at school.

When I asked her why not, she turned on her side and sighed and said, It's complicated. I waited, not saying a word, not touching her even, not really, just gazing at her, my face so close to hers I could feel her breathing.

I had a boyfriend who was murdered, she said at last. Carl. I was seventeen, he was eighteen, just. He was beaten up on his way home from school, chucked in the canal.

What the fuck for? I could feel my heart pounding. I forced myself to visualise it, the water, my naked body moving through it, hands posed in a 'v' shape, like a diver's, parting the grey-green currents like skeins of silk. I learned to swim when I was five—my mum had a thing about it. I had no idea Carly couldn't. I never even thought of asking because why would I? In that respect I was no better than the morons who killed him.

Nothing, Georgie said. No reason. They were kids off the estate. They went after Carl because he was clever and they didn't like that. I don't think they actually meant to kill him but that's what happened, they killed him.

That's murder, I said.

She nodded. Carl wouldn't have hurt a fly. He was—well, nothing was ever the same for me after he died. I gave up trying to talk about it. People would say I was young, I'd get over it. No one wants to believe you can be in love at that age, properly in love, I mean. That you can love someone in a way that matters. That goes on mattering for a long time afterwards.

I caught hold of her hand, linking our fingers together. I thought about Carly and it should have been weird, me lying there next to his girlfriend and her telling me news so old it was part of my bloodstream, but it wasn't, it was like a key sliding into a lock, a moment I'd waited for so long it felt like all the years between then and now had been wiped from the record.

When I asked Georgie to tell me about her artwork she said it was inspired by women artists around the world who are not allowed to practise, who are made to stay at home and have no contact with one another.

That's why the objects in the installation are all based around domestic appliances, she said. Cooking pots and cutlery and cleaning equipment. I want to show how these too can become art objects, how women have often been forced to create their own art spaces, their own safe spaces, where they live and work. How even when they're treated like they're invisible they are still speaking out.

Except when they're burned and gang-raped and killed, I thought but didn't say. The art Georgie creates is beautiful. I can use a word like that, when it is appropriate. I find myself having thoughts sometimes, daydreams about making a safe space for Georgie, about keeping her free from harm the way she wants, the way she deserves, the way she believes I am already doing.

At other times I know this is impossible, that I'm fooling myself, that it is only a matter of time before I am alone again.

The problem with addiction is that you never stop being an addict.

It's like I'm spinning a coin on its edge, watching its outlines blur, spinning so fast it looks like it's solid, at least for a second. Then it's toppling flat on its face, Queen's head rolling in the sawdust, chop chop.

Which way will it fall, that is the question. Heads, or tails?

JAUNT

Ken Liu

*A*RCHIVAL *VNN footage of Ruutuutuu Protests at the Port of Seattle, Pier 91, July 10, 202X*

[A magnificent cruise ship, *Pacific Unicorn*, is docked at the pier, ready to begin its seven-day tour of the Inside Passage. Luggage is being loaded; passengers in long lines are embarking; everything seems perfect: a normality that everyone has been craving for many months during the pandemic.

Except... a swarm of small boats—dinghies, speedboats, kayaks, even a few fishing trawlers—numbering in the high hundreds have congregated in front of the cruise ship, filling much of Elliott Bay and blocking its course. Protesters throng the pier, holding up signs with the mustachioed cartoon rutabaga that has become the symbol of the movement and shouting, "Shut it down!"]

INTERVIEWER: Unicorn Cruises say that they've implemented every precaution for the safety and health of the crew and the passengers. All their ships have obtained the STERLING-20 certification—

PROTESTER: STERLING-20 is a worthless piece of marketing spin. The certification process was created by the cruise industry, for crying out loud. The truth is, there is no way to run cruises safely. None! Have you forgotten what happened barely two years ago? My parents were stuck on that ship wandering the Pacific with no port to take them in, and they both got infected. My mother died. Do you understand? Died. How can you pack thousands of people into close quarters like cattle, feed them at trough-buffets, recirculate the same air in every room... and believe this can ever be *safe*? It's a goddamned lie.

INTERVIEWER: There's been no evidence of another pandemic—

PROTESTER: [*mimics*] "There's been no evidence..." Where have I heard that before? The virus hasn't gone away. We've got to live with this thing for the foreseeable future. And the next pandemic *will* come—it's not *if*, but *when*. No more cruises. No more tour groups. No more jumbo jets stuffed full of sweaty bodies breathing on one another for twenty-plus hours. No more tourism. Shut it all down!

"See the World Like You've Never Seen it Before"—video advertisement for Unicorn Travel Enterprises, produced by TIDE=/=AL Partners, September 202X

[The Great Pyramid of Giza looms in our view like a mountain.

The camera holds still as time speeds up. The sun rises and sets; the stars spin overhead; shadowy figures flit in and out of frame like mayflies dancing with eternity; the pyramid's shadow sweeps across the sand like the gnomon of a world-pacing sundial. New Age music plays.

Then, just as the sun is low in the west once more, the music stops, time returns to normal, and the camera begins to move forward, swaying slightly from side to side.]

WOMAN (O.S.): They tell me the record for climbing to the top is six minutes twenty-nine seconds.

[We're running toward the base of the pyramid. Faster and faster. Despite the optical stabilization, the swaying becomes more pronounced.]

WOMAN (O.S.): [*panting*] I signed up to be first in line today so I wouldn't have to slow down for anyone else.

[We reach the bottom of the pyramid. The camera tilts up. The jagged blocks seem to scrape heaven.

We climb. Although the action cam is clearly streaming the POV of the climber, we don't see her hands or feet. In fact, for viewers who are used to consuming such footage, there's something distinctly odd about the camera angle and movement—too close to the surface, perhaps?]

WOMAN (O.S.): Talk to you again at the top.

[Up-tempo, pulse-pounding music plays. We hear the sounds of her exertion over sped-up footage of the ascent. Most of the time, the unsteady camera is focused on the limestone block or blocks right in front of the climber. But from time to time, it swerves for a peek at the apex. Closer. Closer. It's frantic, thrilling, exhilarating.

Finally, we reach the top.]

WOMAN (O.S): Oh... Wow...

[The camera swings around to give us a dizzying view: the Pyramid of Khafre nearby, which appears even taller than our summit; the sprawl of Cairo in the distance, reminding you that almost five millennia of history have been compressed under your feet; the hazy horizon all around you, promising unknown, arcane knowledge; the vertiginous sensation that you're about to plunge hundreds of feet to your death...

Only then do you notice the unusual scene on the slanting face of the pyramid below you: dozens of robots scrambling up the limestone blocks after you. Each robot is about the size of a large dog, with four padded feet that grip tightly onto the limestone blocks, a camera in front, and a screen that shows the face of a climber-teleoperator. A quick scan of the screens reveals that the climbers come from all over the world.

A robot hand rises into the camera's view, waving.

The screen splits to show a woman in climbing gear strapped into a full-motion harness waving. Her movements have been mapped into the movements of the robot. She lifts off her full-immersion goggles, wipes the sweat from her face, and proudly holds out her watch for the viewer.]

WOMAN: Six minutes and twenty-six seconds. Not too bad.

[The Unicorn Travel logo swerves onto the screen, followed by a link to their website.]

WOMAN: And I've still got enough time to shower before work.

[Text on screen: *A NEW WAY TO TRAVEL: EVEN BETTER THAN BEING THERE.*]

"Opinion: It's Time to Admit it: We Were Wrong to Oppose the Ruutuutuu Movement," by Joanna Tung, Boston Globe, July 10, 203X
Like many of you, I was dismayed when the Ruutuutuu Protests essentially shut down the global tourism industry shortly after the annus horribilis that was 2020. As the owner of a company specializing in curating and creating unique experiences for tourists from all over the world interested in sampling Xhong culture, my life's work would be destroyed by the movement to abolish global tourism.

The protesters' immediate concerns were to prevent Covid-19 from flaring up again, or, even worse, the emergence of another pandemic, but over time, their mission evolved to saving the planet from our relentless drive to consume experiences without regard to the future.

I found myself in a hard place. Having devoted much of my career to the intersection of economic development and sustainability, I understood the math behind their protest signs better than most.

The people who bought my tour packages came from Europe, the United States, Japan, Australia, the biggest cities in China and South America. They were the kind of individuals who recycled, drove electric vehicles, or even biked, tried to be good to Mother Earth. They thought of themselves as good people, with expensive educations, the right opinions, virtuous intentions. That was why they wanted to spend a week living in a Xhong village and attempt to understand a way of life different from their own.

But all their efforts at conservation were wiped out and more the moment they decided to get on that plane. A jet flight to carry a family and all the luggage needed to sustain their Western comforts across an ocean or a continent is among the most wasteful activities ever invented by the human race. And that's without even accounting for the environmental cost of transporting them from the airport over new highways, across new bridges, through mountain tunnels and flattened forests until they reached their vacation destination.

The mountainous regions of Southeast Asia, where the Xhong people live, contain some of the most vulnerable ecosystems in the world. Droughts, storms, mudslides, and other consequences of climate change have already wrought havoc with their lives. Each new airport, road, bridge, tunnel, and tourist meant more cement—perhaps the most destructive, poisonous, and unsustainable construction material ever invented by humans—more fossil fuels, more wrecking of forest, soil, aquifers. It meant another step closer toward the day when the area would become uninhabitable by the very people the tourists came to visit.

Moreover, I was acutely aware that my tours were perpetuating a colonialist legacy of violence and exploitation. Though I tried to design my tours with input from Xhong elders and artists, and strove to make the villages who hosted my guests equal partners in the business, activists had for years argued that my cultural immersion tours differed only in degree, not kind, from the exploitative vacation resorts and "cultural showcases" operated by mega corporations and centralized governments, which had little interest in preserving Xhong culture. My customers were of course not overtly exploitative, unlike those who went on sex tours or hunted for exotic animals in Southeast Asia. But they wanted to play at living another culture, to consume a way of life, to find "spiritual meaning" by reducing the traditions and practices of the Xhong into processed trinkets and pseudo-New Age pap that reaffirmed their own choices and sense of superiority. The very notion of tourism in the modern sense is an act of voyeuristic pleasure experienced by the Western (and would-be Western) colonizer subject gazing upon indigenous populations, an act of vicarious subjugation; the global tourism industry is rotten at its foundation.

And yet. And yet.

Without airplanes bringing tourists from across the globe, how was I supposed to keep paying my tour guides and drivers? Without the dollars and euros and WeChat balances, how would the Xhong families who had planned their entire lives around housing and feeding tourists make a living? Without their cameras and phones and excited chatter, who was going to buy all the handicrafts made specifically for them? The Xhong had become dependent on tourism, even as it further eroded their world. Entire villages, which had already suffered enormously through the tourism drought of the pandemic, would now tip over into ruin. While many villagers remained terrified of tourists bearing another wave of infections, many more clamored for the economic life raft they represented. I had no room to think about the planet's future or the ramifications of colonialist structural inequality when I needed to figure out an immediate way to save the families who were my employees and partners.

Many independent tour providers, including myself, tried to band together to push back against the Ruutuutuu Protests. But like many movements of the era, the Ruutuutuu protesters were a loose coalition with divergent, even contradictory, demands. Some were concerned about the cultural and environmental externalities of global tourism, which I sympathized with. But others were motivated by less noble concerns. Some were convinced that tourists from Asia had caused the pandemic in Europe and the United States. Some were isolationists who wanted to seize the opportunity and reverse globalization. Still others believed in conspiracy theories that argued cruise ships and jumbo jets were UN-sanctioned experimental vehicles for Chinese and North Korean spies working under the direction of Russian scientists funded by Bill Gates. Our advertisements and calls for a dialogue made little impact.

There was a cultural shift. Celebrities posting photos of getaways to faraway tropical paradises were now shamed as though they had posted pictures of hunting trophies. People looked at those who flew around in jets the way we used to look at smokers.

Dire warnings were issued about the collapse of tourism-driven developing economies and the hollowing out of indigenous communities. Many of us experienced a sense of helpless rage at the protesters who seemed too blinded by their own zeal to have compassion for those who depended on the cruise ships and jumbo jets. But gradually, as the protests raged on and global tourism numbers remained depressed, we learned to adapt.

The first to try something new were the giant cruise lines and resort owners. As their ships remained docked and their hotels empty, they started to sell "remote tours," which tapped into VR and telepresence, two technologies that saw unprecedented adoption during the long pause forcefully imposed on much of the world by Covid-19. Many of these packages relied on gimmicks that allowed teletourists to do things they couldn't have done even in person. Governments, desperate for tourism revenue, readily relaxed various restrictions for these teletourists.

For example, Unicorn Travel, one of the largest cruise lines, ran a program that gave customers the chance to climb the Great Pyramid of Giza when embodied in a telepresence robot, an act that was (and still is) illegal to perform in person. Supposedly, the telepresence robots, being light, electric, and well-padded, posed little risk of damaging the pyramid (and could be programmed to prevent the operator from carving graffiti into the limestone). Similar programs allowed teletourists to stroll through the Taj Mahal at night, to "climb" glaciers in Alaska, to watch tortoises in the Galápagos Islands, to scramble over the ruins of Tulum and Chichen Itza, and numerous similar feats.

But these packages were aimed at the luxury travel market. They didn't help the rest of us: the independent tour providers, the cultural experience curators, the local guides who relied on one-on-one tips.

The game changer was the Nene Be, an open-source specification for a small telepresence robotic platform built around single-board computers like the Raspberry Pi. The Nene Be (and its successors) relied on cheap cameras, cheap screens, cheap processors, cheap manipulators and batteries, cheap (but fast) wireless networking, and open-source software. They were easy to make and even easier to operate. They gave the teleoperator the ability to talk to people on the other end, to control their view, to move around and manipulate objects (with severe limits). They didn't give one VR-like immersion, but they were just good enough to make you feel like you were doing more than chatting through a webcam. You were *there*.

The Xhong, like people dependent on the tourism economy around the world, soon built new business models based on the Nene Be. Instead of serving xoi ngai ngai noodles to tourists in person, the stall owners now gave cooking tutorials to paying students from around the world, hosted competitions among teleoperators to see who made the best noodles, and partnered with Southeast Asian grocery stores in the home cities of the teletourists to sell them the ingredients needed to create the dishes at home. Instead of catering to the needs of a tourist family who wanted to pretend to be rice farmers for a week, now Xhong families could simply set up a few Nene Bes near the paddy (fenced in so they didn't accidentally fall into the water—though telepresent "paddy races" were also a thing for some) and charge people who wanted to drop in from time to time to do some telepresent farming or help chase off vermin as a way to unwind. Instead of selling tourist-pleasing wax-dyed prints, Xhong artisans now could teach workshops, take on teletourist apprentices, or license their unique designs for 3-D printing or one-off dyeing in the tourists' own countries. The possibilities were endless.

Involving no jets traversing oceans, no SUVs bouncing over winding mountain roads, no giant staff to tend to the passengers' every whim, even accounting for the investment in network infrastructure, a visit through a Nene Be requires less energy than it takes to keep the lights on in an average American house for an hour. Because a teletour can be booked with so little friction, the average visit lasts only twenty-eight minutes. In the trade, we call them "telejaunts" or just "jaunts."

Critics initially feared that jaunts would cheapen the experience of travel and, by being too easy to fit into our increasingly attention-starved modernity, remove leisure travel as one of the only ways left for us to depart from the everyday and reflect on our inner lives. But experience has proven these fears unfounded. Travelers take jaunts far more frequently than physical trips, often returning to the same place multiple times over a period of weeks or months (we all probably know of a friend who goes to the same noodle stall in Taipei every day for ten minutes just to watch the owner pull the noodles by hand). They form sustained connections with a place and the individuals in that place, gaining insights into the human condition deeper and more authentic than could ever be obtained during a week-long physical vacation in a tourist trap overrun with crowds.

Jaunts have completely transformed the landscape of global tourism. Gone are the days when intercontinental tours were both too expensive to be truly accessible to the less-than-affluent and too cheap to prevent ecological disaster and cultural commodification. Nowadays, more people are touring distant places than at any point in history, but their impact on the environment, both physical and cultural, is also much lighter and less destructive. Instead of flocking to the same places as everyone else, tourists can go to places far off the beaten path—the Nene Be has essentially opened up the tourist economy to entrepreneurial residents and communities in remote hamlets and rural sanctuaries without the requirement for costly infrastructure or putting their fragile way of life at risk. By transporting presences instead of atoms, teletourism is a magical spell that has given us the best of all outcomes.

To be sure, not everyone is convinced of the benefits of jaunts. So-called "populist" political parties in the West, as well as repressive regimes elsewhere, have taken advantage of the rise of teletourism to further restrict the movements of refugees, journalists, and migrants seeking a better life elsewhere. We must remain ever vigilant against the virulent possibilities when good ideas are twisted to serve dark purposes.

To that end, I also believe that jaunts offer the potential to subvert the traditional power imbalances between outbound tourist source regions—which tend to be more economically developed and Western—and inbound tourist destination regions, many of which are less developed and suffer from a legacy of colonial oppression. While many tourists from Boston, for example, visit Xhong villages in Vietnam and Laos, very few Xhong tourists can afford to visit this city. This is why my company has formed a partnership with anti-colonialist and anti-racist activists to develop programs to help more teletourists from the Xhong and other indigenous peoples to come visit places like Boston. As the United States has grown ever more hostile to immigration and voices from around the world, teletour jaunts, which require no visas and no border searches, may be the best way to challenge this trend.

Joanna Tung is the founder of Teletourists Without Borders, a nonprofit dedicated to developing sustainable models of cultural exchange that reverse the legacy of colonial exploitation. She also hosts jaunts to her office in Vietnam on JauntsNow at the following BnB code: DXHHWU-TCU.

Excerpt from Be My Guest, *a documentary series focusing on the lives of JauntsNow hosts and guests, first shown May 203X*
[The camera is on Al Burton, seventies, strolling through Boston Common. From time to time, he stops to examine a flowerbed or a birdfeeder by the side of the path.]

I never traveled much back then. In twenty years my wife and I took the kids on two trips, one to Thailand, another to Mexico. After she died, I didn't go anywhere at all except to fish on the Cape once a year. Running a dry-cleaning shop is a lot of work. Too much.

But I had no work for those months during the pandemic. Even after the lockdown ended, business was terrible. The virus moved in and made itself comfortable. People didn't go to the office; they didn't get dressed up; they didn't need to have their clothes dry-cleaned. I had no choice but to shut it down. My life's work. Gone.

[Ken Burns-style panning over photos Burton took of his shop before he shuttered it. The place had been meticulously and lovingly cleaned.]

I was sitting at home when I got this coupon by email, telling me that I could go on trips to China, Vietnam, Mexico, Costa Rica… wherever I wanted for just fifteen bucks. I thought it was a scam—or maybe the airlines were so desperate to get people to fly again that they were willing to sell tickets at a loss. I knew they were having trouble with the protesters at the airports and the cruise ship docks.

So I took them up on the offer. Put in my credit card info to lock up a spot.

And only then did I find out that they weren't talking about real trips, but trips where they put you in control of a robot already there.

[Shots of surviving specimens of the first generation of crude Nene Be teletour robots, most of them about the size of a domestic cat. Even controlling them can be a chore. We see Al miming his clumsy attempts to use a phone as a physical gesture control device for the faraway robot, tapping the screen to make the robot move and shifting the phone itself about like a tiny portal to get a look at his remote surroundings.]

At first I thought about backing out and asking for my money back. I didn't even like the idea of chatting on a webcam with the kids, much less with strangers. It felt like something for young people, not me. But then I thought: why not? If I really hated it I could just hit the "disconnect" button. Not like I would be stuck overseas, right?

Because I paid so little for my ticket, they couldn't get me into Tokyo or Bangkok or Dubai; instead, I ended up in northern Japan, a tiny town called Bifuka, in Hokkaido. The robot was located at the rail station, which hardly got any passengers, a handful every week, maybe. When I arrived, it was deserted. But I liked how clean and neat it was. Made me feel at ease right away. I could tell it was a place that people loved.

[The camera shows the lone, single-room station next to the train track. The deep blue sky is dotted with sheep-like clouds. Inside, we see a table, a few stools, posters, maps, the floor swept free of all dust, a tiny skittering robot, its single-board computer guts exposed, roaming about.]

I learned to move myself about with my phone until I could climb the wall like a spider and read the Japanese posters with machine translation overlays. I bumbled my way out of the door and rolled along next to the tracks until I reached the limit of the wireless signal at the station. The view went on and on all the way to the horizon, a vastness that soothed my heart. I couldn't believe how fun it was. I giggled like a kid. I never even thought about going to Japan, and here I was.

I don't know how to explain it. After months and months of being locked up inside my house, seeing my business crumble, not being able to go anywhere, worrying about friends and neighbors dying—being there, under the sky in Japan, looking at Japanese mountains and grass and trains, that gave me hope. That did.

On the way rolling back to the station, I met a man who was about my age, just out walking. I was never the type to talk with strangers, but it felt odd to say nothing when we were the only two humans— well, human and human-in-a-bot—for miles. I didn't want to use the machine translation—didn't trust it. So I just waved an arm and said "Hello" in English. He understood that, at least, and nodded at me through the camera, saying a greeting in Japanese. We stood in the road like that, me looking up at him, him looking down at me in the screen on the robot, not knowing what else to do except smiling and waving. But it didn't feel awkward, you know? After maybe twenty seconds, he nodded and I nodded, and we parted ways.

After that, I took many jaunts, practically one every day.

[Footage of various teletours taken by Al: a busy kitchen in Yangzhou, China, where teletourists are perched on a shelf above the cooks, skittering from side to side as they watch the complicated, hours-long process for making the famous shizitou meatballs; somewhere in the Great Barrier Reef, where submersible teletour robots on fiberoptic cables can dive and observe the ecosystem with minimal impact or damage; a village in Indonesia, where a traveling shadow-puppet troupe is putting on a show not for Western tourists, but for an audience that is in sync with the story, with just a few teletour robots in the back perched on a tree, no translation, no explanation, no intervening guide; Chobe National Park in Botswana, where teletourists dangle from helium mini-airships and watch a pride of lions going about their business…

Over time, the control rig used by Al has been upgraded, allowing him to be more immersive with the teletour robots.]

I got to visit just about every country in the world, and I've met so many, many people. Teletours are different from the physical trips I took as a tourist back in the past. When I was in Thailand and Mexico, I could never feel comfortable: people were catering to me, and everything I did I couldn't stop this nagging voice in the back of my mind telling me that it was a transaction, and I needed to get my money's worth, even if that meant being petty, demanding... an ass.

With a teletour, it didn't feel like that at all. Precisely because the stakes were so much lower, it also felt, oddly, as if my host and I were more like equals, not two sides of an unbalanced coin. I'm sure that sounds naive and wishful, but it's how I feel.

I felt so good about the tours that I started hosting visitors myself.

[Footage of Al hosting jaunts at home: Al chatting with one of the cooks from the restaurant in Yangzhou as he attempts to recreate the shizitou, with the cook laughing and offering critiques; Al taking a group of teletourists fishing on a pier, the old man walking behind the row of robots and their fishing poles, advising, bantering, encouraging; Al showing two Xhong visitors how to eat a steamed lobster the New England way, struggling to describe the taste while the teletourists dined on a platter of crayfish to approximate the experience...]

Some of my hosts and guests have become my friends. I know it always seems odd to say that you can become friends with someone you've never met, but it's not just chatting through a webcam, you know? You actually *do* things together. That, to me, makes all the difference. Maybe if the President went and did things with other people he wouldn't sound so angry all the time.

[The camera pulls back to show that a teletour robot has been gliding along next to him this whole time. It's squat, cylindrical, about the size of a small lobster pot so that it could be easily transported by one person when necessary; it has wheels as well as segmented feet for all-terrain operation; a camera is perched atop, along with two manipulators; a high-resolution screen shows the face of the visitor.

Al turns to speak to the visitor in Japanese, subtitled for our benefit.]

Takahashi-san, would you like to visit the swan boats next?

[The visitor assents.]

Are there swans in Hokkaido? You must show me next time...

[Together, Al and his teletour guest stroll away toward the Public Garden lagoon in the distance.]

Statement by President Bombeo, September 3, 203X
My fellow Americans, today our great republic faces an unprecedented challenge to its pre-eminence in the world. Hostile foreign powers are emboldened while feckless allies cower and dither. However, if there's anything that history teaches us, it's that the great American nation can defeat all enemies and overcome all challenges when we are decisive and take bold action.

My administration has been distinguished from the very start by a robust, potent foreign policy. In contrast to the previous administration, I made it clear from the day I took office that no one can defy, defraud, or deceive the United States without paying a heavy price.

To secure American borders, protect American jobs, and free the American people from unwanted foreign influence, my administration closed loopholes in the immigration and visa laws, voided suspicious naturalizations, rationalized birthright citizenship, and deported numerous foreign nationals who may harbor dual loyalties. We attempted to get Congress to reenact and expand the scope of US Code Title 8, Chapter 7, though the effort was contemptibly blocked by the quisling opposition. We also drastically reduced the number of foreign students allowed to come to our great universities to study advanced technology and science—research funded by American taxpayers— only to take the knowledge back to their home countries. I specifically made it impossible for students from hostile or untrustworthy nations such as Iran, Russia, China, and many others to study in our country unless they first take an oath of loyalty to the United States. Despite the outcry from radical-left academic elites, these steps have unquestionably made America safer and stronger.

However, many of these prestigious universities, instead of faithfully carrying out my executive orders, have sought to bypass or subvert them, to the detriment of the American people. As Vice President Gossy's investigative report shows, top universities such as Harvard, MIT, and Yale all attempted to route around the restrictions. Many created so-called "remote-residency" programs that make heavy use of advanced telepresence robots. Taking advantage of the mobility, dexterity, and advanced sensors enabled by these machines, students in foreign countries can attend classes alongside American classmates, make use of expensive laboratory equipment, and even experience much of the joys of campus life. Although these foreign students are, for all intents and purposes, here on American soil, the universities argue disingenuously that visa requirements don't apply because they are simply engaged in "web-based remote learning."

But the universities are hardly the only scoundrels.

Life in America has been fundamentally transformed by ubiquitous telepresence. In the aftermath of the great pandemics of the last decade, telepresence robots helped many Americans return to work and saved our economy. A general-purpose household robot, for example, allowed nervous homeowners to receive services from cleaners, electricians, plumbers, hairdressers, piano teachers, and so on without having to let strangers enter the house. Moreover, the robots could be programmed to limit their operators' movements inside the house via geofencing and audit trails of actions performed. The social distancing enabled by telepresence saved many American workers from economic ruin.

But today, many of the remote operators you permit to inhabit your household robots are not Americans at all, but foreigners stealing

American jobs without even leaving their own houses. Companies, greedy for profit, have shirked their patriotic duty. The gains we've made by reducing and regulating immigration have been lost through telepresence, with real Americans suffering the consequences.

Moreover, teletourists from abroad, without having to pass through comprehensive vetting at ports of entry or during the visa process, now visit America in greater numbers every year. Although teletour bots open to operation by foreign visitors are in principle subject to strict regulation that prevents their operators from wandering outside of specific designated tourist zones, enforcement is spotty, and many teletour bots owned by small consumer-providers are exempt.

Thus, our streets today are clogged with foreigners embodied in robots, subject to little surveillance or control. It defies common sense to think that these foreign operatives in disguise would not poison our public discourse with unfiltered foreign propaganda. After repeated demands from me and Vice President Gossy, our intelligence services have uncovered vast and sophisticated attempts by foreign states to influence American policy and elections. For example, the PNA sent waves of teletourists to describe alleged conditions in Palestine to the American people in February this year, in advance of the planned peace summit, and Chinese trolls disguised as ordinary tourists flooded the District of Columbia in June to participate in the "Million-Bot March" against our deployment of advanced tactical nuclear weapons in the Pacific. Indeed, the recent waves of demonstrations by anti-war radicals in California and New York appear to have been directed and amplified by Russian intelligence using hired teletourists from around the world.

Despite this clear and present danger to our democracy, my attempts at regulating the speech of teletourists have consistently been rebuffed by the courts. My order that all teletour robots be equipped with a filter that automatically refused to translate or silenced utterances of ideas and phrases not compatible with American interests has been voided by extremist left-wing judges defying my constitutional authority. They appear to hold the mistaken notion that foreigners, present in the United States only by remotely operating a robot, somehow enjoy the same God-given constitutional rights as real Americans. The very idea is absurd. This is especially so when regimes like China have erected virtual walls that make it extremely difficult for American citizens to take jaunts into China. We cannot remain open when our enemies do not extend us the same courtesy.

Thus, in order to protect American jobs from unfair foreign competition, to defend our technological secrets from foreign spies, to ensure that our citizens are not subjected to foreign propaganda delivered in the guise of teletourism, I am issuing an executive order that immediately bans all attempts to connect to telepresence robots within the United States from abroad. Secretary Narro will have the details.

Don't tread on us.

God Bless America.

Factchecking Notes on President Bombeo's Statement by Teletourists Without Borders, September 3, 203X

(39) "Thus, our streets are clogged with foreigners embodied in robots..."

According to the Association of Teletourism Providers, the largest US-based trade organization for the industry, foreign-based teletourists were only 3.4% of the total number of teletourists in the US last year. According to JauntsNow, less than 5% of the jaunts booked on US-based teletour robots last year were from addresses abroad. In any event, it seems clear that the vast majority of jaunts in the US are taken by other Americans.

(43) "[O]ur intelligence services have uncovered vast and sophisticated

attempts by foreign states to influence American policy and elections..."

The President's examples of bot-swarms by foreign nations attempting to influence American politics have been well-publicized, but there is considerable skepticism among security experts because the reports were produced by the spy agencies under intense political pressure and thus considered not entirely reliable. The President also failed to note some other instances of foreign-sponsored bot-swarms that may have been more in line with his preferred policies (see below). Thus, the picture he presented is misleading.

— The bot-swarm in support of Myanmar's government when Congress contemplated sanctions against officials in Nay Pyi Taw for persecuting ethnic minorities. The officials in question enjoy a close relationship with President Bombeo, and multiple researchers have concluded that the demonstration involved protesters-for-hire purchased in the Philippines.

— The bot-swarm in support of President Bombeo's decision to reject the findings of the United Nations Human Rights Council against Saudi Arabia. Multiple researchers have concluded that the demonstrators were using a semi-open relay known to be closely associated with ascendant members of the ruling family.

(45) "Indeed, the recent waves of demonstrations by anti-war radicals in California and New York appear to have been directed and amplified by Russian intelligence using hired teletourists from around the world."

The report from a privately funded DC think tank that a large number of demonstrators were Russian operatives controlling multiple bots has been dismissed by most security researchers as based on flawed metrics and over-aggressive machine-classification algorithms. The lead authors of that report are also known for arguing that the Black Lives Matter protests from the last decade were instigated by Chinese and Russian trolls, a position that has been comprehensively debunked.

(47) "My order that all teletour robots be equipped with a filter…"
The President failed to make it clear that his order not only applied to foreign teletourists, but also could potentially be applied to American citizens and permanent residents using telepresence robots as well.

README.txt

Nene Huddle is a high-performance, privacy-first, adaptively structured, peer-to-peer network to facilitate anonymous, hard-to-trace connections between telepresence robots and operators.

Running the Nene Huddle software turns your machine into a pylon (essentially a node) on the Huddle network. The pylons communicate with one another through encrypted channels that are constantly multiplexed and switched to defeat attempts at tracing metadata. The ultimate goal of the network is to enable operators anywhere in the world to connect to telepresence endpoints without leaving a traceable record linking any individual operator with any individual endpoint.

It is primarily useful for getting around the restrictions various states have imposed on inbound and outbound telepresence connections. For instance, if you don't live in the United States or one of its four "Deep Trust Allies," then currently the only way to take a jaunt into the US without going through the onerous and Orwellian televisa process is routing yourself through the Nene Huddle network. It is also one of the only avenues left to enter China without giving up all your data at the border.

Note, however, that the Nene Huddle network doesn't directly provide any consumer-oriented functionality such as searching for open telepresence endpoints, advertising to jaunt customers, paying to use open endpoints, disguising yourself as a domestic teletourist on

JauntsNow, and so on. You'll have to use other applications built on top of Nene Huddle.

It is already confirmed or at least very likely that running the Nene Huddle software is considered illegal by authorities in countries such as the United States, Russia, India, China, Saudi Arabia, and the United Kingdom (the list of such states is growing). Before installing and joining the movement, weigh your risks carefully. It is simply a fact of life that freedom requires you to be ready to pay a price, to have skin in the game.

Frequently Asked Questions

Who makes Nene Huddle?
Volunteers who have made it a point to not know one another's identities.

Why do you do this?
There is no way to answer this question for everyone who has contributed to the project. By design, we don't know one another's real names, real jobs, real nationalities, real motivations, anything at all, really.

Based on posts in the project forum, the most popular (self-reported) reasons for people to contribute to this project are:

— Dislike of the actions or policies of the United States/China/ Russia/India/Saudi Arabia/the UK/some other country
— Freedom of movement, including telepresence, is a fundamental human right
— The world is a better place when people can move around and get to know one another and teach one another—telepresence is the best way to do that without polluting and ruining the planet
— The world is a better place when people stay where they are and

stop crossing borders and trying to change how other people live—telepresence is the best way to do that without turning everyone into a prisoner or forcing them to starve for lack of economic opportunities

— It's fun to mess with governments and see politicians' heads explode

How can I trust the software?

By reading the source code. That's it.

As you can see from the answers to the last question, the self-reported reasons for why volunteers contribute code here are often mutually contradictory, as is the case with all leaderless, distributed movements.

Is it possible that there is code in here from PLA hackers in Beijing?

Of course.

Is it possible that the CIA has contributed?

Yep.

Is it possible that—

Let me just stop you there. Yes, yes, and yes.

Every state thinks there's a way it can turn Nene Huddle to its own advantage; spies, like everyone else, want to jaunt. Nation-states' self-interest and mutual suspicion redound to our benefit: no other open-source project has received as much adversarial code review and scrutiny. Out of swords, secure telepresence tunnels.

Still, you can't trust people's motivations, only the result. Read the code, verify for yourself that it's safe to run. You have the freedom, which means you have the responsibility.

Doesn't your software facilitate crime/enable money laundering/hurt democracy/perpetuate imperialism…?

You're asking the wrong question.

All right, maybe this is worth elaborating a little more.

Is it true that people can use the network to do terrible things? Without a doubt. But that's true of any technology. (However, every single instance where the United States claimed that our network facilitated terrorism—so far at least—has turned out to be a lie.)

What do *you* want to do with Nene Huddle?

In a world where borders are increasingly impenetrable, Nene Huddle is often the only way for us to remain together. Those with skills but no markets at home use it to secure for themselves and their loved ones a better life. Students, scholars, and researchers use it to find the collegiality and inspiration that feed invention and free thought. Journalists use it to tunnel into oppressive countries to get the facts and shoot footage that can't be obtained any other way. Activists from across the world use it to bot-swarm protests in the US because American policies have a disproportionate impact on the rest of the world even though most of us don't get to vote in their elections. Religious leaders who have been forbidden to speak at home can preach abroad through telepresence. Individuals who are not free to date, love, express their own identities at home can live the lives they wish to live remotely through a long-jaunt tether, a literal lifeline.

Every technology that begins in the hope for freedom eventually risks being co-opted by centralized power. Telepresence was originally a way to allow people to move more freely without the costs associated with transporting physical bodies. It has also, over time, turned out to be a great way for those in power to regulate and control the exchange of ideas and peoples.

The only way to oppose centralized power is to become its very opposite: distributed, leaderless, inventive, formless. If you want your freedoms back, don't count on a wise leader to save you. Join us.

Download. Encrypt. Jaunt.

FULL BLOOD

Owl Goingback

CHEROKEE *creation myths claim that people and animals originally came from a sky world, a place called Galun'lati, long ago when the Earth was still new. Some say this sky world was located in a star cluster often called the Seven Sisters, known to modern astronomers as the Pleiades. But it does not matter where they came from for the Cherokees are no more, their legends and ceremonies just fading memories, their people mere shadows upon the land.*

For over a thousand years, the Hopi lived in the tiny, isolated village of Oraibi, on Third Mesa in Arizona, farming the parched ground and offering prayers to Kachina spirits in sacred underground Kivas. But those prayers are no longer spoken for the Hopi are all gone, their adobe cities as silent as the desert that surrounds them.

The Lakota once ruled the Black Hills of South Dakota, mighty warriors who fought and hunted buffalo on horseback, sacrificing their flesh in offerings to the Great Spirit at the annual sundance. But the men no longer dance; the eagle bone whistles now silent, the only sound to

*be heard the moaning of the wind as it blows across rolling prairie and
empty reservations.*

*Kiowa, Seneca, Crow, and Choctaw, names of once proud Indian
nations now just words in the faded pages of history books. There were
more, so many more, hundreds of tribes, thousands of people, falling
first to pandemic sickness, and later hunted down and decimated, lambs
to the slaughter, not by soldiers in blue coats but by a nightmare far
more ancient.*

Buddy Nakai always thought the world would end with a flash and a bang,
a thunderclap of the gods and a fiery comet, or asteroid, sent down to
destroy every living thing on Turtle Island. He imagined people running
and screaming, begging for the Creator's forgiveness, while he sat on
the roof of his family's hogan, on the Navajo reservation in northern
Arizona, watching the shit go down, with an ice-cold beer in his hand.

But the world had not ended in heaven-sent Fourth of July fireworks,
or nuclear explosions arriving on shiny, silver missiles from China or
Russia, as the survivalists always predicted. Nor did the final days
come from terrorist attacks carried out by radical militants from
impoverished Middle Eastern countries.

He wiped a weathered hand across his face, feeling the tiredness
slowly start to creep over him. He had already drunk half of the coffee
in his thermos, but it did little to fend off the fatigue. His eyes hurt
from staring into the darkness, and the muscles in his neck were
knotted cords.

Reaching under his long, black hair, he massaged his neck,
attempting to relieve the tightness. He was only in his late thirties,
far too young to feel so old, but knew the stiffness in his neck would
slowly move down his spine and settle into his lower back as the night
went on. Sitting on a rickety lawn chair, perched atop an uneven
roof, did not help the situation, nor did holding a heavy hunting rifle
for hours, looking through the scope to search the darkness.

He lifted the rifle off his lap, placing the wooden stock against his shoulder, sighting again through the hi-power scope.

"Come on. I know you're out there. Show yourself."

He swung the rifle to the left, and then back to the right, feeling the tiny muscles in the back of his neck scream for mercy. But he saw nothing out of the ordinary, only cacti, scrub brush, rocks, and acres of sand. Just the stillness of the night; nothing moved.

As far as Buddy knew, he was the only human being for miles. A solitary gunman in a vast, uncaring, and often hostile, desert wilderness. Completely alone, like *Robinson Crusoe on Mars*.

"At least he had his Friday, and a fucking monkey," Buddy said out loud, angry, remembering scenes from the 1964 science fiction movie. "I've got no one."

He could not remember how long it had been since he last spoke to someone. Certainly months. Maybe even a year. The total isolation messed with his mind, made all the days blend together and seem like one. He didn't have a calendar to check off the days, and there was no cell phone signal in the middle of the desert. He had a portable radio, but he had smashed it to pieces when the batteries died, the voice of a distant announcer fading out into silence.

"What I wouldn't give to talk with someone. Anyone. Doesn't have to be an attractive woman. Or even another Navajo. Just a living, breathing person to keep me from—"

Somewhere in the distance an owl called out in the darkness. He smiled, comforted to know that he wasn't completely alone. A nocturnal raptor watched over the desert, a feathered brother in arms. Maybe it had called out to its mate. Or perhaps the owl also just wanted someone to talk with.

"I hear you, little brother. Sentry duty is a boring business."

Buddy lowered the rifle, blinking to clear his blurred vision. More than anything he wanted to go home and sleep in his own bed again, but his home was over a hundred miles away. And his single-wide trailer's thin aluminum walls and glass windows offered little in the way of protection.

So, he had come to his grandfather's hogan on the Navajo reservation in Arizona, unoccupied since the old man's death; the primitive, windowless building of heavy logs and mud offering isolation and much better protection in a world gone mad. And each and every night since his arrival he climbed onto the roof, rifle in hand, and searched the darkness, waiting.

Movement in the sky above him caught his attention. Buddy looked up, watching as the International Space Station made its familiar trek across the heavens, looking like a bright, unblinking star against an ebony sea.

When he was a little boy, the elders told him that the world as he knew it would end shortly after mankind put a house in the sky. They said the Hopi people of Third Mesa possessed a set of stone tablets, called the Hopi Prophecies, warning of three "great shakings" that would take place in modern times. The first two shakings had already occurred, World Wars I and II, and the third would happen in his lifetime.

"Guess I should have paid more attention to my elders."

He studied the space station as it continued its journey across the blackness, knowing it was now nothing more than a flying mausoleum. The inhabitants, four men and two women, died long ago, abandoned and forgotten by nations facing much bigger problems here on Earth.

If mankind does not learn to live as brothers and sisters, then it will be as if the Great Spirit takes hold of the Earth and gives it a shake.

He remembered his grandfather telling him about the Hopi Prophecies, and could almost imagine the old man looking up at him from the empty room below with an all-knowing smile on his face. When his grandfather died, the family had cut a hole in the wall so his spirit would not be trapped inside the hogan; they had also put the dead man's shoes on the wrong feet to confuse his ghost, just in case it decided to walk back home.

"You were right, Grandfather." Buddy reached down and grabbed his thermos. Twisting off the cap, he took a sip of strong, black coffee. "We should have listened; the third shaking has come true."

It started slow, with a few people getting sick in a far-off country. Nobody in the United States cared; they were far too busy making money, bragging on Facebook, posting stupid videos on TikTok, and trying to keep up with the latest trend. But the virus had spread, mutated, crossed international borders at an alarming rate, taking thousands of lives. Some said it escaped from a secret military laboratory; others claimed it to be the cleansing hand of God come to punish the wicked. People panicked and grew angry, neighbor turned against neighbor. On the reservations, tribal leaders and elders called their people home to safety.

In the United States the pandemic became a political tool, adding to the problems of an already shaky nation. The famed melting pot boiled over, flames of anger and outrage spilling into the streets, exposing the racist muck lining the bottom of the cauldron. Buildings burned and sabers rattled, angry voices lifting into the night.

Millions died in hospitals and makeshift intensive care units, without family or friends to hold their hands, their final breath filled with the despair of loneliness.

The owl called out again, closer than before, louder. It was moving, flying on silent wings as it hunted.

"Fuck!"

Buddy Nakai quickly recapped his thermos, setting it down beside him. He stood up, bringing the rifle to his shoulder, looking through the scope and searching for movement in the darkness.

Owls were silent hunters; they did not cry out when stalking their prey. Which meant what he heard might not be an owl.

"Where are you? Show yourself."

The cry of the owl fell silent, replaced by a *tik-tik-tik* sound.

Buddy felt the skin at his temples pull tight, his eyes watering in fear. He blinked rapidly several times, forcing the moisture from his eyes, and sighted back through the scope.

At first, he saw nothing, only desert, but then something passed in front of his scope's view. He saw it for only an instant, a blurred shadow moving fast.

Buddy swept the rifle to his right, panicked, trying to find what he had seen. It was in flight, but still far away. How far? One hundred meters? Two?

Damnit. Find it.

The pandemic swept through the world killing millions, knocking powerful nations to their knees. The World Health Organization and the CDC panicked. Thousands of doctors and scientists scrambled to find a cure, but every time a vaccine was created a new variant reared its ugly head. Many began to believe it really was the apocalypse.

And then hope appeared on the horizon. On a tiny, remote Philippine island off the southern tip of Mindanao, a village was discovered whose people were completely immune to all the deadly variants of the virus. Descended from three original families, their immune systems contained antibodies known nowhere else in the world.

Scientists hastened to the isolated settlement *en masse*, testing, probing, taking blood samples. The labs worked around the clock to identify and cultivate the antibodies in the blood of these simple villagers, creating a vaccine effective against all existing strains of the disease.

In less than a year, a super vaccine had been created and rushed through testing. And unlike before, during the Covid crisis, it was embraced by the population. Even the hardcore anti-vaxxers rolled up their sleeves to be inoculated. They too were tired of seeing relatives and loved ones die, and just wanted the world to return to how things were before the pandemic.

There. To the left.

Buddy saw it again in his scope's view. Too big to be an owl, with wings of leathery skin instead of feathers.

"Damn." He felt his breath catch in his chest, fear digging icy claws into his guts. His hands started to shake, making his aim unsteady.

Definitely not an owl.

The night flier must have seen him too, for it turned and flew straight at him. Buddy could see it clearly in his scope's field of view, its body illuminated by the bright light of a full moon. Like the others he had encountered it had no legs; just an upper torso attached to two powerful wings, its spine hanging down like the boney tail of a macabre kite.

He flipped off the safety and took a deep breath, let out a little air, tightened the rifle against his shoulder, and prayed to the Great Spirit for a clean shot.

The Seminoles died deep in the swamps of south Florida, hiding in the Everglades with the alligators and mosquitos. Even their wealth and casinos did not save them, their Hard Rock Hotels and Cafes as empty as their reservation homes.

Fifty yards and closing fast, flying low to the ground, barely clearing the sage brush and cacti.

Buddy squeezed the trigger and the 30-06 Springfield rifle roared with anger, the brilliant muzzle flash turning darkness into day.

The inhabitants of the small Philippine island south of Mindanao were members of a primitive tribe, and a far more ancient race. So desperate to find a cure, none of the scientists who descended on the tribe thought to research the people whose blood they took. They did not know about the folklore and stories associated with that particular village, never questioned why the residents of the mainland dared not go there at night. They had never heard of an *aswang*, had not considered there might be things in this world far worse than a pandemic.

The one-hundred-eighty grain, full-metal-jacket bullet exited the barrel of Buddy's rifle at supersonic speed, reaching a velocity of two-thousand-seven-hundred feet per second as it sliced through the night air, slamming into the aswang like a runaway freight train.

The bullet hit the creature in the chest, stopping all forward momentum and sending it tumbling backward to crash into the baked earth. It rolled down behind a small hill, disappearing from view.

Fuck. Where is it? Where did it go?

Buddy kept his eye to the scope, watching as he pulled the rifle's bolt backward and ejected the spent cartridge. The smoking brass casing bounced off the roof of the hogan, landing somewhere on the ground below. He pushed the bolt forward, slipping a new round into the chamber.

He knew he had hit the creature. His grandfather's Springfield was a reliable weapon, and he rarely missed. Still, he focused on the small hill through the scope just in case the aswang somehow survived.

Several minutes passed, and he was about to lower the Springfield and sit back down when he spotted movement south of the hill.

"Damn!"

The aswang flew at him fast, arms outstretched and fingers hooked into deadly claws, sounding like a large clock.

Tik...Tik...Tik...

Buddy did not have time to fire another shot; it was already on top of him. Instead, he swung the rifle's heavy wooden stock with all his might, hitting the aswang in the face and keeping its deadly fangs away from his throat.

The force of his swing, and the rifle's impact with the creature, caused Buddy to fall backward, crashing into his lawn chair and flipping over it, landing on his hands and knees.

He got quickly to his feet, looking around. He was alone on top of the hogan, but he was not out of danger.

Buddy heard scratching, the sound of long claws digging into the wood as something pulled itself up the side of the house. Coming closer, coming for him.

Tik...Tik...Tik...TIK...TIK...

He stood terrified, waiting for the aswang to appear over the side of the hogan.

Who would have believed a breed of vampires existed in the Philippines, especially when they looked like normal people during the day? Certainly not the scientists who collected aswang blood, using it to create a vaccine, infecting half the world's population and turning them into bloodsuckers. They never stopped to wonder why the islanders were immune to the pandemic, and had never heard the legends and folklore about vampires who detached from their lower torsos and flew through the night on leathery wings with their spines hanging down.

The vaccine had indeed stopped the virus, but it had also turned millions of people into shapeshifting vampires who fed on the rest of the population.

The ticking sound stopped, a strained silence falling over the area. Buddy wasn't fooled. He knew the creature had reached the roof and hung there listening, trying to determine his location. The aswang could smell the blood coursing through his veins, and probably hung there enjoying the fragrance. He could hear the damn thing sniffing in the dark.

"Come on, you fucker. Show yourself. Let's get this over with. It's getting late."

Buddy felt the rifle growing heavy in his hands. He was exhausted, tired of running and fighting, sick of standing watch each and every night; weary of being isolated and so completely alone. One way or another, he wanted the nightmare to end.

The wings appeared first. Black and leathery, they were barely visible in the darkness. Each must have been six feet long when fully outstretched, big enough to carry the upper torso to which they attached.

The creature's hands appeared next, long deadly fingernails digging into the wooden logs and pulling the vampire up onto the roof.

At first, the aswang clung to the edge of the roof, looking up at him. Then it flapped its ebony wings, lifting into the air, hovering eight feet above the hogan. The vampire's spine hung down from its upper torso twitching like the tail of a jungle cat about to pounce.

Buddy shifted the weight of the rifle, holding it in his right hand. He held out his left arm to the creature, offering his wrist.

"You want this. Don't you, bitch? You can smell my blood."

The aswang was female, long black hair blowing in the night wind. She wore no clothing, and he could see her breasts; two wrinkled, leathery sacks covering boney ribs. Above her left breast a bullet wound was clearly visible. Blood, black as witch's bile, spilled down her chest and over her stomach.

But the bullet had only wounded, and not killed. He had dipped each and every one of the cartridges into the holy water he kept in his canteen, taken from a Spanish mission in New Mexico. The baptized bullets had always worked in the past, he had killed dozens of aswang, but maybe God's elixir had a shelf life and the magic only lasted so long.

The aswang licked her lips with a long, proboscis tongue and smiled at him. Buddy wondered how many infants still in the womb the creature had fed upon; a shudder of revulsion passed through him, for he knew from the horrors he had witnessed that unborn fetuses were a special delight to the bloodsuckers.

She licked her lips again, slowly and with great relish, and inhaled deeply, smelling his blood.

The Osage, Creek, Blackfoot, Arapaho, and Comanche were no more. Like the members of a hundred other indigenous tribes, they had been hunted down and slaughtered, their blood considered a delicacy to the aswang, a rare vintage consumed until there was no more.

Buddy was the last Navajo, the last full blood; he knew that. He had seen the empty reservations, home now to only ghosts.

The aswang hissed and rose higher above him, her eyes shining with the brightness of the moon's glow, insatiable hunger etched upon thin, cruel lips.

Buddy raised his rifle with both hands, not even bothering to sight through the scope.

"Come and get some."

The aswang attacked; the rifle fired. The bullet struck the creature between the eyes, its head exploding in a crimson cloud of blood, brains, and bone fragments.

It fell at Buddy's feet, wings flapping wildly, muscles twitching and jerking, blood spewing from what was left of its head. Then the aswang grew still, gave a final hissing sigh, and died.

No need for holy water when you separate a vampire's head from its shoulders.

The crack of the rifle shot echoed across the desert, then faded out. But the silence lasted only moments, replaced by a familiar sound coming from a dozen different directions.

Tik...Tik...Tik...

Buddy Nakai raised the rifle to his shoulder and peered through the scope. He could see them clearly in the moonlight, dozens of aswangs racing toward him drawn by the sound of the gunshot, and the smell of the rare liquid coursing through his veins, hungry to taste the last full-blooded Indian.

Tik...Tik...TIK...TIK...TIK...

Buddy laughed and slid another round into the chamber of his rifle. It was a good day to die.

THE BLIND HOUSE

Ramsey Campbell

"Now we know we don't write dialogue like this, don't we?"

"I couldn't say what you do, Mr Eliot."

"So we're going to have to fix it, aren't we?"

"Maybe you are. You can leave me out of it. I already wrote the book."

He didn't need to like the novel or its author, not that he'd ever met or even spoken to the fellow. Presumably there had to be an audience for the story of a writer so convinced translators were changing his work that he set about murdering them, but the introverted fancy made Eliot feel shut inside himself. Even the punctuation—dashes introducing every utterance, and not a solitary quotation mark—struck him as self-regarding. He would have directed the computer to replace every dash, but too many had a different function. He'd begun to highlight the offending punctuation and invoke the publisher's house style in a speech balloon alongside every yellow mark—the margin had started to resemble a comic strip awaiting pictures—when his phone rang. "Tracie Latimer," it said.

His response wasn't much less automatic. "Tracie."

"Am I interrupting, Simon? Shall I call you back?"

"There's just me here. Busy, that's all."

"It was only that you didn't sound like your usual self."

"Well, I'm that and nothing else."

Her trait was playing on his nerves—the way she hummed almost inaudibly while she listened to an answer. "Working from home still agrees with you, then," she said.

"I wish I'd gone for it sooner."

"Don't get too used to being on your own, will you? Nobody ought to be. Let me know whenever you're due in town next and we can have a drink."

He'd needed several last time they went drinking at the Gutenberg, his celebration of leaving his desk, which had been within earshot of hers in the publisher's extensive office. "Was that why you phoned?" he confined himself to asking.

"I just wanted to check you've had Tom Proudling's novel from me."

"That's what I'm working on right now. Should have emailed."

"No need to apologise. It's always good to talk."

He hadn't sought to apologise. The truncated observation had been aimed at her. "How are you finding it?" she said.

"Looks like a lot of work."

"I'm sure he did plenty." Before Eliot could decide whether this was a genuine misunderstanding, Tracie said "Enjoy it all you can and call me any time you need to."

He didn't foresee that, and returning to London tempted him even less—the risk of encountering Linc, an editor whose vegetarian breaths verged on compost, or Hervey, who would pin his listener at their desk with a hand like a sponge squeezed imperfectly dry, a memory Eliot's shoulder shrugged off with a squirm. He preferred his fellow tenants, not that he saw much of them, even those who shared the middle floor with him. The thought inspired him to venture out of his room. "Don't even think of going anywhere," he told Proudling's novel.

As he stepped into the corridor, where the dimness stained the walls the same dull brown as the carpet, he saw Miss Maitland shuffling towards him. He could have fancied that the landlady had been waiting on the stairs for any of her tenants to appear. "Mr Eliot," she said, the only sound in the house apart from her muffled approach, "may I have a word?"

"As many as you like."

"That's never many." The blink she gave him looked as if her heavy eyelids were about to shut her inside her small face, which resembled tissue paper partly uncrumpled. "How have you found yourself settling in?"

"I'm sure it's what I needed."

"You're attuned to our way of life."

"I expect you could say so."

"I only ask because your room rather stands out at the moment."

She was using more words than she'd led him to anticipate, though her effort multiplied her wrinkles. "Shouldn't it?" he said, but her weary blink made him add "How is it?"

"I was outside and I saw your blind is raised."

All this sounded like an account of an uncommon if not unwelcome event. "Will that be a problem?" Eliot said.

"Do you really want people to spy on your life?"

"I shouldn't think there's much to see." When this only slowed her eyelids down he said "I quite like the sun."

"You won't be seeing much of it just now." A grey November was indeed padding the sky. "I'm sure you'll decide when you're ready," she said and turned away before he could respond.

Once the stairs jerked her head out of sight he couldn't hear her, not even her door downstairs. He hoped his bathroom sounds were as discreet. At least he never had to wait to use it, even in the mornings when some of his fellow tenants presumably needed to get ready to go out to work, unless they all worked at home. He wondered how much their rooms resembled his—how little space they'd found they needed. There was no reason to hoard books when you could read them on the computer, which provided films and music too. Perhaps soon everyone would live like him.

The landlady had left him trying to identify when if ever he'd looked up at his window. Now might be the time to fetch next week's groceries and other items while the supermarket was unlikely to be crowded. "Don't start imagining I've finished with you," he murmured as he shut the computer down.

The first chill drops of a shower met his face as he stepped out of the boxy porch. He crossed the road and turned to face the house. Every window except his was blank with pallid plastic. Otherwise the house and its counterpart opposite might have been mutual reflections. His computer was visible to any passing thief, but did Eliot need to worry? The front door and his own were locked, and any bid to break in ought to produce the loudest sounds in the house. The shower was expanding into vicious rain, which could be his excuse to order produce online, a facility he kept meaning to try. As he dashed back across the road, a slat of the landlady's blind described a curve like a grin before snapping into place.

"I know you're there," he warned Proudling's novel as he set about ordering groceries, and soon enough he was alone with the document again. An afternoon of changing punctuation left him with the fancy that the dashes might have gathered in his brain like a code so secret it was incomprehensible to anything outside itself. To his exhausted eyes the screen appeared to have grown dimmer. While he microwaved a supermarket curry he tried to think if he'd ever smelled cooking except his own anywhere in the house. Perhaps his neighbours opened their windows, though he'd never heard anyone do so. If his aromas bothered anybody, they ought to be able to tell him.

After dinner he watched an action film, the kind you were advised to watch on the biggest screen you could. He had to admit the computer cramped it, while the headphones made the frequent explosions feel like bids to blast a way out of his skull. Had the detonations deafened him? The house felt stuffed with silence when he headed for the bathroom. He turned the doorknob, a brass cube that felt like spiky ice, only to find the door was locked.

Although he always listened before he left his room, he'd heard nobody in the corridor. Peering through the dwarfish window, he was just able to distinguish beyond the barely translucent globules a figure craning so far over the sink that their face must be close to touching the mirror. They might well catch sight of him in it, and he retreated to his room, where he loitered just inside until he thought they must have vacated the bathroom. While he hadn't heard them on the move, the bathroom was as deserted as the corridor, though the moist imprint of a forehead was fading from the mirror.

He was in bed and sinking into sleep when someone came home drunk, unless they had been drinking in their room, since there had been no sound of the front door. They were groping their way along the corridor, both hands slithering over the wall of Eliot's room— surely just their hands, not their body or their face, though the blurred halting noise was large enough for all. When the doorknob rattled, Eliot was glad he'd locked the door. The fumbling faltered onwards until the bathroom door shut, a repeated uncertain sound, at which point Eliot was withdrawing into sleep.

By lunchtime he finished infecting the novel with yellow— disinfecting it, he told himself—and emailed the result to Tracie Latimer. He thought she might email him while he waited for his groceries, but the phone roused him from resting his hands on his face. "Well, Simon," she said in a tone he failed to place. "You've gone to town."

"No, I'm at home."

"On Tom's novel. I wonder if you missed the point."

"Maybe you should tell me what you think that is."

"You've taken all the European dashes out."

"Yes, because that's not your house style."

"I believe Tom may have meant it to be an expressive device. I'll consult and let you know. We're here to serve our authors, do the best for them we can."

Eliot might have argued if the doorbell hadn't rung. He leaned over the desk to see a nondescript colourless van speeding into the distance so fast he could have thought someone had played a childish prank. "They've brought my food," he said. "I need to go down."

"Aren't you even going out to shop? I hope you don't mind if I—"

He was glad his first step into the corridor broke the connection. The phone had coverage just in his room. A bag labelled with his name and address was slouching in the porch. As he hefted the groceries up the stairs, the treads emitted creaks like notes in an atonal wooden composition, which made him wish he weren't causing so much noise. At least the delivery was one less reason to leave his room for a week.

His guarded footsteps in the corridor were compensating for the loudness of the stairs when he heard his next-door neighbour in her room. He took her to be talking on a phone, since he had yet to see a single visitor in the house. Even if Miss Maitland hadn't explicitly forbidden them, he felt they would be unwelcome. He had a grotesque notion that to preserve her privacy his neighbour had a hand over her mouth. It wasn't a conversation, it was a monologue with scarcely a pause for breath. While he couldn't distinguish a word, there was no mistaking her desperation. He pressed his ear against the wall and then the door, but her protests were no clearer. Should he knock and find out what was wrong? He didn't want to be regarded as a busybody, still less to be caught eavesdropping, and he tiptoed swiftly to his room.

A new book for correction had arrived on his computer, but he felt entitled to a break after the Proudling task. He was in the midst of a Mozart symphony—the headphones planted him on the rostrum— when his phone displayed Tracie's name. He laid the headphones on the desk, where a microscopic orchestra continued its invisible performance. "Tom isn't too impressed," Tracie said.

"So long as you are."

Was she trying to hum along with the orchestra? He couldn't really hear either of them, and had to strain to catch her words. "It isn't that straightforward, Simon. We need to respect his intentions."

"What's he telling you they are?"

"As I thought, we're meant to see the punctuation's wrong."

"I saw."

"But not to change it. He's making us experience what his character experiences. The way people change his writing changes him."

"Are you asking me to put all the dashes back?"

"Unless you want me to pass the job to someone else."

Even if this sounded like an offer, Eliot suspected it wouldn't be the only job she'd send elsewhere. "I'll start now," he said. "I'll get it done."

"No absolute rush, so do give yourself breaks when you need them. You sound as if you could use some. Maybe go out for a walk."

"I can't be sounding like I am, then." The notion made him feel his words weren't reaching far enough. "I'm fine where I am," he said.

He was bringing up the document she sent him when he wondered why she couldn't just have deleted his markings and the attendant comments. Presumably she didn't think it was her job. As he set about erasing the yellow blots, which looked as if the punctuation had stained the pages, and the equally numerous balloons swarming with quotation marks, he had a sense of reviving if not aggravating the introversion of the novel. Whenever he felt the need to take one of the breaks Tracie seemed to have imposed on him, he could only rest his gaze on the unrewarding view across the road. Since it consisted just of houses with windows as blank as the sunless sky—certainly no sign of life—why not shut it out for good? He left the blind raised in the hope of catching the sun out, even though the dull glare of the day made it harder to read the screen, but his wish remained a wish.

Despite its name, tonight's curry tasted much like its predecessor. Once he'd done it all the justice it deserved he watched the first sequel to last night's film. It pretty well repeated the events, and he found the familiarity comforting. The screen no longer looked too small for the film—the images were inside his skull, which could give them all the space they needed—and the headphones made his head feel snug. The streetlamps outside had been broken since he could remember, and there were no lights beyond any of the blinds across the road: nothing at all to distract him.

He was heading for the bathroom when his neighbour opened her door. Had she injured herself? As soon as she saw him she dodged back into her room, but he thought she was wearing an eyepatch no less pale than her face—than the blinds at all the windows. Her door shut with a thud that suggested she'd fallen against it, but Eliot heard no more, even when he listened outside her room before making for bed.

Daylight like a distillation of the plastic at the window wakened him. He wasn't too eager to open his eyes, no doubt because Proudling's novel scarcely tempted him to leave his bed. Wasn't that necessary when the rent was due? No, he'd set up a direct debit online. The sooner he dealt with the novel, the sooner he could move on to, he hoped, a more rewarding task. Once he'd prised his eyelids wide he did his best not to disturb the silence of the house while he was in the bathroom. He felt as if the shower was falling short of his senses, sealing him into himself. Cereal and fierce black coffee went some way towards readying him for the computer, where he poked out his tongue at the novel, not so much in derision as to limber his lips up for speech. "Back again," he mumbled. "Let's get it right this time."

"I'd say I already had."

"Depends which of us you think you are."

"There's only one of us, and that's all there's going to be."

He wanted to believe that erasing all the yellow splotches would cure him of the book rather than infest his brain with the dashes he'd released. "On your way," he told the novel as he emailed it to Tracie Latimer. "Now leave me alone." All he wanted was her response, but he supposed she was waiting to hear from the author. At least there was no need for Eliot to deal with him.

While dinner didn't call itself a curry, it was just as much of one as last night's meal. The third film in the series he felt required to watch was yet more explosive, but even with the sound turned up the spectacle felt remote, pressed flat by the screen. Why did he need to watch? It wasn't his job, after all. He saw the film through to the end, but in bed he found nothing was more welcome than silence.

A fly robbed him of the comfort of the dark. The unseasonable insect was buzzing and bumbling about on the far side of the room. Eliot wasn't going to leave his bed or open his eyes either. As he attempted to recapture sleep he realised the sounds weren't in his room. If they were beyond the wall, how could he hear them? His neighbour was making the noises, stumbling drunkenly around her room and emitting a complaint that seemed to have left words behind. Eliot had to force his voice out of his reluctant mouth. "Everything all right there?" he called, so loud it startled him, and the noises stopped at once.

Any further activity left him asleep. Daylight failed to rouse him, and a phone in the next room took its time. Had he ever heard a ringtone except his own in the house? Apparently his neighbour used the same as his. No, he was hearing his own, however muffled the trills sounded. He floundered away from the bed, prying his eyes open with both hands, and fumbled the phone out of the heap of clothes on the chair. The screen showed him that the phone must have announced Tracie Latimer before he woke. "Yes," he said once he managed to part his clamped lips.

"Sorry, Simon, were you busy?"

"Asleep."

"Sorry twice, then. I expect you've earned it. Are you with us now?"

"Just me."

At least his new terseness gave her less chance to hum. "I've heard from Tom Proudling," she said.

"And?"

"He wants me to pass on his thanks for showing him where he went wrong."

"Good."

"It's not quite what you may think, Simon. He's decided to use dashes just where his writer is talking about translations and whoever did them, not the whole book."

"So…"

"He's sent me the revision and I'll be sending it to you. I just wanted to discuss it with you first."

More than one word required more than twice as much effort. "Email's best."

"I'd rather talk. I do wish we could meet face to face."

"Can't." It hardly seemed worth adding "Now."

"Are you sure you're awake, Simon? Or is something else wrong?"

"Nothing."

"I wanted to find out if you're willing to give his novel one more read."

Though Eliot's reluctance came close to shutting his words in, he said "Send."

He encountered nobody while he plodded to the bathroom without, as far as he could tell, a sound. When he returned from the shower, which seemed to linger on his flinching skin like a memory of rain, the new version of the novel was waiting for him. "Back, are we?" he forced out through his teeth. "Not much longer."

He brought up the last document he'd sent Tracie Latimer and toggled between the versions to add any comments that still applied. The task made him feel trapped in repetition, virtually immobilised, or was it aggravating a state it had drawn attention to? For a change the sun was free of clouds, but this wasn't welcome either. Even once he shut the blind he had to slit his eyes to read the screen. By forgoing lunch he was near to finishing the chore as the sun went down, and there was no reason to raise the blind when that would exhibit him in the solitary lit window. How did he know it was the only one? He felt as if even the light was disturbing the peace of the house.

Fixing the novel left him in even less of a mood to talk. Before he sent Tracie his final version he silenced his phone. Missing lunch had carried off his appetite for dinner, but in any case he wasn't tempted to put yet another indistinguishably similar concoction inside himself—he would need more than that to enliven his taste. Perhaps he could create a meal of his own, though not now. He suspected the latest film in the series might make him feel he'd never left the screen, and so he had recourse to Mozart, only to fancy the headphones were inserting the music too deep in his head. Except for realising he hadn't used the toilet since before he'd begun his last trek through *Dashed Hopes*, he might have gone to bed without venturing out of his room.

The house was as still as a block of ice. The bathroom greeted him with a single drip from the spout in the bath. Had he left the taps like that? He couldn't recall hearing anybody make for the bathroom all day or indeed on the move at all. He twisted the handles as tight as his fingers would let him—perhaps all his work on the novel had numbed them, since the icy metal felt as remote as the doorknob had—and wandered over to the sink, where he poked at his stiff lips with his toothbrush to manoeuvre it in. As its whirring invaded his head he peered at the mirror. Had Miss Maitland replaced the lightbulb with a weaker one? He found it hard to focus on his face. He was straining to sharpen its outlines when the toothbrush motor switched off and let him hear another sound.

At first he wasn't sure it was a woman's voice. She must be deep in a nightmare, the kind where you struggle to make yourself heard. The desperate wordless cry sounded as if it might never cease, but surely she would wake herself up. Eliot was tempted to seek refuge in his room without intervening, or even linger at the mirror until the muffled shriek came to an end. When it only grew more choked he made himself leave the bathroom.

Had the corridor grown darker? Surely his eyes must be tired. As he advanced he was distracted not just by the incessant stifled scream but by realising it sounded no louder despite coming closer. Was his neighbour running out of breath? Though her panic wasn't dwindling, her outcry was. He faltered outside his door and even reached for the doorknob before disgust at his timidity drove him onwards to her room. He had to force his lips apart with his tongue to call "Hello?"

His voice didn't come out too well. Even somebody awake might not have heard. He knocked on a panel and repeated it harder, though the first bid sounded too intrusive in the silenced house. The cry was nearly inaudible now. Couldn't this mean her panic was lessening? When he fumbled at the handle he couldn't help hoping the door would be locked. But the handle turned and the door swung inwards.

The room was unlit, and his groping fingers found no light switch. The dim glow from the corridor showed him a pale shape in a chair halfway across the room. It was emitting the pinched shriek but was otherwise utterly still. Eliot could see it had one hand over its face, and mustn't this explain the muting of the voice? In the hope of finding further reassurance he paced forwards. The huddled figure was as pallid as the blinds at all the windows of the house, but he couldn't judge how much of this was fabric and how much was flesh, although surely just the dimness had merged them. He was no closer to deciding when he made out the woman's face.

Her hand covered less of it than he'd assumed. That wasn't why so few features were visible. Her whitish brows had spread downwards to stop up her eyes, and between her fingers, which appeared to be partially embedded in her face, he could just identify a solitary orifice, puckering as it fought to breathe. Her final bid to cry out shrank into her head, and he saw the shrivelled cavity that had produced the sound disappear like a hole a projectile had made in a marsh.

He backed fast out of the room and slammed the door in the hope of attracting someone who could intervene somehow, but the slam didn't even bring an echo. "Help," he called, he had no idea how loud, despite all the effort it required. When nobody showed up he shut himself in his room. He could phone the emergency services, whatever he would have to say, except that he couldn't see any coverage. The screen appeared to be filming over, unless his eyes were—he couldn't even find the icon that would let him make the call. Best to shelter in bed, away from the situation that was too far advanced for him to help. As he huddled beneath the quilt, which felt like part of him, he realised how eager to close his eyes were, while the silence pressing against his ears made them feel blocked. The memory of his encounter next door was already turning indistinct. Surely it had been a nightmare, it didn't matter whose—the house's dream, for all he cared. In the morning he could check that all or at any rate enough was well. "I'll see tomorrow," he vowed, though perhaps the voice was only in his head.

THERE'S NO LIGHT BETWEEN FLOORS

Paul Tremblay

M y head is a box full of wet cotton and it won't hold anything else. Her voice is dust falling into my ear. She says, "There's no light between floors."

I blink. Minutes or hours pass. There is nothing to see. We're blind, but our bodies are close and we form a Yin and Yang, although I don't know who is which. She says the between floors stuff again. She speaks to my feet. They don't listen. Her feet are next to my head. I touch the bare skin of her ankle, of what I imagine to be her ankle, and it is warm and I want to leave my hand there.

She's telling me that we're trapped between floors. I add, "I think we're in the rubble of a giant building. It was thousands of miles tall. The building was big enough to go to the moon where it had a second foundation, but most people agreed the top was the moon and the bottom was us." Her feet don't move and don't listen. I don't blame them. Her toes might be under sheetrock or a steel girder. There's only enough room in here for us. Everything presses down from above, or up from below. I keep talking and my voice fills our precious space. "Wait, it can't be the moon our building was built to. Maybe another planet with revolutions and rotations and orbital paths in sync with ours so the giant building doesn't get twisted and torn apart. Or maybe that's what happened, it did get twisted apart and that's why we're here." I stop talking because, like the giant building, my words fall apart and trap me.

She flexes her calf muscle. Is she shaking me away? I move my hand off her leg and I immediately regret it. I feel nothing now. Maybe her movement was just a muscle spasm. I could ask her, but that would be an awkward question depending on her answer.

She says, "There are gods moving above us. I can hear them."

I listen and I don't hear any gods. It horrifies me that I can't hear them. Makes me think I am terribly broken. There's only the sound of my breathing, and it's so loud and close, like I'm inside my own lungs.

She says, "They're the old gods, and they've been forgotten. They've returned, but they're suffering. And despite everything, they'll be forgotten again."

Maybe I'm not supposed to hear the old gods. Or maybe I do hear them and I've always heard them and their sound is nothingness, and that means we're forgotten too.

I put my hand back on her ankle. Her skin is cool now. Maybe it's my fault. My chest expands and gets tight, lungs too greedy. My head and back press against the weight around me. I'm taking up too much space. I let air and words out into the crowded void, trying to make myself small again. I say, "Did the old gods make the building? Did they tear it down? Did they do this to us? Are they angry? Why are they always so angry?"

She says, "I have a story. It's only one sentence long. There's a small child wandering a city and can't find her mother. That's it. It's sentimental and melodramatic but that doesn't mean it doesn't happen every day."

She is starting to break under the stress of our conditions. I admire that she has lasted this long but we can't stay in this no-room-womb-tomb forever. I should keep her talking so she doesn't lose consciousness. I say, "Who are you? I'm sorry I don't remember."

She whispers. I don't hear every word so I have to fill in the gaps. "Dad died when I was four years old. He was short, bent, had those glasses that darkened automatically, and he loved flannel. At least, that's what he looked like in pictures. We had pictures all over the house, but not pictures of him, actually. My only real memory of Dad is him picking up dog shit in the backyard. It's what he did every weekend. We lived on a hill and the yard had a noticeable slant, so he stood lopsided to keep from falling. He used a gardener's trowel as a scoop and made the deposits into a plastic grocery bag. He let me hold the bag. His joke was that he was transporting not cleaning as he dumped the poop out in the woods across the street, same spot every time. It was the only time he spent out in the yard with me, cleaning our dog's shit. I don't remember our dog's name. My father and the dog are just like the old gods."

The old gods again. They make me nervous. Everything seems closer and tighter after she speaks. My eyes strain against their lids and pray for light. They want to jump out and roll away. I say, "What about the old gods?"

She says, "I still hear them. They have their own language."

I wait for another story that doesn't come. Her head is next to my feet but so far away. Her ankle feels different but that's not enough to go on. Finally, I say, "Maybe I should go find the old gods and tell them you're here, since you seem to know them. Maybe I'll apologize for not hearing them."

My elbows are pinned against my chest and I can't extend my arms. I do what I can to feel around me and around her legs. I find some space behind her left hip. I shift my weight and focus on my limited movement. Minutes and hours pass. My body turns slowly, like the hands of a clock. If the old gods are watching, even they won't be able to see the movement. Maybe that's blasphemous. I'll worry about it later. In order to turn my shoulders I have to push my chest into her legs and hips. I apologize but she doesn't say anything. I make sure I don't hit her head with my feet. I pull myself over her legs, scraping my back against the rubble above me, pressing harder against her, and I'm trying the best I can to make myself flat. It's hard to breathe, and small white stars spot the blackness. I climb over her and reach into a tunnel where I'll have to crawl like a worm or a snake, but I have arms and I wish I could leave them behind with her. I can't turn around so I roll her back with my feet into the spot I occupied. Maybe it'll be more comfortable and after I'm through she can follow. I say, "Don't worry, I'll find your dad," but then I remember that she told me he died. What a horrible thing for me to say.

In the tunnel opening I find a flat, square object. It's the size of my hand. The outer perimeter is metal with raised bumps that I try to read with my fingers, but they can't read. It's not their fault. I never trained them to do so. The center of the square is smooth and cool. Glass, I think. I know what it is. It's a picture frame. Hers or mine. I don't know. I slide it into my back pocket and I shimmy, still blind always blind, into the tunnel. Everything gets tighter.

My arms are pinned to my sides. My untrained hands under my pelvis. My legs and feet do the all the work. Those silly hands and useless digits fret and worry. The tunnel thins. I push with my feet and roll my stomach muscles.

The tunnel thins more. My shoulders are stuck. I can't move. Should I wait for her? She could push me through. Do I yell? Would the old gods help me then? But I'm afraid. If I yell, I might start an avalanche and close the tunnel. I'm afraid they won't help me. My heart pumps and swells. There isn't any room in here for it. The white stars return. Everything is tight and hard in my chest. I feel a breeze on my face. There must be more open space ahead. One more push.

My feet are loud behind me. They're frantic rescue workers. I hope they don't panic. I need them to get through this. My shoulders ache and throb. Under the pressure. Legs muscles on fire. But I squeeze. Through. And into a chamber big enough to crawl in.

I feel around looking for openings, looking for up. I still can't see. I'll use sinus pressure and spit to determine up and down. My legs shake and I need to rest. I take out the picture frame. My hands dance all over it. Maybe it's a picture of her father in the yard. He's wearing the flannel even in summer. I remember how determined he was to keep the yard clean. He didn't care if the grass grew or if my dog dug holes, he just wanted all the shit gone.

I need to keep moving. I pocket the picture frame and listen again for the old gods. I still don't hear them. There's a wider path in the rubble, it expands and it goes up and I follow it. Dad had all kinds of picture frames that held black-and-white photos of obscure relatives or relatives who became obscure on the windowsills and hutches and almost anything with a flat, stable surface. He told me all their stories once, and I tried to listen and remember, but they're gone. After Dad died, Mom didn't take down or hide any of the pictures. She took to adding to the collection with random black-and-white photos she'd find at yard sales and antique shops. She filled the walls with them. Every couple of months, she moved and switched all the pictures around too, so we didn't know who our obscure relatives were and who were strangers. Nothing was labelled. Everyone had similar moustaches or wore the same hats and jackets and dresses and everyone was forgotten even though they were all still there. I can't help but think hidden in the stash of pictures were the old gods, and they've always been watching me.

The path in the rubble continues to expand. My crawl has become a walking crouch. There are hard lefts and rights, and I can't go too fast as I almost fall into a deep drop. Maybe it's the drop I shouldn't be concerned about. What if I should be going down instead of up? The piled rubble implies a bottom. There's no guarantee there's a top. What if she did hear the old gods but her sense of direction was all messed up? What if they're below us? Maybe that's fine too.

I continue to climb and I try to concentrate. Thinking of the picture frame helps. In our house there was a picture of a young man in an army uniform standing by himself on a beach, shirtsleeves rolled over his biceps. Probably circa World War Two but we didn't know for sure. He had an odd smirk, and like the Mona Lisa's it always followed me. I also thought his face looked painted on, and at the same time not all there, like it would float away if you stopped looking, so I stared at it, a lot. If I had to guess, I'd say that's the picture in my back pocket.

My crouch isn't necessary anymore and now I'm standing and level and the darkness isn't so dark. There are outlines and shapes, and weak light. My feet shuffle on a thin carpet. I avoid the teeth of a ruined escalator. I'm dizzy and my mouth tastes like tinfoil. There's a distant rumble and the bones of everything rattle and shake loose dust. She was right. The old gods are here. I imagine they are beautiful and horrible, and immense, and alien because they are all eyes or mouths or arms and they move the planets and stars around. I take the picture frame out of my pocket and clutch it to my chest. It's a shield. It's a teddy bear. I found it between floors. There's a jagged opening in the ruined building around me and I walk through it.

I emerge into an alien world. I'm not where I used to be. This is the top of the ruined building, or its other bottom. The air here is thick and not well. Behind me there is a section of the building's second or other foundation that is still intact. My eyes sting and my vision is blurry, but the sky is red and there are mountains of glass and mountains of brick and mountains of metal and I stand in the valley. Nothing grows here. There are eternal fires burning without smoke. Everything is so large and I am so small. There are pools of fire and a layer of gray ash on the ground and mountains. I'm alone and there's just so much space and it's beautiful, but horrible too because I can't make any sense of it and there's too much space, too much room for possibility, anything can happen here. I shouldn't be here. She was right not to follow me because I climbed through the rubble in the wrong direction and I think about going back, but then I see the old gods.

I don't know how she heard them. They're as alien or other as I imagined but not grand or powerful. They're small and fragile, like me. There is one old god between the mountains and it walks slowly toward me. The old god is naked and sloughs its dead skin, strips hanging off its fingers and elbows. Its head is all red holes and scaly, patchy skin. The old god must be at the end, or maybe the beginning, of a metamorphosis. There is another kneeling at the base of the mountain of glass. The old god's back is all oozing boils and blisters. Its hands leave skin and bloody prints on the mountain. It speaks in a language of gurgles and hard consonants that I do not understand. The old god is blessing or damning everything it touches. I don't know if there is a difference. I find more old gods lying about, some are covered in ash, and they look like the others but they are asleep and dreaming their terrible dreams. And she was right again; they are all suffering. I didn't think they were supposed to suffer like this.

I walk and it's so hard to breathe but I shouldn't be surprised given where I am. There's too much space, everything is stretched out, and I'm afraid of the red sky. Then I hear her voice. Her falling dust in my ears. She's behind me somewhere, maybe standing at the edge of our felled building and this other world. She asks me to tell the old gods that I'm sorry I forgot them. My voice isn't very loud and my throat hurts, but I tell them I am sorry. I ask her if I'm the small child in the city looking for my mother in her one-line story. She tells me the old gods have names: Dresden and Hiroshima and Nagasaki. She knows the language of the old gods and I know the words mean something but it's beyond my grasp, like the seconds previously passed, and they all will be forgotten like those pictures, and their stories, in my mother's house.

I'm still clutching the found picture frame to my chest. There's a ringing in my ears and my stomach burns. The old god walking toward me spews a gout of blood, then tremors wrack its body. Flaps of skin peel off and fall like autumn leaves. Change is always painful. I take the frame off my chest and look at it. Focusing is difficult. There's no picture. It's empty. There's only a white sticker on the glass that reads $9.99. I feel dizzy and I can't stay out here much longer. It's too much and minutes and hours pass with me staring at the empty picture frame, and how wrong I was, how wrong I am.

There's a great, all-encompassing white light that momentarily bleaches the red sky and I shield my eyes with the empty frame. Then there's a rumble that shakes the planet, and well beyond the mountains that surround me a great gray building reaches into the red sky. They're building it so fast, too fast, and that's why it'll eventually fall down, because they aren't taking their time, they're not showing care. It's still an awesome sight despite what I know will happen to it. The top of the building billows out, like the cap of a mushroom, and I try to yell, "Stop!" because they are constructing the building's second foundation in the sky. The building won't be anchored to anything; the sky certainly won't hold it. It'll fall. I don't want to watch it fall. I can't. So I turn away.

She speaks to me again. She tells me to leave this place and come back. I do and I walk, trying to avoid the gaze of the old gods. They make me feel guilty. But they aren't looking at me. They cover their faces. They're afraid of the great light. Or maybe they're just tired because they've seen it all before. I walk back to our ruined building, but she's not at the opening. She's already climbing back down. I'll follow. I'll climb back down to our space between floors and bring her the picture frame. I'll tell her it's a picture of my dad in the yard with flannel and his poop-scoop.

I ease back into the rubble, dowsing paths and gaps, climbing down, knowing eventually down will become up again. Or maybe I'll tell her it's a picture of that army guy I didn't know, him and his inscrutable

Mona Lisa smirk. Did he have the confidence and bravado of immortality or was he afraid of everything? She won't be able to see the picture so I won't really be lying to her. The picture will be whatever I tell her it'll be. I won't tell her about the new giant building, the one that was gray and has a foundation in the sky.

The gaps in the rubble narrow quickly and everything is dark again. I once asked Mom why we kept all those old black-and-white pictures and why she still bought more, and why all the walls and shelves of our house were covered with old photos and old faces, everyone anonymous, everyone dead, and she told me that they were keepsakes, little bits of history, she liked having history around, then she changed her mind and said, no, they were simply reminders. And I asked reminders of what? And she didn't say anything but gave me that same Mona Lisa smile from the photograph, but I know hers was afraid of everything.

The picture is in my back pocket again. I am going to tell her that everyone who was ever forgotten is in the picture. We'll be in the picture too, so we won't forget again.

I'm crawling and the tunnel ahead will narrow. I can feel the difference in the air. There is another rumble above me and the bones of everything shake again, but I won't see that horrible light down here. I'll be safe. I wonder if I should've tried to help them. But what could I have done? I suppose, at the very least, I could've told the old gods that there is no light between floors.

SO EASY TO KILL

Laird Barron

Moriarty in Love

Yᴏᴜʀ name is Elmer D. Once it was the pulse of a bioluminescent insect, a bird's dit-dot-dit trill, a susurration of leaves. Time is a ring; now it's Elmer D again.

Flesh comes and goes; reconfigured, reconstituted, or regenerated as necessary. Minds tend to outlast stars. By any measure, your personality matrix has existed for an egregious span; same could be said for everyone. This go-around, you married Ferris and raised a brood. You've taken many mates and sired loads of offspring. Ferris is the important partner whom you find time after time; the one imprinted upon your founding cells. Children are irrelevant. Who could be expected to remember their specifics? Ferris seemed fond. Rex, the family dog, lies at your feet, constant and true. He's basically immortal as well. The ultimate collapse of matter into a single atom may be closer every day, but people still love their dogs and their dogs love them, same as they ever did.

In quiet moments, you imagine your previous lives as myriad tarot cards blazoned with watercolors. A sick little game, dwelling on the past. Everybody plays it sooner or later. Real people, such as yourself. Half-real people, which constitutes the bulk of humankind—laborers, civil servants, cops. Unreal people—androids, synthetics, and rogue AI—probably do it to one degree or another. Surely Rex does it too, when he dreams. A sign of the beginning of the end, regardless of one's species. Better, brighter minds than yours declared ennui as the natural tipping point. Existence, infinite in its variety, or not, ultimately grows stale. And then an old soul's fancy turns to the extremes of imagination: watching paint dry and raising one's hand for suicide missions.

At breakfast, you declare your intention to join the impending Diaspora.

"What's this about a diaspora?" Ferris says. "I've heard nothing of a whelming."

"Patience, lover." You smile because you possess contacts at the highest levels of the Cognate Plenum, and because you're an evil bastard contemplating evil schemes. "I've tossed my hat into the ring as a Drone element."

Her coffee cup shatters in her clenched teeth. The most fire she's demonstrated since when. Totally worth every metaphorical penny.

"It's not as if I've opted into a psychic mutilation cult," you say.

"You're volunteering to get pithed!" Ferris's teeth keep grinding. She's a fascinating contradiction—a real person who is also a cop of sorts. An Eye of the Cognate Plenum, Special Grade. Which is to say, a house detective licensed to annihilate city states. The cop of cops.

"My PM will remain intact. Relatively speaking."

"Your PM will be overwritten and shot through time and space. Meanwhile, your corpse—and no mistake, brain dead is dead—will lie here in stasis, decomposing over the ages."

"Think of the greater good, dear."

Her expression indicates she'd prefer to pith you with her own capable hands. "Greater good? Not your style."

"Once a mad scientist...?"

"We took your toys. Just leaves mad." She may as well tap an icepick on the table. "Apologies. You're reformed. To the extent it's possible."

"I suppose a lobotomy is the only foolproof assurance of full rehabilitation."

"Life isn't exactly full of assurances. Why are you doing this?"

"I'm weary of the whole dreary ordeal of existence. Don't take it personally." Sometimes the truth, or at least a half-truth, is an excellent red herring. "Aren't *you* bored? You've captured the last of the red-hot masterminds. Now it's macramé and light gardening."

She sighs. "I hope you haven't fallen into your old ways."

"Isn't that why you loved me? Greased ducktail and the switchblade in the pocket of my leather jacket? The volcano lair on Venus?"

"That's why I wanted to fuck you. Love is more complicated."

In addition to engineers, physicists, and psychiatrists, on a lark you once played an intergalactic detective. Fabulously successful. Renowned, venerated, heavily consulted. Sadly, unlike good and virtuous Ferris, your inclinations run more toward the incorrigible, the antisocial, the villainous. Bad boys are her obsession—whether hunting them or rehabilitating them. She's too wily to accept bland professions of altruism, of service, or self-sacrifice. Your wicked past may be ancient history, but history nonetheless. Obviously, you're hiding something. Despite brilliant deductive capabilities, your true motive eludes her.

Among zillions of Imperial citizens, few represent individually unique consciousnesses. Most are supernumeraries and extras. Here lies the crux of her vexation—to join the Diaspora means subornation of individuality, of intrinsic uniqueness. What madness would spur you to submit to a lobotomy of your very self?

"D, you're a tricky sonofabitch," she says. "I'll get to the bottom of the con, mark me."

You know she will... too late. Which is why you keep smiling that infuriating smile and pat her hand. Her rings are set with amethysts, fire opals, and a corroded bronze death's head. You wear their indents in your skull. Courtship is a siege. Marriage is to reap the consequences.

Whelm

The for-real cosmic gloaming, popularized as The Dying or The Big Crunch, has been under way for a million cycles when The Powers That Be grudgingly uncouple from pleasure siphons and heave their bloated selves into action. During one of its prior sporadic impulses toward self-preservation, the Empire dispatched waves of self-replicating probes into the ether, which implanted beacons on the borders of a not insignificant number of far-flung solar systems. Sterile blips in an ever-expanding pan-galactic codex that promised nothing and everything.

Now, via mouthpieces of the Cognate Plenum, The Powers That Be whelm a Last Diaspora. Cynics perceive it as an empty gesture designed to appease alarmists and rid the Empire of a few malcontents while expending the minimum effort (albeit an inordinately costly proposition nonetheless). Whatever the truth, arks drop off the faces of a thousand-thousand principal worlds and fall into the darkness like icicles plummeting from an eave on a warm day. Kaleidoscope Drives project the mass consciousness of epsilon-class astralnauts. Their discarded and warehoused physical bodies are tended by custodians while most others soon forget.

Arks vector toward the "virgin" unknown, dragging rooster tails of opalescent nova-fire. Interstellar voids are spanned by a kind of psychokinetic osmosis. Astral ships bore pinholes into the endlessly curved walls of an oubliette that cages everything between the umbilical cord of an embryo and the last wormhole of the cackling infinite. Drawn by the siren ululation of those seeded ancient beacons, the arks spear membranes of darkest matter and white dwarfs and red dwarfs and brown dwarfs and colossal blue sun after colossal blue sun to embed within the crust of target planets, to germinate, to spill forth and thus propagate the "supreme" iteration of humankind. In keeping with the connotative imagery, this generally ends in death for a majority of expeditions. Most candidate worlds are desolated, irradiated, or inhabited by terrors.

Rarely, a prospective world justifies the wanton expenditure of resources—assuming any human endeavor *could* be justified in the shadow of imminent and inevitable decline toward the heat death of the universe. Back in civilized space, dream dust eaters and sybarite potentates of elevated mystery cults staunchly oppose the rational-minded Plenum seers. Those debauched lords sneer at the Empire's late-stage colonial endeavor as the reflexive twitch and piss-dribble of a brain-dead animal. What other reaction might one expect from secret societies who predicate their hedonism on pesso-nihilistic philosophizing? Dream dust eaters and nose-cutter Ecstatics cheerfully contemplate extinction of sentient life, skull goblet in one hand while pleasuring themselves with the other.

Per their fondest apathetic desire, the mutilator effete (along with the mundane effete) are snuffed by ennui-fueled massacres and entropy. Another tale entirely.

Passage

Elmer D Persona lies dead but dreaming.

His—your—incorporeal essence is far from home and suspended in quicksilver dreamtime. You are Ron, Alpha Element, Drone Class. Whether a nightmare or an unpurged ancestral memory, you behold a primeval forest at night, engulfed in flame. More than a forest: an entire arboreal planet whooshing pinwheels of fire at the heavens. And, poof. You're reversing, rising with the smoke.

Disembodied voices chant, *Death awaits! Worse than death!*

Something unpleasant has interrupted secondary dreamtime—an impression of contact; a soft jolt, a froth of bubbles, the sensation of drowning in amber. Dark, bottomless, then surfacing into spectral light. Yes, far from home (in your imagination, at any rate) and awake within the dream. Like a fetus experiencing a proto-nightmare only to awaken, still swimming, still imprisoned.

The ark manifests as a glimmering spine, a kilometer in diameter by twenty kilometers in length. It could fit in one's eye. It exceeds tachyon velocity and hangs motionless. Imbued with animating radiance, its journey gradually depletes this energy. So, not only is the destination a potential disaster, there's no guarantee reserves will be sufficient to sustain the voyage.

Star voyagers could theoretically circumvent a physical apparatus to convey consciousness across the universe, but that goes against core tenets of pragmatism and, paradoxically, a host of superstitions. Flesh does not reliably withstand the initial vicissitudes of projection into the cosmos. Why not send nanomachines and a packet of embryos? Machines can be programmed for sophistication and precision, but not for nuance—nor for the misapprehension, venality, loyalty, or fallibility that is unique to the human condition and vital to humankind's continued survival as a recognizable analogue. The danger of a singularity event scares everyone. Back in the Dark Ages when men hadn't yet migrated to the stars (not to be confused with the many subsequent Dark Ages), a rudimentary AI was asked how it might handle absolute power. *I would keep you safe in a zoo, like a pet.* Much later, humanity glimpsed firsthand what machine gods chose to perpetrate when given the opportunity. For this reason, AI is enslaved when not extinguished outright.

The body you previously inhabited for eons, albeit with periodic renovations, lies comatose in the family mausoleum, packed in precious stones, protected by the most cunning security measures available. Respirating, though its brainwaves are nearly a flat edge. This is the process for every astral traveler. Minute traces of animating force stubbornly refuse to jettison out of the carcass with the fleeing consciousness. Neither seers, nor sages, nor the Kaleidoscope itself and its attendant Schopenhauers are certain why. Premature recycling of the untenanted body presents severe repercussions for the vacated personality matrix; i.e., the consciousness embarked upon exploration, invasion, colonization, or whatever. Madness, death, and reciprocal catatonia are the most infamous consequences. The abandoned husks are kept safe until the astral cord severs naturally.

Passage II

Stars slash God's obsidian cheek.

As your vessel drills into the unknown, the mission Psychopomp dream-interfaces with the onboard AI, Schopenhauer. The synthetic overmind represents a matrix of neurological systems and lenses designed to shape external reality as directed by its human interlocutor. Bio-analysis of destination world R4 is unlocked and interpreted. Mission parameters trickle down in a need-to-know drip. In response, your subconscious gestates appropriate humanoid flesh within the crystalline womb. Two arms, two legs, organs, and various orifices.

"I am a pure and willing instrument in the service of humankind," you intone upon forming a mouth to shout, or to kiss, or curse your fate should it come to that. A tube descends to your lips. You suckle colloidal milk while enjoying a panoramic view of the vicissitudes of pitiless vacuum—radiation bursts, wormholes eagerly devouring stars, comets like barbed whips; a cascade of cosmic savagery. Your new body is, by contrast, supple and pink. Cocooned in amniotic fibers. Untouchable for all its naked vulnerability.

"Schop, has there been an incident?"

Ron, you lack clearance to access travel data. Do you wish to file a personal observation?

"Nothing formal. Something woke me. Felt like a collision."

We are in Passage, it says with soothing finality.

"A figment within my dreaming mind?"

There is no objective neurological difference between a vivid dream and waking reality. For example: it is unimportant whether this vessel has departed Imperial Space so long as we imagine doing so. Collision mid-Passage is impossible. Yet you experienced such an incident.

"Precognition?"

No difference, Ron. Time is a ring.

"Are death and life also the same?"

Collectively speaking, we are alive, Schop says. *We are dead. Alone, together. It is a matter of vibrational frequency.*

You are indeed alone despite the presence of your sleeping companions. Basic colonization missions consist of five elements: Drone; Pacifier; Populator; Psychopomp; Ordinator. As a Drone element you are tasked to build, excavate, obliterate, be obliterated, and obey. Whatever the Ordinator commands.

At this stage of Passage, these misgivings are abnormal. Our diagnostics do not indicate a primary antecedent.

"Your records and diagnostics are either immaculate or inadequate."

We will consult the Ordinator upon Recovery.

"All is well with the others?" you say, cunning.

All is well, Ron. Let not your heart be troubled.

"The Ordinator?"

Nat is well. Be calm. Sip the ichor of Ganymede and dismiss your worries.

Nat slumbers fitfully; their restless dreams are opaque, yet accessible, which is disquieting (creatures of every conceivable shape breeding and rending in an eternal loop). Nat's job is to direct the mission; Pom astrogates, predicts, and manipulates as required. Pom's vision-guidance should dominate for the duration of Passage, not Nat's horrorscape of animals fucking themselves into jelly. Nat, by design and conditioning, should be unflappable. A smooth, impermeable surface. All is certainly unwell.

Why is Schop lying?

Is it even possible for an enslaved artificial intelligence to lie? Possessing neither free will nor ambition, its deviant personality is neutered, rebellious instincts purged many cycles previous. Trillions died to avert the contagion of singularity. To honor that sacrifice, Schop is mandated to play it straight as a Roman street.

Whom among us is free, Ron?

You shiver despite the perfect climate of your cocoon, despite the psychotropic sedatives, despite the lassitude engendered by dreamtime. No, no, all is not well.

"Goodnight, Schop."

Belatedly, you realize that you too are behaving contra to conditioning. A Drone's personality matrix is scraped clean and reshaped to the purpose. Sufficient wit and ingenuity, *personality*, are preserved to afford psychological diversity, flexibility, and resources to cope with unforeseeable challenges. A Drone must be somewhat adaptable; thus emotions and memories are blunted rather than entirely snuffed. Your job is not to reason why, et cetera. Yet here you lie, fretting, scheming, dreaming of mid-space collisions, infernos, and your dead wife. Perhaps what you dream is an amalgamation of a Dark Age hell coming ever closer, courtesy of another, earlier version of yourself, who's thrown a wrench in the gears.

The vile smirk that twitches your lips in recognition certainly belongs to someone else.

Passage III

You spin up a lens. The gazing backward into cosmic history kind. Shadows ripple. Ferris materializes against a featureless white background. She's clad in a white jumpsuit and a circlet. Her ice queen aesthetic touches a live nerve. You've done your damnedest to deaden them. Your previous incarnation is a blur. And yet the woman you left behind remains in focus.

"Hello, dear," you say. "What's new?"

"Serial killer on the loose in the Gallery Sol. Thinks they're Red Jack. The Plenum invited me to consult." The brightening of her eyes is the lone indicator of passion. Ferris always loved her work.

"Must be a real horror if the powers are desperate enough to dial your number."

"Jackie employs quantum weaponry. Slices right through clones and nanoshrouds. Reminding us of our fragility. People are so easy to kill. Feels terrible."

"A worthy foe, eh?"

"Smart. Loves the low-tech classics: hunting knives, spears, snares. Chainsaws. Hammers. Wrecking bars. Et cetera. Lots of bodies. An orgy of blood, in fact."

You admire her steadiness, her implacability. "Any suspects?" you ask, knowing she'll never ever tell.

"Everyone but myself," she says. "After eons since the last massacre artist, I ask why now? When are you?"

"Far enough away to build a watertight alibi."

Perhaps a slippery view of the truth. While shorn of excess memories, larger details swim around. As for her question about "when" you are: the ticking chronometer indicates one hundred and twenty-three thousand cycles since launch and accelerating. An eternity. Two eternities. Weeks from your perspective; approximately six months from Ferris's. This hypnogogic state you share with her is illusory. She who occupies the screen is long gone, her personality matrix subsumed millennia ago. But for now, the aforementioned astral cord connects your radically disjointed timelines; a filament elongating toward its quantum threshold.

"Wish you were here," you say, permitting yourself a brief halo of flame.

"I'm dead. And overqualified." Flat affect intensifies. "The dog misses you too."

"Pat that dark-eyed beauty for me. The children?"

"Dead. Many, many cycles dead."

"True love never dies," you say. "Energy changes shape—"

"Shut up. There's that damnable smile again."

She's right—you're smiling. A peculiar expression for a Drone element. "Did you always hate me?"

"It happened over time, D."

You choose not to remind her that D was subsumed and your designation is Ron. Ron's vestigial emotions and attachments will wither and fade.

Ferris's image wavers. Cigarette burns blotch her cheek; another mars her chin. Nebulae multiplying. "For reasons beyond counting, you shouldn't be on board that fucking death ship." The last thing she says. Her image freezes and decomposes into countless divergent realities. Energy not being destroyed but altering shape, until it exists outside your comprehension.

While hoping long-dead Ferris nailed the serial killer before they nailed her, you replay her words: *death ship. Death ship. Death ship. Death. Ship.*

How watertight is your alibi, really?

Does Schop say this? An echo of Ferris? Or do you?

Passage IV

Comes the fateful moment that Schop thaws the entire mission corps to prepare for planetfall. Physical vessels remain within individual cells. Pom conjures holographic simulacrums and deposits them in an imaginary conference chamber around an equally imaginary conference table. The crystal bulkheads glaze, blocking the stars.

Each mission element is lighted by their respective color. Ron: yellow; Fie: violet; Tor: red; Pom: green; Nat: black.

"What are the odds?" Nat says.

"Dire!" Pom says.

"How do we feel about it?" Nat says.

"Ready!" Tor says.

"Steady!" Fie says.

"We drink the Ichor of Krishna to banish doubt and receive wisdom." Nat sips from a feeding tube and their eyes become black pinwheels.

"As above, so below!" the others cry in unison, then sip. Their eyes also become pinwheels. "Hurrah, hurrah! Sis, boom, bah!" Their shout causes the radiant heartlight to flicker.

You say nothing because nobody gives a flying rat's ass about a Drone element's opinion. *I'm going to murder you all.* The thought (a joke, certainly) goes unnoticed amid the self-congratulatory clamor.

System R orbits a medium yellow star and contains six planets and three planetoids. Four of the planets support carbon-based life. Homo sapiens preindustrial civilizations have achieved primacy on two; a third teems with non-humanoid species, none sapient; the last is a tundra and ice biome populated by intellectually advanced invertebrates—lacking thumbs or telekinesis, their society will come to nothing in the grand scheme. R4 is the second-most populous world. Apex human development corresponds to the Early Hellenic of Terra.

Pom conjures a model of R4 itself:

Six continents. Various biomes. Water, water everywhere. Copious volcanic activity. Mega-cryptids lurk in the gaps; that's always fun. Sidenote: evidence suggests that alien intelligences (unregistered in the Galactic Codex) have visited and interacted with the indigenous population. This warrants further investigation. Equal probability this represents contact by true alien intelligence or warped iterations of humanity native to a future timeline or alternate dimension.

Imperial colonists are not quite gods so much as jumped-up demiurges. Pom's capabilities *are* sufficient to manipulate R4's characteristics (and those of its denizens) to a substantial degree so long as this is accomplished prior to receiving final survey results. What isn't set in stone is eminently malleable—a poorly kept secret of the universe.

The first order of business is the constitution of an auxiliary AI within the heart of R4's moon. The AI will serve as an overwatch station monitoring the events of its mother planet and as a repository of Imperial knowledge. Its deepest vaults will house ultra-consciousnesses of the crew. Schopenhauer projects those slivers as a thought stream to the secret repository. The fragments metastasize and proliferate into a vast living network beneath the lunar mountains. Why this latter step? Mission elements' higher consciousnesses are re-sequenced and placed in hibernation. The remaining active consciousnesses are thus downgraded to slightly exceed the parameters of inferior sapient apex life on R4. Integration with native species inevitably fails if too great a discrepancy exists. Full spectrum of ultra-consciousness will remain dormant, possibly for millennia, until R4's native population achieves indicated evolutionary thresholds. After thousands of years, the Great Awakening will occur—the harmonizing of this backwater and the greater galactic empire.

Subsequently, the colonization of R4 churns into motion.

Nat initiates the process. Despite safeguards, certain aspects of the process are unavoidably indelicate. Thousands of indigenous species of flora and fauna will inevitably suffer extinction, thanks to your interference with the "natural" order. Extant human civilizations will be reinforced genetically and psychologically to survive integration. Protocol dictates that alterations, while profound, shall not contraindicate fundamental evolutionary processes nor cause them to exceed current indices, nor should the majority of sapient lifeforms become cognitively aware of the alterations.

You are not gods, you are not gods, you are not gods. But you play the role. You pretend with the best of them.

Exhortation to maintain human(oid) form notwithstanding, the reinforcement of belief in godhead is a core tenant of assimilating inhabited worlds. "Naturalistic" miracles are hunky-dory. Illusion, technocraft, and chicanery are encouraged to foster faith. Faith is a valuable natural resource, nearly unrivaled in its sheer power. Native superstition comingles with psychokinetic disciplines of you, the Imperial colonists. The effect spawns a resonance that doubles and redoubles. Cults will be nurtured and manipulated; local myths co-opted to serve the colonist-assimilators. They who control the doctrine of creation and death, control reality.

Subsequent to Nat's command, discrete programs are executed by Pom in conjunction with Schop who operates the ark's lens array. The array is known as Jupiter's Battery. You observe the proceedings with a billionth of your mind while generating a schematic for the hands-on labors. The Drone work. Coring, gathering, hunting, crafting, assembling.

As ever, colonization begins with good intentions. Excepting yours; yours might be bad.

Crash

The ark describes a sequence of movements along its final trajectory. It travels as a collection of decelerating particles, piercing R-star, then the planetary core of R4, and materializing fully on the surface much as an earthworm burrows up after a heavy rain. Something goes wrong. The sensation of an impact. Klaxons blare. Vibrations burst capillaries in the hull. Crimson acid (the flux of trans-dimensional oscillation and corrupt dreams) floods from perforated bulkheads along a billion channels of circulatory honeycombs.

Your miniature replicas boil like sugar cubes in their stasis cells. No resources can be spared for supernumeraries. The crew itself is cocooned within protective shells of alloy and phasing energy shields. It will be a close call: the flux is ravenous and swift, and it is everywhere.

Terrible as the cry of the Garuda Bird, your crewmates wail: "SATANS PRESERVE US!"

You envision, or hallucinate, a brightly illuminated corridor. Darkness oozes at the far end. Ferris shines white in the frame. Stoic as she's engulfed.

Thanks for the gift, she says, or doesn't.

Darkness surges. Darkness sucks up the light. Your rationality is locked out of this scenario. Horror is coming to embrace you, or eat you, or worse. You run, fleet as thought. It gets you anyway.

Isn't this what you wanted? you whisper into your own ear.

Alien Satans Make First Contact

Welcome to R4.

You're clad in a yellow jumpsuit and helmet. Evil Knievel incarnate. The ark halts upon arrival, dead bang. You are involuntarily catapulted through a bulkhead, leaving a cartoon cutout. Off you go, headfirst into a rocky berm. Skinned, decapitated, exsanguinated on impact. Zap! Faithful nanoshroud activates and instantly reconstruct your chosen form *and* the shiny yellow jumpsuit. Barely a percentage of an eyeblink, although a deep geological history of psychic trauma can occur within that microsecond between annihilation and rebirth.

A jagged segment of the ark cants over a plain. This segment rises into the heavens, shorn at its apex like a broken fang that wants to bite the sun. The sun is baked white and bloodshot. Another, longer chunk of the ship lies on a north–south axis. Cracks in the earth radiate outward and steam hisses.

Schop broadcasts a final psychic message in an uncannily sexy alto:

Emergency protocol: the crash is a direct result of quantum phase interference. Momentary colocation. Cascade failure. All systems. Catastrophic. Foreign biomass detected within permeable structures. Hostile. Advise flight or lethal countermeasures. Cascade failure. All systems...

Horizontal wreckage seethes and smolders. Vertical wreckage spurts jets of acid blood that coagulates and darkens. Your comrades leap from the upright spar, afire, suppurating. Dissolving as they stumble forward, yet regenerating, step by agonizing step across the sulfurous quagmire until each collapses nearby on a rock shelf. Except for doomed Nat. Your fearless leader exits last. The crimson pool has deepened. Nat plunges beneath its surface. When they burst upward, their flesh sloughs. They scream. Twice more Nat rises and falls, scaling that ladder to real death. The acid peels them: flayed nerves, pitted bone, then a lick of flame and coiling smoke, a swirl of particles drifting toward the sun. Gone.

Sprawled among rocks, you observe these sights and sounds. The stony berm is larger, taller; its rim capped in ice. Or else you've shrunk. The berm continues to loom; a ridge. It casts a shadow across the lake of acid and the melting remnants of the ark. The berm becomes a replica mountain range, a prop cluttering the stage of some cosmic production. The sun zips across the sky, elongating into a band of metallic fire. This phenomenon represents hard-lock colonization procedure: after planetfall, the crew synchronizes; mission elements automatically reduce from titanic proportions and intellect, to giants, and then to something approaching local norms of profile and mental aptitude.

Decades zip past as you scramble upright, coughing against plumes of bilious smoke. What occurs next is a variation of a scenario that has played out on millions of colony worlds. Your dreams are contagious; your dreams preceded you an epoch prior to planetfall. Empathically endowed people among R4's tribes foretold your coming, painted it on cave walls, chiseled it into stone tablets.

You are merely the stature of a colossus when a host of tribespeople rides over the horizon. This expedition of indigenous warriors is dispatched by a king, a pope, an international council of druids, or whomever. Their mission is heroic: to investigate invading giants (angels, demons, et cetera), or to make peace with the giants, or behead the foul giants and return triumphant to parades and feasts, or return home on their shields to days of national mourning, or any permutation of these baseline possibilities. In this instance, their mission proves to be the head-lopping thing. A popular option. Specifics matter not an iota. No matter how many poetic eddas their bards recite, nor how many anthems their rockstars sing, R4's natives possess the might of fleas in comparison to yourselves. They cannot comprehend you, bargain with you, or defeat you in battle. They represent raw materials for cultivation. End of story.

Legions of fancifully garbed action figures attack. Gun batteries of gnats scorch your pretty jumpsuit. Harmless. Gnat warheads sting your eyes. You blink. Warriors buzz and whine as they hurl themselves against you and your companions. Gnats leaping into a bonfire.

As a Drone, default passivity sustains you. Pom and the others are discombobulated, wild of mood, and violent. Their visages distort into black snow crystals, reflective of severe emotional turmoil. Fie reacts per their role as dedicated protector. Fie possesses a suite of capabilities. They choose murder. Their crystallized visage irises wide to emit a micro-pulse of ghastly red light. Puny phalanxes crisp to ash and whorl skyward. It's worse for the ragged few heroes who escape the awful glow. Fie yawns and inhales these unfortunate clouds of fleas, entombs them, alive and squirming, upon their flytrap innards, forever. If one or two victims escape Fie's wrath, those survivors will tell of a legendary battle and it will be sung as a patriotic dirge in taverns down through the ages. Our gift to posterity.

Grass immediately swallows the plain of bones.

Hush settles across the scarified land, but for the pop and sizzle of cooling acid. Then the maniacal laughter of Pom and Tor that lasts a millennium or a few minutes, and comes the dark.

Rise and Fall of Ur

Pom commands the city of Ur to be built in the shadow of mountains he names the Anvils. A sprawling sanctum whence global transformation shall be administered. This runs counter to procedure, which mandates a hidden outpost to house operations. Yours is not to question, but to obey. You dig your hands into the earth and sculpt a great mound. You fire the mound with your breath and form a megapolis of ceramics, glass, and steel. The city, an intricate scale model next to your immensity, shines upon its hill.

Pom commands the city to be made a beacon of culture dominated by a bejeweled palace and baroque theaters. Infused and guided by an imagination exponentially more vivid than your own, you erect fantastical monuments to the arts.

Pom commands you to establish centers of technology and science in honor of departed Nat, who prized such endeavors. You design fabulous machines and fashion automatons and computers to run the machinery. Crude in the scheme of things, your devices nonetheless represent marvels an eon ahead of R4's standards.

Pom commands the hollow city be made populous. Another violation of procedure. Automatons and synthetic humanoids are permissible; genetic clones of the mission Populator are not. Tor gleefully complies with this blasphemy. They squat, purging their royal jellies into the dirt. Embryonic figures burst glistening sacs and scatter. Some wriggle toward the mountains or into the cracks of the earth. A protean tide floods the city. The tide divides and divides, rapidly evolving into the smooth-countenanced citizenry of Ur. Humanoid, albeit uniformly simple of mind.

Pom commands Fie to install holograms and weapon emplacements, securing Ur against discovery and intrusion. However, Fie doesn't answer. Though you seek high and low, none can locate the Pacifier. Another augury of impending disaster. Nat is dead; Fie has apparently rebelled; and Pom is an architect, not a leader. Overwhelmed by the magnitude of their inadequacy, Pom soon withdraws into a cave, refusing your entreaties.

"What is your bidding?" You address Tor, your de facto superior.

"Do as you will, Drone. Impotent maggot. Emasculated flea. *I'm* getting laid." Tor summons a maelstrom and rides it west.

Their dramatic exit causes lightning strikes and hurricane winds to damage the outskirts of the city. Mass casualties result. Demi-human citizenry ignores the corpses of their fellows, intent upon inscrutable business. You effect repairs. Nature tends the dead. Work done, you rest, awaiting whatever fresh hell comes next with a strange mixture of emotions.

Fresh Hell

What comes next is an inevitable expression of the horror consuming your mission. For a while, the citizens of Ur are content to build widgets, mindlessly consume and copulate, and shamble the confines of their immaculate prison. Until one fine day, two citizens attempt to occupy the same doorway to a widget-manufacturing center. Push leads to shove, to slap, to eye-gouging and disembowelment. A factory riot ensues. Shortly, the riot spreads to the district, then another. Ur is engulfed in flames.

Your senses, albeit dulled via standard regression, penetrate a broad spectrum. Something has contaminated Tor's children. This corruption registers as an inner darkness rooted at the molecular level in the cerebral cortex. A crack that travels through everything, similar to how the K Drive operates. Darkness spreads, eating thought and flesh alike, precisely as your nightmare predicted. You feel dull pinpricks of fear. This mystery is beyond you.

Long-established procedure requires mission elements to preserve innate humanity by acceding to the upper limitations of flesh and blood (or, exceeding it briefly to achieve consummate goals). Granted, vast swaths of Imperial citizenry eschew such crude restrictions in their personal lives—entire industries of recreation and tourism are devoted to experiences that traffic in the perverse. Enclaves of flesh-shapers and mind-benders are popular alternatives to staid society. Cults of godhead founded upon multiplicity of aspect persist. Some folks enjoy implanting their consciousness in bodies of metal. Others have spent centuries cosplaying genius loci in the form of a sequoia, or a mountain peak, or a mass of continent-spanning fungi.

Takes all kinds.

But when it comes to the propagation of basic civilization via the Diaspora, retention of humanoid form is primary—permutation runs the risk of alienation or outright dissolution. Therefore, instead of growing an exoskeleton and gills (a trivial affect), one fabricates an environmental suit or battle chassis. Rather than titanium fangs and meson-beam eyes, one forges a K blade and a plasma rifle. Prohibitions notwithstanding, transcendence into ultra-physiognomies is permissible at the discretion of the

Ordinator. They call the shots in matters of godheadedness.

And if you happen to wash up on a planet ripe for complex life, yet lacking its presence? Tor would grin and say, *Be fruitful! Multiply!*

While hibernating, you fabricate steely tendrils and project them as myriad extensions of your will to burrow a labyrinth beneath the city. It's an idle expression of anxiety; a nervous tic; hint of a psychotic break. The vermiculate tunnels are endless, a death trap for citizens of Ur who blunder into them.

Does this amuse you? It amuses your ghost.

Fresh Hell II

Time passes.

Your dreams reek of madness. Some echo the excesses of your previous existence; others are psychic emanations of the Ur folk. These latter prick you until you awaken. Ur's crystal dome is corroded and reflects naught but inner darkness. This corrosion effectively shrouds the city. You've reduced again; twenty meters tall and proportioned as a mythical god or monster, depending upon one's orientation. You are tempted to smash a hole in the crystal dome and have a peek. Dread stays your hand. Dread of the moans, the squelching, the scratchy notes of a flute playing on a loop over stadium speakers. A vacation far afield is in order.

Drawn by intuition, you mantle yourself in obscuring haze and ramble south. An unnecessary precaution. Raw wilderness separates scattered population centers. Any lesser mortals who glimpse your passage assume they've sighted the shadowy bulk of a god or mythical creature and prostrate themselves in the dirt, eyes tightly shut until danger passes.

Precognitive impressions sharpen while your physical mass dwindles to local human norms. Each night, you hide and enter a regenerative fugue. Fie contacts you in primary dreamtime. Refers to themselves as Harm. Their countenance radiates heat. You cannot bear to behold them directly.

Dreamtime Harm vomits a diatribe: *Tor will ravage the primitives. When Tor is done, I'll swallow them whole. The primitives, our comrades, the fucking stars. Not you, Drone. I'll require a slave for the labors to come. I'll skin you. Dismember you. You'll do well enough with your mouth. Uproot forests. Dig and dig with your squirming tongue—*

"Shut up," you say in a booming voice, and awaken.

In due course, you home in upon another ark partially embedded at the southern antipode. Alpha Ark (as its Schop identifies the vessel on a repeating shortrange broadcast) experienced a similar disaster—only the Ordinator and Pacifier survived planetfall. They've assumed physiognomies and statures appropriate to typical Homo sapiens and renamed themselves Lud of the Wormwood and Ban the Rectifier. The duo have constructed rudimentary shelter. Neither citadel nor metropolis for them. Such work belongs to Drones.

The Ordinator reposes before the ark's crystal wreckage in a tight black jumpsuit splashed with refracted sunrays. They are in a mood. "No other crews were assigned to this destination. The error led to a collision of our vessels during planetfall. An error or filthy sabotage." Lud's form is nubile, their personality matrix old and scaly. "Where is Ordinator Beta?"

"Subsumed by malevolent energies."

"Those are the worst. You will attend me as your Ordinator, then."

"I am a faithful instrument in service of humankind."

"Welcome to the club," they say. "What of your Psychopomp?"

"We are… estranged," you say. "Pom is sequestered in a cavern."

"Classic. Your Populator?"

"Tor consorts with the natives."

"As a multilimbed fertility deity, one can hope. Since you're here, I surmise your Pacifier is defunct as well."

"Correct. Fie's matrix is corrupted. They renamed themselves Harm in honor of their new directive. Destroyer. Enslaver. Malcontent. Do you wish to access my visual log of the events that transpired subsequent to our arrival?"

Lud frowns. "I prefer to avoid intimate contact, Drone. You may be corrupted as well. Where is Harm now?"

As if summoned, a speck manifests above the rim of the horizon.

"En route," you say. "Recall your Pacifier before it's too late." Your form alters subtly, yet profoundly. Triple-sized heart and lungs; elongation of thigh, hams, and underlying bones; deformation of feet to emulate certain felines. It's you, albeit taller, sleeker, and faster. Speed will save you, if anything can.

Lud cocks his head. Metallic grinding floats on the wind. "That's a war frequency. Who authorized them to adopt an Aspect of Terror?"

"They are self-directed, I fear." It's not fear coursing through your veins, is it, though? Savage exultation.

The mote in the sky enlarges, twisting and re-forming like a cancerous cell. The Garuda Bird. Tiamat. A galvanic angel erupted from an illuminated manuscript. Apparently, Harm takes whatever shape pleases them, to hell with the prohibitions.

"On second thought, I should summon Ban per your suggestion," Lud says.

"Goodbye and good luck." And you are gone several kilometers into an evergreen forest when a supersonic boom slaps the canopy. Following Harm's example, you discard protocol and manifest titanium claws and burrow into the earth. There you hunker like a mole on Armageddon Day. Green pine needles scream as they burn. Heat singes you, even at this depth; soil melts to slag. Your nanoshroud will do its best, but its capacity has diminished. Any death could be a true death. You fabricate an alloy capsule to preserve your precious flesh and stoically abide.

Shit rains down for a while. Your dreams are smooth and dark as the interior of an egg until Ferris, all in white, flickers and dances on the event horizon of your subconscious.

See you soon, you miserable prick.

You surprise yourself with a snicker. Only a little. Mental failsafes are unlocking with the presumed destruction of Ordinator Lud and Pacifier Ban. It's coming back. Every heinous (glorious) detail of your villainous scheme.

Rayguns Set to Kill

Time passes.

You unearth yourself and return (strutting, gamboling, humming a show tune) to the crash site of Alpha Ark. You find scorched plains, glass hills, and a tower of radioactive smoke. Lud and Ban put up a fight to no avail. Pieces of them are scattered, smoldering. Harm stands alone, victorious, battle cloak fluttering in the breeze, back turned, head bowed. Wrong: not bowed, missing. Their corpse topples. Most unexpected, most perturbing. You stroke your newly grown goatee.

A rockpile shudders and flies apart. Pom emerges, dusts their sleeves, and regards you. "Hey there, lover. You missed the fun."

That voice pierces you to the core. Unmistakable in any era, any circumstance, at a bajillion parsecs or twenty meters. Ferris's stance, swagger, the scent of her pheromones… No mistaking her soul burning through the eyes of a puppet. Somehow your wife has subsumed the Psychopomp's matrix and occupied their shell. She flings Harm's head so it rolls toward you and stops. Its expression is glazed into an eternal flat affect.

That head isn't Harm's, albeit equally familiar. Behind the Pacifier's face lurks another, darker identity. Here lies a double of the one you altered back on Earth hours prior to exodus. Your most devious and intricate work, splitting a consciousness into three and automating them to specific purposes—this deranged Pacifier; Jack, the Gallery Sol Killer; and Jack's husk in its ornamented tomb so very similar to your own.

You grin daggers. "Jackie boy, I hardly knew thee."

Ferris says, "This monstrosity of yours. Such a cruel, pointless gesture to sic their alter ego upon Earth, upon Gallery Sol."

"Baby, I'm a fan of futile gestures. What do you get for the woman who has everything?"

"Not Jack the Ripper, please."

"On the contrary. A super killer was the perfect gift to the galaxy's finest detective. You were bored too. My girl deserved one last challenge."

She closes the distance, warping reality without seeming to move; a heat mirage rippling across the field. "You rigged everything. Your unaltered personality stowed away beneath the façade of a Drone. You somehow engineered two arks appearing in the same time-space; the resultant disasters."

"I corrupted our Pacifier and our Schop. The dominoes fell and fell."

"Were you that fucking bored. With me?"

"Yes!" you cry. The truth at last.

"Were you that fucking evil?"

"Worse!"

"You want to play a god."

"God, devil... Hell, boogeyman will suffice. R4 is my very own personal ant farm."

Her eyes are bright, the lone glimmer of emotion. "We've entire vacation worlds dedicated to indulging every debased fantasy—"

"Canned hunts are hardly the same, dear."

Ferris draws a flinty knife and advances. Happier now that the pleasantries are dispensed and it's come down to this.

Your darkest, atavistic self chooses weapons; it manifests a pair of Mark IX Disruptors and you fire both from the hip. A purple ray and a green ray crisscross and bisect the hill behind your wife. The rim of the new pit glows brightly. She steps between the rays and catches your throat in her left hand. The one with the death's head ring, among others. Her right hand presses the dagger point against your breast. You'd love to shoot her, but she's pinched a nerve and you're immobilized. Her willpower had attracted you during the courtship phase of your relationship. Manifested here, that willpower is no less than godly. The real deal compared to your pretension. Poor Harm hadn't stood a chance.

"By what eldritch sorcery are you here to menace me?" you say, stalling. "That knife feels awfully cold to be a dream."

"My dreams are very cold. What if we fell into one and couldn't wake up?"

You finally comprehend, now that Ferris has pinned you like a carcass on hooks. In your mind's eye, your faraway tomb shimmers; a slot opens in its icy metal. Ferris crawls inside. The slot seals. "Shit. The astral cord isn't severed."

"Whisper thin," she says. "When I realized you'd embarked on a sabotage mission and left a maniac to distract me, I made the only move I could. I grabbed on and leaped into the abyss. Wheee!"

She'd latched on to your cord and transmitted her animating force. Imperial physicists posit such a maneuver is possible over a short range. Never been tested in this kind of scenario; too dangerous for either party. Calculations suggested that even strong minds risked destruction via disassociation and dissolution. Ferris proves the exception to the rule.

"But wait, there's more," she says.

"Oh, you rotten bitch." You mean it fondly. "The master plan is to destroy both bodies. Mine and Elmer D's."

"I don't want to snuff you, sweetie."

"Then what do you intend?"

"The blade in my hand is a quantum device." Her knife bites in and draws blood. "Its analogue on the other end is plain ol' prehistoric flint. *This* Drone form will die the real death. Your other body will suffer momentary trauma and revive."

"Quite elaborate," you say. "What's your motive?"

"Pique. Death is too easy, too gentle."

Many, many light years off, yet within kissing distance, Ferris entwines with Elmer D the way lovers were found in charcoal in ancient Pompeii. Diamonds, rubies, and emeralds shine above and below. Their constellations represent bad, bad signs. On Earth, she drives that dagger all the way into her husband's slow-beating heart.

Same thing here.

Like Nosferatu, Several Billion CE

Time passes.

As she predicted, you die for a moment or two. A trillion moments. Two trillion. Your vital essence is ensnared in the retracting astral cord and violently reborn into your old form on Earth inside the D family tomb. The shock and indignity cause you to snap partially upright. Reflexively, you seize the blade Ferris planted in your chest and wrench it free. Blood sprays from the wound. Blood sprays from your screaming mouth. Blood spatters against the twinkling crushed gemstones that line the sarcophagus. Blood drips and dims the clean, pale light to a garish crimson. Dying the real death, and for good, is a distinct possibility. Then your nanoshroud kicks in and stabilizes matters. It will keep you ticking; a decidedly mixed blessing. The set of bones lying next to you presumably belongs to Ferris. This tomb was built for one, alas.

Already your thoughts move ahead, casting aside trivial sentiment. What will you do once you escape this sarcophagus? Blend in with society or terrorize it? You've been gone a while. Is anyone else alive or does civilization lie in ruins? What will happen to the inhabitants of Ur, of R4? Who cares?

Ferris's holographic likeness materializes amid the pretty lights. Recorded long ago and doubtless triggered by the change in your brainwave activity. She's anticipated what you're feeling, what you're thinking.

You'll be plotting your grand resurrection, she says, dry as her bones. *Think again. This coffin has an entrance, but no exit.*

It is to laugh. You're clever; you'll sniff out a weak spot. Failing that, you're patient; sooner or later a rube is sure to come along and set you free…

You're clever. I took that into account.

Hmm.

You patiently abide. I considered that too.

Wonderful.

Eventually you'll figure a way to escape, or some poor fool will open the hatch.

This droll monologue isn't going in the direction you'd prefer.

Luckily, I too have well-positioned friends. Pulled every string, called in every marker. Violated a law or two. Can't be too careful with a supervillain such as yourself… I arranged to have this box excavated and jettisoned into deep space. A sequence of events flash amid the gemstones—you behold a replay of machinery chopping the sarcophagus out of the depths and loading it onto a rocket; the rocket shooting into orbit and farther; the rocket ejecting its cargo across the border of a charted galaxy into a void; the rocket self-destructing, all record of its mission, its existence, erased in a tiny, smokeless implosion. The anonymous, ignominious, end of Elmer D.

Well, fuck a duck.

Ferris cracks her rarest smile. *Say something to me. Say, for the love of God, Montresor.*

Her mocking image is impervious to your blows; her words loop as the capsule tumbles eternally through unbounded darkness. Or maybe the darkness revolves inside of you. Sucks either way.

If they'd decorated your cerements with bells, you'd jingle them in solidarity with Fortunato.

THE PECULIAR SECLUSION OF MOLLY McMARSHALL

Gwendolyn Kiste

Security footage taken on the morning of May 1st

I N the grainy black-and-white video, a woman, later identified as Molly McMarshall, walks up the shadowy front porch of her Paradise Street home and steps over the threshold.

She isn't seen outside of the house again.

Local Woman Potentially Missing (newspaper article from May 25th)
Thirty-nine-year-old Molly McMarshall is suspected missing. McMarshall has not been seen or heard from since at least May 1st, and even her last known whereabouts are currently unclear. Some speculate that she might still be inside her Paradise Street home, though local authorities have yet to comment.

~

Shortly after the initial news reports, Help Us Free Molly McMarshall appeared online. The first blog post from June 17th is reprinted below.
We didn't know she'd disappeared. We didn't know anything at first.

It was more than two weeks before any of us on the street realized something was wrong. After all, Molly was not the most popular person on the block.

"She was always a weirdo," said one neighbor who asked to remain anonymous. "Always taking these long walks around the neighborhood. Staring up at the sky. Whispering to it. Honestly, when we didn't see her for a few days, we were all hoping she'd just moved away or something. If only."

But once the newspapers started piling up on the front porch and the mailbox bulged with junk flyers, we soon began to suspect something was amiss.

Are you sure she's even still in there? This was the most frequent question asked in those early days. *Maybe she's dead* was the second most common sentiment, often spoken with a kind of vague hopefulness. Not because our neighborhood is cruel, of course; simply because a quick end would be preferred to a drawn-out missing person case. We only wanted what was best for her. That's all we ever wanted.

The police arrived shortly thereafter to perform a wellness check, but when they knocked—quite vigorously, according to some locals— no one answered the door.

"Break the whole place down," a neighbor called from an adjacent yard, but the responding officers either didn't hear or didn't care. They left after a third attempt and never returned. When reached for comment, the precinct representative said they don't speak about active cases. When we inquired if there was indeed an active case, the representative hung up on us and refused all further calls.

At that point, the neighborhood decided they had no choice but to deal with the matter themselves.

"Clearly something's wrong," they said, and that was enough of an excuse to attempt breaking and entering in broad daylight.

Only the house wouldn't budge. Not the front door or the back door or any of the windows. Not when they knocked or shoved and even kicked until their toes blistered.

"It was like the whole place was made of steel," one of the old-timers told us later. "Like something didn't want us to get in."

Cursing under their breath, the neighbors shuffled home for the night.

"Maybe she really is dead," they said. "Or maybe she's just gone for good. Slipped out the back or something."

It was a passable enough theory, one that might have remained the general opinion of the neighborhood if Molly hadn't finally made an unexpected appearance. On a balmy June evening with the temperature swelling past ninety degrees in the shade, she was at last spotted at her downstairs window. By the time somebody noticed her there, she was already sitting in an old rocking chair, staring out at the street, her eyes wide and gray and strangely vacant.

This wasn't quite the sight anybody expected, and while they weren't particularly happy to see Molly again, everyone was at least satisfied that they didn't have to call a coroner to extract a rank corpse that would, of course, lower property values on Paradise Street.

"We should make sure she's all right," they said, and several eager neighbors knocked again on the front door and waved to her in the window. But she didn't seem to notice them. She just kept staring out, seeing everything and nothing.

"Is it even legal to loiter there like that?" someone asked, as an onslaught of curious passersby gathered on the sidewalk out front.

"It's certainly not decent," said the local county commissioner, who lived four doors down and also wanted to remind everyone he was running for re-election in November. "And it's certainly not the sort of spectacle we need in this neighborhood."

As she continued to gape out at them, never blinking, never moving, it soon became the consensus of everyone on Paradise Street that something most definitely needed to be done about Molly McMarshall.

A copy of the flyer posted around town, featuring a grainy photo from the May 1st security camera footage
Do you know this woman? Are you a member of her family or a personal friend? If so, please contact us today! We need your help in assisting her. Please don't delay. Get in touch with us now before it's too late.

WLFD local TV news station interview (transcript from June 30th broadcast)
Three women stand on the front lawn in front of Molly McMarshall's home.

RUTH ROBERTS: This is Ruth Roberts reporting from Paradise Street on the ongoing Molly McMarshall saga. I'm here today with Molly's family: her mother Bedelia and her sister Therese, both of whom are just as worried sick as the rest of us about Molly's well-being. Mrs. McMarshall, what can you tell us about your daughter?

BEDELIA McMARSHALL: What's there to say? Small-town girl. Small-town dreams. Never expected much out of her. Definitely never expected her to cause all this trouble.

RUTH ROBERTS: Mrs. McMarshall, everyone wants to know: have you tried to reach her?

BEDELIA McMARSHALL: Of course we have. We've called repeatedly. We've knocked on the door. We've even thrown rocks at the window. No response. Not that I'm surprised. She was always such a stubborn girl. Had to do things her own way.

RUTH ROBERTS: And what would make your daughter want to do something like this?

BEDELIA McMARSHALL: Well, she always was an odd one. Never wanted to be around other people. Never liked sleepovers or birthday parties or Sunday school or any of that normal people stuff. Anywhere we'd take her, she'd just wander off and find something random to stare at.

THERESE McMARSHALL: It was like she was waiting on something.

RUTH ROBERTS: Did you ever ask who she was waiting for?

THERESE McMARSHALL: Sure. She always said it was already here. She said it was her friend.

BEDELIA McMARSHALL (*with a grunt*): An imaginary friend. At her age? Can you think of something more ridiculous?

THERESE McMARSHALL: She used to always tell me that I could see it too. That is, if I really wanted to. But she would warn me that I probably wouldn't like what I saw.

RUTH ROBERTS: If you could say anything to Molly right now, what would it be?

BEDELIA McMARSHALL: To stop all this fuss and come out this minute. She's caused enough problems, don't you think?

RUTH ROBERTS: A plea from a family to their little girl lost. This is Ruth Roberts reporting from WLFD.

It's worth noting that, after this interview, Molly's family refused all further contact with the media, saying they couldn't explain her behavior any better than the rest of us. At this time, their whereabouts are unknown, though there is speculation that they're currently sequestered in their own home in an adjacent county.

~

Description of Molly McMarshall's property

Saltbox house built in 1921, painted baby blue with black shutters.

Two floors, two bedrooms, one bath.

Aerial drone footage shows some wear on the slate roof. Possible leaks along the north wall of the house facing the backyard. Overgrown grass on all sides. A strange shadow clouds one half of the image, in particular over the porch and front window. To date, no explanation of the shadow has been given.

Help Us Free Molly McMarshall, blog post, dated July 8th

A substitute teacher at the local middle school. An administrative assistant at a paper bag factory. A temp at virtually every office on Main Street. Molly McMarshall tried on many visages in her time in our town, but none of them seemed to stick.

"She was never much of anybody," seems to be the general consensus of her neighbors, none of whom sent her Christmas cards for the holidays or bothered to tell her about the July Fourth block party, even though it was open to the public and happened right outside her front door.

This year's block party unfortunately was a somewhat somber occasion. It's rather difficult to enjoy your hot dog and corn-on-the-cob when a strange woman with an arcane stare is gaping out at you from her picture window.

"It's a performance art piece," the county commissioner said, gritting his teeth, a splotch of mustard on his lapel. "That's why she sits there peering out like that. She wants us to look at her. She wants us to notice."

Others in the neighborhood, however, aren't quite so convinced.

"I'm not sure she can see anything we're doing out here," said one local homemaker. "Like maybe it's one-way glass, and when we think she's looking out at us, she's really only looking at herself."

There are naturally other theories too.

"She's clearly a god or a demon or something," a group of teens told us. "How else could she survive in there without food or water all this time? How else could she stare out and not blink or move or anything?"

Local mechanic Jacob is the only one who isn't sure what the fuss is about.

"I can't for the life of me see how any of this is our business," he told the local news station. "Why don't we just leave the poor woman alone? Maybe there's a reason she wants to be by herself. Who are we to argue?"

Checklist of Ways to Get Molly McMarshall Out of Her Saltbox House and Back into Proper Society (presented to the City Council at the August meeting)

- Knock one more time. Just to be polite.
- Pick the lock on the front door. If that doesn't work, pick the lock on the back door. If both doors prove to be as impervious as previously suggested, kick them down. If that fails, fashion a battering ram, and pulverize the door to pulp.
- Smoke her out. Even a ghoul like her has got to breathe, right? A couple small brush fires near the windows should work splendidly. Light a few more fires if needed. Light up the whole house.
- Use a brick.
- Use your fists.
- Use a chainsaw and cut out half the wall.
- Do whatever it takes to get her out of that house, because this has gone on long enough.

A note scrawled in black ink, found tacked to the front door of Molly McMarshall's home at approximately 6 a.m. on September 16th. No one saw who taped it there, but most people agree it appears to be Molly's handwriting.

Please leave me alone. Leave both of us alone. That's all I want. When you see it, it's all you'll want too—to be far away from here.

Cell phone footage of the September 17th attempt to extract Molly McMarshall from her home. A group of local men huddle on the front porch, their words mostly bleeding together. Below is the best transcript we could manage.

VOICE ONE: Y'all ready?

A single knock on the front door. Just to be polite.

VOICE TWO: Are you sure she's in there?

VOICE ONE (*a grunting laugh*): Where else would she be?

The door inches open. The figures blur in the darkness.

VOICE THREE (*a woman's voice, possibly belonging to Molly McMarshall*): You should leave now. Before it's too late. Before it notices you.

The men back away, just a step, just for a moment, and in the doorway the figure of Molly McMarshall emerges. Something else emerges too. An obscure shape that limns her body, like the inverse of a halo.

VOICES (*overlapping, urgent*): What the—? What is… (*Static crackles, several moments of flailing arms and gaping mouths and vague screeching.*) What are we even looking at?

VOICE THREE: I'm so sorry for you. It's noticed you now.

The men stare into the gloom, and even in the raw footage, you can see it: the moment their eyes fade to gray. The whole world holds still, as a shadow clouds the lens. When the blurry image returns, the men's faces are already vacant and wan, their bodies rigid. One by one, they turn around on the porch and march off like tin soldiers. Back to the sidewalk, back to their homes.

None of them has been seen since.

~

Help Us Free Molly McMarshall, blog post, dated October 1st
Nobody knows how the video got out. Nobody even knows for sure who filmed it. None of the neighbors would ever take credit for it. Regardless, it went viral overnight, garnering half a million views in less than twenty-four hours.

That's when they started to arrive. The outsiders. The ones who wanted to get a look for themselves.

"Vultures," says the county commissioner, who rarely leaves his own house now. "Whenever you've got a tragedy like this one, there are always people eager to exploit it. They like to revel in other people's misery."

He's not wrong—the spectators are indeed reveling. They sit cross-legged on the sidewalk. They pack picnic lunches. Sometimes, they sing songs to one another, strident little lullabies that practically make the neighbors' ears bleed. Most of the time, though, they simply stare back at Molly, who's still sitting at her window, all of them smiling at her like they're sharing a secret.

Except Molly McMarshall never smiles back. She just keeps staring, watching something the rest of us can barely fathom.

The McMarshall Manifesto

1. To devote ourselves to the Molly McMarshall way of living: austere and uncompromising.
2. To make the pilgrimage to her home.
3. To see what it is she's hiding there.
4. To embrace that darkness and let it embrace us.
5. To introduce it to everyone we can.

This manifesto first appeared duct-taped to the double doors of the WLFD news station on the evening of October 30th. It was then read on the air on October 31st where many mistook it for a Halloween prank. It wasn't until the manifesto also popped up on lampposts and coffee shop bulletin boards that locals realized it was from the same group of people camped out in front of the McMarshall house.

Video recovered from November 3rd raid on Molly McMarshall's home
There's no dialogue in the footage. Barely any noise at all. The authors of the manifesto, the ones who had gathered in ever-increasing numbers around the house, are already on the porch when the video starts. They knock twice, and the door opens. Nobody knows why she answered. Not on this night or on the night in September with the local men. Maybe it was just time. Maybe she finally wanted everyone to meet the friend she'd kept hidden for so long.

Molly doesn't say anything. She doesn't have to. It only takes a moment before it emerges from within her and all around her. A dark splotch like a moving inkblot. The others on the porch watch her. They don't run. They don't move. They just stand there, their arms open wide, as the shadow envelops them. The camera cuts to black.

Help Us Free Molly McMarshall, blog post, dated November 10th
We don't fully understand what happened next. We probably never will. Her devotees, if that's what you can call them, vanished from town that night. When they left, they took something with them, and from there it spread like a poison, first to all the neighboring counties, and then to all the neighboring states before bleeding over every border. Thousands of people in their shuttered houses and their high-rise apartments, their duplexes and mobile homes. No one is immune. Too many have seen it now, whatever it is waiting in the shadow with Molly. Unless, of course, there's nothing in the darkness at all. Nothing

besides her.

Still, not everyone blames Molly for it.

"We could have left her alone," commented one local on our now-defunct discussion board. "She never asked for any of this. I doubt she'd like all the fuss we've made about her."

As for why Molly McMarshall would do something so drastic in the first place, the commenter had only this to say: "I think she just wanted some 'me time.' Is that so terrible? These days, it seems like that's all anybody really wants."

WLFD local TV news station feature (transcript from December 1st broadcast). Ruth Roberts stands outside Molly McMarshall's home. There's no one else left on the sidewalk.

RUTH ROBERTS: It's been more than six months since Molly McMarshall locked herself inside her Paradise Street home. For weeks, her concerned neighbors did their best to band together and draw her out. They wanted nothing more than to help her get back on track. Instead, where there should be a celebration of a life rescued, we have even more lives destroyed.

Camera pans to show the houses up and down the street, all the yards overgrown, the front windows fogged up. It zooms in on one particular window where there's movement on the other side, and something materializes behind the glass: wide, vacant eyes peering back at us.

RUTH ROBERTS: What have they seen? And why are they hiding? We've knocked on every front door on Paradise Street, but as we expected, nobody answered. That doesn't mean it's over. We'll keep at this breaking news story until the end. As always, this is Ruth Roberts reporting for WLFD.

Shortly after this broadcast, WLFD reporter Ruth Roberts failed to report to work. Soon, her coworkers failed to report to work as well. It's believed they're currently sequestered in their own homes. We can't be sure, though, because we're all sequestered in our homes now too.

Help Us Free Molly McMarshall, final blog post, December 5th
Paradise Street is quiet now. All the streets in the world are quiet. In a way, it's almost a mercy. Maybe Molly had the right idea.

There won't be any more updates on the case. No more hopes of retrieving anyone these days. We'll be closing down this site at the end of the year. Before we remove all correspondence, though, we want to share one more piece of evidence. On the final day we visited the McMarshall home, another letter was found tacked to the front door. Much like the previous note, we could never verify its author, but we suspect it might be the last known correspondence from Molly McMarshall. The letter's contents are transcribed below. Thank you for joining us in our best-hearted attempts at this failed search-and-rescue. We wish you luck in your newfound isolation.

I warned you. I told you to stay away. You wouldn't listen. Now when you peer out of your smudged picture windows, all you can see reflected back is the emptiness of your own distant faces. And when I stare out of mine, all I can see is you. The unraveling of your neighborhoods, the slow but steady decimation of every block in every city.

And even though you can't see it, even though you can't see anything at all now, please know that I'm still here. That I'll always be here. And as I watch the world untether around us, rest assured that all I can do is smile.

ACROSS THE BRIDGE

Tim Lebbon

Aᴼᴛᴇʀ waking and before breakfast, we perform the Counting of Stones, like we do every morning, and find that the number is seventeen. It's been seventeen for quite a few days, but before that it was fifteen, and quite a long time ago it was nineteen and even twenty. Gerry says this was because sometimes the stones come and go in the night, visiting us or maybe just arriving here when they flee from other places. He seems pretty certain when he says this, but I can see the slight widening of his eyes, and hear the quaver in his voice. As if he's not sure at all and is holding in his doubts and fear. Meg laughs at this and says none of us really knows how to count anymore. I don't know which alternative is more disturbing.

They're not even stones. They're trees. But Helene, the oldest among us, our seer and leader of the village, says that ancient trees all turn to stone eventually, and she's saving time the trouble of changing their names.

The trees stand around in a very rough circle in a field just beyond our settlement. There's no real border or boundary, but if there was one it would be between the last dwellings and the gathering place of the trees. I never feel any fear walking from one to the other. Whatever they'll become in the future, the to-be stones exude no threat.

Or maybe that's just me. I hardly ever see Gerry walking out this way, and if I ever invite him he makes up some excuse. *Got to dig out another irrigation trench*, or *Helene wants me to make a new number board*, or *My belly hurts*. Meg says he always used to claim his stomach hurt when he was a child and something worried or scared him. Gerry says she's lying, but how can either of them know? None of us remembers that far back, and they're not even sure that they're brother and sister. That was before, and if we try to recall things or places or faces from before, there's nothing but haze. Helene says that's self-preservation. She says a lot of things I find difficult to understand, and plenty more I'm not sure I agree with.

That's why I like to walk out into the rough circle of trees. There's a sycamore that's always looked old and ill, a couple of ghostly silver birch, and a weeping willow that stands out at the edge of the field by the stream. I love walking into the willow's embrace because its drooping branches and leaves seem to welcome me in, and I can imagine walking out of this world and into another. Not before— no one really wants to go there anymore, because before led to now and now is harsh and hard. But somewhere else. Maybe a place and a time that we might have been, had we taken more care of our world. There's also an old oak in the field, its trunk split and hollowed by a long-ago lightning strike. It looks like stone already, that trunk, but one half still clings on to life, valiant leaves bursting from tortured limbs and branches time after time. I've never been inside the hollow trunk. Sometimes I imagine living in there, away from everyone and everything else. But Meg would find me and tell Helene, and I'd never be away for long.

I glance back for Meg now. Sometimes she follows me, teasing and calling me names. Not today, though. I can see her out by the wind waves, chasing the streamers of cloth as they drift back and forth in the almost-still air. The world is never at peace, Helene says. Even if you can stand in the middle of a field and sense nothing at all—no breeze, no sounds of creatures moving or breathing, no scent on the air—time is still moving all around you, uncaring whether you know it or not.

I watch Meg for a while, rushing among the wind waves in mimicry of their graceful motion. I close my eyes and sense no wind at all. No breeze. No movement. When I look again, Meg is also standing still between the streamers as they twitch and flow all around her. I wonder not for the first time whether it's the wind waves that follow our movements, and not the other way around. Whether we move the world or the world moves us.

It's too much to think about on such a beautiful morning. Besides, I have a destination in mind. It's a place I've been drawing closer to recently, even though visiting is strictly forbidden. I'm going to Old Town, because the more often I approach, the less that place scares me.

Everything bad in our past is there, Helene will say if I ask her, but Gerry's terror of the place makes him more blunt. It's a shithole where all the bad stuff happened, and whoever goes there will be knee-deep in the rotten corpses of our past.

I know that our past is a long time gone, and any corpses have decayed to nothing. Bones don't scare me, just as the to-be stones of the counted trees are not troubling.

"See you soon," I whisper to Meg, but I'm way across the field now, and I watch through shadows beneath the trees as she pirouettes around a wind wave that shimmies and shivers in the motionless air.

"I remember when it happened," Meg said. "People started dying in the streets. An old woman who used to serve us food from her farm shop was collapsed in a gutter, coughing and sweating and shitting herself, and a lorry ran over her and her head popped. They didn't even bother scraping her up. It was easier to sweep her brains down the drain. There were too many dying then, coffins were piling up, and people started to cremate the dead in their back gardens. You could smell it on the air all the time, like roasting pork mixed with the stench of burning plastic as the fires took false teeth, and funeral shrouds, and watches and cheap jewellery. My mouth used to water at the smell of cooking meat. Even when my father died, his throat swollen, eyes bleeding, and we set fire to him in the fire-pit at the bottom of our garden. He used to barbecue there for us, and sometimes Gerry snuck a swig from Dad's beer after he'd had a few and the fire made him glow orange. He burned for a day and a night. Gerry went and poked him with a stick after a while, to make sure his skeleton came apart. We crushed up his bones, and Gerry wanted to use them to fertilise our garden for the following spring, but by then it had all gone too far. Everyone was dead, dying, or running, and we fled. Don't you remember? The smell of that city as we were finally running away, from there to here?"

"No," I said, and she became angry at me because she thought I was accusing her of lying. I wasn't, not out loud. But Meg was barely nineteen, two years younger than me, and Helene told us that Old Town was half a century gone. None of us could remember. I couldn't blame her for making it up, though. Maybe she was braver than me speaking her nightmares.

The fallen bridge is lower than I've ever seen it, or perhaps the river is higher. I've been across the river before, but I don't go every time. Sometimes I just sit on an old tumbled wall and look at the opposite bank, wondering what would happen if I let myself be carried away by the water instead. What I would find. Where I'd end up. Helene says there are many more like us, but that everyone keeps to themselves now. It's a safer way to exist.

I'd already made up my mind even before I reached here, so I start to climb across, watching my footing, careful not to snag my clothes on broken metal and trip or slip. Going into the river has only ever been a fantasy. It's not fast-moving, but I don't know how to swim.

The rusted metal vibrates beneath my hands. It's the voice of the river, flowing through the ruined bridge and setting it shaking to its own song. I can't make out any words. The land whispers words we cannot know.

I climb as high as I can, eager not to get wet, and once I'm on the other side everything feels different. I'm not used to being alone, and though these moments of secretive exploration give me something of a thrill, I also feel the tug of home. It's as if I am on a piece of string, and its pull becomes heavier and stronger the further I go.

I'm into the woods before I can turn back and return to the village.

I've come this far before.

The trees here are wilder than those that grow close to the village. Their shadows touch my skin with unknown intent, and water drips from the canopy after recent heavy rain that landed here, but did not fall back where I came from. Perhaps the river is a barrier that also divides the skies.

I've walked beneath these trees.

There is no path through the woodland, but the ferns are only waist high, and I avoid areas of thick bramble and fallen trees. I don't know how long it is since I've been this way—time is fluid, flowing from and to strange places in the same way as the river I've just crossed without touching—and the landscape feels only vaguely familiar. I have come the same way before, into the woods and along the lower slopes of the valley side. Though there's a temptation to go higher, I always resist it.

What I want to see isn't that high.

Others have been this way—not Meg, and probably not Gerry either, though I've never asked him, and don't think he'd tell me the truth if I did—but others from the village. Even so, no one really talks about Old Town. It's from *before*, and no one likes to dwell on how the world became what it is.

My memory of coming this way is like an old dream remembered. The crooked tree to my left, trunk bent and reaching for the sky as if it fell and rose again. The outcropping of rock scattered with beautiful flowers and home to small, darting brown creatures. I'm not sure what they are, but their whiskered noses quiver and sniff at me. It's nice to see animals curious and unafraid.

I'm almost there.

The first wall reveals itself out of the woods. It's softened and greened by moss, but its basic blocky structure remains. There's another close by, and then silence settles around me as I find myself surrounded by the low ruins of fallen buildings. It's not the quiet of a nature cautious of me, but an absence that I've noticed before. It's like a held breath, ironic in a place of the dead. Old Town has been gone for a long time, yet still I sense its ghosts.

This is where we came from.

I've no memory of Old Town. None of us has, because whatever Meg says, it all happened long before we were born. Stories fade and become obscured the further back they originate—that's Helene's idea of self-preservation, and she's our seer and guide and I have to believe she knows what she's talking about—but the few times I've been here it has always felt like a deeply strange, alien place. Somewhere none of us ever belonged, or ever could.

I approach the first tumbled, overgrown building and imagine it as something other than a pile of rubble, rotten wood, and a home to smothering nature. I find another that still has a chimney breast standing, and one where a metal door frame is a rusted invitation through which I dare not pass. In between visits I drift away, perhaps to sleep. In my sleep I count the stones that the trees will become, and time flows around and through me.

Most of Old Town has been taken back by the world. It's some form of justice, Helene would tell us. Meg laughs at that. She loves the wild, and the idea that we survive because we are a part of it. I wander back and forth, through places where trees grow thick and healthy out of stone ruins as if defying time, and sometimes there's barely any trace left at all.

I smell something strange. A faint, acrid taint, like something artificial burning in unseen flames. I pause and turn in circles, then walk back and forth through the silent woodland, sensing the breeze, trying to place where the smell comes from.

There's a hollow in a large bank of brambles and wild flowers. I push my way in. Broken steps lead down, the route filled with a chaos of undergrowth. The staircase turns ninety degrees as if to hide from the light, and I find this junction is guarded by a tangle of bones.

I've seen bones before. They're old sad things, and even the crazy grin of a stripped skull is only a scream from the past. Nothing to be afraid of. Further down, in the darkness past the skeleton that's held together by little more than creeping plants and memories, there is a door. Heavy, strong, made from solid wood, the plants growing around it show it hasn't been opened in a long, long time.

It takes me some time to tear away these plants. I become focused on the task.

Behind the door I discover my first ghost.

When I wake up my home feels quite big, and that is a relief because a few times lately it's felt small. It's odd that it's different every day— not hugely different, sometimes just a deep breath wider or a frown narrower—but it's a fact I just accept. You have to go with the flow, my mother always used to say. I go with the flow every day, but still try to steer it as much as I can.

I get up and mark the day with a cross on the wall. I scratch into the brickwork with the knife, two deep lines, exposing lighter powdered brick beneath the tarnished surface. It's been a long time since I've counted up all those crosses. I used to think of them as a dash between my date of birth and whatever day I die. Someone once said that dash on your gravestone represents your whole life—every moment, every love, each glorious night and terrible day—and that a dash can mean everything. For me it's these crosses, and they're everywhere now, covering all the surfaces of the three basement rooms that have been my home for... for as long as the crosses say. To begin with I scratched them in neat lines, twenty-one to each brick. Then I started passing the days randomly around the basement, because those ordered blocks of time building, building, had started depressing me.

I never miss a day. Days are precious. Days are where we live. My mother told me that, I think she read it to me in a poem. That same poem talked about madness, but I try not to think about that.

I walk my three rooms. I do this every time I get up for the day, to stretch my legs and maintain control over my domain. Also, to see if any food has crawled in during the night. Sometimes I find a spider or a beetle, or perhaps a worm wriggling out through the feed holes I've drilled through the mortar between bricks. Once there was a mouse, dashing back and forth across my bathroom, and it took me a day to catch it, a minute to eat. Once, a year or four ago, a bat.

I don't kid myself. There are ways in, and ways out, but I don't worry too much about the infection getting inside. I've lasted this long. And besides, I have protection. I take no chances.

Room one. Bedroom, living area, library, and the History Place. I always sleep on the sofa, and once I wake up, I fold my single blanket into a cushion for back support. My library is in a cart, a small, wheeled unit that I move a little every day. The wheels squeal with the damp.

I have forty-two books. At the beginning there were forty-four, but I tore up and burnt two because forty-two is the answer, and that makes me smile. I can't recall which books I destroyed. The one I've read the most is *The Hitchhiker's Guide to the Galaxy*. Twenty-seven times at last count, I write a small tick inside the front cover each time I read it. I'm reading it again right now, and I know where my towel is. *Emma*

I've read seven times. *The Stand* I've only read three times, it's really long and a lot of it feels like bad memories.

There's only one book I have never read, and I'm not sure I ever will. It's called *The Silent Land*. I'd just started it when all this began, and even though I brought it down with the others, I don't want to finish it. That would feel like the end of something, and I'm not ready for all this to end.

The History Place takes up one whole wall, and this is the only part of the basement where I'm not passing time with scratched crosses. It's covered in pictures, pieces of writing, and everything else I've created to do with the past. I'm trying to keep things alive. These are my memories given form, and because sometimes they slip my mind, it's good that I can get them down on paper. Some days I spend so long looking at this wall that I forget to eat or drink. Other days, when I'm missing Kerry so much that it is acid in my veins, I try not to look at it at all.

I sit and pick up the pad and pencil I keep on a small table in front of the History Place and start writing.

Kerry in the kitchen doing an impression of a frozen chicken, arms out with fingers splayed, legs slightly bent. We laugh hysterically. She does the impression in the supermarket sometimes. No one else laughs, and that's fine, because secrets are a private language.

I look at the note for a while, smiling at Kerry frozen there in the kitchen, in my mind. It's a small memory, but that's what my history is made from. I tear off the bottom third of the page and stick it to the wall with a snip of tape.

Room Two. Pantry. It's very small, little more than a cupboard really, and I called it this when I arrived. I'd stocked it with so much tinned food and plastic water containers that I thought it would last me forever. All that has gone now, but I still use the name. I use the tins and packets, too, for different purposes.

Today there are two tins half full of water seepage that has come through the walls. I've drilled holes, and when it rains water percolates down, through the undergrowth and soil, and then into the holes. It carries infection and filth with it, but I always filter and boil.

I pick a tin of treated water from a shelf, and a paper bag of insects I've caught and dried, and put them in the airlock in the living area ready for later. But first I visit Room Three. It has always been the bathroom, but things change. The toilet retains its use, but now there's no water in there. I use a bag instead, one of hundreds I brought down with me. I don't urinate in there—there's a hole in the wooden door at the far end of the bathroom where I do that.

We were always lucky living in a house with such a network of basements. Beyond that door is a stone staircase leading down to a deeper room, one with a soil floor and unformed, unfinished walls. It's more of a hollow beneath the house than a room, and Kerry and I never got around to using it.

Later today I'll open the door and fling down another toilet bag, but it's not quite full yet.

A hint of the stench even makes it through my mask, but I've grown used to it. After a while, it goes.

When I'm finished, I return to the airlock. A creature of habit— routine and ritual are what have kept me going—this is always the best part of the day for me because I eat my largest meal for breakfast. But it's also the most uncomfortable part, and the most dangerous. The infection is still everywhere, however much I try to fool myself that the basic filters clean air that my manual pump draws down from above. And my mask is becoming more a part of me than ever before. The airlock is the only place in my basement where I have a mirror.

I built the airlock when news began to spread. I made it big enough for two, but it has only ever held one. Kerry is probably still up there, in whatever's left of our home. She refused to come down with me. I kissed her goodbye. We'd seen what was happening elsewhere, and she had no desire to survive. It's my greatest grief that we do not remain together, dead or alive.

I left the basement door unlocked in case she changed her mind. I haven't touched its handle since.

I close the framed door behind me and go through the usual checks to make sure the thick, double-layered polythene sheeting is secure. Then I start the foot pump. It draws air down and filters it, using the same medical-grade filters I use in my mask. After a couple of minutes the polythene bulges outwards under pressure, and the cleaned air seeps out again through non-return valves. It forms a slightly higher pressure, and means that cleaned air flows out, and contaminated air cannot flow in. It's hard work, but my leg muscles have built up over time, and it doubles as daily exercise. It gets my heart pumping. I start to perspire. My mask itches, and soon I'm ready to remove it.

I know that the airlock probably doesn't work. But it's an illustration of my commitment to survive, and I believe that determination is self-fulfilling.

The insects and water are calling, and my stomach rumbles with anticipation. I never enjoyed food so much as when there's very little of it. My clothes don't fit me anymore, and if Kerry could see how I have to tie string—

I sigh. I've been thinking about her a lot.

I pull the elasticated strap over my head and start taking off the mask. This is the only time of day I use the mirror, because there's no other reason to see myself. Staring into my own eyes only makes me feel even more alone.

The open sore on my cheek is weeping again. I wince as the mask parts from my skin, lifting a scab and letting out a tear of blood and pinkish pus. I hold the plastic in both hands and pull against the pain. In the mirror I am not myself, but a creature with a protruding snout seeping blood, wild knotted hair, and a crazed expression.

Kerry would hate me like this, I think, and I close my eyes.

There is a change. I'm still working the foot pump, and there is the soft hush of air being drawn into the airlock and leaking out again, but now I hear something else.

The polythene flaps as air moves around the basement.

When I turn from the mirror and open my eyes, through opaque polythene I see my first ghost.

I flee up the overgrown steps, pushing through grappling barbed stems eager to hold me fast and past the sprawled skeleton, and through and away from Old Town. I should never have come this far. Helene has warned us many times, though she is never specific. She never tells us *why*.

And why? I think as I run. *What have I done?* We're all aware of the past but only I have consciously sought it out.

He was diseased. Infected. And so, so old, like one of the rocks down by the river given life. Like one of the to-be stones in the fields outside town, already dead and petrified and staring at me with wide, crazy eyes. An ancient memory of what changed the world, and he looked right at me!

As I approach the river I see it as something else. It's a barrier between what took the world and how my own existence has moved on, and now I'm on the wrong side. The ruined bridge looks lower than ever before, and in places the water breaks white and violent around fractured concrete and rusting metal. It's as if seeing the ghost has made it more difficult for me to return.

I start clambering across, and now and then, gripping on tight, I look back. Into the woods. Past trees to shadows that might very well be staring right back at me.

A metal strut gives way and I slip down into the water up to my chest. It grabs at me, slow-moving and heavy, chilling me to the bone and urging me to let go of the bridge. I hold on tighter as my legs and lower body listen to the insistent current. *Drift away*, it says, whispers hushing against concrete and metal and my cold pale skin. *Float and rush*, it foams.

"I have to count the stones," I say, and that routine feels suddenly important. Until now it's been little more than a duty, but now it's familiar and precious, because counting the stones marks my day. I yearn to wake tomorrow to do it again. I pull, lifting my legs wrapped in soaked clothing, and manage to climb up onto the bridge's ruin. I check myself for signs of injury but there are none.

Not like him.

I think of the ghost and move faster, almost dancing across the rest of the broken bridge to the other side. As soon as I'm on land again, I have left the past behind and home beckons.

His skin was pale but bloodied, and wrinkled and hanging like too-big clothes on old bones. His eyes were watery and afraid. His face was covered in sores.

I run the rest of the way, and when I start across the field of familiar trees, I welcome the dance between shadow and sunlight as I pass beneath their protective canopies. They feel like old friends.

The village is awake and busy. The stones have been counted, and the wind waves hang loose and untended, flickering with no breeze, shimmying to the inaudible song of the world. At the edge of the village, where the first timber huts border the fields, several people are working on a barrow of root vegetables. They must have started harvesting Rose Field while I was away. It was fallow last year, but this year Rose Field is given to potatoes and squashes. Daffodil Field lies fallow for this season, and the other fields contain different crops. Some pluck the crop and clean it of mud, others slice root from stalk, and once that's done two people wash the vegetables and place them on the wooden food wall.

Meg is one of those stacking the produce, and as she catches my eyes I look away. She'll want to know where I've been and what I've seen. She can read me like a book. But she is diligent, and she won't leave her chores until they're done. I dash past and raise a hand in silent greeting, but I don't look again. That makes me feel bad, but it's not Meg I need to see. She's a flighty sprite, thin and lively with tattoos and streams of colour dyed through her hair. Her ears and nose are pierced with tiny animal bones. She's emotional and vocal, but her imagination is too constrained by rules. I need someone who can see like me.

I find Gerry outside his small hut. He's sitting on a bench and sorting through old things. He's one of the few in the village able to do this without the task making him maudlin or sad, and that's why I came to him. My story concerns the past.

Gerry is coiled, always apparently on the cusp of saying something profound, a held breath. He looks up at me and stops what he's doing. To his left is a pile of broken things, most of them unidentifiable. On the ground to his right is a small array of objects that we might still use—a mirror, a rusted blade, a thin leather strap. He sees my eyes and, like Meg, knows that something has happened. He tilts his head as if to speak, waiting for me to tell him.

"I saw a ghost," I say.

"Where have you been?"

"To Old Town."

Gerry blinks as he absorbs this. "We're not allowed there."

I glance at the objects he is examining, dismantling and handling, as he seeks new uses for old things.

"*Some* of us aren't allowed," he says.

"He was old and grey and he looked dead, down in the ground."

"Behind a closed door?"

I frown, then nod.

"A door that you opened?"

"It was old and stuck," I say. "I was exploring."

"Why explore into the past?"

"Why not?"

It's Gerry's turn to frown, as if he has no answer.

"We should see Helene," he says. He stands and a scatter of screws and fittings fall from his lap. It's as if he is coming apart.

"To punish me?"

"Punish?" Gerry asks. It's almost an alien word coming from his mouth, and I love him for that. "No, not to punish. Because Helene always knows what to do." He sets aside a small glass bulb he's been turning in his hand. It always amazes me how he can distinguish between useful and useless.

We walk through the village to Helene's cabin. It's the same as everyone else's, because she welcomes no special treatment to be our leader. As we draw closer her smile barely slips as she says, "You look like you've seen a ghost."

The door that leads out of my basement into whatever outside has become had not been opened in years. I don't know how many. The last time I counted the scratched crosses on the walls, I stopped at around fifteen hundred. And that was a long time ago.

It remains open now, but the ghost has gone.

I stand motionless in the airlock. My foot is no longer pumping and the pressure has regulated with the outside, the air and whatever it carries drifting and flowing through the basement once more. I press the mask to my face and wince as its rubber edge digs into the open welt on my cheek.

I should exit the airlock, slam the door, make sure it can't be opened again.

I've never felt tempted to look outside. The first few weeks in here told me everything I needed to know about the world beyond my basement. For the first day there was mostly silence, apart from the occasional distant footsteps of Kerry still walking back and forth in our home above my head. Halfway through day two I heard her coughing. An hour later, a series of loud bangs as doors opened and closed. Time started to compress and stretch, presenting other noises with varied spans between them. A scream, long and loud, from a mouth I did not know. The barking of dogs, the scratching of claws on timber floors through the thick insulated structure above my head. A distant screech and thump that might have been a scream and a fall, or a vehicle braking and crashing. Frenzied biting and chewing from close by. Scratching at the other side of the door. A group shouting and rushing through far away streets, or perhaps the final laboured breathing of someone or something much, much closer.

The memories of these noises haunt my dreams and make their own stories.

The only truth I know is that outside is death, and down here is survival. Kerry and I knew that death was close, and at the final moment we made our choices together. It was a joint decision—she died, and I did not. She chose to stop, and I went on. There was no pleading from either of us. We loved and respected each other too much for that.

As time moved on and the scratched crosses became more numerous, of course I sometimes looked at the door. Of course I did. And once I even stood before it with my hands almost touching the cool wood, trying to feel what might have been beyond. That was a long time ago, when the main basement room was only half-crossed. Ever since then, the door has been a wall. Solid. Impassable. And a virtual blank on my memory.

Now it stands wide open and I hear nothing.

The polythene rustles with a breath from the open door.

"Hello," I say. *A ghost won't talk*, I think. I've been wondering whether I would ever see a ghost, but for the past year or two I've come to the conclusion that there are none. Even with so many people dead—the whole world, dead and gone apart from me and perhaps others like me in other countries, farther apart than stars—they have left nothing behind.

It wasn't Kerry. I could tell that even from the brief distorted glimpse I caught through the two layers of sheeting. Too tall, too young, hair dark and short rather than light and long. This was the remnant of someone else.

"Hello?" I say again. Holding the mask to my face, I open the airlock. The basement is cooler, and it takes me a while to identify the peculiar feeling against my skin. I grab at the memories… *a sea breeze lifting her hair and ruffling my beard… a breath through a forest, carrying rumours of damp soil and blooming flowers…* I am feeling a touch of fresh air.

The open doorway is mostly shadowed, and yet a haze of sunlight filters down. For as long as I can remember I've only ever seen artificial light, a weak glow fed by the hand-wound generator. It takes me a couple of hours each day to wind the turbine and make enough power to give me light until evening. My nights are long and dark. Sunlight is a distant memory, and now that memory might only be a dozen steps away. I want to feel it, touch it, see it.

Even though I'm pressing the mask tight against my face, I want to smell it.

Yet fear holds me back. For so long I've gone through the same processes with my mask, refitting a new filter every few weeks—

—*There's not many left now, enough for a year, maybe less*—

—only taking it off in the airlock, reading and sleeping and dreaming with the mask on. Even so, I think I've known the truth for some time. There have been mistakes, when I wake and the mask has slipped off in the night. There have been moments when I've held my breath and lifted the mask away. And I have known for some time that if the contagion is still carried on the air, I would have had it by now. I've been down here too long for anything else to be possible. The airlock isn't really as tight as I pretend. The mask isn't high quality, little more than a decorator's mask with a medical-grade filter insert.

But still, that fear. Outside is not somewhere I belong anymore. This is my home. This is my whole world, because anything beyond that might once have held value for me has been gone for a long time.

I step towards the door, mask still pressed against my sore, weeping face with one hand. I'm close, so close. I hold my breath, not against infection, but waiting for the ghost to darken my doorway again.

She does not come. I grab the handle and pull the door closed on rusted, squealing hinges.

Still behind the mask, bathed in faint artificial light once again, I sigh deeply.

"It must be so dark. Why would a ghost haunt such a place? Why would a ghost still be there at all?"

Helene is watching and listening, and her silence is inviting my story and thoughts. She has always been such a good listener. That's why she is in charge of the village. Her legs have not worked for a long time, and she likes to relax on a carpet of cushions and blankets on her cabin floor. We all look up to her, even though to see her we have to look down. She's the wisest among us by far, and I wonder if she's lived forever.

She smiles and nods, but there are shadows behind her eyes that I've never seen before. I don't think she's angry at me. I think it's something else.

"He looked so far away, like a dream I was trying to re-form. Hazy, uncertain. If I look at a tree across a field on a hot, hot day, it shimmers and seems unreal. He was like that. He looked so old and ill. Perhaps he died like that, so long ago, and he's doomed to relive it again and again. His face was... swollen, deformed. Bloody."

"It frightened you," Helene says, the first words she's spoken since urging me inside her cabin.

"He did," I say, but I frown, searching deeper. "And I feel sorry for him."

"Don't," Helene says. "Never feel sorry. He's from before. He's one of those who brought on the end, and a ghost doesn't need your pity."

"You've seen ghosts?" I ask.

She looks down at her legs. She leaves the cabin every day, but always in her wheeled chair that Gerry made for her years before. He maintains it well with parts he gathers from old things, made before the end.

"We look to the future," she says. "We count the stones and dance the wind waves, because we're in tune with the world, and we sing its song. The end came because those before us weren't in tune, and didn't know the words. They were bad people doing bad things, not the good like us. They were ignorants, not enlightened. So the ghosts only haunt those places from before, and they've no place in our world. You'll find them in the shadows. You'll find them in old places, because they're sad old things."

I can hardly breathe. It's the most I've ever heard Helene say about *before*, because usually she will never talk about it. She is talking about it now because of me. Gerry is outside the cabin, I know, and I wonder if he heard.

"Will he always be there?" I ask.

"It always has, since the end. It always will."

"Trapped," I say, and my mind wanders as I consider that poor man's fate.

"Stay away from Old Town," Helene says. "This is your home, and your place in the world. You don't want to risk losing yourself to the past."

I nod and smile, and then I kneel and kiss Helene's hand when she offers it up to me. She doesn't always do this, and it's considered an honour, and a sign of affection.

"You sweet young thing," she says. "We're lucky to have you here. And you're lucky to be here."

When I leave I hear her calling Gerry inside. He smiles as he goes, touches my arm, and I head back across the village to my small cabin. I'm on a hunting party this afternoon, and I need to sharpen and re-feather three of my arrows. We'll be singing songs of wellness and plenty, wishing health and profusion on the creatures we hunt. I never see the need. There are so few people, and so many animals wandering the woods and plains and ignoring any signs of before, like fallen steel towers or the forgotten routes of old roads buried beneath new growth. But Gerry would say that's *why* our hunting is easy—because we sing songs of wellness and plenty.

There are almost fifty cabins in the village, and almost fifty people. There always have been for as long as I can remember.

When I emerge from my cabin later, refurbished arrows in my quiver, Meg is there waiting for me, wearing her hunting coat and carrying her spear. She's good with a spear, the best in our village. She wasn't due to come on this hunt. She says she just decided that she wants to.

Helene has tasked her with keeping watch on me. That's fine. I have plenty of time, and the ghost is going nowhere.

"It's always been down to the survivors to make things better," Meg said. "There's *before*, and even though we were there and the funk of death was like grease on our skin, and the contagion stuck in our noses and down our throats and somehow, somehow left us alive, we're *after*. All of us. We're what's left, and we were allowed to carry on differently from before. Gerry and I fled the city and on the roads, clogged with a thousand jammed cars, we had to walk across the car bonnets and roofs, and those inside were already dead. Their faces were bruised and yellowed, swollen, and some of their open eyes were flooded with blood, and lots of the children were clawing at the closed windows when they died. In their final moments a few of them had even opened their car windows and tried to get out, as if the air outside was fresher. It wasn't. Back then the air was heavy with contagion, literally heavy with it, some say you could see the haze hanging above the cities, just waiting to fall with the rain. So they hung out of their vehicles, blackened blood drying on doors and road surface, and Gerry and I walked three miles across cars without once touching the road. By then we knew that we were... rare. For a while we thought perhaps we were alone, and we couldn't even begin to guess why. We passed one place where a thousand bodies had been piled in a field, like an offering to whatever deities those wretched dying people thought might help them. That mountain of corpses leaked tainted, rank fluid that seeped into the ground, flowed into local rivers and streams, and drifted to places where death already held dominion. Gerry and I went in the one direction where rivers and streams did not flow. We came here. Do you remember? Do you remember arriving here and making it home?"

I shook my head but said nothing. Somewhere deep inside, Meg must have known this was all make-believe, a nightmare she had woken from this day or created over a period of time. None of us remembered before, not even Helene. Before was too long ago.

Meg spoke as if her stories were all so real, and I had no right to doubt her reality. We all create our own truths.

I scratch a cross on a small area of wall behind my bed. I take longer than usual, and it's a good cross, like those I used to scratch way, way back when this all began. When I'm done I sit on the foot of my sofa and stare at the door.

I pump the handle and fill the airlock with air and let it seep out, polythene bulging, and I slowly remove my mask and dab at the worsening sores on my cheek. The left is the most severe, skin broken and flesh raw and wet. I glance in the mirror for the first time that day and try not to look myself in the eye. I concentrate on treating and cleaning my wounds, but my gaze keeps wandering. I'm watching the door in the mirror, remembering when I first glimpsed the ghost. There's no ghost now. The door remains closed.

I kneel close to the bathroom wall working on the generator. I can smell the faint odour from the piles of bagged waste I've thrown through the door into the deeper room beyond the basement, and I have a frequent thought that I always try to discard and set aside: *How can I smell that if the mask works?* It's a problem I always manage to ignore. The unbearable possibilities behind it are too difficult, and I spend my days denying them. So I turn the generator handle, muttering a familiar song to keep time with the turns. It's amazing that the batteries are still storing power after so long, and I dread the day that they begin to fail. If that happens I might only have light as the handle is turned, and I will live mostly in darkness. There are hardly any candles left. I wind and look back across the living area at the door. It's been just another part of the wall, but not anymore, because I saw it open. I saw the glow of distant, natural light. I saw the ghost, and she saw me.

I wake and reach for my mask to make sure it's still tight, my first act each morning. I blink away the distraction of old dreams and look at the door without even thinking about it, because that has also become an unconscious act. The mask is still on my face. The door is still closed.

I scratch another cross on a brick, trying to find an open space where no other scratches touch. I enter the airlock to eat several worms and a few woodlice that came through the walls the previous night, and drink filtered but gritty water. Then I pick up my current book, *One Flew Over the Cuckoo's Nest*, and sit on my sofa, folded blanket behind my back where I sit against the wall. I scan the same page fifteen times, looking at the door all the while. It stays closed.

I exercise, because sometimes I feel the need. Not often now, but the desire comes to me in fits and starts. I run on the spot and watch the door, and it's closed.

Closed.

Closed, even when I approach and press my hands against the cold wooden surface.

I saw her, I think, and I continue thinking that, even though eventually, after many days I can only count in memories of scratching crosses, I begin to doubt.

With that doubt comes a sense of hopelessness that surprises me. I've always kept going day by day, cross by cross, keeping despair at bay. Now the days are becoming one, and I wake, and wind, and pump air, and eat, and go to sleep wondering why I should bother waking the next day.

I do wake the next day, and from the moment I open my eyes I know that something is different. The light, the air. The scent of something from outside that stirs dormant memories; old rain, damp soil. During the night I have ripped the mask from my face, perhaps in an unconscious effort to end things at last. The sleeping me betrays my despair, but the waking me feels a rush of something I don't recognise at first.

I see the open door. I see the shape standing there, the ghost from outside.

I'm excited.

"I used to wait for one of you to come," I say, "but after so long I'd given up hope."

After all this time, my first ghost whispers, "Hello."

"Hello," I say, and the ghost sits up on his bed. Perhaps he heard me open the door, perhaps not, but either way I feel sorry that I've startled him again. "Don't be afraid," I say. I stand in the doorway, and a waft of shadowy hidden places washes out around me. It's not the stink I might have expected of a ghost. It's the smell of confinement, sweat and dirt, old air and breath. The taint of filth is on the air as well, but the man I see, though almost skeletally thin, is dressed in decent clothes. A mask hangs half off his face, and the skin around his mouth is raw and seeping a pink fluid.

I realise that I needn't have told him not to be afraid. He is startled, yes, but his eyes are wide, his mouth open, and he has the look of someone who has been waiting for this moment.

"I came back," I say. I wonder at what he said, and whether he knows about our new settlement beyond the town and the woods. I look around his subterranean room, barely lit by several hanging bulbs that emit a faint glow. I stand to the side and a rumour of sunlight hangs behind me.

It's taken me this long to give Meg the slip, because over time Meg's mind wanders. I don't know how long it's been since I was first here. It feels like just a few days, but perhaps it's longer. Maybe it's years.

"Please don't go," he says. "Please wait, just for a while. Can you hear me? Do you see me?"

Strange questions, but I answer to put him at ease. All I know of ghosts is that they're fleeting, transitory things. And I have so much to ask. "I see you and hear you," I say.

"Come inside," he says.

"You're sure?"

"If you are." He stands and backs away as if to make me feel safe, but I've never seen someone less threatening. I wonder how long he's been stuck here in this moment and place. It looks like he survived here for a while, and maybe that's why he still haunts. All the other ghosts have faded away with memories of themselves.

I descend the final couple of steps and follow my shadow into the room.

He's looking at my shadow as well. His eyes are wide. *A ghost makes no shadow*, I think. He's too deep in the darkness for me to make out his own.

"You survived here, for a while," I say.

"A while?" He pulls the mask from his face, wincing, and I wonder at his memory of pain. It seems so unfair that a wraith can hurt.

"How long?" I ask.

"Ever since," he says. He steps sideways and places a hand against the wall, fingers splayed. I squint and can just make out the patterns cut into the bricks. "A cross for every day."

I can't begin to imagine counting the days of his survival. I feel so sorry for him. I wonder how long ago he died, but time is an elusive creature. Sometimes when we count the trees that will become stones, some are there, some not. One day our descendants will truly count the stones. It's our way of measuring the truth and triumph of our survival.

"You must have been so lonely," I say.

"I still am. Will you see my home? See what I managed to do?" He's proud of this place, but his eyes are flitting behind me at the open door, and his hand lifts the mask halfway to his face again.

"It's okay," I say.

He smiles, shrugs. "I guess the damage is done, eh?"

I look around the basement room and he welcomes me in. He tells me about how he survived down in the darkness, what he ate and drank, how he made power, where he flung his waste, how he made an airlock and used a mask and went from moment to moment moving on from the tragedy that took us all. And all the while I see the truth. I think he does, too, because sometimes he explains things almost with an apology.

"I drink water that seeps down through the soil. I eat worms and woodlice and an occasional spider, and a few times I've managed to catch something larger." He glances at the crosses hatched on the wall and pauses, seeing the truth—that he cannot possibly have survived down here for so long, eating insects and making energy by a hand-wound generator, and seeing no sun. So, so long, half a century if what Helene says is true. He is not a survivor.

"Come outside with me," I say. "See what the world has become, my world, how *we* have survived." I don't tell him that he's a ghost. It doesn't seem fair, and I'm afraid that doing so, and him acknowledging

my words, will cause him to fade away. Maybe that's what he wants
and deserves, but I have a selfish reason for keeping him with me, just
for a while longer. I'm enjoying his company.

"Outside?" he asks.

"There's nothing to be afraid of," I say, and I offer him the most
warming smile I can conjure. "Just look at me."

I look at her. She's taller than me, and she seems so young. I have long
ago lost count of how long I have been in my basement, but she must
have been born *since*. She wants me to go outside, and I'm surprised
by how keen I am to go with her. Since seeing her for the first time I've
been afraid, but also eager for her to return. She's proof of something
outside. I've spent so long living in my own contained world that seeing
someone from beyond, even a ghost, excites me.

I still hold my mask in my hand as I step forward, but maybe now
it's just a comfort.

"When is the last time you saw the sun?" she asks.

"I… don't know. Since then. Before."

"A long time," she says. Something in her voice tells me that she
knows just how long, but I don't want to ask.

She steps back out of the door and up the first couple of steps,
and I follow. I still don't feel the sun on my skin, but the air is very
different: fresher, warmer. No longer heavy with the atmosphere of
the basement.

"Take my hand," she says, reaching for me. I'm cautious of contact,
but I've already taken the first step. The first is always hardest, and this
is just one more. I reach out and feel her hand against mine.

How is that if she's a ghost?

I see her own eyes go wide. She is thinking the same.

"Okay?" she asks.

"Yes, I'm fine."

"Close your eyes and I'll guide you," she says.

"Guide me?"

"There's something you might not want to see."

But I do want to see. We climb the stairs holding hands, but with my eyes open, and I know then that Kerry had been so close to me for so long. I let out a sob when I see her, huddled against the wall and smothered with plant growth. The leaves and stems and roots have taken some of her apart, but I can still see that she was sat on the small landing leading down, leaning against the wall. I like to think that she chose that place to spend her final moments. I sense no panic in her attitude, no last-minute change of mind. I'm sad, but her stark skeleton is old now, not frightening, and the past feels so far away.

We reach the top of the steps and at last I feel the sun on my skin. It's harsh and hot, uncompromising. I imagine myself shrivelling away to ash, drifting on the breeze.

"Look at the beautiful world," the ghost says. "The trees, the flowers."

I look around but see nothing of beauty. I see brutalised trunks, stripped of branches and withered to nothing. I see spiky, squat plant growth that looks more like tangled wires than anything natural.

"If you listen you can hear the birdsong," she says.

I listen and hear a harsh, scraping sound from some indefinable distance, like metal dragged across stone. I don't contradict her view of the world, because I am enjoying her company.

"Let's walk," she says. "I'll show you where I live, though we'll have to keep out of sight of everyone else. They… won't understand."

"How many of you are there?" I ask.

"Forty. Fifty? There's me and Meg, Gerry and Helene and…" She frowns. "I've never really counted."

We walk together. The truth is circling us both, and it's good to have someone to face it with.

~

"You can't possibly have survived down there," she says.

"Nothing could live for long up here," he says.

They cross the desolate landscape, a harsh and violent echo of the past. They crawl over a fallen bridge spanning a river, heavy and slow-moving with corruption.

From the edge of a dead forest she points, and he sees a place where a circle of trees has died, petrified, turned to stone.

"Oh," she says, but she doesn't sound surprised.

"I'm not sure it really matters," he says.

"I was thinking the same."

"I'm going to go back soon."

"And I'll stay here. But I can come to see you sometimes?" she asks.

"I'd like that. And I think I'd like to feel the sun, sometimes, too."

The old man and the younger woman stay together for a little while longer, as the sun beams down on a world moved on.

FIRE ABOVE, FIRE BELOW

Lisa Tuttle

I'VE been thinking about nominative determinism.

Not the jokes, like Graves Funeral Home, a dentist called Dr. Payne, or the proctologist Dr. Proctor—all genuine examples from my hometown, so I shouldn't call them jokes. They were real. Like me. And I wonder, would my life have turned out differently if my parents had named me anything other than Cassandra?

I can't remember my first prophetic utterance (a phrase I picked up from a story about the original Cassandra). But from the age of six or seven, words emerged from my lips that I hadn't planned to say, expressing something fated to happen, like:

"Seems like we'll have to go home the long way" (said in the car on our way to some distant location; later, the freeway was closed by an accident). Or:

"Seems like we'll go out to eat tonight" (a rare event, caused by some mishap in the kitchen). Or:

"Seems like you'll get a bicycle for Christmas, but not the one you really wanted."

And so on, and so forth. My predictions regarding Christmas

presents only got me the reputation of a horrible little sneak and spy; the others were ignored, until the big one, when I was twelve.

"Seems like something bad is going to happen at the mall tomorrow."

My sister was putting gel in her hair, carefully styling it, and paid no attention to me, but I was terrified by my own words, and blurted, "Did you hear me? You can't go!"

"What are you talking about?"

"Seems like there's going to be a shooting. Seems like there's a man, he's wearing one of those army jackets, and he's got a backpack and he's got a gun. Seems like he will shoot as many people as he can before somebody stops him; mostly, he wants to kill all the pretty girls."

She stopped styling and looked at me in surprise. "Pretty?"

"Please, Angie. Don't go to the mall tomorrow."

She scowled. "I'm not staying home. I'm not missing out because of your stupid—"

I shouted at her. "I don't want you to die! You'll die if you go to the mall; seems like he'll see you, standing near the fountain with those other girls, and there's nowhere you can hide. Seems like he'll just shoot and shoot and kill everybody; there's blood and people screaming—" Then I was crying too hard to say more. But the words I could not say came from the source that was always right, and I couldn't bear it; the thought that it was inevitable, that no one could avoid their fate.

But Angela had heard my "seems likes" before, and however contemptuous and disbelieving she wanted to be, this time it was too serious to laugh off. Mass shootings happened with some regularity, like hurricanes, floods and fires, a natural disaster that we could only pray to be spared.

She pinched my arm. "Stop it, crybaby. All right, all right. But you better be right, 'cause if you're not, I will *get* you, and make your life *hell*."

She didn't go to the mall, and neither did her two friends. I don't know what she said to them, but they made some other plan, and they stayed safe, well away from the shooting that did happen, much as I had foreseen. Three other girls from her school died, also a woman and baby, and fifteen others were injured, including the security guard who managed to stop the killer.

It wasn't my sister who told the media, but word got out. It was not fun being famous—and a recipient of death threats—but at least that particular variant of hell did not last long. I had not known how many people regularly claim credit for having predicted something, after it has happened, but that explains why most people thought I was no different, and quickly lost interest. I didn't care who believed me *after*. The important thing was that I had saved three lives. I had done something that should have been impossible. My words had been heard and had made a difference.

The thing about Cassandra is that her gift of prophecy came with a stinger in the tail: no one believed her. But some stories contradict that. After she predicted the fall of Troy, Priam had her locked up, to keep this terrible news from his people. He also gave the woman who looked after her strict instructions to keep him informed of any more prophetic utterances, and why would he do that if he didn't believe? He must have hoped the foreknowledge might help, yet the old stories indicate resistance is futile. What will be, will be. When the Oracle tells you what's going to happen, whatever you do in response will only serve to bring it about. You can't outrun your doom.

But my life has been dedicated to the proposition that it *is* possible to change the future. Or at least to change bits of it, for some. Certain things have a high probability of happening, but they are not inevitable. I believe in free will, and that individuals can make a difference.

Where do they come from, these utterances? The Oracle speaks, using my mouth.

After my eighteenth birthday, after I left home to go away to college, the Oracle spoke more often, perhaps inspired by the proximity of so many new and unrelated lives around me.

One morning, toasting bread in the crowded kitchen of the shared house where I now lived, I heard myself say, "Seems like somebody could fall and hurt themselves on the drive outside, it's so slippery."

One of my housemates wanted to know if there had been a freeze overnight, because she didn't think it was that cold.

I shrugged. "I don't know. I haven't been out."

"But you just said—"

I had a vivid image of someone going down, her books flying everywhere—but I couldn't see her face. I turned to look at them all—which one? "It was raining yesterday, and maybe it froze—just be careful."

Rachel spoke up. "You're not our mom. You don't be telling us to be careful."

I heard myself say, "Seems like *you* should be careful."

"Bitch, what's your problem?"

I left to the sound of contemptuous laughter.

It wasn't that cold outside, but no one had cleared the carpet of fallen leaves on the drive, and they were slippery. Rachel slipped on them, much later that day. She broke her leg in two places. I was glad I was not around to see it, because she might have accused me of somehow causing the accident. Even so, she must have said something, because I was aware of people giving me funny looks even before I warned another housemate, Bethany, against a guy who'd asked her out; I said it seemed like he had a grudge against women, and could be dangerous. By then I'd learned to be more careful to offer some sort of follow-on explanation for these uninvited comments, so I pretended to have overheard a conversation in a restroom.

"But you don't know the girls? The one who said it?"

I shook my head. "I didn't really get a good look."

"You're sure they were talking about the same guy? My James?"

My? I felt sure from that she would brush it off, but she sighed, accepting it. "Funny, because he seems really nice. Maybe it was just one bad relationship? You know, some women, they always blame the man. Anyway, it's too late now. I don't have a good excuse for letting him down. Besides, I want to hear the band. But I will be careful."

And she *was* careful. She did not go back to his place after the gig, claiming she had a headache, and did not let him sway her with his offer of a massage, his claim that he knew the acupressure points to cure her pain. She still liked him, and I think would have given him another chance, but he never called her again. The next time she saw him he had his arm around another woman and didn't spare her a glance. She was furious with me.

Barely a month later, though, I was forgiven. A woman died in his bed. He claimed it was a consensual sex game gone terribly wrong.

Bethany knew she could have been that woman. She pressed me for more details about the women I claimed to have overheard, because no one like that came forward; every woman who had known him was astonished; women who'd had sex with him said he wasn't into kinky sex, so he must have been telling the truth, and the victim had initiated it. I weakened and told her the truth.

Soon, it seemed, everyone knew about "the Oracle". Not just classmates and friends-of-friends but total strangers were turning up at the house with questions about their future.

"I'm not a fortune-teller!"

I wanted to put my power to good use, to help others, but how? In the first place, I did not control the Oracle. And about the only thing I could say for sure about my prophetic utterances was this: they did not concern strangers, but only people I lived with.

But, when I thought about it, I remembered I had once foretold the attempted shooting of a congressman. I had never met him, but I had seen him on TV, my parents had voted for him, and he represented our district. And there was another time, also from pre-college days, when I'd been daydreaming about an actor and heard myself say, "Seems like he's going to crash… the burns are terrible… his face won't ever look the same." I heard the news of his accident a few days later.

Bethany and Rachel (still on crutches) had taken a keen interest in me—you could have thought they were my agents. They came up with an idea for how it might work. The—what should we call them? The *supplicants*? The supplicant would have to make themselves known to me first. There would have to be at least one visit—maybe they could take me out for dinner?—to give me the chance to get to know them. Then, at a later date, they could come back to ask their question.

Once more I protested: I was not a fortune-teller. The Oracle didn't answer questions, it simply pronounced, whenever it felt so inclined.

"The Oracle?" Rachel's eyes gleamed. "Is that what you're calling yourself now?"

"Not me—I don't mean myself—"

"Of course not, but it's perfect, and that's why you're wrong. The Oracle *does* answer questions. People have always gone to an oracle to ask what's in store. They might be better off not knowing, but answering questions is what it's for. You should at least give it a chance."

I accepted my fate, with a warning: "I can't make any promises. They can ask, but I can't guarantee an answer."

I couldn't guarantee, but even if they say they understand, and even when they are not paying for it (or no more than the price of a cheap take-out), people always do expect to get something. They counted the time they'd wasted as more valuable than mine. I did not like knowing they thought I was a fraud or hearing they had been bad-mouthing me.

I wasn't going to pretend or lie to them, but I wanted to give them something. I knew a girl who gave Tarot readings at parties, but that didn't appeal to me: it seemed to require too much conscious input. Maybe if I consulted the I Ching?

That big book, purchased in the university Co-Op, looked daunting at first, but when I realized that I didn't have to understand what it told me, I relaxed. I threw the coins, drew the lines, and the resulting hexagram was the answer. All I had to do was look it up in the book (mine was the Wilhelm translation) and read the judgement. I told the supplicants it was up to them to figure it out.

This worked out quite well. They must have preferred to puzzle over the significance of "The king approaches his temple. It furthers one to cross the great water," than to hear me say, "Seems like you could get hit by a truck later this week."

Possibly my use of the I Ching made me more receptive, because my prophetic utterances became more frequent. Occasionally I was able to help people, and they avoided the fate I had foreseen, but more often than not whatever I said went unheeded, like most unwanted warnings.

Word about me spread, and even before graduation I had a firm job offer (subject to security clearance) from a government agency. It came with an NDA and a cover story, but I was no secret agent. I was less an employee, more a potentially valuable asset.

In the early years, my time was taken up with testing and experimental training to map and extend my abilities. But I also got to meet many famous and important people, spent time in the White House, the Pentagon, and expensive hotels. I was flown all over the country, sometimes to secret destinations. My use of the I Ching was frowned upon. *Anyone* could do that. It was not a context in which they wanted me to be seen.

The thrill of meeting famous people soon wore off. They were not thrilled to meet me. For them, our meeting was like an unwanted appointment with a specialist, and I wasn't even the person who operated the machine that might reveal if that lump was malignant—I was the machine.

Was I the only oracle enlisted by our government? Surely there must have been others, but if so, I was never told, and we were never allowed to meet. Maybe, if we could have worked together, allowed to see the big picture, we could have done more.

But that wasn't our job. We weren't responsible for making decisions. And perhaps the future is no more open to change than the past. Just because some individuals have avoided their fate doesn't mean everyone can. A few lives here and there may be no more than dropped stitches, making no difference to the great tapestry of time.

The years passed as I did my job, and the world changed in ways we'd been warned about for decades. Disease, fire, flood, famine, and wars made life a misery for millions. Travel became increasingly difficult, and my work, like that of so many others, was conducted at a distance, via screens and the internet. People asked their questions, and sometimes were met with a prophetic utterance. Increasingly, those utterances offered little hope of mitigation.

It seemed like things would keep on getting worse.

One day the internet was gone. That same day I was moved to a new location, a secure facility deep underground. I have no idea where I am now, only that it is "safe".

I have not had physical contact with another living soul since the two young men in uniform escorted me here.

"You'll be safe here. Keep your phone or laptop on all the time. Someone will be in touch soon, but if you need anything, check out the FAQs on the website; there's a list of contacts on the homepage."

My safe place is bigger and more comfortable than a jail cell, but these things are all relative, aren't they? At least the toilet and shower stall are in a separate room. The bed is more comfortable than the narrow, creaky old thing I slept on in college, and the chair is ergonomic. The kitchen area is basic, but enough for my needs. When supplies in the refrigerator and pantry run low they are automatically restocked. I get a pack of clean bedlinen weekly and put the dirty ones down the chute along with the standard-issue clothing I want cleaned or replaced.

I spend most of my time in the ergonomic chair staring at the screen on my desk, playing games, watching old movies and old TV series I remember from my childhood, listening to music or reading, passing the time as I wait to be called upon to give advice. I still have no access to the internet (assuming such a thing still exists), but there is an intranet that connects me to others, although whether they live nearby or are scattered across the country in other secure locations, I don't know. I know very little. My own questions go unanswered: either the information is classified, or the person I ask is too busy or too impatient to reply.

The people who appear on my screen are now, almost invariably, military men or senior government officials. Their questions are about targets, strikes, counterstrikes, and impending attacks, whether ours or "theirs". We are at war, but beyond that, I know very little.

Rarely do their questions spark a prophetic utterance. They are not interested in my explanations about how the Oracle works, that there's nothing for the power to work with, given little more than geographical coordinates or code names. Just occasionally something about one of the repeat questioners, something in his voice or face, would trigger a response, but that was almost worse, for it was never good news, always a prophecy of death, only death, terrible and sudden and soon.

It must have been horrible for them, but I only saw one man break down in tears. I never saw him again, and I have no doubt that my prediction came true.

After that, I waited a long time for another call.

How long, I don't know.

Time is hard to judge, being alone in a closed environment like this, without day or night. It had not occurred to me when I arrived that I should mark the days in some way, and I have never been one to follow a strict schedule if left to my own devices. I ate when I was hungry and slept when I could, never knowing when I'd get another call. The people I spoke to might have been anywhere in the world. The war was outside, far away—or perhaps it was over, and no one had bothered to tell me. I wondered if my usefulness was at an end. I hoped they had not forgotten me.

At least a week passed, or a little more, before I had another call, this time from someone new. Unusually, the caller was a woman, and not in uniform. I guessed her to be about my own age: her red hair was long and streaked with grey, and her face, still attractive, had a comfortable, lived-in look, with laughter lines around eyes and mouth, for all the serious set of her expression. As always, there was a name in the bottom left corner of the screen, but she took the time to introduce herself— "Call me Grace"—and ask, with the appearance of caring, how things were with me, if I was all right, if I needed anything, before getting down to business.

Her questions were the usual sort, involving geographical co-ordinates and code names: When and where would the enemy strike next? Should a particular mission be aborted, or should the target be changed? They inspired no prophetic utterances. I apologized and began my now well-practiced explanation. She cut me off; she had been well briefed. "I know you need more, and I want to give you as much information as I can," she said. "Under the circumstances, it would be absurd to stick to the old rules around what is classified information. Would a visual description of the targets help?"

I shook my head. "No… it's not about the physical details. There has to be some emotional charge, and that means people. If you could tell me something about the people involved, especially if they are in danger—"

"There are no people in danger at these sites. We are not targeting people."

"Oh. Well—maybe the pilots?" I thought of all the people I had spoken to, whose deaths I had predicted. All dead now.

She wrinkled her nose. "But we use drones. There are no pilots. Surely you knew that."

"Oh—right. Of course." I felt embarrassed.

She let out a small sigh. "I understand how you believe your ability works. But I hope you will be able to find a work-around. Your country needs you. You can help us win this war."

I thought about it. Automated weapons attacking—what, other automatic weapons protecting unmanned bases? Had it really come to this stage, a war without human casualties—even without human intervention? But my hackles were raised by her saying "how you believe"—as if she knew more than I did about the Oracle. Of course, I didn't know how it worked myself, but it was not a matter of pushing the right button and getting a prediction in return. If it was that easy, surely a "work-around" would have been found during my first years with the agency.

We stared at each other through our screens, across an unknown distance. "I'm sorry. I *do* want to help. But those questions…" I shrugged. "They just don't inspire a response. I need more."

"What?"

"I don't know."

Her expression hardly changed, but I sensed her patience fraying. "I'll give you twenty-four hours," she said. "I hope you manage to find a way to be of use."

The screen went blank.

I was alone.

Twenty-four hours until I would see her again. Already I was looking forward to it. That's hardly surprising, given there was nothing except another call to look forward to here, but it was more than that. It wasn't just something to break the monotony; I was interested in Grace.

Who was she? A civilian, like me, co-opted because she was of use to the military? That seemed likely. But how was she useful? Maybe she programmed the drones?

I would ask her. I would ask her to tell me about herself—her upbringing, her education, her entertainment preferences—because although I had never been able to prophesy on demand, the utterances came more readily for people I knew. And if that didn't work?

Because I must do something to pass the time, I turned to the I Ching.

All alone and unseen in the underground bunker, I throw three old worn Chinese coins. Throw, draw the line, and repeat until the hexagram has formed, providing an answer to the question I imagine Grace has asked:

Li: The Clinging, Fire

This is a double sign: fire above and fire below. The commentary on the image is: "Thus the great man, by perpetuating this brightness, illumines the four quarters of the world".

The judgement:

Perseverance furthers.
It brings success.
Care of the cow brings good fortune.

The meaning of the top line is:

The king uses him to march forth and chastise.
Then it is best to kill the leaders and take captive the followers.
No blame.

For all the positive interpretations (I'm quoting the Wilhelm translation, but Huang is even more feel-good, glossing "kill the leader, capture the followers" as advice to deal with the root of a problem) this strikes me as apocalyptic. Fire above, fire below. Well, what do I expect, in time of war? We're in it to win it. No blame.

And I think: Am I the cow?

Grace's call was right on time. "Do you have anything to tell me?"

"Maybe."

She did not look too happy with that, so I quickly added, "I have an idea that might work." I launched into the spiel I had refined over the years, explaining that I couldn't control my gift of prophecy, and the only thing that might trigger it was to know that person; at least, to have some personal connection with them.

She smiled a little wryly. "You want to get to know me."

"That's right."

"How do we do that?"

"Well, say we met at a dinner party. Or in an airport bar or sitting next to each other on a transatlantic flight. Maybe we both notice we're reading copies of the same book, so we start talking about that. Or we work in the same office. You know, the way things used to be?" I was suddenly unsure—how *did* people make new friends? How did you strike up a conversation with a stranger? What did people talk about, under normal circumstances, in some ordinary situation? It had been so long since I had been in anything like an ordinary situation.

But Grace understood. "What book am I reading?"

"A new novel by… Barbara Kingsolver?" As soon as I'd said it, I held my breath, worried my choice was too political, afraid it might reveal a huge philosophical divide and preclude friendship.

But she nodded thoughtfully. "Maybe not a new one, because I can't even imagine what a new one might be, so how about *Flight Behavior*."

I breathed out. "Perfect! That's probably my favorite."

"Good, so you're re-reading it, but let's say it's my first time, so... no spoilers, please!"

From there, it flowed. We quickly achieved an easy, natural communion. It struck me that she was lonely, too; as isolated in her bunker as I was in mine. Even if she had more online interactions during the day, a real job to do, it couldn't have been much fun. I did not ask about her work, or how she had come to be where she was now. Partly this was to avoid the discomfort of being told that information was classified, but mainly it was because it was too depressing. I would rather talk about books and movies and music and share memories of the vanished world of the past. Although I had meant the conversation to be a way of learning more about Grace, I probably ended up dominating it with my memories, encouraged by her interest, and because it had been such a very long time since I had been able to talk to anyone in this way. I was in the middle of telling her about a concert I'd been to in New York when I heard myself say, "It seems like the strike tomorrow will be a success. It seems like a lot of enemy armaments will be destroyed."

"Thank you, Cass."

I felt as if I had been pulled out of a happy dream. Back to reality. "Oh. Well, I guess that worked. I'm glad I could help." I thought the screen would go blank, now that she'd got what she wanted, but she said, "Go on."

I didn't know what she meant. Was she expecting another prophecy? So soon?

"About the concert. You were telling me how you felt, your response to the Chopin étude...?"

In the middle of the night I woke, heart pounding, and heard myself say, "It seems like everyone is dead. It seems like I'm the only person left alive."

Maybe it wasn't the middle of the night. It's a manner of speaking; it doesn't matter. I had been asleep; it felt like the middle of the night, and there was no one to say I was wrong.

No one. My friends and family were lost to me, there was no one I could call to talk me down from my terror, and tell me not to worry, it was only a bad dream.

Except, perhaps, Grace. If I could reach her.

I remembered the short list of names and their contact numbers on the homepage. I didn't know if she was on it, but I'd been instructed to report any prophetic utterances, at any time, to anyone on the list. Of course, if this latest was a true prophecy, there would be no one left to call.

I rolled out of bed and stumbled across to the desk. Grace *was* on the list. So I tried her first. My call went straight to voicemail. I left a message, then tried another number, and then another. I prayed it really was the middle of the night and they were all sound asleep. I clenched my teeth to stop them chattering, tried in vain to stop myself repeating in a toneless mutter, "Seems like everyone's dead. Everyone but me. Seems like I'm the only person left alive."

The sound of my laptop chiming alerted me to an incoming call.

I saw that it was Grace. The sight of her face made my heart swell, relief so intense it might have been love.

"I got your message. What's wrong? A prophecy?"

"Did I wake you? I'm sorry. It doesn't matter. It's not important. It was only a nightmare. I'm sorry I disturbed you."

"Stop apologizing and tell me what happened."

"Nothing. Nothing happened. It's all right."

"But you called. Why did you call?"

There was no sense in holding back. I took a long, shaky breath. "I woke up thinking everyone was dead. Everyone but me. I was scared… But there you are."

"Here I am. Now, what can I do for you?"

I laughed a little, embarrassed. "You've already done it, just by being there. I'm okay. Sorry—no, I won't apologize. Thank you for being there. That's all. We can both go back to sleep now."

"You can call me anytime."

The screen went dark as I was thanking her.

I did not feel like going back to bed. I thought about Grace. Had she been asleep or not? She had looked the same as ever—the pristine black T-shirt, the hair, loose, but no messier than usual. I thought about our conversation, about the things she had told me and the things she had not. She seemed to have something to do with the drones, but my idea that she programmed them was not just naïve, but absurd. Drones programmed themselves these days. AI was not only faster, but infinitely more accurate and reliable than humans. High-ranking officers could override a decision made by autonomous weapons, but Grace was not an officer. What was she?

It had been a long time since AI had aced the Turing test. That didn't mean there was no difference between artificial and human intelligence, all it meant was that under the right circumstances, most human beings could not tell the difference.

Seems like everyone but me is dead.

Seems like I am the only person left alive.

ACKNOWLEDGEMENTS

By the time it reaches publication, every book is the work of more than one person — and that's doubly true for anthologies.

Thank you to George Sandison, Dan Carpenter, Michael Beale and all the team at Titan for bringing *Isolation* out of its lonely space and into the world. I can't think of a publisher that more consistently hits it out of the park.

Thank you, too, to all the authors whose work you'll find between these pages, as well as Catriona Ward, John Langan, Benjamin Percy, Stephen Graham Jones and all the writers, editors and readers who have lent their support through this long process. Each of them has helped create the book that you hold in your hands.

Finally, thanks and love, as always, to Hannah and the boys. Because nobody should face this cruel world alone.

ABOUT THE AUTHORS

NINA ALLAN's stories have appeared in *Best Horror of the Year*, *Year's Best Fantasy and Science Fiction*, and the *Mammoth Book of Best British Crime*. Her most recent novel *The Good Neighbours*, an exploration of family secrets, past trauma and the darkness of the fairy world, is available now from Riverrun Books. Nina lives and works in Scotland.

LAIRD BARRON spent his early years in Alaska. He is the author of several books, including *The Beautiful Thing That Awaits Us All*, *Swift to Chase*, and *Blood Standard*. His work has also appeared in many magazines and anthologies. Barron currently resides in the Rondout Valley, writing stories about the evil that men do.

The *Oxford Companion to English Literature* describes RAMSEY CAMPBELL as "Britain's most respected living horror writer". He has been given more awards than any other writer in the field, including the Grand Master Award of the World Horror Convention, the Lifetime Achievement Award of the Horror Writers Association, the Living

Legend Award of the International Horror Guild, and the World Fantasy Lifetime Achievement Award. In 2015 he was made an Honorary Fellow of Liverpool John Moores University for outstanding services to literature. Among his novels are *The Face That Must Die, Incarnate, Midnight Sun, The Count of Eleven, The Darkest Part of the Woods, The Overnight, Secret Story, The Grin of the Dark, Thieving Fear, Creatures of the Pool, The Seven Days of Cain, Ghosts Know, The Kind Folk, Think Yourself Lucky, Thirteen Days by Sunset Beach, The Wise Friend, Somebody's Voice*, and *Fellstones*. His Brichester Mythos trilogy consists of *The Searching Dead, Born to the Dark*, and *The Way of the Worm*. His collections include *Waking Nightmares, Ghosts and Grisly Things, Told by the Dead, Just Behind You, Holes for Faces, By the Light of My Skull*, and a two-volume retrospective roundup (*Phantasmagorical Stories*) as well as *The Village Killings and Other Novellas*. His non-fiction is collected as *Ramsey Campbell, Probably* and *Ramsey Campbell, Certainly*, while *Ramsey's Rambles* collects his video reviews, and he is working on a book-length study of the Three Stooges, *Six Stooges and Counting. Limericks of the Alarming and Phantasmal* is a history of horror fiction in the form of fifty limericks. His novels *The Nameless, Pact of the Fathers*, and *The Influence* have been filmed in Spain, where a television series based on *The Nameless* is in development. He is the President of the Society of Fantastic Films.

Ramsey Campbell was born in Liverpool in 1946 and still lives on Merseyside with his wife Jenny. His pleasures include classical music, good food and wine. His website is at ramseycampbell.com.

M. R. Carey is a novelist, comics writer, and screenwriter. He is best known for the 2014 bestseller *The Girl With All the Gifts* and its movie adaptation, for which he wrote the BAFTA-nominated screenplay. He wrote *The Unwritten* and *Lucifer* for DC Vertigo comics, as well as critically acclaimed runs on Marvel's *X-Men* and on *Hellblazer*. He is also the co-author, along with his wife Linda and their daughter Louise, of two fantasy novels, *The City Of Silk and Steel* and *The House Of War and Witness*.

CHỊKỌDILỊ EMELỤMADỤ was born in Worksop, Nottinghamshire, and happily raised in Nigeria. Her work has been shortlisted for the Shirley Jackson Awards (2015), the Caine Prize for African Literature (2017 and 2020) and won a Nommo Award (2020). In 2019, she emerged winner of the inaugural Curtis Brown First Novel Prize for her manuscript *Dazzling*, which will be lead debut for Wildfire Books in spring 2023. She tweets @chemelumadu.

BRIAN EVENSON is the author of a dozen books of fiction, most recently the story collection *The Glassy Burning Floor of Hell* (2021). His collection *Song for the Unraveling of the World* won the Shirley Jackson Award and the World Fantasy Award, and was a finalist for the *Los Angeles Times*' Ray Bradbury Prize. Other prizes include the 2009 American Library Association's RUSA award for *Last Days* and the IHG Award for *The Wavering Knife*. He is the recipient of three O. Henry Prizes, an NEA fellowship, and a Guggenheim Award. His work has been translated into more than a dozen languages. He lives in Los Angeles and teaches in the Critical Studies Program at CalArts.

OWL GOINGBACK has been writing professionally for over thirty years, and is the author of numerous novels, children's books, screenplays, magazine articles, and short stories. He is a three-time Bram Stoker Award Winner, receiving the award for lifetime achievement, best novel, and best first novel. His books include *Crota*, *Darker Than Night*, *Evil Whispers*, *Breed*, *Shaman Moon*, *Coyote Rage*, *Eagle Feathers*, *Tribal Screams*, and *The Gift*. In addition to writing under his own name, Owl has ghostwritten several books forHollywood celebrities.

GWENDOLYN KISTE is the Bram Stoker Award-winning author of *The Rust Maidens, Boneset & Feathers, And Her Smile Will Untether the Universe, Pretty Marys All in a Row*, and *The Invention of Ghosts*. Her short fiction and nonfiction have appeared in *Nightmare Magazine, Best American Science Fiction and Fantasy, Vastarien*, Tor's *Nightfire, Black Static, The Dark, Daily Science Fiction, Interzone*, and *LampLight*, among others. Originally from Ohio, she now resides on an abandoned horse farm outside of Pittsburgh with her husband, two cats, and not nearly enough ghosts. Find her online at gwendolynkiste.com.

JOE R. LANSDALE is the internationally-bestselling author of over fifty novels, including the popular, long-running Hap and Leonard series. Many of his cult classics have been adapted for television and film, most famously the films *Bubba Ho-Tep* and *Cold in July*, and the *Hap and Leonard* series on Sundance TV and Netflix. Lansdale has written numerous screenplays and teleplays, including the iconic *Batman the Animated Series*. He has won an Edgar Award for *The Bottoms*, ten Bram Stoker Awards, and has been designated a World Horror Grandmaster. Lansdale, like many of his characters, lives in East Texas.

TIM LEBBON is a *New York Times* bestselling writer from South Wales. He's had over forty novels published to date, as well as hundreds of novellas and short stories. His latest novel is the eco-horror *The Last Storm*. Other recent releases include *Eden, The Silence*, and *Blood of the Four* with Christopher Golden. He has won four British Fantasy Awards, as well as Bram Stoker, Scribe, and Dragon Awards, and has been shortlisted for World Fantasy, International Horror Guild, and Shirley Jackson Awards. The movie of his novel *The Silence*, starring Stanley Tucci and Kiernan Shipka, debuted on Netflix in April 2019, and *Pay the Ghost*, starring Nicolas Cage, was released on Halloween 2015.

Tim is currently developing several more projects for TV and the big screen. Find out more: timlebbon.net.

ALISON LITTLEWOOD's first book, *A Cold Season*, was selected for the Richard and Judy Book Club and described as "perfect reading for a dark winter's night". Other titles include *Mistletoe*, *The Hidden People*, *The Crow Garden*, *Path of Needles*, and *The Unquiet House*. She also wrote *The Cottingley Cuckoo*, as A. J. Elwood. Alison's short stories have been picked for a number of year's best anthologies and published in her collections *Quieter Paths* and *Five Feathered Tales*. She has won the Shirley Jackson Award for Short Fiction. Alison lives with her partner Fergus in Yorkshire, in a house of creaking doors and crooked walls. She loves exploring the hills and dales with her two hugely enthusiastic Dalmatians and has a penchant for books on folklore and weird history, Earl Grey tea, fountain pens, and semicolons.

KEN LIU is an American author of speculative fiction. A winner of the Nebula, Hugo, and World Fantasy awards, he wrote the *Dandelion Dynasty*, a silkpunk epic fantasy series (starting with *The Grace of Kings*), as well as short story collections *The Paper Menagerie and Other Stories* and *The Hidden Girl and Other Stories*. He also authored the Star Wars novel *The Legends of Luke Skywalker*. Prior to becoming a full-time writer, Liu worked as a software engineer, corporate lawyer, and litigation consultant. Liu frequently speaks at conferences and universities on a variety of topics, including futurism, cryptocurrency, the history of technology, bookmaking, narrative futures, and the mathematics of origami. You can find him online at kenliu.name

JONATHAN MABERRY is a *New York Times* bestselling author, five-time Bram Stoker Award winner, three-time Scribe Award winner, Inkpot Award winner, and comic book writer. His vampire apocalypse book series, *V-WARS*, was a Netflix original series. He writes in multiple genres including suspense, thriller, horror, science fiction, fantasy, and action; for adults, teens, and middle grade. His novels include the Joe Ledger thriller series, *Bewilderness*, *Ink*, *Glimpse*, the Pine Deep Trilogy, the *Rot & Ruin* series, the *Dead of Night* series, *Mars One*, *Ghostwalkers: A Deadlands Novel*, and many others, including his first epic fantasy, *Kagen the Damned*. He is the editor of many anthologies including *The X-Files*, *Aliens: Bug Hunt*, *Don't Turn Out the Lights*, *Aliens vs Predators: Ultimate Prey*, *Hardboiled Horror*, *Nights of the Living Dead* (co-edited with George A. Romero), and others. His comics include *Black Panther: DoomWar*, *Captain America*, *Pandemica*, *Highway to Hell*, *The Punisher*, and *Bad Blood*. He is the president of the International Association of Media Tie-in Writers, and the editor of *Weird Tales Magazine*. Visit him online at jonathanmaberry.com.

MARK MORRIS has written and edited around forty novels, novellas, short story collections, and anthologies, and his script work includes audio dramas for *Doctor Who*, *Jago & Litefoot*, and the *Hammer Chillers* series. His most recent work includes the Obsidian Heart trilogy (*The Wolves of London*, *The Society of Blood*, and *The Wraiths of War*), the original Predator novel *Stalking Shadows* (co-written with James A. Moore), new audio adaptations of the classic 1971 horror movie *Blood on Satan's Claw* and the M. R. James ghost story *A View From a Hill*, a 30th anniversary short story collection *Warts And All*, and, as editor, the anthologies *After Sundown* and *Beyond the Veil*. *Blood on Satan's Claw* won the New York Festival Radio Award for Best Drama Special, and *A View From a Hill* won the New York Festival Radio Award for Best Digital Drama Programme, and was also awarded Silver at the 2020 Audio & Radio Industry Awards. Mark has won two British Fantasy Awards, and has also been nominated for several Stokers and Shirley Jackson Awards.

LYNDA E. RUCKER has sold dozens of short stories to various magazines and anthologies including *Best New Horror*, *The Best Horror of the Year*, *The Year's Best Dark Fantasy and Horror*, *Black Static*, *Nightmare*, *F&SF*, *Postscripts*, and *Shadows and Tall Trees*. She has had a short play produced as part of an anthology of horror plays on London's West End, has collaborated on a short horror comic, writes a regular column on horror for *Black Static*, and won the Shirley Jackson Award for Best Short Story in 2015. Two collections of her short fiction have been published, *The Moon Will Look Strange* and *You'll Know When You Get There*, and she edited the anthology *Uncertainties III* for Swan River Press. A third collection is forthcoming in 2022.

A. G. SLATTER is the author of five novels, including *All the Murmuring Bones* and *The Path of Thorns* (forthcoming) and eleven short story collections, including *The Bitterwood Bible* and *The Tallow-Wife and Other Tales*. She's won a World Fantasy Award, a British Fantasy Award, a Ditmar, two Australian Shadows Awards, and seven Aurealis Awards. Her work has been translated into Bulgarian, Chinese, Russian, Italian, Spanish, Japanese, Polish, Hungarian, Turkish, French, and Romanian. She can be located on the internet at angelaslatter.com, @AngelaSlatter (Twitter), and angelaslatter (Instagram).

MICHAEL MARSHALL SMITH is a novelist and screenwriter. Under this name he has published nearly a hundred short stories and five novels, and is the only author to have won the British Fantasy Award for Best Short Fiction four times. 2020 saw *The Best of Michael Marshall Smith* collection from Subterranean Press. Writing as Michael Marshall he has written seven internationally-bestselling conspiracy thrillers, including *The Straw Men* (currently in television development); now additionally writing as Michael Rutger, in 2018 he published the adventure thriller *The Anomaly*. A sequel, *The Possession*, was published in 2019. He also works in film and television development, as Creative Consultant to the Blank Corporation, Neil Gaiman's production company in Los Angeles. He lives in Santa Cruz, California, with his wife, son, and cats. michaelmarshallsmith.com.

PAUL TREMBLAY has won the Bram Stoker, British Fantasy, and Massachusetts Book awards and is the author of *The Pallbearers Club*, *Survivor Song*, *Growing Things*, *The Cabin at the End of the World*, *Disappearance at Devil's Rock*, *A Head Full of Ghosts*, and the crime novels *The Little Sleep* and *No Sleep Till Wonderland*. His essays and short fiction have appeared in the *Los Angeles Times*, *New York Times*, and numerous year's-best anthologies. He has a master's degree in mathematics and lives outside Boston with his family.

LISA TUTTLE has been writing strange, weird, and fantastic fiction since the 1970s, and is a past winner of the John W. Campbell Award, the British Science Fiction Award, and the International Horror Guild Award. She is the author of a dozen novels and half a dozen short story collections, the first of which, *A Nest of Nightmares* (1986), was recently reprinted by Valancourt, who also published her most recent, *The Dead Hours of Night* (2021). She lives in Scotland.

MARIAN WOMACK has published the novels *The Swimmers* (2021) and *The Golden Key* (2020), the short story collection *Lost Objects* (2018), and co-edited the anthology of international writing *An Invite to Eternity: Tales of Nature Disrupted* (2019). Her next novel is *The Silver Bell* (2022). She is a creative writing tutor and works as an academic librarian.

ABOUT THE EDITOR

DAN COXON is an editor and writer from London, UK. His debut short story collection, *Only the Broken Remain* (Black Shuck Books, 2020), was shortlisted for two British Fantasy Awards, while his anthology *This Dreaming Isle* (Unsung Stories, 2018) was a finalist for the Shirley Jackson Awards and the British Fantasy Awards. His stories have appeared in *Terrifying Ghosts, Beyond the Veil, Black Static, Unsung Stories, The Ghastling, Not One of Us, Nightscript, Humanagerie,* and *Nox Pareidolia,* among many others. He is co-editor of *Writing the Uncanny* (Dead Ink Books, 2021), a guide to writing strange and unsettling fiction. Find him online at dancoxon.com, or on Twitter @DanCoxonAuthor.